P9-CQQ-544

THICKER THAN WATER

ALSO BY MEGAN COLLINS

The Family Plot

Behind the Red Door

The Winter Sister

THICKER THAN WATER

A Novel

Megan Collins

ATRIA BOOKS

New York • London • Toronto • Sydney • New Delhi

ATRIA
BOOKS

An Imprint of Simon & Schuster, Inc.
1230 Avenue of the Americas
New York, NY 10020

This book is a work of fiction. Any references to historical events, real people, or real places are used fictitiously. Other names, characters, places, and events are products of the author's imagination, and any resemblance to actual events or places or persons, living or dead, is entirely coincidental.

Copyright © 2023 by Megan Collins Hatfield

All rights reserved, including the right to reproduce this book or portions thereof in any form whatsoever. For information, address Atria Books Subsidiary Rights Department, 1230 Avenue of the Americas, New York, NY 10020.

First Atria Books hardcover edition July 2023

ATRIA B O O K S and colophon are trademarks of Simon & Schuster, Inc.

For information about special discounts for bulk purchases, please contact Simon & Schuster Special Sales at 1-866-506-1949 or business@simonandschuster.com.

The Simon & Schuster Speakers Bureau can bring authors to your live event. For more information or to book an event, contact the Simon & Schuster Speakers Bureau at 1-866-248-3049 or visit our website at www.simonspeakers.com.

Interior design by Dana Sloan

Manufactured in the United States of America

1 3 5 7 9 10 8 6 4 2

Library of Congress Cataloging-in-Publication Data

Names: Collins, Megan, 1984– author.
Title: Thicker than water: a novel / Megan Collins.
Description: First Atria Books hardcover edition. | New York: Atria Books, 2023.
Identifiers: LCCN 2022049289 (print) | LCCN 2022049290 (ebook) |
ISBN 9781982196240 (hardcover) | ISBN 9781982196257 (paperback) |
ISBN 9781982196264 (ebook)
Classification: LCC PS3603.O454463 T55 2023 (print) |
LCC PS3603.O454463 (ebook) | DDC 813/.6—dc23
LC record available at https://lccn.loc.gov/2022049289
LC ebook record available at https://lccn.loc.gov/2022049290

ISBN 978-1-9821-9624-0
ISBN 978-1-9821-9626-4 (ebook)

In memory of Nicole Whidtfeldt,
who spoke with strength and stunning clarity,
lending her voice to those who had not yet found their own,
and who was fiercely defiant in the face of injustice

Chapter One

JULIA

We don't talk about the wallpaper. Not its age: thirty years, hung there by Sienna and Jason's mother when they were still in grade school. Not its condition: faded in places, peeling in others. Not even its pattern: fist-sized splotches of blood.

"It's *not* blood," Sienna said the one time I mentioned it, two weeks into my marriage to her brother. Her eyes tightened with irritation, and that was enough for me to clamp my reply between my teeth.

She was right, though; it isn't blood. It's roosters. Dark red roosters with bulbous chests and feathery combs, stamped onto gauze-white paper that lines the family room walls. I've lived here, in Jason and Sienna's childhood home, for fifteen years—a little longer than Aiden's been alive—and still, as I look around, I don't see roosters; I see wounds.

"Our mom loved roosters," Jason said, shrugging, that single time I brought it up. Unlike Sienna, he wasn't irritated, just sad, like

1

I'd offended the woman I never got to meet. "I can't imagine taking it down."

So we didn't. Sadness, irritation—those aren't emotions I want to inspire. But I've tried to cover the paper as best I can, hanging my favorite photographs on the walls: Jason, Sienna, and me on the courthouse steps the day Jason and I got married; Aiden cheering on Jason's shoulders at a Red Sox game; Sienna and me doubled over with laughter in front of the ocean.

Still, behind and around it all—blood.

"Jules, are you listening?" Sienna asks now. "These people think a woman did it."

It being murder. The reason I'm watching the walls instead of the news. On Friday night, someone stabbed Jason's boss, Gavin Reed, then smothered him, before sewing up his lips like a rip in a seam.

"Only a woman has that much anger," Gavin's neighbor tells the reporter, averting her gaze. Just before the camera cuts away, it catches her swallowing, and in that swallow, there are words left unsaid. I recognize it immediately, her stuffed-down silence.

Another neighbor, a man this time, agrees the murderer was female. He chuckles before launching his opinion: "Everyone's still all 'Me Too' these days. He probably called her 'sweetheart' or something."

Sienna scowls at the TV. "Fucker."

Gavin's murder has been the lead story in Connecticut ever since his body was discovered two days ago. Like these neighbors, people have been quick to theorize, desperate to make sense of it—how a successful, respected businessman can turn up dead.

And not just dead. Sewn.

"We're breaking the rules," I say.

Movie Night is for movies, *not* TV, not even the made-for-TV movies we like to dub with our own script. (Sienna's specialty is turning crime stories into sitcoms; I like making every character Swedish.) But when we turned on the TV and heard Gavin's name, Sienna stiffened, and my eyes drifted, the roosters snagging my gaze.

"Shh!" Sienna says.

The reporter is reminding viewers of the facts of this case. Gavin Reed's body was found in the backyard of his lake house. He was forty years old, owner of Integrity Plus Home Services, a home improvement company he took over after his father's death six years ago. Gavin was last seen leaving a regional sales conference (*Jason's conference*, I reflexively think) on Friday. But on Sunday, a kayaker on the lake spotted Gavin, prone and unresponsive on his lawn, his clothes still drenched from the sobbing, furious rainstorm that began late Friday night and continued until Sunday morning, washing away the killer's DNA.

There was a cut, three inches long, across Gavin's abdomen, and he'd been suffocated, but without fibers in his lungs, it seems likely that someone did it with their bare hands. Gavin had been drunk—his blood alcohol level over twice the legal limit—something that might have made him easier to take down. But those aren't the details anyone cares about. It's Gavin's lips they keep coming back to.

"He was sewn up!" The news is back to the interview with the male neighbor. "Clearly the work of a woman! I don't think I know a single man who even owns a needle and thread. Let alone knows how to work 'em."

"Seriously, fuck that guy," Sienna says. "Jason's known how to sew since he was twelve. Our mom taught him so he could sew on his boy scout badges himself." She nudges her chin at the man on TV. "This guy can go choke on his own tongue."

Cool your fire, I'm about to say. It's my usual mantra for Sienna, words meant to soothe her anger. But Sienna speaks first: "I bet Gavin deserved it."

I snap my gaze toward her. "How can you say that?"

"Because most men deserve it."

I consider the flush in her cheeks, the same shade of pink that swamps her skin whenever we speak of her ex-boyfriend. "Is this about Wyatt?"

"What? No," Sienna scoffs. "I haven't seen Wyatt in months. I'm over him."

"Clive Clayton?" I ask carefully. Not an ex. But someone who ruined her all the same.

"*Everything's* about Clive," she seethes. "But also, no, just in general: men are trash."

Sienna's assertion reminds me of my mother, who raised me with a single warning: *Never trust a man.* She repeated it so often that, for much of my childhood, I thought it was a regular household proverb—something to be embroidered onto pillows, woven into welcome mats.

"Oh, really," I say. "So, Jason's trash?"

"My brother is an impeccable human being."

"What about Tom Hanks? Is he trash?"

Sienna waves a dismissive hand. "Tom's fine."

"And your nephew?"

"Hmm," Sienna considers. "I don't know." She mutes the TV and shouts toward the ceiling. "Aiden!" We listen for movement upstairs before she tries again. "Aiden! Help! Your mom got bit by a rat!"

I swat at Sienna, and then we hear it: the creak of Aiden's door, the thud of his footsteps. He hasn't spoken to me all day, which is not so different from other days lately. When he got home at 2:45, I asked him how school was, and his response was to trudge up the stairs.

Now, appearing on the threshold between the family room and front hall, he's dressed in Jason's old Wilco shirt, strumming a guitar pick against his thigh, as if unable to stop practicing for even a moment. Sienna once told me that Jason used to be the same way. In high school, he'd play an invisible trumpet at dinner, working on his "marching band muscle memory"—and I find it sweet, this echo of Jason in Aiden, who would echo everything about his father if he could.

"Aiden," Sienna says, "are you trash?"

"What? I thought you said something about a rat."

Sienna and I share a glance. We haven't gotten used to his deeper, decidedly teenage voice.

"Forget about that. Are you trash?" she repeats. "Do you do things that would make someone sew your lips together?" She gestures toward the TV.

"You mean, like, Dad's boss?" Aiden asks, straightening. "Why, what'd he do?"

"Nothing. Well—something, I'm sure, but I'm just saying: You better not be trash."

Aiden chuckles. "I'm not trash, Auntsy," he says, the name a holdover from his childhood, when his toddler mouth couldn't handle *Aunt Sienna*. "I'm writing a paper on toxic masculinity in *Lord of the Flies*."

"You are?" I ask, and the way Aiden stiffens at my voice is so noticeable that I can tell it embarrasses us all. I lower my gaze to the coffee table, where there's a stack of travel magazines I haven't touched in months.

I feel Sienna watching me. She wants me to address it, whatever *it* is—teenage aloofness or a shift in hormones or some grudge Aiden's holding against me. But my mouth won't open, my throat won't speak, and in a few seconds, Sienna speaks instead.

"That doesn't impress me," she says, inspecting her nails. "I'm sure the teacher assigned you that topic."

Aiden shrugs.

She cocks her eyes toward him. "Do you cheat on your girlfriend?"

"I don't have a girlfriend."

"Your boyfriend, then?"

Aiden rolls his eyes.

"Do you leer at girls in gym class, with your greasy little eyeballs?"

"My eyeballs are greasy?"

"I don't know," Sienna teases, making her thumb and finger into a circle, then peering through it like a monocle. "Are they?"

Aiden shakes his head. "I have no idea what's going on right now."

"Sure you don't. Just don't come crying to either of us when you get . . ." She mimics sewing up her lips. Aiden's eyes go wide.

"Sienna!" I scold, and she looks at me—almost proudly—before backtracking.

"I'm kidding. It's terrible what happened to Gavin Reed." She nods solemnly before adding, "Unless he deserved it."

I lob a pillow at her. Sienna's been rabid about injustices for as long as I've known her—cussing at her computer when our clients are late with payments, yelling at drivers who cut her off, starting fights with internet strangers in response to sexist tweets—so I know the news struck a chord with her tonight; as soon as someone theorized a woman might have done it, Sienna's sympathy switched from the victim to the perpetrator. Never mind that Jason's never said anything bad about his boss at Integrity Plus. All Sienna needed was the suggestion that a woman had an ax to grind with Gavin, and the tenor of the story changed. I can practically see the images in her eyes: Gavin forcing a secretary's head toward his unzipped pants; Gavin, out at happy hour, slipping a pill into an unattended cup. The signs Sienna made for the first Women's March said, "Believe Women." Even hypothetical ones, apparently.

"I thought everyone loved Dad's boss," Aiden says. "Didn't he, like, save the company by turning in some dude for fraud?"

"The merger thing?" Sienna clarifies. "Big deal."

This is not the first time Jason's boss has been in the news. A couple years ago, Gavin had been set to merge Integrity Plus with a rival home services company, Higher Home Improvement. But when Gavin discovered that his soon-to-be partner had been falsifying financial records, he reported him to the IRS. *Our name is Integrity Plus for a reason*, Gavin told a reporter, who'd caught wind of the failed merger, and in the end, when Higher Home folded—the fallout from an enormous fine and a mountain of back taxes—Integrity Plus absorbed a lot of their customers anyway.

"Anyone can do the right thing once," Sienna continues. "It's the bad things they do that define them."

"Guess we can't define you, then," I joke, "since you're a literal angel."

Sienna feigns a bashful smile. Then she lifts one hand to just above her head, moves it in tight circles as if rubbing something invisible.

"I'm polishing my halo," she explains.

"It's very pretty."

"Here." Sienna mimes plucking the halo from the air and placing it above my head. "You should borrow it, since you're an angel, too, and your halo is . . . at the cleaners," she improvises.

"It'll go with *everything*!" I say, and Aiden rolls his eyes again, impatient with our antics.

"Can I go now?" he asks.

Sienna dismisses him with a wave. Aiden takes a couple steps but stops before turning the corner. Without looking back, he asks, "When's Dad getting home?"

It takes me a moment to realize he's addressing me. "Oh! Prob-

ably not for another hour. He had a late sales call. Why, do you need
help with something? I can—"

"No," he says. Then he clomps through the front hallway and
plods up the stairs.

Sienna arches an eyebrow at me. "That's partially on you, you
know."

"What is?"

"*That.*" She gestures to the space where Aiden stood. "You need
to speak up. Tell him he's being weird and dismissive and it's bum-
ming you out."

I shake my head. "I don't want to make it worse."

"Jules. Did you learn nothing from *Liar Liar*? We *just* rewatched
it." She shoots her arms above her head, affects Jim Carrey's shrill,
victorious voice from the final courtroom scene: "And the truth . . .
shall set you free!"

"He could be depressed or something," I say, "and I'm not sure
how to navigate that. I've been thinking I should call his doctor."

Sienna drops her arms. "Maybe. What's Jason say?"

"Nothing."

"What do you mean 'nothing'?"

"I haven't brought it up. And he hasn't seemed to notice. He's
been distracted lately, even before what happened to Gavin. He's up
for that big promotion—although, who knows if that'll even be a
thing now that his boss is dead—and he and I—"

I stop myself from mentioning it: the night in December that un-
raveled something between us.

"And you and him what?" Sienna asks. She never misses when I
swallow my words.

Jason and I haven't spoken of it much, except for his assurances
that he'll make things right. Still, it's shadowed our interactions
for months: quiet dinners, Aiden's head shooting between us as if

keeping score of our silence; the flinch of my hand whenever Jason reaches for it; the travel magazines he keeps bringing home for me, even though I've removed all my multicolored tabs from the ones I already have; the way I feigned sleep on Friday night when he slipped into bed, finally home from his post-conference dinner.

But Sienna doesn't know that things have changed between me and Jason—it's the rare secret I've kept from her—so I distract her from the question by letting her win. "Nothing. You're right, I'll talk to Jason about Aiden."

Before this shift in Aiden's demeanor, my son was softer, easier. He'd tell me about the play he wanted to audition for, the study hall teacher who lets him practice guitar instead of doing his homework, the kid in his English class who thought Julius Cesar wrote *Romeo and Juliet*. But back in December, he became stiff and guarded around me, like his skin, his muscles, had been replaced with armor, and I can't help but wonder what he might have overheard between me and Jason. Or wonder, if he did overhear, why his resentment is aimed at me instead of his father.

"In the meantime," I say, before Sienna can push the issue harder, "can you watch how you talk to Aiden? You shouldn't scare him with the Gavin Reed stuff."

"Oh, come on. He knows what happened."

That's exactly the problem. Aiden, Jason, and I were eating pizza on Sunday evening, local news playing in the background, when the story of Gavin's murder blared across the screen. Jason dropped his slice then, not even wincing as the hot tomato sauce splattered his lap. He sat there, wide-eyed, wide-mouthed, unchewed crust adrift on his tongue, and his shock hooked my attention so completely that it took me a moment to process its source: Jason's boss had been killed.

Later that night, I tumbled through dreams of Gavin's stitched-up mouth—until something woke me. A sound from down the hall led me to Aiden's room, where his light was still on at two in the morning. Peeking inside, I found him sitting on the edge of his bed, hunched over his phone with his brows drawn, his feet digging into the carpet like he was crushing cigarettes beneath them. *You okay, hon?* I asked, and he startled, flipping his phone upside down.

I'm fine, he said, but he skated one finger over his lips, as if thinking of the thread that wove through Gavin's.

"The news stories have freaked him out," I tell Sienna now. "You don't need to tell him the guy might've deserved it, too."

"Well, what if he did?"

"Nobody deserves to be murdered. And especially not like *that*."

Three assaults to his body: the postmortem sewing, the suffocation that killed him, the stab wound in his stomach. I glance toward the wall, at those bloodred roosters, and shudder.

"Maybe not," Sienna says. "I'm just saying: carrying this horrible thing that someone's done to you, knowing every single day they got away with it—" She smooths her blunt dark bob. "It's enough to make a person snap."

I take a long breath before asking: "Are you saying *you're* going to snap?"

Sometimes I wonder. It's been seventeen years since Clive Clayton downed six shots of Jaeger at a party, drove across a double yellow line, and killed Sienna and Jason's parents on impact. Sixteen years since he was sentenced to only three in prison. Fourteen and a half since he got out on parole. But it was just last week, working on the splash page for a new A&A client, that I saw Clive's Instagram among the open tabs in Sienna's browser. And yesterday, Sienna scowled at a post about his new car, a growl low in her throat.

"No, I won't snap," Sienna says. "I have you." She boops my nose. "But not everyone has a Julia to hold them together."

She reaches for my hand, and it takes less than a second for our fingers to lock together, perfectly grooved to each other like gears in a machine. The first time we held hands like this, we'd known each other less than two hours. We were twenty-two, Jason twenty-four, and I was pregnant, though nobody but Jason and I knew that yet. I'd only been dating him for three months, and I was hoping that meeting his sister would solidify a connection with him. I liked him, of course—was probably going to love him—but everything had happened so fast, and his proposal had been with a twist tie he'd shaped into a ring. I wasn't wearing it the night I met Sienna—dinner at Olive Garden—because I hadn't answered him yet. I'd only kissed him when he asked, smiled without my teeth, and told him I'd think about it.

The dinner was awkward to start. Small talk and small laughs. When the waitress asked what I'd like to drink, I was about to second Sienna's order of a cosmo—maybe it would relax me, turn me into someone more interesting to Jason's cool, tall sister with the blistering blue eyes. But then I remembered the two lines on the pregnancy test, shaped like a road I'd travel forever, and I switched to cranberry juice. So we went on: small talk, small laughs, until Jason, spearing a tomato with his fork, proclaimed, "Mmm, these are good motatoes." At Jason's fumbled word, Sienna and I looked at each other, sharing a panicked gaze as we struggled to pinch back our laughter, our mouths filled with fresh sips. But as soon as Jason corrected himself, so earnestly—"*tomatoes*, I like these *tomatoes*"—we exploded into simultaneous spit-takes, spewing bright red juice all over our salads.

The night rushed ahead after that, with Jason edging more and more toward the periphery. Sienna and I leaned toward each other, hunting for everything we had in common: we both love foods that are sweet and savory (we later dipped our breadsticks into the raspberry sauce on our cheesecakes); we both graduated from UConn; our names both end with A, a fact that Jason contributed dully, as if it barely warranted a mention. But Sienna and I latched onto it, latched onto each other, too, our hands locking together for the very first time across the table. And four years later, when naming our two-person brand development business—Sienna as designer and coder, me as copywriter—it took us only three minutes to decide on A&A Brand.

On the ride home from Olive Garden that first night, I said to Jason, "I love your sister!" Then, my heart buoyant, veins buzzing as if I really had ordered that Cosmo, I added, "And I love you too."

I hadn't said that to him yet, and the sentence felt stiff on my tongue. But I kept going, trying to loosen the words, soften them up.

"I love you and we're having a baby." I said this second part as if it were shocking news—which it still kind of was, the ink on my diploma barely even dry. "I love you and—I think we should get married."

I didn't allow myself to wonder: if I hadn't just bonded with Sienna so intensely, would I still be saying yes to Jason? Or, in time, would we decide to raise our son in separate houses, loving each other but not in love?

Jason jerked to a stop on the side of the road. Cupping my face in his hands, he told me he loved me too. But then—because he knew about my mother, the phrase she'd repeated my entire childhood, drilling it into my head like an emergency phone number—he asked if I was sure. And briefly, like so many times before, I heard my mother's warning: *Never trust a man.*

I silenced it with another kiss.

Now, Sienna nods toward the TV, where the news has moved on from Gavin's murder. "We should start the movie," she says. "But first: *motatoes!*"

Since our initial Olive Garden dinner, Sienna and I have referred to food as *motatoes*. It doesn't matter what kind. Soup is motatoes. Cupcakes: motatoes. Nachos: motatoes with cheese. Jason always rolls his eyes, but Sienna and I smile every time.

"What do you want," I ask, "chocolate popcorn, or pretzel cookies?"

I need comfort food right now, something to distract from the warning that's wormed its way back: *Never trust a man, never trust a man*. My mother's been dead for eight years, but in the wake of that December night with Jason—my laptop open between us, my finger shaking as it aimed at the screen—I've been hearing it more and more. And every time, it's as clear and precise as if she's standing beside me, whispering it into my ear.

"Pretzel—" Sienna starts, but my phone cuts in. The ringing fills the room like a siren.

I squint at the screen, not recognizing the number, but pick up anyway. I have to answer unknown calls; Jason's always letting his cell phone die, forgetting to charge it or just not caring to, so there's always the possibility he could be calling from someone else's phone.

But the person on the other end isn't Jason. It's a woman, and as she speaks, something turns off inside my head. I don't hear the caller's voice, or the ghost of my mother's, or even Sienna's as she registers my expression—*What's wrong? Who is it?* I read on her lips.

I ask the woman to repeat what she said, and as I press the phone tighter to my ear, I can just make it out: Jason's name, then *hospital*.

When I hang up, I say only this: "Jason's hurt." And as Sienna and I lurch for our keys, our shoes, I see on the muted TV a shot of a residential road. Lights from several cars strobe against the trees, back and forth, over and over, switching between the color of blood and the color of a bruise. They're pulsing, insistent, will not be ignored: blue and red, and blue and red, and blue-red-blue-red-blue.

Chapter Two

SIENNA

I don't recognize my brother.

His face is bruised to deep indigo around his nose and eyes. There's an IV taped into place on his hand, which is specked with blood the nurses missed. A bandage circles his head, the gauze stretched tight, and his body is hooked to so many wires he looks like a fuse box. Strangest of all is his mouth, stuck open with the plastic tube snaked into his trachea.

Julia and I stare at him, holding hands so tightly we feel each other's pulses. Julia's hammers; mine whips. The air in the ICU is colder than it should be, especially for April, and when I shiver beneath an air vent, Julia shivers too, as if the movement coursed from my body into hers.

The last time we were in a hospital like this was eight years ago, when Julia's mother was dying. My role was easy then: support Jules, advocate on her behalf to nurses and doctors, demand information when they were stingy with it. I hunted down tissue boxes. I crushed up potato chips to sprinkle onto cake from the cafeteria—a makeshift snack, sweet and savory, that made her smile. And in every other moment, I stood beside her, anchoring her between Jason and me.

Now, though, Julia and I need each other equally. Her hand in mine is the only thing holding me together as Dr. Brighton, a woman we've waited hours to see, explains the mechanics of Jason's crash. How he drove off the road and slammed into a tree. How his head snapped forward as his airbags deployed, breaking his nose and the bones around his eyes. How the paramedics intubated him at the scene.

"Was there another car involved?" The question squeezes my throat, identical to the one I asked seventeen years ago, the night Jason called me at college to tell me our parents had been killed in a crash. It's a reflex, how quickly I picture Clive Clayton, his suit and smooth hair at the sentencing. My entire body clenches, waiting for the doctor to answer, same as it clenched in the courtroom waiting for the judge to speak.

"They said there were no signs of another vehicle," Dr. Brighton says, and I loosen, just a little. "It's possible he was driving distracted, though. On his phone, maybe?"

"No," I say, resolute. Jason doesn't text or call while driving. Jason hardly texts or calls at all. He treats his phone like it's the same one our parents bought him when he first got his license—an early, clunky model that was only for emergencies.

Dr. Brighton continues, this time with technical stuff, and here is where her words dissolve for me, where each syllable is only a sound floating from her mouth, reaching me slowly, liquidly, as if I'm listening from underwater.

Bilateral, subdural, hematoma—these are words from another language.

When she says *subarachnoid*, I picture spiders. Then blood. Then blood spidering through my brother's brain. Because that's what Dr. Brighton is talking about. Brain bleeds. Brain injuries. They have him in a medically induced coma now—the doctor emphasizes *medically induced*, as if to soften the blow of *coma*. She tells us what drugs he's on, but the names mean nothing to me.

"Every morning, we'll turn down the anesthetic to reassess his neurological function," Dr. Brighton says, "and at that time, we'll recalculate his GCS score."

"GCS?" I'm not even sure which of us asks it—me or Julia.

Dr. Brighton smiles politely. I see it in her face: she's explained this already.

"Glasgow Coma Scale. It's how we measure the level of consciousness in a patient after a traumatic brain injury."

We nod. "Right," one of us says.

"We'll repeat this process," Dr. Brighton adds, "until he's responsive enough and breathing well enough on his own for us to take the tube out."

"And when will that be?" I look at my brother, the blue mosaic of his face. Can he hear us talking? If I bent toward his ear, said, *Hey, punk, I'm gonna freeze your bra if you don't wake up soon*, would he want to roll his eyes, tell me that surely, in a hospital of all places, I can lay off him for a while?

"We can't say for sure," Dr. Brighton answers. "And I can't promise anything. But we're hopeful we'll see improvement over the next few days."

She leaves us then, no closure to the conversation. I crane my neck, watching through the doorway as she leans across the counter of the nurses' station, reaches for a cup that one of them holds out to her. When I hear laughter—from Dr. Brighton or a nurse or some inconsiderate visitor—I grip Julia's hand like a stress ball.

"I can't believe this," Julia murmurs. She's staring at Jason, who's still unfamiliar, still bandaged and tubed like a goddamn extra on *Grey's Anatomy.* "And what if she's wrong? What if he *doesn't* improve?"

"Hey. We can't think like that." But the same questions pound through my head.

"I know, but—he looks so bad. So wrong. Almost like a stranger."

"He's not, though," I say. "He's still Jason. Just the Hospital Chic version. New wardrobe. New color palette. New"—my gaze lingers on the gauze around his head—"accessories."

The joke, painfully inappropriate, doesn't land. Julia's face remains tight with anxiety.

"It's just," she says, "what if that's it? What if he never wakes up and everything between us is still—"

She stops herself, and like always, I can practically see the words she's forcing back. I don't know what they are or why she won't say them. I only know they're stuck inside her throat.

"Everything between you is still what?" I prompt, picking up the scraps of her sentence.

She shakes her head, already downplaying whatever it is. "Jason and I have just had trouble connecting lately. He's been so busy with that promotion he wants, and you and I have been slammed with work, and we just—we haven't spent much time together."

"Well, you will. Soon. He'll wake up and the two of you can get back to planning your big trip. You'll have tons of time to connect in Paris. And Venice. And Prague. And wherever else you've added to the list."

Usually, just the thought of their second honeymoon is enough to make Julia smile. When she and Jason got married, they were more concerned with affording a stroller and crib than a lavish vacation, opting instead for a couple nights at a Berkshires cabin. But their fifteenth anniversary was in January, and Julia's been collecting travel magazines and curating Pinterest pages since at least their tenth, all in preparation for their European tour later this year. Now, though, Julia's face darkens even more, as if I've only reminded her of something else she might lose.

"He's going to be okay," I assure her. Assure myself, too, because it's difficult to fathom *okay* with Jason's body laid out like a corpse in front of us. I lean closer to inspect his face. Did our parents look like this, purple and bloated, after Clive Clayton drove drunk and killed them? Or did the stopping of their hearts keep their capillaries from breaking, their blood from pooling? By the time I saw them in their coffins, they'd been scrubbed clean, made up, had their organs scooped out. Only their fingertips, tinted the faintest blue, outed them as dead instead of sleeping.

"He *has* to be okay," I insist. "Because I can't stop thinking about Clive Clayton. I know this is different, but—" I pause as Julia squeezes my palm. "I can't lose another family member to a car crash. Jason's the only reason I survived the last time at all."

When our parents were killed, we inherited our childhood home, and my brother urged me to ditch my campus apartment to stay with him there. I only lasted a few weeks in my old bedroom, haunted by phantom echoes of my parents, but during that time, Jason shelved his pain to make space for mine. He cooked me blueberry pancakes for breakfast, reenacted funny scenes from my favorite movies over dinner, coaxed smiles from me I didn't know I was capable of.

"He's always been so good to me," I say, "helping me whenever I needed him. And I can't do anything for him now."

With her free hand, Julia strokes Jason's arm, careful not to disturb his IV. Then something like a laugh gurgles in her throat.

"What?" I ask.

"Nothing. It's not appropriate."

"Say it."

"It's just that story you guys tell—about him putting dead bugs on your pillow."

"Um, don't forgot how he also *named them,* so I'd feel sad about throwing them out."

Julia rubs the space between her eyes. Another laugh escapes her, breathy this time. "You said he's always been so good to you, and that popped into my head—the bug pillows, which is *not* being good to you."

A chuckle punches out of me. "To be fair, I put bugs on his pillow first."

She's right, though. As kids, Jason and I tortured each other. I'd spit in his cereal bowl; he'd spit on my toothbrush. I'd hide the controllers to his video games; he'd hide under my bed to grab my ankles. In the back seat of our parents' car, we were always poking and pinching each other, twisting each other's arms.

"But you know what I mean," I say. "He's been good to me since Clive."

Julia nods. She knows this story, too, knows I'm not thinking of my parents' crash anymore. I'm thinking, instead, of a night six years before that: the first time Clive Clayton tried to wreck my life, and the night that changed everything between Jason and me.

Something beeps on one of his machines, yanking me from the edge of that memory. A nurse bustles in to fiddle with Jason's IV, check his tube, press something on his monitor, before exiting with a smile. I'm jealous of her knowledge, her easy ability to quiet a machine, keep my brother breathing.

"Oh god," Julia says, startling. "I have to call Aiden. It's been hours!"

Earlier, as we scrambled out the door, Julia yelled up to him, voice choked with fear, to come down for a minute. Instead, he stayed at the top of the stairs, staring at us warily, and Julia told him that Jason had an emergency, that she'd call when we knew more.

"It's okay," I say. "He's probably asleep by now."

Julia shakes her head. "He was up late the other night—two in the morning, on his phone. For all I know, he's up late all the time now; he's a teenager, that's what teens do—" She stops, mid-ramble. With the hand not holding mine, she grabs her phone, then gapes at it like she has no idea what it's for. She looks at me, hazel eyes wet and red. "What do I say?"

Even now, I test her: *One . . . Two . . . Three . . .* I count like this, slow and steady in my head, whenever I'm hoping she'll find her own words and feel confident enough to speak them herself. Normally, I make it the whole three seconds, uninterrupted—which always disturbs me a little, the way she's so content to be quiet, to keep such distance between her thoughts and her words. This time is no different. On *three*, she's still just blinking at me, lashes dewy with tears.

"For now, just text him that you're on your way back."

Julia's gaze darts toward Jason. "I can't *leave*. Not yet. I—"

"You heard what the nurse said earlier. They recommend we go home overnight. I'll stay, though—*you* go tell Aiden in person. And try to get some sleep. Jason would want that."

"But what do I say?" Julia asks for the second time, and I give her a script, parceling it out slowly so she can rehearse each phrase aloud. When she repeats the final sentence—*don't worry, Dad will wake up soon*—it comes out shaky. Unsure.

"You've got this," I say. "Drive safe. I'll call you if anything happens."

But our hands won't come unclasped. We look at them, then look at each other, and when we separate our fingers, slowly unstick our palms, it's like we're ripping stitches that have sewn us together.

Just before she leaves, we hear a couple nurses in the hallway, gossiping about Gavin Reed. We share a final glance, and I know Julia's thinking the same as me: it was only hours ago we were talking about Gavin ourselves. But with Jason in this bed, hooked to these machines, his boss's murder no longer has anything to do with us.

"So they stabbed him, suffocated him, *and* sutured his lips?" one of the nurses says. "Why all three? And why bother with the mouth at all when they'd already killed him?"

"I don't know," another answers. "But speaking of mouths: that cut on his abdomen? I hear it looked like a smile."

· · ·

Twenty-four hours after we first arrived at the hospital, my brother's condition remains unchanged. We've spent the day staring at Jason, pinching off bites of muffin from the vending machine, walking loops around the long hallways, just to feel our legs again. Not once today have Jason's eyes so much as flicked with dreams beneath his lids. Nurses have come and gone, regarding us with compassionate nods, and while I swiped again and again to Clive Clayton's Instagram, checking for new posts, new anger to distract me from despair, Julia sent sporadic texts to Aiden about food in the freezer, bringing the mail inside.

She said she messed up the script I gave her. She rushed through some of the words, stumbled over others, and when Aiden asked if Jason would be okay, she said, *Yes, he'll be fine, they just put him to sleep.* She covered her head with her hands when she mentioned that part to me—*I told my teenage son that the doctors put his dad to sleep. Like a dog. Like killing a dog.* Then she looked at me with horror that quickly melted into hysteria, both of us laughing so hard it counted as an ab workout.

None of this is funny. We know that. But we don't have much practice with sustained seriousness. Even earlier, when we scanned the contents of the vending machine, it was my instinct to ask which *motatoes* Julia was getting. But the old joke, Jason's exquisite mistake, stuck to my tongue, tasting like tears.

Now, for the millionth time today, I study my brother, desperate to detect a change. His hands are so still they look fake—props attached to his wrists. His bruises shine. Dry skin flakes at the corner of his mouth, and his lips gape around the tube, a fish on a line. *Nothing new to report*, I say to myself, the same thing the nurses have been telling us all day.

Movement by the door pulls my gaze away from my brother, and when I turn my head, my eyes instantly widen.

My ex-boyfriend is here, in uniform, standing at the threshold of the room. A transceiver chirps on his belt, hisses static, before a woman's voice relays a code and location he ignores.

"Wyatt," I say, and I'm conscious of Julia's surprise in the chair beside me. I speak his name as if this is the first I've seen him since we broke up a year ago. Because as far as Julia knows, it is.

The edges of his Hillstead Police badge glow under the lights like a reflector. Of course Wyatt would know about the accident; someone, at some point, told us it happened in Hillstead, Wyatt's town of jurisdiction. But still. The gall of him, showing up like some kind of boyfriend.

"What the hell are you doing here?" I ask him, standing up.

Julia stands, too, muttering so quietly only I can hear it: "Cool your fire."

I take a deep breath. My lungs are hot and tight, but the mantra does what it's supposed to. It loosens me, turns down the temperature of my anger. Still, it's not as effective as usual, because Julia has misread my stiff posture. She thinks I'm mad at the sight of Wyatt, which I am, but mostly I'm panicked that him being here will make it obvious that he and I are hardly estranged.

Julia and I tell each other everything, but I haven't been able to tell her this: for the last six months, I've been sleeping with Wyatt again. Even though he cheated on me at a bachelor party. Even though I broke up with him immediately, deleted all our pictures, repainted my apartment so it would look nothing like it did when he slept inside its walls. So many times, almost as a reflex, I've opened my mouth to share this with Julia, but I've found there's no way to explain why I keep a list in my phone called "Plan for Punishing Wyatt," which goes: (1) text him to come over, (2) pull him close, (3) undress us both a little, (4) back away suddenly, (5) button my shirt, and (6) leave him breathy and throbbing as I tell him to go. And I really don't want to tell Julia my recurring problem—because it's a part of myself I don't even recognize, a part it would humiliate me to admit: in the moment, I always forget number four, *back away*, and then the next thing I know, I've got my legs clamped around Wyatt's hips, my teeth sinking into my bottom lip, his words hot against my ear: "I've missed you, Si. I miss you all the time."

"Sienna," he says now, and I'm relieved he's using my full name, for Julia's benefit; I've made clear to him that she needs to think we're still estranged. "I've been calling you."

Julia shoots me a puzzled glance. Every time Wyatt's name lit up my screen today, I flipped the phone upside down.

"And I've been ignoring you," I say.

But there was part of me, damn it, that had wanted to pick up. Wanted to place my pain in Wyatt's hands.

"In case you can't tell," I add, "I'm busy."

Wyatt looks over my shoulder, his eyes landing on Jason, comatose and discolored, and he swallows. He lingers on my brother for a few moments, then shakes his head. But the expression on his face isn't one of sympathy. It's the one he wore that night he confessed to cheating on me. It's a mix of anguish and dread, a crinkle around the eyes that usually accompanies his laughter but on that night was the wince of knowing he had to hurt me.

"I'm actually here," Wyatt says, "on official business. The calls were— I wanted to warn you."

"Warn me about what? Is this about the crash? Did they find out somebody hit—"

"No, no." Wyatt turns to scan the hallway before facing us again. "Listen, Beck's in the bathroom, I was supposed to wait for him, but—"

"Beck? The detective?"

Jerry Beck. One of Wyatt's colleagues. I hung out with him several times over the two years Wyatt and I dated, department barbecues where I was a reluctant plus-one, and his presence—loud and commanding, desperate to be the smartest person in the room— always rankled me.

But why is he here?

"Spit it out," I say when Wyatt hesitates, and my heart thrashes, an echo of the night he told me about the woman at the bachelor party, whose name he didn't even remember, whose body he only knew he entered because of the condom he woke up wearing in her bed.

"It's not even supposed to be me," Wyatt says. "I'm only here because Sam's kid got sick. But God—I don't want you to hear it from Beck first, so I—"

"For fuck's sake, Wyatt."

"Jason's a suspect."

Julia and I exchange a look, brows equally furrowed.

"A suspect?" I repeat, whirling back to Wyatt. "A suspect for what?"

He rubs the back of his neck. Shifts from side to side. "The murder of Gavin Reed."

Chapter Three

JULIA

I choke on my own gasp.

"What the hell, Wyatt?" Sienna says, pounding on my back. "Is this a joke?"

"I wish it was." Wyatt watches me, waiting for my fit to pass. When I gulp in a breath, then successfully push it out, he continues. "But with the crash yesterday, they found evidence linking Jason to Gavin Reed."

"Of course he's linked to Gavin Reed," Sienna hisses. "Gavin's his boss."

Wyatt glances into the hallway, sweeping it with his eyes. "They found a knife in Jason's car that—"

"You mean his pocketknife? Our dad gave it to him. He carries it everywhere."

"They found traces of blood on it."

Blood? Jason uses that knife to tighten screws on Aiden's desk, to open packages, to snip loose threads from his sweaters.

"And the blade itself," Wyatt adds, "is consistent with Reed's wound."

My mouth pops open again, but nothing—neither words nor air—comes out.

"So?" Sienna says. "Now everyone with a pocketknife is a suspect?"

"No, but"—Wyatt lowers his voice—"they also found Gavin's phone. In Jason's car."

I stare at Wyatt, forcing myself to breathe, but Sienna takes only a second to absorb this information.

"That makes my brother a murderer?"

"No," Wyatt says. "It makes him a suspect."

"Yeah, of murder. That's what you said. That my brother—the same guy who had to close his eyes during the Red Wedding on *Game of Thrones*—somehow stabbed his boss? And smothered him? And stitched up his lips?"

Wyatt shakes his head. "All they have right now is the knife and the phone. They've submitted the blood for testing. They should know within a few days if it's a match, but—"

"It won't be," Sienna cuts in.

"But for now," Wyatt continues, "protocol dictates that—"

"I don't care about your protocol! Wyatt, you *know* Jason."

How well do you know this man?

I touch my left temple, where my mother's voice rings loudest. It's what she said to me, years ago, when I told her I was marrying Jason, defying her warning to never trust a man—a conviction she clung to after marrying my father at twenty-one, then losing him at twenty-two, when he went out for diaper cream and never came back. For most of my childhood, my mother wore her misery and regret like a too-tight wedding ring, and instead of confetti or well wishes, she threw doubt on my decision to commit to Jason. *I under-*

stand there's a baby involved, she said, *but really, Julia, how well do you know this man?*

It disturbs me how the question comes back to me now, as Sienna's ex-boyfriend, an officer of the law, informs us that Jason is somehow, impossibly, a suspect in a murder investigation.

A voice rumbles in the hallway, where a stocky man with salt-and-pepper hair leans across the nurses' station. Wyatt whips his head toward the sound, then back to Sienna, piercing her with his stare.

"Try to be calm when Beck's here," he whispers. "Otherwise, he'll keep you in the dark."

He turns toward the man—Beck, apparently—who's approaching us now. "I figured I'd wait for you up here," Wyatt says.

"No problem. I saw a doctor I knew from an old case on the way up, so it took me a—"

His gaze snags on Sienna.

"Wait," he says, looking at Wyatt. "Isn't this . . . ?"

Wyatt nods, lips pressed together.

"Sierra, right?" Beck asks.

Sienna crosses her arms by way of an answer.

"Sienna," Wyatt supplies. "Sienna Larkin."

Beck's eyes go hazy as he mutters to himself, "Jason Larkin. Right." He shakes his head at Wyatt. "Jesus, Miller, why didn't you say anything?" When Wyatt only shrugs, Beck turns back to Sienna. "Always the bleeding heart, am I right?" He pitches his thumb at Wyatt. "Even when it could get him in trouble."

He puts his hand on Wyatt's shoulder and gives it a squeeze. "I won't tell anyone," he says quietly. "But you're to steer clear of this case, all right? I don't care if Sam's kid explodes into a million pieces and he's out for a month on bereavement. You're off this one."

"I know," Wyatt agrees.

"Your case," Sienna says to Beck, "doesn't make any sense. I don't care what you found in his car—my brother didn't kill anyone."

Beck shoots another disappointed glance at Wyatt, who steps away a little, hands behind his back as if waiting to be cuffed.

"I'm Detective Beck," he says to me, reaching out a hand. On instinct I take it, my grip limp in his, easily crushed. "You're Mrs. Larkin, I presume?"

I nod.

"Good to meet you," he says. "Listen, I understand this is a difficult time, but I'll need to ask your husband a few questions."

"Well, good luck with that," Sienna says. "He's in a coma."

Beck's eyebrow lifts as he looks past us at Jason. There it is again: the bruises, the bandages, the tube, my husband's mouth stuck open, as if in perpetual surprise.

"I, uh . . . didn't know that," Beck says.

"I didn't either," Wyatt murmurs. His eyes, soft and imploring, reach for Sienna's, but she turns her cheek, shielding herself from his gaze.

Beck clears his throat. "Did the doctors say when he'll regain consciousness?"

"If you think we're sharing that information with you, you're insane," Sienna says.

Beck rocks on his heels, brow furrowed in thought. "We can speak with his doctors. In the meantime"—he pivots toward me—"Mrs. Larkin, could you please confirm: Your husband attended the HomeGrowth Conference at the Hillstead Marriott on Friday, correct?"

He reaches into his jacket to pull out a notepad, then yanks the pen from its spiral. Flipping to a clean page, he waits for my answer, but now my thoughts are stuck on that conference. According to the news, it was the last place Gavin was seen alive.

"You don't have to say anything," Sienna says, hooking her hand onto mine. Her palm is hot, her skin almost scalding, and it's only at her touch that I realize how cold I am, how the room feels walled with ice.

"No, it's—" My voice quivers with the first words I've spoken since Wyatt arrived. "It's fine, I— Yes. He went to the conference."

"And do you recall what time he got home?"

"Um. I went to bed early that night. But I— I think it was eleven thirty?"

Sienna squeezes my hand, bolstering me through my stammer, as Beck scribbles a note.

"Did your husband mention any stops he made between leaving the conference and arriving back home?"

"Stops? No. There was a dinner. At the Marriott. He came home right after."

Beck's hand pauses as he glances at me above the notepad. "You sure about that?"

The follow-up is pointed, like he knows something I don't, and it catches me off guard. Because no, I guess I can't be sure. On Friday, I was surprised when it was nine, and then ten o'clock, and Jason wasn't home yet. He hates the after-hours networking at conferences, always wants to duck out as soon as the last presentation is over. When I texted at ten to get his ETA, the message went undelivered—his phone dead again.

"Of course she is," Sienna says, filling my silence, but Beck lingers on me, waiting for an answer.

My throat shrinks. If I say I'm sure, then I'm lying to a cop. But if I tell him the truth, I risk validating his suspicions, giving him space to wonder where else Jason went that night.

I compromise with a nod.

"All right," Beck says. He clicks the top of his pen and slaps his notepad shut. "Thanks, Mrs. Larkin. I'll reach out to your husband's medical team."

"You're wasting your time," Sienna says, but Beck is already swiveling toward the door, nodding to Wyatt to follow him. Wyatt hangs back, though, and Sienna continues her thought, aiming it at him instead of Beck. "Jason has nothing to do with what happened to Gavin."

He stretches out a hand—as if his instinct, after all these months, is still to touch her—but he drops it at the sharp lash of her gaze.

"Miller," Beck calls to Wyatt. "Let's go."

And then we're alone again, Sienna and me, our hands knotted together, Jason laid out behind us like a body in a morgue.

. . .

I've never loved our house.

As we pull into the garage, this is what I think of. Not Jason's coma. Not the blood on his knife. Not the dead man's phone in his car.

The house is too big, too boxy, too similar to all the others in our town of Willow Creek. But when Jason first invited me to move in with him, I was soothed by the message it might send my mother: *See? It doesn't matter how well I know him. He's not going to leave me. He'd have to leave his own house, his own history, too.* So I kept my opinions stored away like the box of childhood mementos I brought with me. I pretended not to mind the pee-colored tile in the master bath, pretended it didn't haunt me to sleep in his parents' old room. Day after day, I looked at the rooster wallpaper downstairs and I said nothing, pretending it didn't look like a crime scene.

For a moment, though, this house I don't love is a comfort, a thing unchanged when everything else is warped and wrong. There's the dent in the garage's drywall where Aiden, careening in from the driveway, crashed his bike when he was eight. There's the fort, stacks of brick and wood, Jason helped him make in the corner at ten. And there's the spot, empty now, for Jason's car—which is smashed up somewhere, a gnarl of seats and steel. Evidence, apparently.

I stare at the vacant space, lingering behind the wheel even as Sienna rips off her seat belt beside me. "Come on," she demands.

Numbly, I follow.

Inside, Sienna slams her purse onto the counter. "This is so stupid," she says, a proclamation she threw out repeatedly on the drive back. "Who the fuck does Beck think he is?"

"Cool your—" I start, but the mantra's words are lost beneath her own.

"There could be a million reasons why Jason had Gavin's phone!"

I frown at that—because I haven't been able to think of any. So I've tried not to think of it at all.

"He could have given Gavin a ride home from the conference," Sienna says. "Maybe Gavin got sloshed at that dinner—Jason wouldn't let him drive drunk—and the phone slipped out of his pocket in the car. Or maybe Jason saw Gavin leave it behind at the Marriott and figured he'd give it to him at work on Monday. Either way, it doesn't mean he *killed him*, and the cops are off their fucking rockers to think so."

"The cops think *what?*"

We wince at Aiden's voice. He shuffles into the kitchen, brown hair rumpled, cheek pillow-creased. I lurch toward him. "Honey . . ." But he recoils from my outstretched hand.

"Why do the cops think that?" he asks.

Silence oozes through the room. I'm struck mute by Aiden's loose lounge pants that, even with his recent growth spurt, make him look like a little kid. They're Jason's, actually—bigger than Aiden's old ones, but still too big overall. The plaid pantlegs pool around his heels, threatening to trip him up.

"It isn't true," Sienna says.

"But why do they think it?"

"Because they're idiots. And because—"

I glare at her in warning. Aiden was troubled enough by Gavin's murder, awake but zombie-faced in the middle of the night; the specifics of the cops' suspicions will only disturb him even more. But Sienna barrels ahead.

"—there was a tiny bit of blood on his pocketknife. And Gavin's phone was in his car. But it doesn't even make sense. Who would kill someone and leave that evidence lying around?"

Aiden stiffens, then goes completely still. His gaze hollows out like a sleepwalker's. "Whose blood is on the knife?" he asks.

"Probably your dad's!" Sienna stomps toward the cabinet to pull down a glass, then fills it at the sink. "He probably got clumsy and nicked himself."

She tosses her head back, draining her drink in only three gulps, and as she reaches for a refill, my attention drifts toward the living room walls—the splotches of blood Sienna insists are only animals.

"Um. How—" Aiden's voice is hazy, as if speaking from inside a dream. My focus snaps back onto him. "Can't Dad just explain to the cops what's going on?"

"No, not yet," I say. "He's still in the coma. But pretty soon he'll . . ." Pretty soon he'll what? Wake up? Dr. Brighton was clear with us: the timeline for Jason's recovery isn't guaranteed. I look to Sienna, hoping she'll take over, but she's still at the faucet, drinking from her glass. "The doctors are very hopeful he'll get better soon."

Aiden sways on his feet. Side to side, slow as a pendulum. I inch toward him, hands in front of me in case I need to catch him. "Aiden?"

He doesn't answer, but his face grows pale. His brows pinch together.

"Aid?" I try again. This time, I touch his cheek, and when he doesn't spring away, I pull him into a hug. He stands like a statue in my embrace, and my heart aches, remembering how he used to ask me to hold him, to engulf his entire body with mine. *I'm the ice cream and you're the scoop!* he said once. And I answered, *How can I be the scoop if I'm the one eating you up,* as I nipped at his neck, drank up his squeals of laughter.

Now he wrenches out of my embrace, speaks without meeting my eyes.

"How do you know Dad didn't do it?"

Sienna's head jerks toward him. "Do what? Kill his boss?"

Aiden nods, and I step away from him, blown back by the question.

"Because he *didn't,*" Sienna says, her nonanswer doing little to alter Aiden's posture.

"Because he's Dad," I try. "Because we know him."

Because Jason would never hurt someone. Quite the opposite: he obsesses over keeping people safe. He bought me an escape tool for my car, on the off chance I ever drive into a lake and need to break the glass. He mostly ignores his own phone, but he figured out how to set up parental controls on Aiden's so if our son ever edges too close to danger, we'll be alerted. And it's not just with us. He missed Aiden's fifth birthday party because he witnessed a hit and run, and even after the police took his statement, he drove to the hospital, sitting vigil for the victim, who was a twenty-year-old woman with no family in the area. Despite the distance I've kept from him lately, Jason is a good man. To us and to others.

"Maybe you don't know him as well as you think you do," Aiden says.

The sentence clangs inside me, ringing a bell whose sound is too familiar.

"What?" Sienna says. "Why would you say that?"

The hair on my arms lifts up, hundreds of tiny antennas. He knows. Our walls aren't particularly thick; he easily could have heard Jason and me, that night we fought in December. I'd tried to be quiet, to say as little as I could, but my voice was shrieky with the shock of my discovery.

Ten thousand dollars missing from our bank account.

It was almost a fluke that I noticed it at all. Jason handles our bills and transfers; it's not very often I log in to the accounts. But our fifteenth anniversary was approaching, and I was eager to finally start booking the second honeymoon Jason had promised me since our tenth. That year, we marked the occasion with takeout at home, candles on the table, an impromptu slow dance in the kitchen. Then, in a whisper against my ear, Jason told me he'd opened a new bank account, one specifically allotted for the big, multicity European vacation I'd always dreamed of. Growing up with a single mother—who could barely afford vacations in New England, let alone other countries—I never had a chance to travel, and after we had Aiden, the farthest we went was Virginia Beach. But Jason planned to change that. He told me he'd already deposited his recent bonus in the new account, and for the next five years, we'd save as much as we could. *I want to dance with you*, he said, his palm warm on my back, *just like this, in as many countries as I can*. The line was clearly rehearsed, but still so sweet, and it reminded me that I'd been right, ten years before, to commit to a man I'd only known for a handful of months.

But this past December, I was checking the account's balance, and instead of all deposits, I saw a stunning withdrawal, its zeroes lined up like beads in an abacus. I pointed it out to Jason, at first imagining that he'd booked our trip himself—planning, perhaps, to gift me the itinerary for Christmas. But his face flooded with color, his expression darkening, and I knew then, before he explained anything, that whatever he'd done with the money was not a surprise, but a secret. Instantly, my mother's voice, bitter and suspicious, barged into my head: *Never trust a man.*

He called it a bad investment, one that had been pitched to him as a sure thing, a way to double what we'd saved. *Well, then, un-invest,* I said. *Get the money back. We can't go anywhere with this.* I gestured to the amount left—barely enough for plane tickets—and Jason paused for a long time, chewing his bottom lip, something like fear streaking through his eyes. Then he told me that someone had screwed him over. Those were his words: *he screwed me over, the money's gone, I'm so sorry.* And he got on his knees in front of me, like a strange proposal, promising to fix it, to work like hell to get the promotion he was up for, the salary of which would earn back our honeymoon money in no time.

Since then, I haven't asked him more about it, haven't even spoken of it, really—just drifted from his touch, skirted his gaze, answered his jokes with a courtesy smile. It spooked me too much, this thing he did behind my back, the dream of mine he shattered, and it made me wonder what else he's done that I never could have guessed at.

Now Sienna repeats her question. "Aiden, why would you say that?"

I hold my breath, scared he's going to say it—that he heard everything. That I failed to protect him from my hurt. That I hurt him in turn, marring his shiny vision of his father. That, for as few words as I said to Jason that night, I still said too much.

"Just forget it," he says instead, and I release a morsel of air. "I'm going back to bed.

"Aiden, you're clearly upset," Sienna says. "Let's talk about it. We can make you some hot chocolate."

She sings the name of the drink, trying to entice him, trying to do for me, for him, what I can't do myself. Because the only sentence I can conjure now is his—*Maybe you don't know him as well as you think you do*—which is, of course, unnervingly similar to my mother's: *How well do you know this man?*

"I'm fine, Auntsy," Aiden says to Sienna. "Goodnight." He swishes out of the kitchen, pantlegs catching beneath his feet.

"Come on—" Sienna calls, but she's cut off by her phone, ringing in her purse.

Our eyes snap toward each other, blaring the same thought—*the hospital!*—but when she launches for the phone and reads it, the hope slumps out of her. In a moment, her cheeks are stained with a familiar pink.

I crane my neck to see the screen: Wyatt.

Sienna declines the call. I know she doesn't let herself speak to him; she hasn't budged an inch on that self-imposed rule since their breakup. But maybe Wyatt could be an inside source for us on the investigation, a luxury that most families of suspects—I blanch at the reminder that Jason's a suspect—probably don't get.

"What if he had news about Jason?" I ask. "About the . . . evidence."

"You heard Beck. He's off the case. He's probably just using this as an opportunity to—I don't know—worm his way back into my life."

Sienna crosses her arms, holding herself rigid. She's trying to appear unfazed, but the flush in her skin tells me otherwise.

"Are you okay?" I ask. "I know it was probably hard. Seeing Wyatt after all this time."

A muscle jumps in her jaw, but before she can answer, her phone rings again.

"Jesus," she says. "Twice in a row?"

"He might know something," I say. "I think you should pick up."

She unfolds her arms, then cups her phone, head tilting from side to side as she wavers over the decision. Finally, she groans, stabbing at the screen.

"You're on speaker," she says. "Julia's right here."

It's an odd, cut-to-the-chase greeting. But then again, any exchange with Wyatt probably feels too long for Sienna.

"Oh. Hey," Wyatt says.

"Do you know something?" she asks. "Did the blood come back on the knife?"

"Uh, no. That'll probably be a few days. I just— I wanted to tell you something, before I left the hospital, but Beck had me on a short leash after warning you about the evidence."

"Okay, well, what? Why are you calling?"

There's a hiss of static as Wyatt blows out a breath. "I think you should get a lawyer."

Chapter Four

SIENNA

On Thursday morning, Gavin Reed is everywhere.

In posts on the NextDoor app: *Be careful everyone. That stitched-up mouth? That screams serial killer to me. I wouldn't be surprised if—*

On the TV in the hospital lobby: *Police say they're continuing to follow leads, and while they don't believe Reed's killer poses a threat to the public, they're cautioning—*

On the lips of people in the cafeteria: *The woman who does my hair? Her father-in-law lives on the victim's street, and he said he's seen someone skulking around at night and I just know it's—*

But inside Jason's room, Julia and I haven't mentioned Gavin's name. We've been too busy watching the nurses, beaming them hopeful looks whenever they check on Jason, then deflating when they note no changes in his condition. We've also been pecking at our laptops, fielding messages from clients we've ignored over the past couple days. In between, I've been on my phone, waiting for it to glow with one specific call—and fuming over Clive's Instagram.

Early this morning, he posted a picture where he's crouched beside his toddler daughter, his back to the camera, pointing at the sunrise like his kid couldn't find the sky without him. *Light of my life*, he captioned it, and as I scan it again now, I feel the sun in every part of my body, a nuclear fusion setting me on fire. How dare he enjoy one moment with his daughter when my parents can't enjoy any with theirs. How dare he have any light at all, other than the kind in prison cells.

I picture him in a space like that, dim and desolate, and try to relish the image—but too quickly, it gets away from me, morphing to a moment from my freshman year of high school. Clive's voice in the dark. A postered wall. My pulse thumping, first to some distant music, next to some internal alarm. Then Jason, out of nowhere—

"What are you doing?" Julia asks, cutting the memory short.

My thumb hovers above Clive's head like a laser sight on a gun. I point the screen toward Julia, showing her the photo for the second time today.

"Nope," she says. "Back to work."

Huffing out a breath, I set my phone aside, then force my attention back to my laptop. I groan at our inbox, where Dale Stapleton is impatient for an update on when his new splash page goes live.

"What's the Out of Office message," I ask, "for 'Our brother-slash-husband is in a coma and the cops think he murdered someone so give us a break for a while'?"

"I wouldn't lead with 'brother-slash-husband,'" Julia says. "It sounds . . . gross."

I pout at her. "You don't want to be my sister wife?"

"Ew, please stop."

I chuckle deviously before turning back to the email. "I'm telling Dale we have a family emergency. And also that he can suck it."

Julia's fingers pause on her keypad. "I know you're joking, but I also know you're stressed. So let's be careful not to have a Lashley Incident."

The reference tugs a smile from me. Ashley Lattari was one of our first clients. She was getting her salon off the ground the same time Julia and I were learning how to run a business together. So far, our journey had been relatively bump-free—no surprise to us; our closeness and complementing talents made us uniquely qualified for partnership—but when Ashley's check bounced, after we'd already sunk weeks into her project, my eyes burning from perfecting each pixel of her Lashley logo, I didn't even think, just reached for my laptop, then funneled my rage into an email, caps lock engaged. When Julia caught sight of my screen, she gasped and grabbed my hand. "Cool your fire," she urged—and I took a moment, breathed in the mantra like it was oxygen, and deleted the draft so Ashley would never receive it.

Not even moments later, our email pinged with an apology: I'm so sorry, I think my check bounced?? There was a delay on my recent deposit, but it's all set now. I'll drop off a new check today.

Julia and I gaped at Ashley's message, processing the split-second sequence of events.

"Oh my god," Julia said, "you almost blew up our business before it really began."

"Uh-huh, uh-huh," I said, not bothering to deny it, "that's a fair assessment of what just happened. But hey, this is why we're partners, right? So you can keep us . . . un-blown-up?"

Our eyes slid to each other, and we shared an uneasy silence. Then we burst into laughter, giddy with relief at the near miss.

"As long as Dale behaves," I tell Julia now, "I won't have to Lashley him." Her gaze dashes toward me to make sure I'm joking.

On the armrest of my chair, my phone lights up. I slap my laptop shut. "It's Lou!"

Lou Ackerman, my dad's old golfing buddy—and a defense attorney.

Last night, I'd resisted Wyatt's recommendation to get a lawyer. Actually, according to Julia, I sniped at him about it. But the suggestion stabbed at me. How could Wyatt, whose life Jason literally saved one time when Wyatt choked on a hot dog, think that Jason was capable of murder? *That's not what I'm saying,* he insisted. *But it's in Jason's best interest to have someone representing him, before this gets worse.*

"Lou, hi," I say into the phone. "Did you talk to the cops? Did they give you anything?"

When I spoke to him a few hours ago, he was shocked to hear that Jason was a suspect. *Jason's a good kid,* Lou said, as if my brother were thirteen, not thirty-nine. But his next sentence—*don't worry, I'll take care of him*—relaxed my spine for the first time since Detective Beck trudged into Jason's room.

"Uh, yeah," Lou says, voice deep and gravelly, just like I remember from my childhood. I switch to speaker so Julia can hear. "I'll be able to do more once the blood from the knife comes back, but in the meantime: Do you know where Jason went on Friday night, after the conference?"

Julia and I hold each other's gaze over the phone.

"He went home," I say. "We already told them that."

"Turns out that isn't true. Police have footage from the hotel security cams that show Jason leaving around eight thirty p.m. The cameras don't have the best view of the parking lot, so they can't tell what direction he went, just that he left at eight thirty."

Julia's forehead scrunches. Yesterday, she told Beck that Jason got home at eleven thirty.

"We . . . didn't know that," I tell Lou. "But I'm sure it's nothing. Friday night   that was when it was really nice out, right? Before that big rainstorm? He probably just went somewhere to enjoy the night, or maybe he grabbed a beer with a co-worker before going home."

"Definitely possible," Lou says. "But it's important we—"

"And if they have Jason on the cameras, what about Gavin? Did they see him leave with anyone?"

"It's hard to say," Lou answers. "He departed the same time as Jason—seems a group from Integrity Plus left all at once—but again, the camera angles didn't allow the police to catch where he went once he left the building. What's important right now, though, is plugging that gap in Jason's timeline. And since we can't ask Jason himself, I'd suggest you check his credit cards, debit cards, see if he made any purchases during those hours that could verify his location."

I point at Julia's laptop and she opens a browser.

"Okay, I'll let you know if we find anything," I say. "But—can't the cops just figure out where Jason was through his phone? The cell phone towers he pinged or whatever?"

"Phone was off," Lou says. "Last data they can pull has him in the area of the Marriott, around that same time, eight thirty."

I shoot an annoyed glance at Jason in his bed, trying to ignore the protruding tube. "It must've died. We *always* have to bug him to charge it."

"Right," Lou says, "I'm sure it was something like that. But I'll be honest: the police could use it to build a case for premeditation. They've got three hours unaccounted for, and now they can say he switched off his phone upon leaving the hotel because he didn't want his location to be traced."

I scuff out a laugh. "I don't think Jason even knows his phone *can* be traced. It's basically a paperweight to him."

"Be that as it may," Lou says, "the best thing you can do for him right now is to determine where he was from eight thirty to eleven thirty the night of the murder—and to do it as soon as you can. I'll keep a line open with the police and update you accordingly."

There's something different in his tone now. Gone is the friendly buffer from earlier this morning; instead, his words are edged with gravity, urgency, like someone whose client is actually in trouble.

When Lou and I hang up, I turn to Julia, hunched over her laptop.

"Find anything?" I ask.

She shakes her head, twisting strands of her dark caramel hair. "I checked his personal credit card *and* the one we use for household purchases and there's nothing from Friday night."

"Okay." I take her hand to keep her from knotting her hair. "That's . . . not ideal. But look, this won't even matter once the blood comes back."

Julia blinks at me, eyes big and anxious, and I squeeze her palm—maybe a little harder than I intended to, because it annoys me, that anxiety, like she thinks the case against Jason is careening toward an arrest.

Then again, maybe she's right to worry this much. Don't I know, as well as anyone, that justice isn't guaranteed, that it's as slippery as oil, that police and prosecutors and legal systems can easily fuck things up? I'd expected Clive Clayton to be sentenced to the state maximum of ten years, but when the judge said *three* that day in the courtroom, my shock and anger flashed so bright I stopped seeing the wooden bench, the attorneys' tables, the back of Clive's head. Jason tried to wrap his arm around me, but he couldn't protect me from this unfathomable knowledge: you can choose to drive drunk, you can crush someone's parents—literally crush them—and in the end, the number of years in your sentence will barely exceed the number of people you killed.

I grip the hospital chair as my stomach plummets.

Justice failed us then. What if it fails us now, too?

A knock, gentle and tentative, snaps my attention to the doorway. There's a woman there—tall and glossy with long, red hair and a chic, slim-fit blazer.

"Maeve!" Julia says, jumping from her chair.

I blink, surprised to see her here, cut from her usual context: grumbling with Jason about colleagues, laughing about hijinks at Integrity Plus. Maeve Dorsey is Jason's best friend from work. I've only hung out with her on a handful of occasions, one of which was last Thanksgiving, when a snowstorm canceled her flight to her sister's, but I know enough to like her. She has a cool, easy confidence that, at first glance, makes her seem unapproachable, but she nerds out with Jason all the time, the two of them using their lunch breaks for "competitive crosswording" or crafting things out of office supplies—a cabin from pencils, a coat from packing tape and Post-its.

Julia bounces to the doorway and stands on tiptoes to hug Maeve.

"I'm on my lunch break," Maeve says, "so I can't stay long, but I wanted to— Oh god." Her eyes latch onto Jason over Julia's shoulder, and she drops her arms, takes a step back. "I know you said *coma* in your text, but this—" She gestures to my brother, whose bruises are more waxy than shiny today, a marginal improvement. "I didn't picture his face looking so . . . wrecked."

I nod, understanding her shock. "Come in," I say, but she lingers at the threshold, as if unwilling to see Jason up close, his wounds even ghastlier beneath the room's harsh lighting. "Or we could talk in the family lounge?" I offer.

We move down the hall to the dim, unoccupied space with stiff couches and too many tissue boxes. Maeve plops her canvas bag beside her, and I recognize the design as one of her own creations, a mix of hand-painted leaves and embroidered petals. For years, she's supplemented her work as an office manager with an online store where she sells totes and wallets, shirts and scarves. Her pieces are beautiful. Classy and stylish, like Maeve herself. The first time we met, we connected over the design aspect of our jobs, though I envy Maeve's florals and ivies and intricate patterns, all more elegant than the flashy web pages most of our clients want.

"How's your store coming along?" I think to ask. At Thanksgiving, Maeve mentioned she was working on transitioning from an online shop to a brick-and-mortar store. But it was taking more from her than she'd realized—time, money, energy—so the process had been slow. *Guess you'll be stuck with me at Integrity a little longer,* Jason had said, smiling at her over a forkful of mashed potatoes.

"That's sweet of you to ask," Maeve says. "I don't know if Jason told you, but I finally secured a space."

"Oh, wow—where?"

"In Hillstead, so I can zip back and forth between there and my house. It's in that little strip mall, near the Barnes & Noble, between a salon and yoga studio, which I think will be good. There's reno to be done—I'm going to HGTV the hell out of it—but I've got my fingers crossed for an August launch. I was going to contact you both about some branding work, but"—she gestures to the walls around us, the dull beige paint, the same anonymous art you'd see in a motel—"this isn't the time to talk about that."

"It's fine," I say. "We'd love to set up a meeting, once Jason's better."

"And congrats," Julia adds. "That's amazing."

"Yeah, thanks." Maeve fidgets with the strap of her bag, an anxious gesture that's out of sync with her usual poise. "Do they think that'll be soon—Jason getting better?"

"The doctor told us on Tuesday she expected improvement over the next few days," I say. "But it's been two days already and nothing's changed, so it's agonizing."

"I bet," Maeve says. "I still can't believe it. Jason was *fine* on Tuesday, and now— God, his *face*." She shakes her head. "This has been the craziest week."

"What's it like at work?" Julia asks. "With Gavin . . . gone."

Maeve lets out a breath. "The police were there Monday and Tuesday, taking statements, searching his office. And the phones have been ringing off the hook. If you can believe it, this has actually been *good* for business. But it's so weird there. Everyone's just tiptoeing around, almost like they're . . . suspicious of each other? As if one of us was the one who killed him."

A shudder ripples through Maeve, but Julia and I stiffen.

"Do you think that's possible?" I ask. "Is there someone at work with a grudge against him?"

"The police asked the same thing, but—I don't think so? Nothing I noticed, anyway. A lot of people still treat him like he's a god because of the whole merger thing. Remember that? How Integrity was supposed to merge with Higher Home Improvement but Gavin turned the owner in to the IRS instead? I'm sure Jason told you that Integrity was struggling before that—we were heading toward layoffs—but then Gavin managed to get most of Higher Home's customers without having to split any profits. So, some people still really respect him for that. But others . . ." She trails off, shrugging one shoulder.

"Others what?" I press.

"I don't know, he can be"—Maeve pauses, searching for the right word—"inappropriate. Making jokes about women during sales meetings—not to their faces; all our sales reps are men right now—but Jason's told me stories. Like, Gavin will talk about someone he rode up in the elevator with, saying he wouldn't mind giving her *a different kind of ride*."

"Ew," Julia and I say together.

"And at the dinner after the conference, he was downing drink after drink—which isn't that weird; a lot of people get pretty loose at those dinners—but he kept trying to chat up the women from other companies, inviting them to 'keep the party going' back at his lake house."

My pulse thrums beneath my skin. "Do you know if any of them did?"

Maeve shrugs again. "I doubt it."

I think of the news story from Tuesday night, the interviews with Gavin's neighbors. *Everyone's still all "Me Too" these days. He probably called her "sweetheart" or something.* It boiled me up at the time—that absurd, reductive take on the movement—but even then, something about it resonated. The brutality of the murder, those stitched-up lips, like someone was punishing Gavin for something he'd said. *Only a woman has that much anger,* another neighbor told the reporter. And I know what she means.

Maybe a woman from the conference went home with Gavin—for a nightcap, for the promise of a great view: the lake behind his house sparkling with stars. And maybe Gavin crossed a line. First with his words. Then with his hands. And maybe, by the time the woman left, there was a body, stabbed and smothered and stitched, lying in his backyard.

The theory zips up my spine, a tingle of potential.

"So you were at the conference?" Julia asks Maeve. "It wasn't just Gavin and the sales team?"

"Yeah, Gavin likes me to get some face time with the vendors, since I'm their main contact at the office."

"Okay, so—" Julia clears her throat. "Do you know what happened with Jason that night?"

My head whips toward her.

"What do you mean?" Maeve and I ask at the same time.

Julia looks at me, brow puckering, before returning her attention to Maeve. "Did you see Jason leave? Do you know where he went after the conference?"

Maeve's eyes fog over a little, as if perplexed by the question. "Jason? No. I assumed he went home." She tilts her head. "Why?"

I stare at Julia, her parted lips, the flick of her tongue behind her teeth.

Is she actually planning to tell her? We didn't discuss it, but I assumed we were on the same page: Lou's the only person outside the family we're sharing this with. Nobody else, certainly not Jason's colleague—good friend or not—needs to know what the cops are so stupid to think.

"The police are investigating him," Julia says—and a flicker of something, like a pilot light, ignites in my chest.

"Jules," I say.

"For what?" Maeve asks, frowning. Then her mouth pops open. "Wait—for Gavin? As a suspect?" She swivels toward the door as if Jason might be standing there, waiting to explain. "*Why?*"

I laser a look at Julia, but if she feels the heat of my gaze, she simply ignores it. And she tells Maeve everything—Gavin's phone in Jason's car, the blood they're testing, the time we can't account for.

I study Maeve's face as she listens. Her eyes bulge. Her features contort with horror. "But that's impossible!" she says. "They can't seriously think it was Jason."

I relax a little. She's on our side. Jason's side. And it feels good— her sputtering disbelief, the validation that the cops are out of their minds—especially after Lou's terse phone call, his insistence that we plug up Jason's timeline like it's a leak in a boat.

Julia was right to include Maeve.

"Do you know why Jason might have had Gavin's phone?" Julia asks. "Sienna thought maybe Gavin left it at the Marriott and Jason picked it up for him. Or maybe he drove Gavin home that night and he lost it in his car?"

Maeve is slow to shake her head, eyes pinned to the wall as if watching her thoughts play out there. "I don't know. Gavin might've left it behind, I guess. But I seriously doubt Jason would've given him a ride home."

"Well, if Gavin was drunk," I explain. "You know our history, right? With our parents? You said Gavin was knocking back drinks, and Jason wouldn't let him drive like that."

"No, I know, it's just—Jason was pissed at Gavin last week. And he definitely wasn't thrilled to have to spend the whole day with him on Friday."

Julia and I exchange a puzzled look.

"Pissed at him?" she asks.

"Yeah, you know," Maeve says, "about the promotion. The sales manager position."

The line in Julia's forehead deepens, a shallow trench dug into her skin.

"Right," she says, "he's been anxious to hear about it."

"Oh—no." Now it's Maeve who looks confused. "Jason didn't tell you?"

Julia straightens in her seat. Her lips curl inward, sealing together, but otherwise, she's remarkably still.

One . . . Two . . . Three . . .

"Didn't tell her what?" I ask.

Maeve pivots toward me. "Gavin picked somebody else. He announced it last Monday."

Julia's lips part. Her eyebrows cinch together. "Oh," she says.

I sit back in my chair, sympathy whooshing through me. For months now, Jason's been talking nonstop about that promotion— the extra hours he's been working, the sales he's been racking up—

and I was actually surprised it was so important to him. It's not like home services is his dream job; he'd planned to go to grad school for architecture, but when Julia got pregnant, he took a crew position at Integrity Plus, which was close and hiring and willing to train him. Then, after seven years of sunburns and callouses, of smelling like a warehouse whenever I saw him, he was promoted to sales rep, a job that plays to his strengths: he has a deep interest in people's needs, and he cares about helping them.

"Sienna, did you know?" Julia asks, an odd tremor to her voice.

"No. But he was probably just processing it still. We know how badly he wanted it."

The job seems awful to me—managing other people, no thanks—but it would have provided a significant salary bump, which Jason had been fixated on.

"But Maeve," Julia says, face stamped with a dark expression, "you said he was pissed at Gavin about it? At the conference, too?"

"Well, yeah. But I just mean, he still seemed kind of raw about it. Scowling at Gavin, stabbing him with his eyes." Maeve chuckles a second, before sucking in a breath. "Oh god, terrible word choice, with the knife and the blood and everything. I didn't mean it like that. He was upset about it, sure, but he wouldn't . . . I didn't mean he'd—"

"It's okay," I say. "It sucks that Jason didn't get the job, but that had nothing to do with Gavin's death."

Still, I know from my years with Wyatt: if the police catch wind of Jason's anger toward Gavin, they could view it as motive.

"Right," Maeve agrees. "Of course not."

I look at Julia. She blinks, as if her vision's gone blurry. Then, meeting my gaze, she gives a curt nod. "Of course not," she echoes.

And I don't understand it—the speckle of doubt I see in her eyes.

Chapter Five

JULIA

By the time Sienna drops me off at home, streetlamps halo the sidewalk. I head to the front door, ignoring the newspaper tossed onto our driveway. I already know its headline—Community On Guard as Killer of Local Business Owner Remains At Large. It glared at us from kiosks as we left the hospital, and now the neighbors prove it right: up and down the street, all the porchlights are on, shining through the night like eyes keeping watch.

Sienna's high beams swish over me as she reverses out of the driveway. I told her not to come in. Told her I wanted to talk to Aiden, make sure he's okay. But our house is dark, the shades pulled tight. He must have gone to bed early—and it's terrible how relieved I am, how I can breathe a little easier than I did in Sienna's car. *How do you know Dad didn't do it?* Aiden asked last night, and I'd never heard him sound so cynical or suspicious about his father. It's made me worry what else he might press me about, what other questions he might have when my mind already swarms with so many of my own—sharp, stinging ones I've tried all evening to swat away.

Inside, I linger in the foyer, pressing my forehead against the front door, pushing back against the ache that's pulsed there since Maeve's visit. Why didn't Jason tell me about the job? For an entire week before his accident, he knew he didn't get the promotion, but he never uttered a word. I try to think of the last time he mentioned it: how the new position would fix everything, how it would allow us to replenish our honeymoon savings, fund a trip even bigger and better than the one we'd planned. But in truth, I'd started to tune those comments out. Because even though I'd been anticipating our vacation for years—learning basic phrases in French, Spanish, and Italian; doodling the Eiffel Tower in the margins of grocery lists—it wasn't the money, the lost trip, I was most concerned about. It was the furtiveness of it all, the fact that he hid it from me, that his story about the bad investment, the secret someone who'd lured him into it, was so vague and incomplete that it seemed obvious there were even more secrets he was squirreling away.

I know Sienna's suspicious of my reaction. At red lights on the drive home, I felt her examining my face, wondering about the tight, agitated expression I'd been struggling for hours to loosen. But more than ever, I can't tell her about those ten thousand dollars, can't explain why Maeve's revelation about the promotion has me so rattled. Sienna's already on the defensive, deflecting details that continue to confound me: Gavin's phone in Jason's car, the gap in his timeline. If I told her what he did, how he explained it, she'd skip right over Jason's betrayal of my trust and focus only on the way *he* got hurt, the part where someone screwed *him* over. The injustice would be too much for her, and her reaction—defending Jason instead of supporting me—would only devastate me more. So I've buried my discontent from the beginning, entombing it deep inside me.

I lock the front door, shuffle into the kitchen to set the timer on the coffeemaker, then head upstairs. Jason's absence is everywhere. It thickens the air like humidity. Working from home, I'm used to being here without him. But that's during the day, when his return is a promise. Now his absence feels more like a presence, a shadow hovering above me, even as I flick on the stairwell light and darkness skitters away.

The door to Aiden's room is ajar, but when I peek in, I find that his bed is empty. I look across the hall at the bathroom—empty, too—and concern seizes my throat.

"Aiden?" I choke out.

I yank my phone from my pocket, hoping for a text, a missed call, a voice mail in which he begrudgingly keeps me in the loop. Maybe he went to a friend's house after school, got picked up by someone else's mother. But I have no messages, no notifications.

I type out a text to him, pausing only at a sound down the hall: a drawer sliding open. I whip my head toward the master bedroom, a crack of light leaking through the space where the door isn't totally closed. I hurry to my room, push inside, and finally breathe at the sight of Aiden, his back facing me, earbuds in, hands rummaging through Jason's nightstand.

"Aiden?"

He doesn't respond. I touch his shoulder and he jolts like I've electrocuted him.

"Jesus!" he says, ripping out an earbud.

"Sorry! I was calling you, but—"

"Why are you home so early?" His question is sharpened to an accusation.

"It's not early. It's eight forty-five."

"What? No it's not." Aiden pulls his phone from his hoodie, pauses his music, then squints at the time. "Whoa." He takes a step back, setting a hand against the wall. He looks disoriented. Suddenly unstable.

I leap forward to support him. "Honey, are you okay?"

He jerks upright. "I'm fine. I just—didn't realize what time it was." His gaze drops to the open drawer of Jason's nightstand. He closes it with his thigh, then stares at his Converse, the white toes marked by handwritten band names.

I stare at them, too. I've seen these sneakers hundreds of times, but suddenly, there's something about them that gives me pause. A vague anxiety hums in the back of my mind.

"Are you sure?" I stall, waiting for the thought to clarify.

Aiden digs the toe of his shoe into the carpet, like he's squashing a bug, and that's when it strikes me, a detail I didn't register until now. On Sunday night, when Aiden couldn't sleep—spooked by the news of Gavin's murder—he was wearing these sneakers. But it was two o'clock when I found him like that, hours since he'd gone up to bed.

"Did you go somewhere Sunday night?" I ask.

His brows knit together. "Huh?"

I point to his sneakers. "You were wearing those when I talked to you, in the middle of the night. Did you leave the house?"

I'm careful not to say *sneak out*—which is what teenagers do, right? It never occurred to me that Aiden would, but he's been so bristly lately, so unlike the boy I've known, and now I wonder what he does when he thinks we're asleep.

"No," Aiden says, scornful, as if I'm being ridiculous. But I see his shoulders stiffen.

"Why were you wearing them, then?"

"I wasn't. You must have imagined it. You were, like, half-asleep."

I shake my head, but I can't exactly prove I'm right. It nags at me, an odd sense of unease, but I table it for now, turning my attention to Jason's nightstand, still open a crack.

Gently, I ask, "What were you doing in here?"

"Nothing, just—looking for something."

"For what?"

Aiden's foot scrapes the carpet again. "Dad's cuff links. The semiformal's on Saturday and he told me on Monday I could borrow them."

The semiformal. I completely forgot. And only a week ago, I had Aiden try on his suit to make sure it fit.

"You still want to go?" I ask.

"It'll probably be stupid, but"—he shrugs—"all my friends are going."

"Yeah, but—honey, are you sure you're up for it?"

His eyes spring to my face. "Why wouldn't I be up for it?"

I sit on the edge of the bed, prompting a groan from the mattress, one I hear at night whenever Jason rolls over.

"Because of Dad?" I say, and I don't know why it comes out as a question. I guess I expected something different from him tonight— more distress, more need. At the very least, I assumed he'd ask me about Jason: Did he wake up? Is he still a suspect? I knew not to picture him throwing his arms around me, but I still thought this week, these astonishing troubles, might be a bridge between us.

When he was a baby, Aiden's innate neediness clawed at me, leaving me shredded. My nipples felt like spigots, nothing more than a mechanism of my breasts, even as they stung from Aiden's tiny, gnawing mouth. Sleep came only in snatches, the slippery pauses between Aiden's endless cries. In my worst moments, I resented him. I was barely out of college; I should have been sleepless by choice, from staying out too late, from talking to men I'd later gossip about with friends. But then I'd nuzzle into Aiden's neck, inhaling his milky smell until my annoyance softened into awe.

Now I wish his needs were as simple as they were back then: food, comfort, love. But this—his forced coolness—signals a darker, more nuanced need, one I don't know how to approach, let alone fulfill.

Still, I try: "Do you want to talk about any of this? We haven't really discussed it much, and I know it's really upsetting. Or"—I pivot at his visible apprehension—"if you don't feel comfortable talking to me, I could always find someone else for you to speak to."

Aiden's eyes narrow. "Someone else like who?"

"Like . . . a doctor."

"A shrink?" His voice spikes in pitch. He stuffs his fists into his pockets, backing away as he shakes his head. "No. No, Mom, stop. Can't you just—let me pretend this isn't happening?"

My heart contracts. My arms ache to hold him. "I don't know that that's the healthiest idea, sweetie."

"Why not? *You* do it all the time."

His words land a punch. I stare up at him from the bed, struggling to absorb the blow.

"What does that mean?"

He answers my question with one of his own. "Did Dad do something bad?"

"What? No. He didn't kill Gavin, honey, the police just—"

"*Before* that," he interrupts. "Like a week before Christmas. I heard you argue about something. And since then, you've been weird and distant with Dad."

My stomach drops.

"So, what did he do?" Aiden asks. "Did he cheat on you?"

"Oh—god, no." I stand up, cup his shoulder with my palm. "No."

He pulls away so my arm drifts back to my side. "Then what?"

I sink onto the bed again, the same place I perched, gut-punched and stunned, that December night. Jason knelt down in front of me then, hands on either side of my body, as I asked how he could do this. And when I saw that he didn't have an answer, only a promise to make it right, fear tornadoed inside me—*how well do you know this man?*—buckling the foundation of what I believed.

It was so unlike him, this secrecy, disloyalty. Because loyalty is as much a feature of Jason as his blue eyes, his dark hair. It's one of the qualities that made him so easy to love, back when I was newly pregnant, when I'd decided to commit to him and needed that love to follow. Jason still sees the same dentist he did when he was a kid, despite the tremors in Dr. Tatro's hands. He still buys a dozen bagels a week from the bakery in town because it was something his mother did, and when she died, he didn't want the shop to lose the sale. Every time it snows, he rushes out to shovel our elderly neighbor's driveway, even though she's offered to hire a service to do it. But gambling away ten thousand dollars of our money, money we'd saved, together, for an experience I'd been dreaming of my whole life—where was the loyalty there?

As Aiden waits for my response, dread covers me like a lead blanket. It's a familiar feeling, one I get whenever I have to—or should—say something important, something that might make waves, might expose a painful, unchangeable truth. And now I can't bear to burden Aiden with another thing. His father's in a coma, a suspect in a murder; he doesn't need my own hurt to be heaped onto his plate, doesn't need a reason to reexamine who he thought Jason was. I want Aiden to always see Jason the way he did as a kid, when he'd follow him around the house, dubbing him "President of Everything!" or would vault into his arms, eyes glittering with delight, as soon as Jason got home. Even after Jason missed Aiden's fifth birthday party—choosing, instead, to stay at the hospital with the woman whose hit-and-run he witnessed—Aiden welcomed his dad home with the widest grin, the widest arms.

"It was nothing," I say. "I was just— I overreacted about something."

Aiden crosses his arms. "Overreacted," he repeats, voice coiled with contempt.

I nod, then pick at my thumbnail, expecting him to push it, to demand to know what that *something* was I overreacted to. Instead, he chews the inside of his cheek, eyes avoiding mine as he shakes his head, and in his silence, I hear the grumble of his stomach.

"Have you eaten?" I ask. "I could order takeout."

"I'm fine. I found a frozen pizza."

"Found it, huh?" I try for levity. "I *thought* I'd lost a pizza."

When he doesn't respond, I walk to the dresser, on top of which is a small black box where Jason keeps his tie clips and cuff links. I would have thought Aiden knew about that. As a little kid, he used to watch us dress for date nights, deeming himself a *fancy man* as he clumsily pinned Jason's clips into his hair.

Longing pumps through my chest as I pick out a pair of cuff links. I return to Aiden, and when he holds out his palm to receive them, I cradle the back of his hand. For a moment, he does not draw away.

"Thanks," he mutters. Then he spins toward the door and leaves.

He's angry with me, but I don't regret my lie. For a long time, I've known it's best to keep trouble clamped between my lips, to swallow it down, no matter how bitter.

My mother taught me that.

Even before the cancer that killed her, my mother's skin was often tinged with gray. As a child, it made sense to me; clouds grew gray when they held in rain, so why wouldn't my mother, whose bitterness brewed inside her like a storm, turn that color too? It didn't take much to change her pallor—a commercial for a couples vacation, an extra shift she had to pick up to pay the bills—but every time, she'd look at me and grumble, *Never trust a man*, her skin as drab as ash.

But when she met Bob Sullivan, the color rushed back to my

mother's cheeks. I had just turned thirteen that month, the month of Bob, and for those four blissful weeks, I basked in my mother's blushes like someone tilting their face to the sun. Bob was kind of boring, always recounting his days at the Honda dealership, but he brought flowers to my mother on Fridays, and finally, it seemed, she would be happy. Or at least less bitter. Less gray. For twenty-nine days straight—I counted—she never uttered her catchphrase, never so much as scoffed at a rom-com she caught me watching.

But then, as my mother made dinner for the three of us one night, I found Bob standing over her purse in her bedroom, saw him fold up a stack of twenties, saw him slip it into his pocket. Then he opened her wallet, pulled out her credit card, and stared at it for a long time, mouth moving in silence.

I rushed to my mother and told her what I'd witnessed. I expected her to flush with anger, to run to her room to confront Bob. I also expected a smidge of gratitude. Surely she'd want to know that the one man she'd gotten close to since my father was actually a thief; surely she'd appreciate the chance to not repeat her biggest regret: attaching herself to someone undeserving of her trust. And I was right; she was angry. But not at Bob.

"That's ridiculous, he would never do that," she spit out.

But that night, I heard my mother and Bob arguing, heard the front door slam, a car drive away. Then she tore into my room.

"I told him what you said," she seethed. "And he says you're delusional, that he makes more than enough money to ever have to steal from me. And now he's gone. He said he wouldn't take that kind of accusation, that clearly you're not going to accept him into your life. Is that what this is? You weren't content just to drive your father away, you have to take Bob from me too? You can't just keep your mouth shut, can you? That's why your father left us, you know. Because you wouldn't stop screaming every night. You made us delirious. So now this is two relationships you've fucked up for me. And here I am, alone again. You happy?"

No. I wasn't.

I wished I'd kept quiet about Bob, who might have only been folding up his own money, or simply puzzling over her credit card, which had a different surname—my father's—than the maiden name my mother had started using again. Maybe I'd misinterpreted the scene, been too quick to judge, to speak, and now I watched as my mother's skin faded from the bright red of her anger back to a sheen-less gray.

Later, she apologized for the worst of what she'd said—that it was my fault my father left—but over the years, her words remained in me, glass shards that cut me deeper each time my thoughts pressed against them. And when she scoffed at my news about marrying Jason, huffing out, "How well do you know this man?" I squeezed my lips together so I couldn't speak the truth: that I wanted my mother's support, not her bitterness; that her question didn't sound like a warning, but an almost hopeful promise that I would end up as miserable as her.

"I know him really well," I had answered her.

I take stock of our room, where Jason confessed what I still suspect was only part of the truth about the money. The dresser is a bit off, the lip of each drawer sticking out in a pout. There's something wrong with the closet, too. It hangs open, a gap no thinner than a cell phone, but a change I'm acutely attuned to. I like tidy edges, neat lines; I'm always careful to keep things closed.

Jason's nightstand. The closet. Every single drawer.

That's a lot of places for Aiden to look for cuff links. What else was he searching for?

I retrace Aiden's footsteps. I flick through hangers in the closet, shake out Jason's shoes, shove past socks and pants and shirts in the dresser. I dig through the bulging hamper on my knees, tossing out my sweater from yesterday, the pants I wore Tuesday night, our first in the hospital. It's only once I extract a pair of Jason's own pants—the ones he wore Sunday, when we learned of Gavin's murder; I know them by the crust of pizza sauce on the thigh—that I realize my search is no longer about Aiden.

I dig deeper into the hamper, clawing now for one particular outfit: the blazer, shirt, and pants Jason wore to the conference—memorable to me because I thought he looked especially handsome. The blazer, a pale blue one I've always loved, is nowhere to be found, but I weed out the salmon button-down and light gray slacks. Shaking them out, I notice something flutter from the pants, and I feel a spike of triumph.

Jason always does this, leaves the detritus of his day in his pockets, tissues or business cards that form stiff clumps in the dryer—and this time, he's left a receipt. Jason's credit cards couldn't tell us where he went after the conference, but if he bought something afterward—a beer, maybe, or a snack—he could have used cash.

I snatch up the paper, then slump back as I read the details. The receipt isn't from Friday night; it's from that morning, a coffee before the conference—zero help. But ink bleeds through on the other side, and when I turn it over, I find an address—scrawled in Jason's hurried handwriting.

I pull out my phone, attempting a reverse address search, but with only the house number and street name written on the receipt, I have to guess at the town. Nothing comes up for Willow Creek, where we live. I try Hillstead—where Integrity Plus is, where the conference was, where Jason crashed his car on Tuesday night—and there's a hit this time: *This address has 1 current resident.*

I drop the receipt.

It's the address for Gavin Reed.

Chapter Six

SIENNA

My pulse is ticking, hot and fast. I feel it in my neck, my fingers, my temples, the countdown to an explosion.

There it is, a few driveways down—Clive Clayton's house.

This isn't my destination. I'm on my way to Wyatt's. I called him after dropping Julia off, asked if it was okay to stop by, and he said, *Of course, can't wait to see you*, as if this visit is for comfort or pleasure.

But to get to Wyatt's, I have to pass Clive's first. I couldn't believe it, when we first started dating, that Wyatt lived in Clive's neighborhood—an address I knew from my cyberstalking. Now there's something cosmically correct about it, the nearness of these two men who hurt me, and as I approach Clive's house, I don't look away. There's a masochistic part of me that needs to see it, same as I need to see his Instagram photos—him and his daughter laughing as he hugs her, him and his wife crouching in front of a Christmas tree.

Julia once described my anger as a lighter. "You keep flicking and flicking it," she said, watching me stare at my phone, "and the whole time, you're only burning yourself."

She was right, of course. Even as she said it, my skin felt freshly singed by Clive's latest post: a video of him braiding his daughter's hair.

"Well, what's the alternative?" I asked her then. "Ignore that he just gets to move on and live his life? Look at this." I scrolled through his grid, showing her pictures I knew every pixel of by now. "It isn't *right* that he gets to celebrate holidays and string up piñatas for his daughter's birthday."

"But you don't need to look at it. You're only burning yourself," she repeated.

"I'd be burning either way!" I said, snippier than I'd meant to be—and I was glad, for once, when Julia tucked her lips between her teeth, the telltale sign that she would not push it further. I saw her swallow her response and I didn't encourage her to speak. Instead, I returned to the latest video, where Clive ran gentle fingers through his daughter's hair—as if he was a good father, a good man. As if he didn't take two lives and ruin mine. As if he hadn't tried, years before he killed my parents, to ruin me a different way, too.

That time, I was a freshman at Willow Creek High, and Clive was a senior—so popular that passing him in the halls felt like a brush with a celebrity. When he started flirting with me at a party one night, I was flattered, if not a little shocked. I giggled into my third Smirnoff Ice, the room strobing gently around me. Clive slid his arm over my shoulders, asked if I wanted to go upstairs, and I nodded, then leaned against him as we climbed each step. I thought it was cute, how he helped me; I didn't know it meant I wasn't steady enough to walk on my own. And in the bedroom, he backed me against a wall, kissed me like I'd seen so many boys do on the teen dramas I loved, and I closed my eyes, melted into it, melted into that wall, imagined the music that pulsed from the floor below was a soundtrack playing just for us. My first kiss. My first drinks. And soon, the two firsts blurred together, my mouth growing clumsy, my hands unable to bat Clive's away as one crawled up my shirt to squeeze my breast, and the other tugged at the button on my jeans. *Shh, just relax*, he said, and I'd seen this, too, on my teen soaps, how a kiss could go so terribly wrong.

My eyes shot open, panic gushed through me, and then—as if sensing I needed him—Jason burst into the room. He yanked Clive off me, threw him onto the bed, and whisked me out of the house. In the car on the way home, he kept asking if I was okay. And I was. I was shaken and stupid and suddenly sober, but I was fine—all because my brother had saved me. *I will never let him hurt you, okay?* Jason said, blue eyes bright, even in the dark. *Never. I promise.*

He couldn't have known, of course, that Clive would eventually hurt us both, that six years later—still clinging to his high school stardom, still living in our little town of Willow Creek—Clive would drive drunk from a kegger and crush our parents' car. But even then, when Jason, too, was gutted by grief, my brother rushed in to rescue me.

Now, as I pass Clive's house, I feel that burn Julia warned me against, decades of anger scorching me anew. His windows glow softly, a picture of warmth and security, fit for his social media feeds. You'd never imagine, looking at Clive's from here, that the man inside spent eighteen months in prison.

As I round the corner, the house disappears from view, and my fire eventually cools.

I'm closing in on Wyatt's, but I don't look at his front window to see if he's watching for me, don't wave like I always used to, back when we were together. Instead, I park like I've arrived at the post office, the grocery store, just an errand I'm running on my way back home.

Outside, it's a sharp April night, the cold like a blade held against my throat, and when Wyatt opens his door to me, dressed in the hoodie I bought him two Christmases ago, I have to fight the urge to hurry toward him, to bury my face in that soft, warm fabric that would smell like sandalwood and cloves. Instead, I step inside, harden my voice to steel.

"Thanks for letting me come over. I won't stay long. I'm just wondering what you can tell me about the case."

"Nothing," he says. "I'm not on it."

But cops talk. He told me that once. Details slip like loose papers from a folder. Even the desk clerk picks things up.

So I try another tactic, a familiar one. I drop my purse in the entryway, guide him to his bedroom. Then I press my palms against his chest and tug on his lower lip with my teeth.

"Come on," I whisper, my mouth skating over his. "There must be *something* you can share."

He surprises me by drawing away. His eyes search mine, flicking back and forth like a doctor's penlight, before he pulls me back in, folding me into an embrace.

"I've been so worried about you," he says. "I know you're going through hell."

I go slack in his arms. Not in resistance—the way Aiden did last night when Julia tried to hug him—but in surrender. It feels good to be held, by Wyatt in particular. He straps himself to me like his body is a life jacket, the air an ocean, and all I have to do is float. A moan of release slips out of me, and he responds by holding me tighter.

My eyes snap open, reminders flooding in. I picture the woman he cheated on me with, even though I have no idea what she looked like. Don't know her name, either, because Wyatt himself was too

wasted to remember it. He'd always been an affectionate drunk—
just a few beers and he'd turn boisterously sweet, complimenting
everyone, pulling his friends in for hugs. But I never could have
imagined he'd take it so far. A year later, and it's still embedded in
me, the hot knife of his betrayal.

I push him away. His expression flickers between surprise and
confusion before settling into empathy, resignation. "Si," he tries—
but I shut him up, thrusting him onto the bed, where I climb on top
of him, pulling my shirt over my head.

If sex with that woman had been nothing, then I can be nothing
too. I rock my hips, arch my back, imagine myself weightless, blood-
less, heartless. When Wyatt reaches up to stroke my cheek, I clamp
my hand around his wrist and pin it to the bed.

Afterward, I roll off him, sweaty and panting, my body returning
to me in a rush. "Fuck," I mutter.

Wyatt hums in agreement, misinterpreting the curse as one of
satisfaction. He turns onto his side, skims my arm with his fingers. I
feel the admiration in his gaze even as I stare at the ceiling.

"That was awesome," he says. "You're amazing, Si."

I grope for my shirt on the floor, livid with myself for fucking up
this visit. When I'm clothed again—from the waist up, at least—I
swivel toward him. "Wyatt."

"Sienna."

He gulps from a glass of water by his bed, then holds it out to me
in offering. He always used to get us beers after sex, whatever new
IPA he was obsessed with—usually from a brewery we'd recently
toured—but ever since we started these meaningless hookups, he's
been respectful of the fact that I don't like to linger.

"No—thanks," I say, declining the water. "What do you know
about the case?"

He sets the glass back down, then sighs as he crosses his arms, forcing his gaze away from me, toward the bathroom door. "I can't talk about that."

"I won't tell anyone," I promise. "Except Julia, obviously, but—please. Can you at least tell me who the other suspects are?"

Wyatt tents his knees beneath the sheets. "Listen," he says, "forget I'm on the Hillstead PD. I'm just me. You can talk to me about Jason. How's he doing? How are *you* doing?"

He rubs my back the way I like, thumbing circles beneath my shoulder blades, but I hold myself stiff. I cannot, will not, sink so swiftly back into the comfort of his touch.

"I'll be a lot better," I say, "as soon as I know this nonsense with Gavin is tied up. Because it's a lot—having no idea when Jason's going to wake up, and on top of that, I've got Lou acting like it's life or death that we know every single step Jason took on Friday night."

"Who's Lou?"

"Our lawyer. He seems all concerned that there's a few hours missing from Jason's 'timeline'"—exaggerated, sarcastic air quotes—"and Julia seems all nervous, too, and it would be great if I could put her mind at ease by telling her that Jason is *not* the only suspect in this case."

Wyatt pulls his hand from my back, his eyes probing my face. Finally, he exhales, resistance hissing out of him like air from a tire.

"They *have* looked into other people," he says.

My stomach fizzes. "Great! Like who—other Integrity Plus people?"

Wyatt hesitates. "I really shouldn't talk to you about this." He pinches his lips together, reminding me of Julia.

"Wyatt, please."

I hear the pleading in my voice, the second *please* I've uttered in minutes, and swallow back a surge of self-hatred. I'm not supposed to need him. That's the rule I set for myself, the way I justify responding to his texts, initiating messages of my own. I can scratch an itch with him, I can punish him by offering my body while withholding my heart, but I can't be vulnerable. Can't relinquish my sense of control.

It's working on him, though—my sticky, acidic need. I see it dissolving his remaining reluctance.

"There was someone they looked into right after the body was discovered. Did Jason tell you about the guy who accosted Gavin, about a week before the murder?"

I straighten and shift on the bed. "Accosted him where? At work?"

"No. At a restaurant where Gavin was eating." Wyatt tilts his head in confusion. "Jason didn't mention it?"

My grunt is hoarse with annoyance. "Wyatt, no. Jason doesn't talk to me about Gavin. Beyond being the guy who signs his paychecks, he's not an important part of Jason's life—which is why the idea of him *killing* him is so absurd in the first place! So keep going: What happened at the restaurant?"

Wyatt watches me a moment, eyes conflicted, before blowing out a breath. "The guy had some kind of beef against Gavin, saw him there while he was a few drinks deep at the bar, and began shouting at him. A server called the station, and he was still causing a scene by the time the officers showed up. They arrested him on drunk and disorderly."

"That's—perfect. Someone with a motive, a recent incident of abuse against him."

"I wouldn't call it abuse," Wyatt says. "The guy was just a mess. His life imploded recently; his wife left him—"

"Left him for Gavin? Is that why the guy wanted to attack him?"

"No, no—it was nothing like that. It sounded more . . . financially motivated. And I think he just saw Gavin there that night and jumped at the chance to express his anger."

I narrow my eyes. "You're being pretty sympathetic toward someone who got arrested."

Wyatt shrugs, but it's not a casual movement. The gesture is heavy, like it takes some effort to hike up his shoulders. "Alcohol makes people do crazy things. Things they'd never dream of doing otherwise."

He's talking about himself. The party. The woman. "Or it just brings out something that's already there," I say, my tone appropriately thorny. But I need to skip past this, can't let this potential lead get lost in the rubble of us. "So who was the guy?"

Wyatt dips his head and shakes it, as if chastising himself for sharing so much. "I can't tell you that. And it doesn't matter anyway. He has an alibi for the night of the murder."

My shoulders sag. "What kind of alibi?"

"I've already said too much. I want to be here for you, you know I do. But you can't . . . I can't . . ." He lifts a hand into the air, a gesture of helplessness, and I pinch the space between my brows.

I know he's conflicted—between loyalty to me and loyalty to his department—but it's times like this when Wyatt's job gets under my skin. I went into our first date already holding it against him. He'd sent me a message on a dating app, and when I saw his occupation in his profile, I was about to delete his words unread. All I could think about was the cop who'd been called by the prosecution to testify at Clive Clayton's sentencing only to behave like a minion for the defense, describing the "agonizing wail" Clive emitted, "a sound of true despair like I've never heard before," as Clive "realized the results of the crash."

The results.

But something about Wyatt had hooked me anyway. In his profile picture, he had the gently scruffy face of an L.L.Bean model, but he was wearing an Eeyore T-shirt, which was so dorky and adorable

I couldn't help but look twice. Under the prompt "I Can't Live Without . . ." he didn't try to be clever like some men, who made me gag
with answers like *Oxygen, baby!* Or *You, I hope.* Instead, his response
made me laugh: *I can't live without ranch dressing because, at this point,
my blood is like sixty percent Hidden Valley.* I liked that he used punctu-
ation correctly, that his message asked what my favorite board games
were, that he explained, in a later response, his career was something
he'd never expected. He'd been coasting through business school
when a police officer saved his father's life. After that, he wanted to
pay it forward, protect someone else's parent if he could.

Our first date was at a restaurant we deemed "hipster Italian."
When Wyatt's prosciutto appetizer arrived with two pale, skinny
breadsticks crisscrossed over the top, he eyed the dish like he was
apprehensive about it. *Okay,* he said, *I'm not really sure how to do this.*
Then he picked up the breadsticks, wielded them like chopsticks—
which, I suddenly realized, he thought they were—and flinched in
surprise when they snapped between his fingers.

For our first anniversary, I bought him actual chopsticks, NOT
BREADSTICKS scrawled in a tiny font across the wood, and even
though we broke up a year ago, he still has them here, in his room,
propped on top of his bookshelf.

Now I glance at them, feeling a twinge in my chest.

"Who else is a suspect?" I ask. "Besides the drunk and disorderly
guy."

Wyatt drags his hand over his face. "Si," he says, weary of my
questions, disappointed in my persistence. He doesn't continue, but
his eyes bolt from mine, making the answer clear.

"No," I say. "It's *just* Jason? How is that possible?"

Wyatt sighs. "When that evidence turned up in your brother's
car, they had no choice but to narrow the scope onto him."

"So they're just assuming he did it, blood results be damned?"

"No, they're still waiting on the blood. And in the meantime, they're trying to get a handle on Jason's relationship with Gavin."

"I told you, he didn't have one! Not outside of work, anyway."

Wyatt reaches for his boxers on the floor, then slides them on under the blankets, face pointed firmly away from me.

"What?" I ask, touching his arm, his skin so soft beneath my palm. He looks at my hand, and the tenderness of his gaze feels as intimate as a kiss.

"Nothing, just—" He reaches for his shirt at the foot of the bed. "They re-interviewed Jason's colleagues this afternoon. And the consensus was that Jason seemed really stressed over the last few months. A little anxious around Gavin in particular."

My heart drops. If the police asked people at Integrity Plus about Jason, then it's not just Maeve anymore who knows he's a suspect. And I can't stand that, the image of them gossiping about him, shifting glances toward his empty desk, recalibrating their idea of him from colleague to killer.

"Of course he's been stressed and anxious," I say. "He's been working his ass off for some big promotion."

Wyatt shrugs. "Okay."

"Okay?" I pluck up my underwear and tug it on, careful to keep myself covered. "Wyatt, you don't think any of this means anything, right? I mean, I assumed you'd be on Jason's side, but if you—"

"Hey," Wyatt murmurs. As he reaches toward me to squeeze my shoulder, I brace myself. "I'm on your side, always."

I bristle at that. If he was truly on my side, always, there'd have been nothing to confess after that bachelor party. He wouldn't have had to explain how he kept downing shots, how the time between the third bar and someone else's bed was a black hole in his mind.

"My side is Jason's," I say.

"I know." He lets go of my shoulder, but the heat from his palm lingers. He stretches his arms out, yawns, then gets up to head toward the bathroom. "I need to get some sleep, my shift starts early tomorrow." He pauses with his hand on the doorframe. "But you should stay."

"No." I tear back the blankets and spring from the bed like it's scalded me. Wyatt knows I don't *stay*.

He moves closer as I step into my jeans. I button them up, and Wyatt leans in. He arches, nearer and nearer, stopping only once his mouth is inches from mine.

"Can I kiss you goodbye?" he asks.

My lips tingle, as if with static electricity. My head tips forward—muscle memory—almost closing the space between us.

At the last second, I remember to veer, pecking him on the cheek.

Wyatt scratches his jaw, and I know he's trying to mask his disappointment. My chest pings, a single note of pain I do my best to mute.

"Thanks for the info," I say, sliding into my jacket, zipping it up. "I know you could get in trouble for that, so . . . I appreciate it."

On my way to the front door, I pick up my purse, Wyatt shadowing me to see me out. "But when the police get that blood test back," I add, turning back for a moment, "they're going to kick themselves for wasting all this time. Because Gavin Reed's killer is still out there, and he's *not* confined to a hospital bed."

Chapter Seven

JULIA

Aiden tries to leave for school without me noticing.

I'm at the kitchen island, holding a mug of coffee, the receipt with Gavin's address—in Jason's handwriting—laid flat in front of me, when I hear him creep down the stairs.

"Aiden?" I call, and there's a measure of silence, as if he's wavering between joining me in the kitchen and making a run for it. But then he lumbers into the room, backpack and guitar case slung over his shoulders.

"You weren't going to say goodbye?" I ask. "Or have any breakfast?"

"I'm running late."

I look at the time on the microwave. "You still have twenty minutes until the bus."

"Parker's mom is picking me up. We're going to practice a little before school."

"Oh, you and Parker's mom jam out together now?" I ask, but he rolls his eyes at the joke. I open a cabinet, pull down a pack of Pop-Tarts to toss to him. "Here."

"Thanks," he mumbles, catching it. He turns to go.

"How 'bout I pick you up from school today," I say, and he freezes mid-step. "I'll take you to the hospital so you can see Dad with me and Auntsy."

His back is rigid as he answers. "I have drama club."

"I can email the teacher. I'm sure they'd understand."

Aiden spins around, mouth drawn back in a snarl. "What would be the point? Dad's still in a coma. We can't ask him to explain why the cops are after him—about a guy who had his *lips sewn together.*"

His animosity surprises me. Not the tone of it, but the target. I think of him in our room last night, all the ways he'd left it open and undone. Was that what he was doing, searching for an explanation that Jason can't currently give?

"Kids at school are calling whoever did this the Triple S Killer," he adds.

I frown at the moniker.

"Stab, suffocate, stitch," Aiden explains. "They say it was, like, a ritual. That that's why the killer used three kinds of violence. They say he's prowling the streets with a needle and knife in his pocket. And the cops think that's *Dad.*"

I hold back a queasy sigh, hating that, even at school, Aiden can't escape the gossip, the rumors, the news. I stifle a shiver, too. *Knife in his pocket.*

"Honey, I know it's confusing," I try, "about the police and—"

"The evidence," Aiden cuts in.

I resist glancing at the receipt on the counter. "Right. But that'll all be cleared up soon."

"And what if it's not?" he asks. "What if they only find reasons to look at him harder?"

"Like . . . like what?"

There's something dark in his expression, a specific hostility I've never seen before. For one unnerving second, I worry he knows what I don't: where Jason was for those missing hours after the conference.

His phone chimes with a text. He pulls it out and steps backward. "They're here. I'll see you later." As he turns away from me, he adds, "*After* drama club."

I should stop him from leaving. Any other mother would. They'd tell him that visiting his father is nonnegotiable. Or they'd draw him closer, speak until they found a way to sand down his edges. But there was something of my mother in him just now, something bitter and suspicious, ominous as her warnings, that felt like glass beneath my skin. I can see it backfiring, any grasp for honesty, for understanding between us. So I let him go and I don't say a word.

In his absence, I stare at the family room wall, the giant photographs with which I've tried to cover the roosters. In one, Aiden is six years old, perched on Jason's shoulders at a baseball game. He's exuberant, cheering, stretching his arms up high. He doesn't hold on to Jason; instead, he trusts his father will keep him stable, keep him safe. And suddenly, it's difficult to see them as the same boy— the joyful one in the photo and the sullen one in Converse who just walked away.

Those Converse, though—the ones I'm sure he was wearing in the middle of the night. They're troubling me again, despite Aiden's insistence that I'd only been seeing things, that he hadn't put them on that night to leave the house.

I grab my phone and load the app for our home security system. We hardly ever set the alarm—Jason only had it installed for his occasional business trips, when Aiden and I are home alone—but the app logs every time the front and back doors open and close. I scroll down to early Monday morning, then pull in a breath

Someone did leave the house. I picture Aiden lacing up his Converse, easing down the stairs so he wouldn't wake us, and feel my gut clench. Except—according to the app, he didn't leave just once, but twice. The first time was at 1:41 a.m., and it appears he returned only three minutes later. Then, at 1:58, he left again, coming back at 2:03, shortly before I found him in his room, nervous and disturbed.

Why was Aiden outside so late? I return to my concern from last night that he might have been sneaking out—but he was gone for such a short time. Was he meeting someone? My mind conjures quick, impossible images of a late-night drug deal on the corner of our street. I almost text him, begging for answers, but I know he'll ignore the message. Instead, I remind myself that, whatever Aiden did that night, he was home safe in the end. I can ask him about it later.

Searching for distraction, I refill my coffee, then move toward my laptop. I take Jason's receipt—one more mystery clouding my thoughts—and flatten it against the kitchen table. For a single moment of respite, my palm obscures Gavin's address, but when I lift my hand again, there it is: Jason's hurried handwriting, whipping my heart into a gallop. I flip it over, practically smacking the table. Now it's just a regular receipt, a simple coffee order. Nothing suspicious at all.

I force my attention onto my computer. Sienna will be here soon, and in the meantime, I can settle my nerves by touching base with clients, clearing out messages in our inbox. Right now there's one email from Dale Stapleton, a craft brewer, and seven from Angie Price, the owner of Sweet Love Bakery. As I scan Angie's emails, I find they're all stream-of-conscious notes about her business's history, mission statement, and upcoming product launches. I'm used to her spontaneous, scattered approach; it's why people need copywriters in the first place, and the act of it—translating complicated, nuanced thoughts into words that are simple and succinct—is as soothing to me as tidying a messy room.

It was Sienna's idea for us to go into business together. Before that, we were both freelancing; Sienna made graphics for marketing agencies, and I wrote ad copy for talk radio. It was a good way for me to stay home with Aiden while he was young, and sometimes, when Sienna felt cooped up in her apartment, lonely without co-workers, she'd bring her laptop and sketchbooks over so we could work side by side while Aiden played at our feet. The days felt easier with her around—not only because she helped with Aiden, but because we bounced ideas off each other and laughed at our mistakes together (the time I mistyped "public" as "pubic" in an ad, the time Sienna drew a tree that we decided resembled "a penis with problems"). *We should do this for real*, Sienna suggested one day. *Be a team, start our own business. Think how much time we'd get to spend together*—and I grabbed her hand, already giddy with the idea.

Jason was skeptical at first. He worried we might clash over projects in a way that could crack the core of our friendship. But Sienna and I weren't concerned. We knew that our core was uncrushable, fortified by all the ways we offset each other's flaws. Sienna would handle our more difficult clients, communicating with a clipped, no-nonsense swagger I could never even attempt, and if those conversations escalated, I would keep her from boiling too hot, from spewing anger like lava onto the people whose money and referrals we needed.

This is why, looking at our inbox now, I ignore the message from Dale Stapleton in favor of the ones from Angie Price. Dale tends to be abrasive and arrogant, which means that dealing with him falls firmly into Sienna's territory. The first time we met with him at his lodge-like brewery, he noticed me taking a back seat in the conversation. That was nothing unusual—I got tongue tied during pitches, whereas Sienna delivered them effortlessly—but Dale seemed almost offended by my silence.

"And what about you?" he asked, nudging his chin at me. "What's your part in all this?"

"She's the copywriter," Sienna said. "She'll make the descriptions of your products sound like poetry."

"My product is beer," he replied, eyes still leeching onto me. "No need to get all Shakespeare and shit. I'm a simple guy." He adjusted the brim of his trucker hat. "I'd like to keep things simple, all right?"

"Of course," Sienna said. "We're happy to accommodate whatever style you prefer."

I nodded in agreement, but Dale wasn't satisfied. He chuckled—meanly, Sienna and I agreed on the drive back home—and flicked another comment my way: "You always let her speak for you?"

I actually flinched, as if he'd thrown his foamy beer in my face. The question seeped into me, reaching someplace deep, and as I clamored for an answer, seconds accumulated—one, two, three—before Sienna uncrossed her legs and planted both feet on the floor.

"Julia is perfectly capable of speaking for herself," she said, "but I'm helping her out today, because she's got laryngitis." At that, Dale leaned back, as if worried I might infect him. "From allergies," Sienna added.

Later, in the car, I apologized for my awkwardness, to which Sienna reached into the passenger seat and squeezed my hand. "Don't worry about it," she said. "That guy was a dick." A dick who ended up hiring us, not just for the initial lucrative job, but also for frequent web updates and annual merch designs—and every time, I've hardly even communicated with him.

Now I flag Dale's email with the red "Sienna" label and return to Angie's messages, which stir no discomfort in me. I don't get very far, though, because in a minute, the front door opens, Sienna's feet swishing over the mat.

"I brought *motatoes!*" she calls, and enters the kitchen carrying a doughnut box. Inside are two maple bacon, our favorite, but not even the glistening bacon or thick maple frosting is enough to stoke my appetite. Sienna shoves hers in her mouth, devouring it in four ample bites.

"What's that?" she asks as I pick at the bacon. She points to the receipt on the table before licking her fingers.

"I found this in Jason's pocket, in the pants he wore to the conference." I push the paper closer to her so she can see her brother's handwriting. "That address? It's Gavin Reed's."

Sienna freezes, one finger still in her mouth. Then she wipes her hand on her pants and picks up the receipt. "Hmm," she says.

"Hmm? That's it?"

"Well—yeah." She narrows her eyes at me. "Why, you think this means something?"

"I have no idea *what* it means, but I'm struggling to understand why Jason had Gavin's phone in his car and why he wrote down his address—on the night Gavin turned up dead."

"Okay, first of all, you don't know he wrote this down that same night."

"Turn it over. The receipt's from Friday morning."

"Ooo-kaaay," Sienna says, stretching out the syllables. "Well, your answer's in the question. He wrote down Gavin's address *because* he had his phone. Like I said before, he probably saw that Gavin left his phone at the conference. So maybe he got his address so he could return it to him that night."

"Except he didn't," I say.

"Didn't what?"

"Return it to him. Jason had it in his car."

"Okay, so maybe he *tried* but Gavin didn't answer the door."

"So he took it with him instead of leaving it for him? On his front porch or something?"

"Yeah! Phones are expensive. Jason wouldn't just leave it there for any old neighbor to take. And—ooh!" She perks up, bouncing on her feet. "If Jason did try to return it to Gavin, then that explains where he went after the conference!"

I rest my forehead on the heels of my hands. "The scene of the murder, you mean?" Even with my eyes fixed on the table, I see Sienna deflate.

"Oh. Right. Well, obviously he wouldn't have been there *during* the murder, but . . ." She trails off, and I can practically hear her mind paddling through ideas, trying to keep her theory afloat, despite the holes I'm poking in it.

"And Gavin lived in Hillstead," I remind her. "I mapped it out, he's twenty minutes from us, thirteen from the Marriott. So even if Jason did go there after the conference to drop off the phone, and even if he did leave without giving it to him, he should have been home within an hour. Not three."

"Ooo-kaaay," Sienna says, and again, she tugs on each syllable until it's taut. "So, what are you saying, Jules?"

I shake my head, grinding deeper against my palms, targeting the ache that's threatening to throb. "I'm not saying anything. I just have questions." I lean back in my chair, sip my coffee, and avoid Sienna's piercing gaze. "Have you talked to Wyatt at all?"

"What?" Sienna's spine goes rigid. "Why would I talk to Wyatt?" She crosses her arms, as if she can armor herself against her ex's name.

I do hate to mention him, especially as the usual flush creeps into her cheeks. But I still believe her connection to him could be an asset for us.

"Maybe he could tell us what's going on behind the scenes. Info that even Lou can't access. Something that could put our minds at ease, or . . . or even just help us prepare in case—"

"No. I'm not—you *know* I don't talk to him. You think I'd do that?

If I were to talk to him, Jules, or even . . . even voluntarily see him, what kind of message would that send? That he gets to betray me and still be in my life?" She forces a laugh, sputtery and high-pitched. "That would be, like, completely unhinged of me."

I'm surprised by the shine in Sienna's eyes. Not tears, but— shame, maybe? As if she, too, wants to reach out to Wyatt, but has to extinguish that urge, smother any embers of love that still smolder in her. No matter what she promises or how hard she bristles at his name, I know she hasn't stopped loving him. Even the night after they broke up, when we ate our weight in chocolate pretzels and made a list of all his faults—leaves the toilet seat up, points out plot holes in movies, drags her on monthly brewery tours, even though, according to Sienna, "If you've seen one, you've seen them all"—I knew it wouldn't be so easy, wrenching her heart from his.

Sienna's previous boyfriends had always seemed so seasonal, like coats she'd wear for only a few months before switching to another. But with Wyatt, it felt different from the start. She looked nervous as she introduced us to him, watching Jason and Wyatt shake hands as if searching for chemistry in their grip. And at that first cookout together as the four of us, Sienna pulled me aside while Jason and Wyatt fussed over the grill. *He's perfect, right?* she asked, her palm a little sweaty against mine. *Like, if we forget the whole cop thing, he's just so . . . good, you know? Just a completely good man.*

Right away, I wanted to caution her: *Don't set yourself up for failure. Don't think of him as someone incapable of disappointing you.* I was thinking of my mother, of course, how her cynicism had been softened by Bob Sullivan, to the point where she refused to believe me when I darkened her vision of him. But the advice felt too familiar, too *never trust a man,* so I nodded at Sienna instead, let her keep building the pedestal for Wyatt that I knew he'd have no choice but to fall from.

Not that his betrayal was Sienna's fault, or she was wrong to break up with him. But over this past year, I've seen her work so hard to pretend she only hates him, and I can't help but wonder, if she hadn't thought of him in terms so absolute—*completely good, perfect,* the same way she thinks of Jason—would she be better equipped to admit to herself that it's possible to love someone who did something bad?

"Okay," I say now, "we won't go to Wyatt. I'm sorry for suggesting it."

"It's fine," she says, waving a hand. "Already forgot—"

The doorbell rings, slicing through her sentence. Our eyes jolt toward each other.

"It's a murderer," she whispers, an old joke of ours that's only half in jest, a side effect of bingeing too many crime shows. *I don't think murderers are usually so polite,* Jason once said to us, when Sienna and I shrank lower on the couch at the sound of the bell. *That's exactly what they want you to think!* Sienna hissed.

But now there's nothing funny about it, not when one murder in particular is hogging so much of our headspace, not when high school kids are whispering about a Triple S Killer. And there's something about it—this early visitor when it's only eight a.m.—that sends me hurrying for the door, Sienna on my heels. Before I open it, I picture a nurse on the other side, or Jason's doctor; I imagine that something's gone so wrong with his care that they felt it warranted a house call. As I turn the knob, I brace myself.

It's Detective Beck on our porch. Relief surges inside me, but it quickly curdles into fear. He's flanked by two other officers, and there's a strange but subtle smile on his face, one he tries to cover by scratching at the gray hair near his temples.

"Good morning, Mrs. Larkin." His voice booms as he holds up a piece of paper. "We're here with a warrant."

Chapter Eight

SIENNA

Beck's smile bleeds into a smirk.

Julia gapes at him, and I don't measure her silence, don't count to three, don't waste a second waiting for her response. "A warrant for *what*?" I demand.

He hands it to Julia, and I squint over her shoulder at print that's mockingly small.

"For seizing Mr. Larkin's computer and his financial records from the last three years."

"Financial records?" I spit out. "What the hell do you need those for?"

He ignores my question to address Julia instead. "Tax records, as well as credit card and bank statements. If you don't have hard copies, you can turn them over electronically." He pulls a flash drive from the pocket of his suit, holds it up like a winning hand in poker.

"Again—*why* do you need that?" I ask. "How could that possibly help you?"

"Mrs. Larkin?" Beck says. Julia's still staring at the warrant, and I don't know if she's even registered his voice. "If you could lead the way please?"

"Lead the way?" I repeat. "You want her to escort you like you're fucking guests?"

And it's that—the swearing, I think—that jump-starts Julia's attention. She's seen me curse at cops before, like the time one pulled me over for going five miles over the speed limit when a guy in a growling pickup had just blown past me, or the time one hit on me while writing me a ticket for a broken taillight. *Are you fucking kidding me?* I asked both times, prompting Julia to seize my hand—same as she does now.

Her skin is cold against mine, her eyes almost pleading. "Cool your fire."

But unlike those times in the car—when I *had* been speeding, when my taillight *had* needed to be replaced—the mantra's power fizzles out, like a hose only trickling water.

"My fire's pretty fucking warranted," I mutter. Then I hurl my gaze onto Beck. "There's an actual killer, somewhere out there, roaming free, and instead of searching for them, you're standing here asking for—" I laugh, a grating, scraping sound. "For my brother's *taxes*?"

"We can search for everything ourselves," he says, sidestepping my question, avoiding the accusation of incompetence, "but this will go a lot easier if we have your cooperation."

"You do," Julia says before I can respond. "Everything's upstairs, you can follow me."

My mouth drops open. "Jules."

Music blares from the kitchen. My phone's ringtone—"Call Me Maybe"—sends me stomping away from the door, Carly Rae's bouncy vocals needing to be silenced. But when I see Lou Ackerman's name on the screen, I accept the call.

"The cops are here with a warrant," I say. Their footsteps thud up the stairs. I picture their shoes tracking dirt on the floral runner my mother once installed.

"Yeah, that's why I'm calling. I just got off the phone with the PD. They want his computer and financial records."

"But *why?*"

"My assumption is they're looking for motive, other connections between Gavin and Jason besides Integrity Plus. Now, is there anything you can think of that they might find?"

"For *motive?*" Heat rockets through me. My eyes fall on the receipt Julia found in Jason's pants. I snatch it up, shove it in my pocket, glance toward the front hall to make sure no one saw.

"For possible connections," Lou says.

"I'm telling you, Lou, Jason hardly ever talks about Gavin. That's why this is so ridiculous. I mean, what do they think they're going to find on his computer? A Word document with a ten-point murder plan? And in his credit card statements? A charge at Joann Fabric for the thread from Gavin's lips?"

"The statements and tax records are for motive, too. I don't know the specifics, but it seems there's a possibility Gavin was involved in some shady financial dealings."

"Okay, and why would that have anything to do with Ja—"

I stop before I finish my brother's name. Because that phrase, *shady financial dealings*, has pinged against a memory: Wyatt in bed last night, telling me about the man who accosted Gavin a week before his murder. He was *financially motivated*, Wyatt said, but he hustled me away from the subject as soon as I pressed for more.

"If Gavin was doing something shady," I tell Lou, "Jason wouldn't go near it, *especially* if it had to do with money. He's way too responsible. Like, pays-his-bills-the-second-they-come-in responsible. And he definitely wouldn't do anything illegal. One time, at this barbecue he and Julia had, his friend wanted to play blackjack for money, and Jason literally googled whether gambling at home was legal in Connecticut."

Lou chuckles. "Smart man."

"Sure—smart, lame, tomato, motato. My point is: if Gavin had some financial scheme going on, Jason's not the one with ties to it, and the police should be looking at whoever does, because maybe *they're* the real killer."

Before I continue, I turn toward the entryway, making sure Julia can't hear me. She isn't there, of course. She's upstairs, giving the cops her *cooperation*. Still, I lower my voice.

"Please don't repeat this in front of Julia, but I talked to my ex, who's a cop, and he said that someone recently attacked Gavin— verbally, but still—and it seemed to have to do with money. He also said the guy had an alibi for the murder," I admit, "but it still seems like the police should be looking closer at him."

"Look," Lou says, "I haven't seen your brother in years, but from what I know about him, I agree that it seems unlikely he'd be tied up in any financial crimes."

"It's not *unlikely*, it's—"

"And that there certainly could be people who *are* connected to Gavin in that way, people who might have an incentive to hurt him. But the issue here is, right now, the police believe they have a lot of reasons to be suspicious of Jason in particular. The phone, the knife, the mystery of his whereabouts on Friday night. So that's why their focus is on him at the moment, and they're going to keep digging until something—the blood test, we hope—disproves their assumptions."

I don't like how he says that: *we hope.* As if he worries the blood on Jason's knife might actually turn out to be Gavin's.

"And like I said before," Lou adds, "the best thing you can do right now is determine your brother's movements after leaving the conference."

I pick a piece of bacon off Julia's doughnut, grind it between my teeth. "And what if we can't? We checked his credit cards and there was nothing. And short of building a time machine so I can go back to that night and follow him myself, I don't know how to figure that out."

"So we wait for the blood," Lou says, like that's so easy—waiting. "Or we hope another lead pops up that shifts the focus elsewhere."

I consider that, stealing a sip of coffee from Julia's mug. "Like a lead about Gavin's financial fuckery? Oh—pardon my French, Lou. But a lead about that, and whoever might have actually been tied up in it?"

There's a pause before he answers. "That would be . . . helpful, yes, if it points away from your brother."

And there it is again—*if*—another uncertain word. My hand tightens around Julia's mug.

"But I should caution you, Sienna, not to go investigating into anything like that on your own. For one thing, it could hurt your brother's case. The police might wonder why you're getting so involved, what you're trying, perhaps, to cover up. And another thing, it could be dangerous—you don't want to risk catching the attention of Gavin's killer."

"I think it would be obvious why I'd be getting *so involved*— they're after the wrong guy." At the top of the stairs, Beck's voice rumbles, and I cock my ear, listening for his descent. "Lou, I've got to go. Thanks for the info—keep me posted."

The rumble was a false alarm. Fifteen minutes pass before anyone comes down, and I spend them sitting with my arms crossed, squinting at the ceiling whenever I hear footsteps above me. When the officers finally march down the stairs, I spring toward the entryway, where Beck holds the door open for his men.

"Thank you, Mrs. Larkin, Sienna." He nods at each of us, Jason's laptop tucked under his arm in a clear plastic bag. "You have a good day now."

"Oh, you too," I call out as he leaves. "Just a sparkling, spectacular day. In fact—"

Julia closes the door before I can say more. Misery swims in her eyes.

"I can't believe you handed it all over," I say.

Her brows spike. "They had a warrant. I didn't have a choice."

"Still." I head back toward the kitchen. "You didn't have to make it so easy for them. But listen—Lou called, and he said that Gavin might have been involved in something shady, financially speaking. Which is great information, because I *also* found out that someone—"

I stop myself. I can't share what Wyatt told me without outing myself for talking to him in the first place—a thing I swore to Julia in this very kitchen that I could not, would not, do. But I'm also struck by Julia's reaction. Her eyes have shot wide, and her face looks drained of color.

"What?" I ask.

"They think Jason's involved with that? With—Gavin's financial stuff?"

Her gaze goes distant, obscuring whatever thoughts are leaping through her head.

I wave away her worry. "They're grasping at straws. Lou says they're looking for motive. But listen—I think we should look into this. Did Jason ever tell you he thought Gavin was doing something sketchy at work? Or even outside of it?"

Julia shakes her head slowly, eyes attached to the wall behind my head. "No," she says, something a little haunted in her tone. "Jason never talked to me about money."

I take her hand, which is limp and clammy. It does not grip me back. "Jules? Are you okay?"

She blinks, which seems to focus her, and her fingers fold around the back of my hand. "Yeah. It's just—not every day the cops arrive with a warrant."

I purse my lips, narrow my eyes. There's something she's not saying. Her silence forces a gap between us, a disconnect, even as our hands remain linked. Still, I carry on, no time to waste.

"Which is why I think we should get a little more proactive," I say. "Do you think Maeve would have an idea what Gavin was up to? She's the office manager, so she does the bookkeeping, right? I wonder if she's noticed anything . . . off. I think we should call her. It's before nine, so she might not even be at work yet. Do you have her number?"

"Well, yeah, but—"

"Great." I drop Julia's hand to swoop up her phone. Then I punch in her passcode and call Maeve, putting it on speaker.

"Julia?" Maeve answers. "Is everything okay? Did something happen with Jason?"

Her words are blurred with fear, all of them mashed together in a breathless rush.

"Oh, no, sorry," I say. "Jason's the same. And this is Sienna, actually, but Julia's here too. We wanted to ask you something."

Maeve's exhale shushes against the phone, and in her moment of hesitation, I imagine her with her hand on her chest, settling her surge of nerves. "Okay. What's up?"

"It's about Gavin. Have you ever seen him doing anything suspicious at work?"

There's a beat before she responds. "Define suspicious."

"I'm not sure exactly—something to do with Integrity Plus's money?"

At Maeve's silence, I look at Julia, who doesn't return my gaze. She's staring at the table, her palm pressed against it, like she's propping herself up.

"Maeve?" I prompt.

"Yeah, sorry. I do the bookkeeping, and everything's always above board with it. The cops took a look at it all on Tuesday. I hope you know I would never let Gavin put me on the hook for something illegal."

I plop into the nearest chair. "Right, no, I didn't mean—"

"But . . . did Jason tell you?"

Now Julia's eyes zing toward mine. "Tell us what?" she asks, leaning toward the phone.

"About the warehouse?" Maeve continues.

Julia shakes her head, and I answer for us both: "No. What about it?"

Maeve's quiet once again, and as seconds pass, my skin prickles with anticipation.

"I mean, it could be nothing," she finally says. "But a few months ago—like, early December—I'd swung back to Integrity around nine at night because I'd forgotten this custom piece I'd brought in to work on at lunch; the buyer had requested a quick turnaround."

"Uh-huh," I say, impatient with her extraneous details. But Julia doesn't seem to mind. Her gaze is hooked to the phone again, her brow dented in concentration.

"And as I was leaving, I drove out the back way, which takes you behind the warehouse—and I saw that the door was ajar. Which—I don't know if Jason mentioned it, but in November, Gavin had to fire a crew member because he'd caught him stealing from the warehouse. So I was nervous he might've come back. Or someone else might've been stealing."

"Who was it that got fired?" I ask.

"Dave Morgan," Maeve says.

I look at Julia, who shrugs. The name is unfamiliar to us.

"So I checked it out," Maeve continues. "I had my phone in my hand, ready to call the cops if I needed to. But then I heard this sound. Like a metal clang. Coming from the boneyard."

"The boneyard?" I repeat.

"It's this corner in the back of the warehouse where they store things too big to throw out. Damaged inventory. Broken power tools and ladders. There's even stuff from the office itself: old desks, obsolete printers. It's all junk. The crew strips things for parts sometimes, but mostly it just keeps accumulating. But when I heard the clang from that area, I crept in deeper to get a better look. And it wasn't Dave Morgan or another member of the crew. It was Gavin."

"Doing what?" I ask.

"Well—I don't really know. He was kneeling next to this old gutter machine—"

"What's a gutter machine?"

"It's like . . . a long metal box with a giant spool attached to it. They're usually in the trucks so the crew can measure and cut the gutters on the jobsite. But this one's been in the boneyard for a while—as long as I've been here, I think—so it was weird he was doing something with it. And even *weirder* that he'd unscrewed the lid and was, like, rummaging around inside it. And the reason I'm even thinking about this at all is because you asked about money, and . . . there was a stack of cash on the floor, right where he was kneeling."

"Cash?" I slide to the edge of my chair. Julia sinks into the one beside me, clutching her stomach like she's fighting a wave of nausea. I stretch out my arm to squeeze her hand, flash her an encouraging smile. "How much cash? That *definitely* sounds sketchy."

"I don't know. As soon as Gavin noticed me, he threw it into the gutter machine.

"Okay, sketchy times two," I say. "Did you ask him about it?"

Maeve's pause stretches so long that I check to make sure the call wasn't dropped. "I did," she says.

"And?"

"He tried to distract me, which only made it weirder. He steered me away from the boneyard, cornered me against a stack of insulation."

"Cornered you?"

A sense memory: my back pressed against a bedroom wall, the sheetrock hard against my shoulder blades. Clive's crawling, squeezing hands.

"Yeah, like, backing me up to it, standing super close. Then he was like, 'Oh, it's funny, I had a dream that started just like this, you and me, alone in the warehouse, late at night—but oh, I shouldn't tell you more details, that would be *bad* of me.'"

It's a husky purr, the way Maeve says *bad*, and it, too, speeds me back to Clive, his mouth damp against my ear: *Shh, just relax.* I shudder beneath the ghost of his fingers.

"That's disgusting," I say. Julia nods, eyes big and solemn as she stares at the phone.

"Yeah, well, I told you he's inappropriate."

"But that's textbook sexual harassment. Did you report it?"

Maeve laughs. "Gavin owns the company. There's no one to report it *to*. But it did light a fire under me to get things going with my store so I wouldn't have to work for him anymore."

"But what about that night?" I ask. "How did you react?"

I riffle through my mental Rolodex, all the things I thought to do to Clive at that party only after I was already safe: knee him in the balls, rake my nails across his face, scream until I ruptured his eardrum.

"I left," Maeve says. "The dream thing was clearly a diversion, so whatever he was doing, with the cash and the gutter machine, I figured it was best not to know about it."

"But Jason knew?" Julia asks. Her hands are clasped together on the table, knuckles almost white. She looks like a patient waiting for bad news from the doctor. I catch her gaze and beam out questions with mine: *What's going on? Why are you so nervous?* She shakes her head in answer, then clarifies for Maeve: "You asked before if Jason told us what you saw. So he knew about it?"

"Yeah, I told him the next day. I wanted to know if he had any idea what Gavin was up to in the warehouse, but he said he didn't. He was much more concerned about the harassment."

"That sounds like Jason," I say.

"Right," Maeve replies after a moment, her voice dim with distraction as a key fob chirps in the background. "I'll admit, I *am* curious what Gavin was up to. I was kind of hoping Jason would check it out at some point, but if he did, he never shared it with me."

Music blares through the phone, sudden and loud, but Maeve is quick to silence it. "Sorry, that was the radio in my car. I'm on my way to work now. I should probably—"

"Wait," I say, an idea sprouting. "Do you think the police will be back today, at Integrity Plus? I know they were there yesterday, interviewing everybody about—"

My throat clamps shut, keeping me from revealing another thing I only know from Wyatt. I slide my gaze to Julia. If she noticed, she isn't showing it, her eyes glazed and opaque, like she's deep inside a memory.

"Not that I know of," Maeve says. "Why?"

"Well, I'm just thinking: say that, hypothetically speaking, a couple people were to go to the warehouse, to check out Gavin's little gutter machine themselves. Would there be any way for those people to get in undetected?"

Now Julia looks at me, eyes piercing.

"You want to investigate it yourselves?" Maeve asks. There's a clash of notes in her voice: dubious and intrigued.

"It feels like we have to." I meet Julia's stare. "The cops came with a warrant for Jason's financial records. Our lawyer said they're fishing for motive. So if they think the killer might've had financial ties to Gavin, maybe there's something there, in whatever sketchy thing he was hiding in the warehouse, that could point their attention to someone else."

As Julia shakes her head, she doesn't blink. Her gaze stays fastened to mine, and I know what I'm proposing—sneaking around, searching for Gavin's secrets—will not be an easy sell.

"It's the only lead we have," I say—to her as much as to Maeve. "And I'm sick of sitting around, waiting for the cops to be proven wrong. If I were in trouble, there's no way Jason would just sit back, twiddling his thumbs. He'd do anything to help me."

The memory flashes: Jason wrenching Clive away from me. In that moment, it felt like he was freeing me from a room that had caved in on top of me. Clive had three inches and twenty pounds on my brother, but Jason tossed him aside as easily as debris.

On the other end of the phone, Maeve is silent. I picture her squinting at the road with a skeptical gaze. But when she finally speaks, it's exactly the answer I want.

"Don't show up before ten this morning," she says. "After that, the crew will be out at the jobsites, and it'll give me a chance to warn you if the police are there. But if all seems clear—" As Maeve pauses, I smile across the table at Julia, whose face is still tight, whose lips tuck inward. "I'll leave the door unlocked for you."

Chapter Nine

JULIA

What if we get caught?"

I'm holding on to the door handle as if I might thrust it open and roll from this moving car. I watch the speedometer creep ten, then fifteen miles above the speed limit.

"We won't," Sienna says. "The warehouse will be empty, and Maeve will warn us if we need to leave."

"We should be at the hospital, though. With Jason."

I've been trying not to picture him there, alone, sunlight rolling across his bed as the day drives ahead. Since the moment the cops asked for Jason's financial records, my nerves have rattled like chains, my mind whirring with things I don't want to wonder, things I can't even discuss with Sienna. Still, I hate to think of it: Jason lying in that room, bruised and tubed, with nothing but sterile air to hold his hand.

"We'll go there after," Sienna says. She readjusts her grip on the steering wheel as if she's worried it might squirm out of her grasp. "But right now he doesn't need us there. What he needs is for us to get the cops off his back. That way, when he wakes up, he can recover in peace, *without* Jerry Beck and his smug little warrants."

For a moment this morning, as he stood in my doorway, Beck's mouth had curved into a smirk. But up in Jason's office, where I uploaded files onto the flash drive, the detective's lips were pinched with pity—and I can't decide which expression was worse.

"But," I say to Sienna, "I'm still not sure what you're hoping to find."

She heaves out a sigh, her answer laced with impatience: "What Gavin was up to in the warehouse. Why he was hiding all that cash."

"Right, but—how will that help us exactly? It'll only give us more information about *him*. We won't have anything that can clear Jason's name or provide an alibi."

"Unless," Sienna says, "we find out who was involved in what Gavin was up to. Because they might be the real killer."

"Why are you so convinced that anyone else *was* involved? Or that, if they were, they'd be motivated to hurt him?"

Sienna opens her mouth, then quickly snaps it shut. She slaps her blinker, indicating the turn toward the industrial park where Integrity Plus resides. Her silence fills the car, and her eyes flick across the windshield, as if trying to find an answer on its glass.

"Sienna?"

"The cops are looking for motive in Jason's financial records, so they obviously think Gavin's killer was tied up in whatever shady shit he was doing. And since we know that *Jason* wasn't the one tied up in it, then that means someone else was."

My fingers shook this morning as I clicked the trackpad to dump our bank statements into the flash drive. I thought of what the police would find there: a December withdrawal for ten thousand dollars. I have no idea who Jason gave that money to. *It was a bad invest-*

ment. *He screwed me over.* But with Beck demanding Jason's financial records for a murder investigation, it's hard not to wonder if that person—the unnamed *he*—was the murdered man himself.

Sienna pulls into Integrity Plus's lot. "No cops," she notes, driving around back to park behind the warehouse. "The trucks are gone, too, so we're good to go inside."

My palms are slick, my hairline damp, because even my skin is aware we're entering someplace we don't belong. Sienna has done this before, dragged me into trespassing. A couple years ago, when Clive Clayton posted that he was on a family vacation at Disney World, Sienna made a pitstop on our way to Wyatt's. She'd told me she needed to pick up some sketches she'd left there, but first she parked in front of Clive's vacant house. *I just want to see, up close, what his life looks like*, she said after I took her hand in protest. And when she tugged free of my grip, I had no choice but to follow her out of the car; it's always been my job to keep her in check.

As Sienna peered into Clive's window, I hung back, heart pounding. I could see from her shoulders that her breathing had quickened—tight, searing huffs. When I hissed her mantra, she turned, then winced. *This is unhinged, isn't it?* she asked, and I nodded, letting out a tight breath of my own. *I just miss them*, she said, batting away a tear as if it had betrayed her. *My parents are dead, and Clive's on a damn vacation.*

It's a memory that always stings, both from the pain in her eyes and the way she'd lied to me beforehand, telling me we were going to Wyatt's when she only wanted to scope out Clive's. This time, Sienna hasn't lured me here under false pretenses, but as she exits the car, I feel that day in my body again, feel all my muscles clench with our impending transgression.

"Wait," I say. Sienna's hand pauses on the warehouse door. She looks back at me, expectant, but when I don't continue, her mouth sinks into a frown.

"Jules, come on. Don't you want to help Jason?"

Of course I do. But I don't have words for the threads of thought tangling in my head: the bad investment, the promise of a promotion, Jason keeping silent when he didn't get the job, the warrant for financial records. For months now, I've kept Sienna in the dark about the ten grand Jason took, and now I can't reveal my concerns without also revealing I've kept something from her. I can't explain why I'm so nervous—not just about sneaking into the warehouse, which is bad enough, but about digging into Gavin's secrets. And I definitely can't tell her what, as of this morning, I'm most afraid of: finding a tie between Gavin and Jason I didn't know was there.

And anyway, she's already decided. I can no more keep her from this warehouse than I could once keep her from charging up Clive's lawn. I nod at her to open the door.

Inside looks like a Home Depot without any aisles: boxes of downspouts and garage doors, a section for fireplaces and venting pipes, coils that look like huge rolls of duct tape. Shoved against one wall are piles of pallets, while another supports a selection of wire shelves. There's insulation, too, stacked like staircases, and I think of what Maeve said, how Gavin cornered her in that very spot, dripped his dream into her ear like a poison. I shudder and Sienna waves me onward.

We navigate to the back left corner, where Maeve told us the boneyard would be, and it's exactly as she described it. Clunky desks sit under ancient desktop computers. Aluminum ladders are wedged against file cabinets. A printer squats beside machines I can't even identify, each of them tagged with "Out of service, do not use."

"This must be it," Sienna says, pointing to a particularly large piece of equipment. "Long metal box: check. Giant spool: check." Sienna crouches in front of it, trying to remove the lid as if it were the top of a sarcophagus. And it is like a coffin, the size of the box. I brace myself for the moment it opens, as if something dead lies inside.

"It's screwed on," Sienna says. She looks up at me. "Do you have a screwdriver in your purse?"

"Is that a real question?"

"I don't know, you're a mom. You have all kinds of things in there."

"Yeah, like tissues and Tylenol. Not *tools*."

"Ugh, so unprepared. Fine. I'll try to do it with my keys, but can you see if there's one lying around?"

I spin from the boneyard, examining the floor as if loose tools will be littered there. Then I circle the rows of supplies until my eyes latch onto a rusty toolbox on a metal shelf. I pull out the first Phillips-head I find.

"Here," I say when I thrust it at Sienna.

"Thanks." She drops her keys, and as she works at the screws with the correct tool, I wander far enough away so I can watch all the doors at once—the one we came through, the one that connects to the office, and the loading door where trucks pull up. Even though Maeve assured us we'd be alone here, my heart rate spikes as I imagine tires on gravel, the beep of a truck reversing, the pop and slide of a door suddenly opening. I focus on breathing to steady myself, the warehouse's air sharp in my nose.

I've never been here before, but the smell is so familiar. It transports me to my early days with Jason, back when he had just joined the crew and I was still getting used to it all—loving him, caring for Aiden, being a wife and mother at only twenty-three. Every evening, Jason would come home with this same warehouse scent on his clothes, a strange mixture of mustiness and burnt cookies. As I hugged him hello, my own clothes stained with Aiden's spit-up, I'd make a show of holding my nose, and Jason would tear off his T-shirt, then chase me around the room, as if the dirty cotton were a net he would catch me with. Inevitably, I'd melt into laughter, and Jason would wrap his shirt around me, roaring with delight.

It's been a while since Jason and I greeted each other playfully. Over time, he's taken to squeezing my shoulder as he passes me in the kitchen, my hands busy with whatever I'm cooking, and in return, I mime a kiss in his direction. These last few months, it's been even less. When he isn't talking up the promotion, he's cautious around me. He walks through the door and only waves hello, as if I'm on a phone call he shouldn't interrupt. I could ask for more, set aside the vegetables I'm chopping and wrap my arms around his waist, but I haven't known how to be close to him, his betrayal still a phantom space between us I can't bring myself to cross.

"Jules, come here!" Sienna calls, and I return to her at the gutter machine, where she's cupping a palmful of screws. She sets them down, then attempts to lift the lid again. This time, it actually budges. "Here, help me," she urges, and I hold back a sigh before grabbing the opposite end. Together, we place it on the floor, then step forward to stare into the cavity we've exposed.

"Shoeboxes?" I ask. There are seven in total, and as Sienna reaches in and opens one up, I think at first that there's really going to be shoes inside. Beige paper conceals the contents, just like they do in stores. Sienna peels back the paper, and even though Maeve mentioned this on the phone, we both gasp.

Bundles of cash, held together with rubber bands.

It looks like a shot from a movie, one Sienna and I might stumble upon as we scroll through our options on TV, one where nefarious people do nefarious deeds and the pile of cash is the first damning clue. I blink at the shoebox, as if doing so might switch the channel, but the scene remains unchanged.

Sienna opens the other boxes, too, careless with the lids. It's all the same, down to the color of the bands that keep the stacks neatly in place—and Ben Franklin's face, over and over and over. There must be tens of thousands of dollars here.

"I—I don't get it," I say. "Why is this *here*, in this . . . defunct machine of all places?"

Sienna sits back on her heels, forehead scrunched in thought. "Well," she says, "he's obviously doing something illegal. Maybe he's . . . pulling a *Breaking Bad*? Selling drugs? Using Integrity Plus as a front? I don't know. But this is a pretty brilliant hiding spot."

"Brilliant?" It's an odd word for *something illegal*.

"Think about it: if the cops ever caught wind of what he was up to, they'd search his home, his office, maybe even the warehouse, but they wouldn't think to unscrew a broken machine, sitting among all these heaps of junk, and check for mounds of cash inside it. They'd look for safes, right? False panels in the wall, that kind of thing. But he's been hiding it under everyone's noses."

"You sound impressed," I say.

"Not impressed. Excited." Sienna picks up a stack, flicks through it with her thumb. "Someone might have killed Gavin for this money. Someone who's *not* Jason, obviously."

A chill curls around my spine, but before I can even shiver, I notice something else in the gutter machine, standing flush against one of its sides.

"What's that?" I ask, pointing.

"Ooh, good catch." Sienna reaches in and extracts the object—a leather notebook.

She holds it out with flattened palms, expression almost reverent. "How great would it be," she says, "if this was, like, a journal confessing to all his dirty secrets? And somewhere in here it's like: *hey, if I'm ever murdered, look into Dick Dickerson*, or whatever."

Her laughter bounces around the warehouse, and I fight the urge to clamp a hand over her mouth. I shush her instead, then listen for footsteps or doors.

"No one's here," she insists.

As she opens the notebook to its first page, I hover over her, struggling to read the bulky handwriting. It's not a journal. Not in the traditional sense, anyway; there's nothing narrative about it at all. There are four columns: one for dates, one for names, and two for dollar amounts—one labeled *Price*, the other *Cash*.

Sienna riffles through the book, but only the first half is filled up, all in the same format. The dates at the end are recent—one from last month, a few others from late last year—but the dates at the beginning are from a decade ago.

"I have no idea what this means," Sienna says. "Maybe he really *was* selling drugs, and these are his customers?"

She returns to the final columned page, and I squint at the list of names. "No, look," I say, pointing to one in particular. "I don't think it's individual people. Linear—that's that new gym in Hillstead. And this one up here, Zigoris—that's a furniture store a few towns over."

Sienna zips her gaze up at me. "How do you even know that?"

"Because they're—" I pause. Dread pools in my stomach at the realization. "They're Jason's customers. They're contracts he brought in. His commission from the Linear project paid for the HVAC work we had done on the house last summer."

Sienna looks back at the names, the numbers, her brow crumpling in confusion. "These are all *Jason's* customers?"

My legs are shaking now, rickety as an old ladder. I kneel down beside Sienna on the cement floor, grateful for its stability. I glance at the shoeboxes of money, my insides churning, before skimming the column of names again.

"Those are the only ones I recognize."

"Okay, so why would—" Sienna starts, but the rattle of a doorknob silences her. We grab hands, eyes flitting over the gutter machine, open like a body during an autopsy. We don't have time to cover it or return the lids to the boxes. The door—the one connected to the building, hidden from view by the stacks of insulation that border the boneyard—pops open, and footsteps clap inside.

We lurch in sync toward the section of discarded desks, then crouch behind them, our hands tight as vises around each other. The footsteps draw closer, hurrying their pace, an exact match for my heartbeat. Sienna narrows her eyes, pointing them toward the approaching sound, and I try to quiet my breathing, which tumbles out of me in panicked huffs.

The person stops, the silence as sudden as a light switched on, and though we can't see them from behind these desks, I know they're staring into the gutter machine, taking stock of the screws Sienna removed, the lid we pushed aside, the money in all those boxes.

"Julia?"

I spill out another breath, my lungs loosening. My hand releases Sienna's as she slumps in relief. We take a second to recover, then spring up in unison.

"Jesus!" Maeve says, hand flying to her chest. "You scared me."

"You scared us," Sienna says.

"I came to check on you, see if you found anything." Maeve looks into the gutter machine, shaking her head in bewilderment, disbelief. "I guess you did. That is a *lot* of cash."

"Yeah, but look at this," Sienna says. She picks up the notebook and opens it to the page with Linear and Zigoris. Nausea swims inside me at those familiar names.

"Does this mean anything to you?" Sienna holds the notebook out to Maeve, who takes it with a skeptical squint. As she scans the page, I focus on swallowing.

"It kind of looks like a job log," Maeve says. "But these dollar amounts . . . Why are there two for every date?"

She chews on her bottom lip as she continues to read. Her finger runs across the page like a highlighter, pausing at times to linger beneath a name, then speeding up again. Finally, she sucks in a breath, her eyes flashing bright as high beams. "Oh my god!"

"What?" Sienna and I say together. Sienna lurches closer to Maeve.

"I think Gavin was cooking the books! Look: for every row, there are two dollar amounts, price and cash. And the price is always greater than the cash, see?" Maeve jabs at one example in particular. "Here, the price for the job is forty thousand, but cash is only thirty. I think he was offering certain customers a discount if they paid in cash."

"But—why?" I ask.

"To keep it under the table. Classic tax evasion."

"Tax evasion?" Sienna spits out. "Isn't that what he blew up that merger over a few years ago? Because his would-be partner had committed tax fraud?"

Maeve nods slowly. "It sure is."

"What a fucking hypocrite!" Sienna says. "There were, like, news stories about that! And he was all 'Our name is *Integrity* Plus for a reason.' I remember the exact quote because I thought it was so stupid."

"Yeah." Maeve scrapes out a scoff, still staring at the open notebook. "I *feel* so stupid. I had no idea this was going on."

"Do you think Jason did?" I ask, the question blurting out of me, loud as a belch.

Sienna's gaze whips toward me. "Are you kidding? Of course he didn't."

"But those are *his* customers," I say to Sienna. "Two of them are, at least. How could they have gotten this discount without him knowing? Wouldn't Jason have been the one to send them their contract?"

"Wait, some of these are *Jason's* customers?" Maeve asks.

I nod and she scrunches her nose, musing over the page some more.

"Well, if that's true," she says, "Jason wouldn't necessarily know about the discount. Every now and then, Gavin steamrolls over the sales reps and sends a contract off himself—writes out a little note of thanks on his personal stationery. He insists it's the kind of 'attentive touch' that elevates us above the . . ."

As Maeve trails off, Sienna cringes. "'Attentive touch' is a really gross phrase. I feel itchy now."

Maeve doesn't respond to Sienna's quip. Instead, her eyes probe the air a few inches above the notebook, swinging back and forth.

"Oh god," she finally says. "That's what he's been doing this whole time. It wasn't about a personal touch; it was so *he* could manipulate the price! Keep control of the money. I am *such* an idiot. Of course 'attentive touch' is bullshit."

Maeve looks winded by the realization. She passes the notebook back to Sienna, who snaps it shut.

"See?" Sienna says to me. "Jason wouldn't have known."

It nags at me, though, tugging my mind in different directions. I can't find the connection between Jason's "bad investment" and the cash from these backdoor deals, but for some reason, I keep trying to tie them together, keep thinking of our drained vacation account when I look at these shoeboxes of money. I know it doesn't make sense—it was a withdrawal from our account, not a deposit—and a few months ago, I wouldn't have even considered it possible that Jason might have participated in fraud. But that was when I knew my husband to be practical, protective, not a man who'd secretly gamble a chunk of our savings.

How well do you know this man?

Not enough, it turns out, to believe without a doubt that he's innocent of Gavin's scheme.

"Maeve, you need to tell the police about this," Sienna says.

"What?" Maeve falls back a step. "Why?"

"Because this could be evidence in Gavin's murder. Maybe one of these deals went bad. Or maybe he was partnering with someone and they wanted to take the money all for themselves."

"Then why is it still here?" Maeve asks.

It's a good question. And when my mind flits to Jason in his hospital bed—incapable of moving his own body, much less piles of cash—I swat the thought out of my head, forcing my attention back to the women in front of me.

"I don't know," Sienna says. "But the cops are looking for financial motive. And from where I'm standing, there's thousands of motives right here in these boxes."

Maeve shakes her head, her shiny red hair swishing over her shoulders. "I can't show this to the cops."

"Why not? What's the point in protecting Gavin? He's dead, for one thing."

"I'm not protecting Gavin, I'm protecting myself!"

Sienna's gaze whittles to a sharp point. "What?"

"What if they think I'm involved? I do the books!" Maeve shifts farther from the gutter machine. "No. No way. I told you yesterday, I'm trying to get my store off the ground—I can't do anything to jeopardize that." As if to demonstrate, she tugs at the hem of her sweater, which I recognize as one of her own pieces by the delicate emerald leaves along the collar.

"Well, *we* can't turn it in." Sienna wags a finger between the two of us. "Our lawyer specifically advised us against investigating—"

"He did?" I interject.

"—and it'll be suspicious as hell if the family of the primary suspect just happens to stumble upon all this evidence."

"Well, what was your plan, then?" Maeve asks coolly. "Why'd you come looking for this if you couldn't do anything with it?"

"I was hoping," Sienna says, "to find something that pointed toward a *specific* suspect. Which—okay, maybe that was optimistic of me, but it's not like I have practice investigating murders." She runs her hands through her hair, her fingers raking over her scalp. "And anyway, *you* were the one who tipped us off in the first place. *You* left the warehouse unlocked. So you made yourself involved."

"I wasn't thinking that *this*—" Maeve gestures to the gutter machine, her arm arcing wildly. "I didn't know he—"

"Look," Sienna tries, "can't you just call it in anonymously?"

"Can't *you?*" Maeve retorts.

Sienna grunts and spins away to pace through the narrow gaps in the boneyard.

"Jules," she says, "help me out here, tell her she needs to do this."

My lips stick together like Velcro. I don't dare tell Sienna what I really think—turning in the evidence is not Maeve's responsibility, and more important, it might only hurt Jason's case in the end—but I don't know what to say instead. I'm used to opting for silence, but Sienna's staring me down, her eyes like sirens blaring her need.

My phone rings then, barreling through my quiet. I fumble for it in my pocket, expecting to see it's the hospital or even police calling—but the number on my screen is the one that, before this week, I dreaded most, believing its appearance in the middle of the day would signal some unbearable tragedy, or at the very least some trouble.

I look at Sienna, whose face is already mirroring the concern I feel.

"Hello?" I say into the phone.

"Hi, Mrs. Larkin?"

"Yes."

"This is Mona Pickett, assistant principal at Willow Creek High. We need you to come here as soon as you can. There's been an incident with your son."

Chapter Ten

SIENNA

Julia keeps her hand on Aiden's back as she guides him into Jason's room. My nephew's steps are so reluctant, he looks like a prisoner, cuffed at the ankles, led by a guard.

He hasn't explained The Incident yet, not beyond what the assistant principal told us. According to Mona Pickett, Aiden shouted at another student in the hallway, loud enough to lure two teachers from their classrooms, then shoved the kid into the lockers. Julia and I stared at the woman in shock, certain she must have mixed Aiden up with another student; he's simply not a violent kid. Once, during Movie Night, there was a spider in the living room, which Aiden caught in a gentle, welcoming palm before bringing it out to the yard, while I was still standing on the couch screeching at him to kill it. He quit karate after two classes because even kicking the instructor's foam shield felt "too brutal" to him. But today, as he sulked in Pickett's office, he told us, "I don't want to talk about it," confirming that there was, in fact, something to talk about.

On the way to the hospital, Julia tried only once to pry it out of him, and instead of answering her, he asked, "Can't you just take me home?" His voice was snarly and impatient, and I waited for Julia to call him out on it, to insist he explain why the hell he'd hurt another student, but instead, she sealed up her lips, like a letter she was too afraid to send, and stared out the passenger window. In my head, I rushed through my usual count—*one, two, three*—before informing Aiden we'd discuss it after he saw his father.

Now he stands beside Jason's bed, still as a mannequin. He glares at his dad like he's furious with him, and I don't understand it, not the scowl puckering his mouth, not the tightness of his body or the dip of his brow. I get that Aiden's a teenager, mad at the world, mad at this shitty situation. But why does he seem mad at *Jason*? His eyes could drill holes in his dad's face.

"Okay, fess up," I say—since Julia clearly isn't going to. "Why'd you attack that kid?"

He slaps his attention onto me. "He attacked me first."

"He pushed you?" Julia asks, palming his elbow.

"No, he was going off about Dad. Saying he's the Triple S Killer. That people better keep their distance from me in case I 'pull a Larkin' and suffocate someone."

My head rears so far back it feels like whiplash. Julia told me earlier about the snappy little nickname the kids have given Gavin's murderer, but I'm shocked to hear they've now applied it to Jason. Julia's gaze, wide with alarm, flicks between me and Aiden.

"That's not—" she says. "He didn't—" But she doesn't finish either sentence.

"How would this kid even know to connect him to the case?" I ask. "The police can't name him as a suspect unless he's been arrested."

Aiden shrugs. "His mom's a cop in Hillstead. I guess she said something."

"Oh, *did she*. And what's this kid's name again?"

"Nate Hyde."

"Great, I'll be right back."

"Sienna—" Julia tries, but I stalk out of Jason's room, and before I even reach the lounge down the hall, my phone is at my ear.

Wyatt answers in the middle of the third ring. "Sienna. Are you okay?"

"No, actually." I march into the empty lounge. "Do you work with a Hyde?"

"Um. Yeah? Hold on, I'm at the station, let me step outside a second."

"She told her son that Jason's a suspect. And the little punk harassed Aiden about it."

"Jesus," Wyatt says—and I like that, how quickly he agrees it's a fucked-up thing to do.

During his slow intake of breath, behind which I can hear the swish of cars, I pace the room, lapping between the stiff couches, almost banging my leg on an end table.

"I'll let the chief know," he says, "and he'll talk to her."

"*Talk* to her? Suspend her is more like it."

"Well. We'll see what happens. But yeah, of course—she shouldn't have done that. Is Aiden okay?"

"No, he shoved the kid into a locker."

"*Aiden* did?" Wyatt says—and I like that, too. He knows my nephew is not the type to willingly harm another person. I can picture Wyatt shaking his head, massaging the space between his eyes. "I'm so sorry this happened, Si. That's the last thing you all need right now."

I don't respond. I'm too busy rubbing my sternum, where an ache has sprung. It's a specific pain I've felt before, one that only seems to waken at the sound of Wyatt's voice, and right now, my fingers dig into it, intent on burying it beneath the bone.

"How's everything else going?" Wyatt asks. "Can I do anything for you—besides take care of this Hyde thing?"

I stop in my tracks, my hand dropping from my chest as my mind leaps back to the warehouse. Before Julia and I sped off to Aiden's school, I snapped pictures of it all: the money, the gutter machine, the pages in the notebook, all those prices and dates and names.

"Actually, yes. I could use some professional advice. Jules and I found some evidence that I think the police will be interested in, but I'm not sure how to bring it to their attention."

In Wyatt's hesitation, I hear the honk of a horn, a gust of wind. "What kind of evidence?"

I relay the story of our morning, beginning with Beck's warrant—which he admits he already knows about—and ending with Maeve's conclusion about Gavin's boxes of cash.

"She's refusing to turn it over to the cops. She's worried they'll think she has something to do with it—which ticked me off at first, but you know what, maybe she's right, given how your department likes to put all their resources toward investigating innocent people. But they need to know about this, right?"

"Sienna, no," Wyatt says, quick and clipped. "Whatever you saw in that warehouse—you need to forget about it."

"Forget about it? Someone might have *killed* him for it!"

"You don't know that." There's an edge of anger in his voice that surprises me. "And you really shouldn't have investigated on your own."

I punch out a grunt. "You sound like our lawyer. Can't I call in an anonymous tip?"

"Did you use gloves when you handled it? The money, the equipment."

"What? No."

"Then your prints are all over it. Not exactly anonymous. And you get how that would look, right? That the suspect's sister has touched it?"

I pause at that. It never occurred to me to be so careful, to snap on latex gloves like a detective, to protect the evidence—and protect myself, my brother, against it.

"And not just touched it," Wyatt adds. "Planted it, maybe."

"You think I *planted* boxes of cash?"

"Not me. But they might. They could see it as you trying to stir up suspicion elsewhere, sending them on a wild goose chase away from Jason."

"That's ridiculous! And anyway, it's not like my prints are in the system. I've never been arrested or anything."

"Doesn't matter. It's too big a risk. Just—forget you found it, okay?"

"Are you fucking serious? This is a lead! I know it is! It's—"

"Hold on— Yeah?" He responds to someone who's called out to him. Their words burble through the phone, swift and indecipherable. "Got it, be right there," he says after a moment, and when he returns to me, his voice is low but firm. "Si, I have to go. But promise me you'll stop digging. Figure out where Jason was on Friday night, follow *his* movements, *his* actions, but stay away from warehouses and anywhere else associated with Gavin. Do you understand?"

Chest searing with every breath, I don't reply, and in a few seconds, I end the call.

• • •

I burn my mouth on molten cheese.

We're back at Jason and Julia's, huddled around a Hawaiian pizza, and I'm not like Aiden or Julia, who blow on each steaming bite to cool it down. My teeth are tearing through dough and ham and pineapple, because any minute now, Lou Ackerman's going to call me back.

I contacted him right after hanging up with Wyatt, but his assistant told me he was in meetings all afternoon and would reach out after six. That was at two o'clock, and four hours seemed an impossibly long time to wait. As I watched my brother in his bed, noting the changes in his bruises and bandages, the tick of my pulse felt like the tick of a clock, each second wasted, each second another chance for Nate Hyde to taunt my nephew, for the cops to get this wrong.

Julia's phone pings with an email. "Oh!" she says as she reads it. "Good news! Ms. Pickett says they're still letting you go to the semiformal tomorrow." She beams at Aiden, forcing cheerfulness, but Aiden only chews his pizza, avoiding her gaze. "She says she understands you've got a lot going on, and they'd be happy for you to make up for the fight with two detentions next week."

"Does Nate Hyde have detention?" I ask.

Julia's smile slips a little. "She didn't say. But that's good, right, Aid? I know you were excited about the dance."

"I'm not *excited* about it. It's just a thing to do. But all people are going to be talking about now is Dad. Nate was telling everyone he's the Triple S Killer."

"I take it back," I say. "Detention's too good for Nate. Let's send him to the stocks! Or, hey, how 'bout that island where the *Lord of the Flies* kids go?" I lean toward Aiden to nudge him with my elbow. His lips twitch for a second, but he doesn't smile.

"Look," I try instead, "if Nate or anyone else gives you any shit, just tell them the truth."

"Yeah?" Aiden says. "And what's that?"

There's venom in the question. It feels like poison spit in my face. I look at Julia, but she's focused on her pizza, scrutinizing the cheese, picking at the crust.

"That your dad is innocent," I say. "That the cops are complete and total screwups, and anyone who would act like Jason's been convicted when there hasn't even been an arrest is just a know-nothing lowlife who's talking out their ass. That the last person on earth who would ever hurt someone, let alone kill them, is your dad, because he's good and kind and—"

"Okay, Auntsy, stop!" Aiden cuts in. He jolts his chair back, the legs scraping against the floor with all the suddenness of a record scratch. He stares at Julia. "Can I eat in my room?"

Julia blinks at him, as startled as I am by the interruption. "Uh—sure, honey," she says. "Just take some extra napkins."

He picks up his plate, grabs the stack she holds out to him, and stomps away from us. I wait until he's out of earshot before whirling toward Julia. "Take some extra napkins?"

"In case he gets pizza on the carpet."

"Yes, I know what napkins are for. That's all you have to say to him?"

"I already talked to him at the hospital." She takes a large bite, then chews and chews and chews, until I'm sure the pizza is nothing more than mush in her mouth. "While you were reporting Nate Hyde's mom to the police chief," she finally adds.

I hold my gaze steady, gesturing for her to continue. When I lied to her, back at Jason's room, telling her it was the police chief I'd called instead of Wyatt, I felt a pinch of guilt at how easily she believed me. It was mostly true, though. Wyatt said he'd tell the chief, so I simply revised the story to cut out the middleman. No need to explain why my ex was the first person I thought to call, or what he said about the money in the warehouse.

"And I told Aiden," Julia says, "that violence is never the answer, even if he was provoked."

"Okay, but what about the way he keeps talking to us, or even how he's talking about Jason? He seems so . . . pent up with anger—not that I blame him, but he doesn't need to be angry at *us*. It's not

Jason's fault he can't defend himself, and you and I are doing every-thing we can to prove his innocence."

Julia stalls by taking another bite. I wait her out, crossing my arms, but just as she swallows, my phone rings on the table.

I spring up from my chair, jabbing at the screen to accept the call. "Hey, Lou, thanks for getting back to me."

"Of course," he says, "but I'm sorry to tell you I don't have any-thing new to report."

"That's fine, because I do."

I run through it all again, our discovery in the warehouse, the names Julia recognized as Integrity Plus's customers, and when I'm done, there's a long pause before Lou sighs.

"I specifically advised you not to do something like this. You un-derstand you've compromised that evidence, right?"

"Yes, yes, I'm sorry, okay? But this has to be a lead. There must be some way we can tip off the police about it. If not about the boxes of cash, then about the customers they should look into. I have pictures of all their—"

"And you say the names in the notebooks were *Jason's* custom-ers?" Lou asks.

"Not all of them. Only a couple."

Lou sighs again. "Sienna." He says my name with all the disap-pointment of a parent who's caught their kid breaking the rules. "We can't do anything with this. Not only because you handled the evidence, but also because the police could use this *against* Jason. Say you're right about what Gavin was doing. Since Jason brought in some of those customers, they could say he was working with him, that maybe their partnership took a turn, or maybe Jason wanted to reap the rewards all for himself. You'd be handing them motive. Or at least a heap more suspicion."

Acid burns in my stomach. "But Jason *wasn't* working with him."

"You don't know that."

I pause, taken aback. "Um, yeah, Lou, I do. Because I know my brother."

"Regardless, if this makes it to a courtroom, a prosecutor could still construct a narrative in which Jason was very much involved with Gavin."

I march into the family room, circle the coffee table like it's a suspect I'm questioning. "So what am I supposed to do? I *know* this is connected; I can feel it. And what did you expect when you told me Gavin was into something shady? How could I not look into it?"

"I understand you're anxious and frustrated." Lou's voice is pinched, like he's biting back a stronger retort. "But you can't be inserting yourself into the investigation. Is that clear?"

His tone needles me, so similar to Wyatt's from earlier: *Do you understand?* Like I'm a child in need of chiding. Even still, I do understand: from now on, whatever leads I follow, I'll have to be more careful.

Lou continues through my silence. "You need to leave the issue of Gavin's finances—and anything else that comes up—to the police."

"But why are they suspicious of his finances in the first place? Because it doesn't seem like the cops have found what's in the gutter machine."

At the kitchen table, Julia has set aside her dinner in favor of her laptop. She hunches close to the screen, forehead pleated with confusion—or maybe concern.

Lou waits a beat before answering, as if reluctant to move on from scolding me. "Well," he says, "you actually mentioned it yourself this morning. There was an arrest made a week before Gavin's murder. A man lashed out at him in a restaurant, causing a scene."

Hope bolts through me. "And you know why the man attacked him?"

"I haven't seen the arrest report yet, but I got a brief rundown.

When they booked him, he kept urging them to look into Integrity Plus's finances, insisting Gavin was committing some type of fraud. My assumption—since the police *are* interested in Jason's financial records and how they might tie him to Gavin—is that they have reason to believe the claims were credible."

I shoot my fist into the air, miming my triumph. At the table, Julia doesn't look my way or cock her head to question my reaction. Her gaze is pasted to her computer, and the reflection from her laptop makes her eyes shine, as if she's reading the screen through a glaze of tears.

"Who's the guy?" I ask Lou. "Who did they arrest?"

Again, he hesitates. "His name's Henry Hendrix."

My fist loosens. "Wait."

There's something familiar about that name—the alliteration, the obnoxious repetition. Maybe it was in Gavin's notebook, one of the customers he offered a discount. I'm about to pull up my pictures from the warehouse when Julia releases a groan so deep in her throat, it sounds like she's wrenched it straight from her heart.

"Jules?"

Her mouth is twisted in horror, her expression haunted. My skin breaks out in goose bumps. I rush toward her, Lou's voice already shrinking in my ear: "Sienna?"

"Sorry, Lou, I've got to go. Thanks." I drop the phone onto the table. "Jules, what is it?"

At first, her mouth moves without sound. Then she manages some words, so tortured and raspy they sound like a retch. "I'm in Jason's email."

"What? Why?"

A tear slices down her cheek. "I wanted to check his Google Drive— The names. His customers in Gavin's notebook. See if he kept documents about them."

"On his personal drive? Why would he? And why are you bothering with that? We know he had no idea what Gavin was up to."

Julia shakes her head. "The cops took his laptop. I wanted to see what they might find. But— I saw his email, and . . ."

She trails off, then presses her hand against her mouth like she's going to be sick. She stares up at me, her wet, worried eyes rendering her a younger version of herself. For a second, I'm thrust back to the day she was in labor with Aiden, when a nurse snapped at Julia for asking what time the doctor would arrive. *Oh come on, don't be one of those*, the nurse spat, *he'll get here when he gets here*—and it wasn't Jason, gripping her right hand, who Julia turned to; it was me, on her left. She signaled the same panic she's showing me now, and I chewed the nurse out, promised her I'd file a complaint if she spoke to Julia like that again. That day, Julia's need was easy to translate from only a single look, but I'm not sure how to read her now.

"And what, Jules? Come on, finish your sentence."

She still doesn't speak. Her fingers cage her lips. But she rotates the laptop toward me and points to the screen. I bend toward it, where an email thread is open. A quick scan reveals a brisk back-and-forth between Jason and Maeve, but I hold off on reading the messages before checking the date for context: last Saturday at 3:52 p.m.

Jason emailed first: I want to apologize again about what happened last night. And I need to know that you're okay. You're not answering my calls, so if I don't hear back from you soon, I'm coming over.

Maeve was quick to reply at 3:55: Don't come over. I told you when you left the house last night that you need to stay away from me from now on, and I meant it.

I narrow my eyes at the screen, pull the laptop closer.

The whole thing was a big mistake, Jason responded, but I'm hoping we can find some way past this. You mean too much to me. Please, let's talk. I need to know that everything's okay.

When I back away, Julia's wiping her cheek with her wrist.

"I don't get it," I say. "What is this about?"

Julia's answer is choked, her words thick with misery. "Jason cheated on me."

I leap back a step. "*What?* No he didn't. How did you get *that* from *this?*"

"Something happened between them, at Maeve's house, it sounds like. Something he felt the need to apologize for, something he's worried about losing her over. What else could it be?"

"Um, literally anything else," I say. But as I reread the thread, I understand her thought process. The pieces are there—*a big mistake; you mean too much to me; I told you when you left the house last night*—but Julia's conclusion doesn't make sense when applied to Jason.

"They did *not* have an affair," I promise her.

Because Jason isn't the guy who cheats. He's the guy who gave me half his allowance one summer, when he knew I was saving up for a pair of purple Skechers. He's the guy who slept on my bedroom floor for three nights in a row after he rescued me from Clive at that high school party. He's the guy who checks my smoke detectors whenever he's at my apartment, who covers me in our mom's quilt when I fall asleep on his and Julia's couch. Jason is thoughtful and dependable and so thoroughly *good*. There's no room for infidelity in a man like that.

Only a year ago, he comforted me about my breakup with Wyatt. He's a wimp for blood, but he pushed for slasher films during Movie Night and encouraged me to "picture Wyatt's face on every corpse." There's simply no way he watched what I went through after Wyatt cheated on me, then turned around and did the same to Julia. Jason wouldn't. He *wouldn't*.

But Julia's still staring at the messages, her eyes pinched with anguish.

Normally, it would offend me, Julia entertaining this absurd theory. But I understand how disorienting it is, just the idea of betrayal. The moment Wyatt confessed to me, the room reeled around me; even the light fixtures spun.

I take Julia's hand, which is limp in my grip. "My brother is the most loyal and honest person I know. You know that, Jules, come on."

"I'm not so sure anymore," she says, her voice distant now. "He's kept so much from me. Maybe an affair with Maeve is just another of his secrets."

I tilt my head in confusion. "Huh? What secrets has Jason kept from you?"

"The promotion. Where he went after the conference. The money."

"He didn't know about the money!"

"Not Gavin's money," Julia says. "Or, I don't know, maybe it *was* Gavin's money. Maybe that's who he gave it to."

"Huh?" I say again. I let my hand separate from hers. "Who he gave what to? I don't know what you're talking about. And in terms of where he went last Friday night, we've been over that, he was probably just—"

Our eyes jerk toward each other, hers damp, mine wide. I can almost hear the synchronized click of our minds as the timeline—the conference on Friday, the emails from Saturday, Jason's apology for *what happened last night*—snaps into place.

"Oh my god," I say. "Jason was with *Maeve* after the conference! Only— That bitch! We specifically *asked* her at the hospital if she knew where he went. And she told us no. And then! When you told her the cops were focused on Jason, she was like, 'That's impossible!' I assumed she meant it's impossible because Jason's not a killer—but no! She meant it was *literally* impossible that he could have done it.

She knew he didn't, because she was with him at the time. And she didn't say a thing!"

Julia's shoulders sag. Her gaze drifts away. "Because she didn't want me to know they slept together."

"No—it has to be something else. I have no idea why she lied to us, but—" I march toward the kitchen counter, dig through my purse in search of my keys. "We're going to find out."

Chapter Eleven

JULIA

On the drive to Maeve's in Hillstead, I can think only one thing: how foolish I've been. Sienna's chattering in the driver's seat, headlights cutting through the dusk. Again and again, she tries to convince me that Jason would never cheat, but my body tells me otherwise. Reading those emails tonight, I felt the same punch in my gut as I experienced in December, when Jason explained what he'd done with our Europe fund behind my back. And now the betrayal sits hard and huge against my belly, as if I'm held to this seat by a boulder instead of a belt.

Even with my mother's warnings, I never saw this coming. Not when Jason bought Maeve a birthday present—some earrings from a farmers market we went to together. Not when he invited her to Thanksgiving last year, even before a snowstorm had canceled her flight to her sister's. Not when he paused movies, retracted his arm from my shoulder to return Maeve's texts.

If my mother were still alive, she would have sniffed this out a long time ago. *Never trust a man.* Pregnant at twenty-two, I was desperate not to repeat her misery, so I opted for the opposite. I buried my feelings that, even with Aiden growing inside me, marriage was too sudden a step, and I decided to trust Jason. Then I latched onto that trust as if it were a trapeze, like if I ever let go, I'd plummet through the air with nothing to catch me.

In December, my grip began to slip, fingers loosening, palms sweating, and now I'm no longer suspended there at all. My nausea feels like a free fall, like a crash is coming. I grip the door handle to brace myself, watching the GPS close in on our destination.

When Sienna parks in front of Maeve's town house, I don't move to unbuckle my seat belt. The house has a gray brick façade, its windows and door bordered by sleek black trim, sharply lit by the porchlight. Last time Jason and I were here, I remarked how well suited to Maeve the place is. *Classy and stylish, just like her,* I said, and Jason hummed his agreement. Now I wonder how many times he's been here on his own since then. Was it only last Friday? Or have he and Maeve been sleeping together for a while?

"Hey," Sienna says, squeezing my hand. "I really do think there's another explanation for why Jason was here that night, but I know this isn't easy right now, coming here when you're misinterpreting the emails like that. So I'll take the lead in there, okay?"

I'm grateful and annoyed. I love that she knows I need her to be the one to speak to Maeve. But her phrasing just now—*misinterpreting the emails like that*—feels like she's invalidating my response, like she's stuffing my voice even deeper down my throat.

It's my fault, though. How can I expect Sienna to imagine her brother being unfaithful when she has no idea about the money he siphoned from our account, or that this is not the first time he's betrayed me in the last few months?

"And this is good," Sienna says, voice springy with excitement. "We're about to get Jason's alibi."

Opening the passenger door, I'm overwhelmed by the need to run. Instead, I follow Sienna up the walkway, then stand in her shadow as she rings the bell.

"Come on, come on, come on," Sienna mutters, bouncing on her toes to peek through the window at the top of the door.

I close my eyes against a surge of vertigo, praying that Maeve isn't home. But then I hear the swoosh of the door opening, and there she is, Jason's . . . girlfriend? Lover? The woman I hugged just yesterday in the hospital?

"Hey, guys . . ." Maeve says uncertainly. She's swapped the work clothes we saw her in this morning for a pair of black leggings and a white T-shirt, through which I glimpse the outline of her black bra. Her hair is pulled back in a ponytail, and she's removed her makeup, but she still looks beautiful, her skin clean and bright, a stray red lock framing one side of her face. For a second, I picture Jason sliding that hair behind her ear, and flinch so hard that Maeve must notice.

"What's going on?" she asks. Her expression clouds with concern. "Is it Jason?"

"In a manner of speaking," Sienna says. "You lied to us, Maeve."

Before Maeve squints in confusion, I think I see a flash of panic in her eyes. "What—" she starts, but Sienna breezes past her.

Maeve remains still for a second before following Sienna into her own living room. I trail behind, gaze pinned to Maeve's slippers: gray, furry things that remind me of Aiden's old Bugsy Bear. Has Jason ever seen them? Did they make him think of Aiden, who once howled himself hoarse when I put Bugsy in the wash? Or did he not even consider his son at all, these slippers just the things that Maeve kicked off before she and Jason—kissing, laughing—rushed into bed?

"Lied about what?" Maeve asks.

The living room floor is cluttered with tote bags, which transform the hardwood into some kind of garden: hand-painted hydrangea and peonies, branches of cherry blossoms and wisteria.

"Sorry," Maeve says as Sienna navigates the mess. "I'm doing a shop update, and—"

"We know you were with Jason last Friday," Sienna says. "After the conference."

Maeve's lips pop open. "No, I wasn't, I—"

"Don't." Sienna takes out her phone and pulls up the shot she took of Jason's emails, then aims it at Maeve.

Maeve leans toward the screen, eyes flicking back and forth across the messages—until they stop, freezing in recognition, in fear.

"We asked you yesterday," Sienna says, "if you knew where Jason went after he left the Marriott. You told us no. And just *hours* ago, you helped us look into Gavin, which we wouldn't have even needed to do if we knew Jason's alibi. An alibi *you've* been keeping from us, and I sure would like to know why."

With each new sentence, Maeve takes a step back, her feet tangling with the tote bags strewn across the floor. When her legs collide with an armchair, her knees give out. She falls into the chair like a marionette whose strings have been snipped, but her spine remains erect. Across from her, I let myself sink onto the couch. Only Sienna stays standing.

"Julia has a theory about why you haven't told us," she says. "And it doesn't paint you in the most favorable light."

As Maeve shoots her gaze to me, color floods her cheeks, blaring her guilt and shame, staining the air I'm trying to breathe. Even without her saying a word, that blush is all the confirmation I need.

"We—we didn't intend to hurt anyone," Maeve says. "You have to trust me on that."

"*Trust* you?" The question bullets from my mouth. "Maeve, I *trusted* you and you slept with my husband."

Surprise blasts across Maeve's face before backfiring onto mine. I hadn't meant to chime in, hadn't wanted the brunt of Maeve's attention, and now I recoil on the couch.

"See? That's Julia's theory," Sienna says. "I, for one, am sure it was something else, but what I'm not sure of is why you'd keep it from us. So tell us what's going on."

Maeve's eyes sweep across her bags on the floor. Her brow pushes down, in sync with the pull of her mouth. Then she chews her lip, teeth digging so deep I'm sure they'll draw blood.

She's silent for long enough that Sienna takes a step forward, sucking in a breath to prompt her again. But Maeve returns her gaze to me, the blush on her face now bleached to a clammy gray.

"I'm so sorry," she says. "It didn't start— We didn't— I just invited him over to show him the designs for my new store. I'd received the mock-ups from the designer the day before, and I figured he deserved to see them, after everything he did for me to get to this point."

Even as pain lashes me, I cock my head at that. What had Jason done for her?

"And after he looked them over," Maeve continues, "we moved to the couch and—"

She stops, wincing, and it takes me a second to realize why: it happened on the couch, where I'm sitting now. Right away, the cushion burns beneath me. I want to leap away, but I'm pinned into place by my imagination. I see them, only inches from me—Maeve straddling Jason, Jason dragging his lips along her neck, Maeve gripping his shoulders, hips rocking and rocking. As my mind forces me to watch, tears simmer in my eyes.

"I had a couple drinks," Maeve rushes ahead. "And then—I don't know. Something came over me, and I just—kissed him. I don't know what I expected. I didn't think we'd— But he surprised me by actually kissing me back. And then one thing led to another and we—we slept together."

"Wait, *what*?" Sienna says. She laughs for a second. "You can't be serious."

"I'm so sorry," Maeve says again, the words a rush of desperation. "Like I said, we didn't intend to hurt anyone. It wasn't planned. We never so much as flirted before that. But I think I . . ." She looks into her lap, where her hands are clasped together, and for a moment, I don't even recognize her. The vulnerable hunch of her shoulders is a posture I've never seen her wear.

"I think I'd had feelings for him for a while," she finishes, "ever since—"

"I don't give a fuck about your feelings," Sienna fires. "Jason wouldn't— He would never—"

But Maeve cuts in, as if committed to shattering my heart.

"We knew it was a mistake as soon as it was done. He made me promise I wouldn't say anything, that we'd act like it never happened." Maeve swallows, knotting and unknotting her fingers. "Which was fine with me because I was so ashamed. I *am* so ashamed. I'm not the type of woman who—" She shakes her head, cowardly, unwilling to name the thing she's done to me. "I told him we couldn't be around each other anymore, that we should keep our distance at work, too. And he agreed that was for the best. But then he sent me that email the next day. To check on me." She scoffs then, something bitter in the sound. "As if I'm so fucking fragile."

She focuses on me again. "He doesn't love me, Julia. He loves you. And Aiden. And your life together. He'll hate me when he finds out I told you. He'll deny it, I'm sure—the last thing he wants is to lose you—but I can't pretend I haven't been conflicted this week, every time I've seen you, spoken to you. He's hidden something so huge from you."

Maeve blurs in front of me, like I'm viewing her through rain-smeared glass. Tears swamp my vision, then spill in silence down my cheeks.

The man she's describing—the man who'd let one thing lead to another, who'd allow that *one thing* to happen in the first place—is a man I don't know at all. Even after Jason lost our money, I never considered I'd end up here, listening to the story of his adultery. Maeve might as well be talking about a fictional character, relaying scenes from a movie where the husband was always a stranger, and the wife was always a fool.

"I can't—" Sienna says. "Are you fucking serious? I can't believe he'd—"

She doesn't finish her sentence. Her eyes stick to the wall across from her, and I see the shock waves of Maeve's confession rippling through her. I lean forward, my hand wanting to latch onto hers. We've both lost something. Twin chasms have opened inside us, and our connection, our fierce and faithful love, is the only thing that can keep us close to whole.

I stretch toward Sienna, but she doesn't notice. She drops into an empty chair, then puts her elbows on her knees, her head in her hands.

"I'm sorry," Maeve says to me again. She isn't crying, but her voice is thick, as if the tears are in her throat instead of her eyes. "I don't even know why I— I just started to see him differently, after December. I've been so grateful to him for lending me that money, and—"

"What?" The word launches out of me, startling Maeve. "What money?"

Her forehead creases, as if she isn't sure the question is serious. "The money to help me open my store," she says. "The only reason I was finally able to secure a space."

Sienna picks her head up from her hands, looking from me to

Maeve, then back to me again. I feel her studying my face, radiating questions, but I can't meet her gaze, can't turn away from Maeve. My blood roars in my ears.

"How much money?" I ask.

Maeve bites her lip, gnawing at the plump, pink flesh.

My throat threatens to close, but I push out the question one more time. "How much?"

"Ten thousand dollars."

The room shrinks—walls tilting, ceiling sinking. Breath tumbles out of me, and my heart wavers on the verge of collapse.

This is where the money went. It wasn't a bad investment. It wasn't linked to Gavin Reed or tied to the shoeboxes of cash. It was something Jason gave to Maeve—a startling sum, stolen from our special account.

"Jason gave you *ten grand*?" Sienna spits out.

Maeve stares at us both, apparently blindsided by Jason's secrecy. And there's something almost funny about that. Shouldn't she know how easily my husband keeps things from me?

"He— My store, I—" she stutters. "After I told Jason how I caught Gavin in the warehouse that night, and how Gavin—how he cornered me after, talking about that dream, Jason told me I should quit. That I should stay away from Gavin. And I told him I'd love to quit, I'd wanted to for a while anyway so I could start my store, but I didn't have the money to make that happen yet."

"So *Jason* gave you the money?" Sienna asks, incredulous. But then she straightens in her chair, as if buoyed by a thought. "Actually, you know what? That's the first thing you've said tonight that actually sounds like him."

Sienna's right. Jason's always rushing to people's rescue. I just never imagined that him helping someone else would end up hurting me.

But even as that thought crosses my mind, I'm wondering if it might not be true. I think of Aiden's fifth birthday party, the one Jason missed because he was at the hospital with the hit-and-run victim. As he explained his absence to me on the phone, I couldn't understand it. The woman was going to be fine; she'd already made her police report, he'd already made his own statement, so why did he need to be there with her? After I hung up, still confused, unsatisfied, Sienna said it was "so sweet" of Jason to stay with the woman, deemed the whole thing "exactly like him," but I remember watching Aiden tear into presents, gobble down cake, with something cold and cloying in my stomach, like the sick, sticky feeling of eating too much ice cream.

And that's not the only example. On our tenth anniversary, Jason and I had to forfeit our fancy reservation—one we'd had to book weeks in advance, one with only a tiny grace period for tardiness— because, on the way there, Jason stopped to change a woman's flat tire. *It's okay*, the woman said, seeing Jason's suit, the shoes he'd recently shined. *I can call for roadside assistance.* But Jason insisted it was no problem, he'd do it himself, and I watched him from our parked car, love and frustration drumming inside me on different beats. Afterward, we attempted to salvage the night by ordering takeout, lighting candles, dancing in the kitchen. And it was then, Jason's hand on the small of my back, that he told me about the account he'd opened for our second honeymoon. *I want to dance with you in as many countries as I can*, he said—a moment so sweet it rendered the missed reservation just a blip in our celebration.

Now, I sway on Maeve's couch, other memories pushing to the front of my mind: the morning Jason shoveled our elderly neighbor's driveway, even though I needed the extra hand with ours to make it to a meeting on time; the day he didn't show up to Aiden's parent/teacher conference because his co-worker needed a last-minute ride to the airport. Where once there were separate, distinct anecdotes,

I see now a constellation of behavior. Jason is desperate to rescue people, even if it's to the detriment of his own family.

And what about him rushing to propose to me as soon as I got pregnant? Is that what the start of our family was to him—a way for Jason to rescue me?

"He told me he talked it over with you," Maeve says. "That you agreed to lend me the money. I wrote a thank-you card for him to give to you, but—I'm guessing you never got it?"

I shake my head, covering my mouth against a wave of nausea.

How many betrayals is this now? I'm quickly losing count. And I'm not sure how to manage it all at once: not just Jason's cheating—which has already cut me to the bone—but his lies, too, each one a layer of secrecy he built around the truth.

"Wait," Sienna says to me. "Jason took ten thousand dollars out of your account, and you never even noticed?"

I bristle at that, the implication that it was my fault for missing it. But I know she's struggling, same as I am, to understand how Jason could be this man: duplicitous and cruel.

"I noticed." My voice is small, barely a shard of sound. "But when I questioned it, he— I guess he lied to me. He told me someone talked him into a bad investment. And when I told him to get the money back, he said he couldn't, because the person he gave it to had screwed him over."

Maeve's eyes bulge. "I didn't screw him over."

"No, you just screwed him."

Sienna's comeback is quick and vicious, like a cat batting a mouse. Maeve's gaze darts to her lap, instantly chastened, but it's me who feels the swipe of Sienna's claws.

Fighting more nausea, I grip the arm of the couch—a move that draws Sienna's attention. She's at my side in less than a second, blanketing her hand over mine: "Jules, are you okay?"

I don't respond, but she nods as if I had; she can read my posture, my grimace, the room: of course I'm not okay.

"You did this to her," Sienna says, whipping her head toward Maeve. "She's only ever been kind to you, and this is how you repay her, by sleeping with her husband? Did you even *think* about her that night?"

"No," Maeve says without hesitation. "I wasn't thinking at all. I was only acting."

"Yeah, acting like a—"

Whatever insult Sienna's about to hurl is cut off by a shrill ring. Maeve frowns toward the entryway, then scurries away to answer the door.

Out of sight, there's the rumble of a man's voice, followed by the clomp of footsteps. I straighten, swiping tears from my face, uncertain who we're about to see, and for a dizzying second, I think it's going to be Jason; I think I'm about to see him and Maeve laugh and twirl into the living room, tangled in each other's arms.

But the man who enters is not my husband. It's Detective Beck.

"Oh, thank god," Sienna says, "*finally* you're on the right track. You saw the emails, right—when you searched Jason's computer? We beat you to it, but *she's* his alibi! *She* can account for his missing hours on Friday night."

Sienna points to Maeve—and though her finger is stiff and accusing, it's clear that her anger has short-circuited. It's rewired into something lighter, giddier. The pitch of her voice is high with anticipation, and I want to wince at it like it's a shriek of feedback. Instead, I keep my face blank, my own voice tucked inside my throat, and I try not to feel Sienna's thrill as its own kind of betrayal.

Beck turns to Maeve, whose gaze darts across the floor. "Is there somewhere we can speak in private?" he asks.

"No need!" Sienna says. "You can talk to her all you want. We're done with her."

She casts a blistering glance at Maeve before pulling me to my feet. Then she kicks through tote bags, purposefully sending them askew, to guide me past Maeve and Beck. As my shoulder brushes Maeve's, I shrink into myself, my skin feeling scraped beneath my clothes. I let Sienna lead me to the front door, which she thrusts open before nudging me through.

"For the record, I don't care that he's my brother," Sienna says as she slams the door shut. "I'm furious that he cheated on you. I'm a million percent livid with that idiot."

But she isn't. I know Sienna's fury, and this—her jaunty steps down the porch stairs—isn't it. Because Jason hasn't been unfaithful to *her*. He's disappointed her, sure, likely ripped open her Wyatt wounds, but no matter what, he is still her family, her blood; he didn't break any vows the two of them made.

Mine and Jason's had been generic (*in sickness, till death*), because we hadn't been together long enough to be more specific. It was only on our eighth anniversary that we opted for a "do-over," each of us scrawling into cards the promises we now knew to make. That night, beneath our blankets, we read our do-overs aloud, Jason laughing when I said I'd always warn him, from now on, when the avocado he thinks he's about to eat is actually a chunk of wasabi, and me rolling my eyes when he said he'd love me even when I left him sleepless during allergy season by "snoring like a clogged tuba."

And now I'm the one who'll be sleepless, tortured every time I close my eyes by Maeve's couch, Jason's lies. It's impossible to reconcile—Jason's promise to "always save the first dip into the peanut butter jar" for me with someone who could be so reckless with my trust.

I settle clumsily into Sienna's passenger seat, my legs heavy and cumbersome, like columns of granite. Sienna eases in.

"We didn't intend to hurt anyone," she says, mocking Maeve's voice, the excuse she first gave us, as if intention means anything, as if their sex was so fiery it burned all thoughts of me from their minds. "What a bitch."

She pivots toward me. "But now we have an alibi. And this will all be over. So at least there's a silver lining to Jason's affair."

It snatches my breath, how insensitive she sounds. Not to mention inaccurate. Jason's affair—god, his *affair*—has already plunged me into such darkness that the silver can't possibly shine through. As I buckle my seat belt, I don't respond—because I shouldn't be surprised. Sienna is hardwired to love her brother. She simply isn't equipped to criticize him for long.

But there's something else, too—a question that's slow to form, gummy from my grief. If Maeve is Jason's alibi, why did he have Gavin's phone in his car, his address in his pocket?

Could it be as simple as Sienna originally said? Maybe Gavin forgot his phone at the hotel. Maybe Jason picked it up to drop it at his house. And maybe—my stomach twists—Jason forgot that errand after leaving Maeve's, his mind fogged by sex and guilt.

"Jules," Sienna says, squeezing my hand, "why didn't you tell me about the money?"

Even in this lightless car, I see her face darken with confusion and hurt.

"I saw you in there," she continues, "when you figured out what Jason really used it for. You seemed almost as upset about that as you did about him—him cheating. And you've known about it for, what, months now? But you never even mentioned it to me."

For a moment, my knuckles pinch in her grip. I adjust my hand, forcing hers to loosen.

I don't tell her the real reason that comes to mind—that I was sure she'd take Jason's side, stung by the injustice of someone screwing her brother. Instead, I tell her a different truth: "He took the money from our Europe account. There's barely anything left."

Sienna's jaw drops. "Oh my god."

"And what am I supposed to make of that?" I continue. "He was the one who called the trip our second honeymoon, he knew how much it meant to me, and he just . . . took it. I didn't want you to think he and I were having problems—that our marriage wasn't—"

Without warning, I gasp out a sob. Then I hunch forward, twist my hand out from under Sienna's and cry into my palms. My despair ricochets, a desperate sound that bounces off the walls of the car, crashing into our ears.

"Oh, fuck, Jules, fuck, fuck, fuck." Sienna rubs the length of my spine, nestling her forehead against my shoulder.

I hiccup breaths, my back lurching as if with dry heaves.

"I love you," she says. "I'm here. I'm sorry. I love you."

She stops speaking to let me sob, and I love her too—so much—because she doesn't try to shush me. Despite her knee jerk allegiance to Jason, I know that she's still devoted to me, that she understands exactly what I need right now: to curl up with this anguish, to feel it fully, to figure out the future—mine and Jason's—another time.

But then she says one more thing: "You and Jason will work this out."

And I feel walloped anew, deep in my stomach, as my sob trembles with a sigh.

Chapter Twelve

SIENNA

I wake up in the wrong bed.

Sunlight needles through the windows, gritty and intrusive as sand in my eyes. Wyatt's arm snakes around my body, tightening the space between us as he breathes against my shoulder.

I pick up his wrist and move his arm away.

It was such a sloppy move, coming over two nights in a row. This should have been the last place I'd choose to go. But when I pulled into Julia's driveway and snapped off my seat belt, she'd put her hand on mine to stop me from opening my door. *Not tonight*, she said, tears still crowding her eyes. *I just want to be alone.*

I nodded at first—because for a few seconds, I didn't comprehend what *alone* really meant. To me, it meant Julia and me together, nobody else. But as she unbuckled her own seat belt, opened her own door, planted one foot on the pavement, she said she'd drive separately to the hospital tomorrow. And I knew then what *alone* really meant: Julia wanted me gone.

But I'd tried to be strong for her. I'd promised that everything would be okay. I'd reminded her that, if nothing else, Jason would be safe from the police's suspicion, now that he had an alibi. I'd framed it for her as a silver lining, a shimmering strand of hope, but as I reversed out of her driveway, all I saw was a swamp of darkness. And I knew then that to survive the night, I'd need a distraction. I'd need to dissociate from my scuffed-up heart, keep my mind from circling that alibi and everything it meant, keep my mind from doing anything at all.

I'd need to be only a body: hot skin and fiery nerve endings and loud, pulsing want.

I drove on autopilot to Wyatt's. When I passed Clive Clayton's house, I swallowed the sharp ache in my throat, suppressed the memory of Clive's hand on my breast, the well-worn image of his car crossing a double yellow line. Because thoughts of Clive would lead to thoughts of Jason, how my brother pulled me from that man's wreckage again and again. And I didn't want to think of Jason. Didn't want Maeve's confession to keep on skinning me raw.

Now Wyatt nuzzles against me, his fingers inching up my arm before working at the space between my shoulder blades. It feels good, and I almost lean into it, reach back to clamp him closer. But the sun stings my eyes—a reminder that I shouldn't even be here.

"No," I say. "It's morning."

He retracts his fingers, but his laughter tickles my neck. "I can only touch you at night?"

"Yes. No. I don't know." I tear off the sheet and fumble for my clothes. Walking around the room half-hunched, I pick them up piece by piece.

Wyatt rolls onto his back, setting his eyes on the ceiling. He's seen all of me, every scar and freckle and unruly hair, but he's giving me the illusion of privacy. I step into my underwear, clasp my bra, then shove my head into my sweater.

"We could do this more often," he says, voice slow and distant, like he's slipping back to sleep. "I love waking up with you."

I pause, my jeans halfway up my hips. "I didn't intend to stay the night."

But what did I intend to do? Blunt my pain with sex. Drown out my thoughts. Check and check. But what does it mean that I found out my brother—*my* brother, of all people—was a cheater, and I ran straight to the man who cheated on me?

"It was a mistake," I say.

Wyatt's face tightens—almost a wince. His eyes close as if he's steeling himself. And since he doesn't answer, I have to keep going, have to make sure we both understand.

"It didn't mean anything. It was nothing."

The words have the rusty taste of a lie. Because looking at him now—his bare chest blanketed by sun, his hair flattened by his pillow, a portrait of so many mornings from our old life together—it isn't nothing I feel; it's everything.

I feel our Sunday afternoons, weaving through flea markets, inventing origin stories for cracked porcelain dolls. I feel our Saturday nights, playing "One-star Bartender," a game to see who could mix the most repulsive drink, before we'd abandon our tumblers, kiss with boozy lips, whisper-laugh against each other's mouths the names we'd given our concoctions: Ditzy Ostrich, Jaunty Street Sweeper, Bashful Teacup. I even feel the plush skin of Wyatt's earlobe, which I'd tug sometimes when we were in public, a signal that I wanted him, that we should hurry off together, find some private space.

For a moment, I want all of it again—as equally, perhaps, as I want to run out the door.

"Sorry for accidentally crashing here," I say. "I have to go, though. I need to shower and change before I leave for the hospital."

His eyes still shut, he shifts his jaw back and forth, as if considering whether to speak.

"What?" I prompt.

"Nothing. I know you'll say no, but—just so it's clear: you can always shower here. Your extra change of clothes is still in your drawer."

My gaze jerks to the drawer he's referencing—the top left of his dresser. I dig my thumb into my palm, my hand remembering the shape of the drawer's knob.

"You kept that?" I ask.

He turns his head, opens his eyes. "I kept everything."

My palm throbs beneath my thumb. I swallow before asking: "Like what?"

"Well, there's the proton pack you built me for Halloween."

I dig harder into my hand. Two years ago, I'd been inspired by a story he told—as kids, he and his friend decided to dress up as Ghostbusters one Halloween, but while his friend's mom went all out, making the most realistic proton pack outside of the actual movie prop, Wyatt had only a plain, unpainted carboard box with a vacuum hose duct-taped on. So ahead of a costume party we'd been invited to, I went all out, too, studying stills from the films so I could replicate each button, each wire, each coil. When I finally presented it to him, Wyatt's reaction was adorable, his mouth morphing back and forth between wide-open shock and giddy grin.

"The box from the care package you made me when I had the flu," he continues, "the one you collaged with labels from my favorite beers. The sticky notes you left on my bathroom mirror of different animals in love; my favorite was always the kitten and the caterpillar. And"—he shrugs—"I don't know, all the things like that."

I look away from him but find myself staring at the set of chopsticks propped on his bookshelf. NOT BREADSTICKS, they read, and I'm whirled back to our first date, to Wyatt's endearing fumble with his appetizer, to our first anniversary when he told me he'd cherish those chopsticks as if they were actually made of bread.

I wonder how he does this, holds on to all our artifacts when they're only reminders of all that we've lost.

"I have to go," I say again, forcing myself to sound insistent this time.

Wyatt nods, eyes returning to the ceiling as if resigned to my departure. And as I exit his room, his house, his sun-soaked street, I do everything I can to keep from looking back.

· · ·

At the hospital, my vision wavers, warping my brother into an unfamiliar shape, an eely, slippery thing inside his bed.

Julia stands at the window, staring at the street below. As soon as she arrived today, I could tell she didn't sleep last night. Her eyelids were so puffy they looked like pillows. Lines fissured her forehead. And as I held her hand, watched her work so hard to keep her gaze away from Jason, it was as if I could feel her heart, clawed-up and mauled, inside my own body. Now she runs one finger over the windowsill, pushing dust back and forth.

As usual, there isn't much for us to do. I've already called Lou to let him know about the alibi, and though he paused after hearing about it—absorbing, no doubt, that his old friend's son is a cheater—he didn't so much as tsk or sigh in response. Instead, he promised to hop on the phone with the Hillstead PD to see if they've dropped Jason as a suspect. *If?* I asked, voice screechy with indignance, and Lou floated an idea that hadn't occurred to me yet: the cops could think it isn't enough, having only one woman's word that Jason's time was accounted for.

And not just any woman, I thought but didn't add. *The woman he slept with.*

Someone's changed Jason's bandages again. They're bright white against his bruises, almost garish, and I'm inspecting them, scrutinizing each fiber of the fabric instead of Jason's face, when a pair of footsteps shuffles into the room.

"Good morning," Dr. Brighton says.

I stand to greet her. At the window, Julia pivots, but doesn't come closer.

"I have some positive news for you both."

I slingshot my gaze back to Jason, as if I might find him blinking awake.

"Not yet," Dr. Brighton says, reading my thoughts. "But we're thinking it'll be soon. This morning, during rounds, Jason responded a little to the spontaneous breathing trial."

"Responded? Did he say something?" I ask.

Dr. Brighton shakes her head. "Not that kind of responding. He's unable to speak with the breathing tube. And we don't think he's ready to breathe on his own just yet, so we're continuing to sedate him. We don't want to get into a situation where we remove the tube, only to have to reinsert it, so we generally err on the side of caution. We'll try again tomorrow, and it's very possible that at that point we'll be able to take him off the sedative."

"And take out the tube?" I ask.

I flash her a hopeful smile. Without the tube, Jason will look more like himself, less like a part of a machine. I have a fleeting image of our reunion, giving him shit about how his bruises look like a toddler did his makeup. *Most dramatic nap ever*, I can tease.

"And take out the tube," Dr. Brighton confirms.

But my smile stutters a little, twisting toward a grimace. Because now I'm seeing the rest of our reunion, the moment when the relief sours, when I remember that something's changed, that we can't just jump back to normal. The moment when I ask him, *How could you,*

Jason? The moment, without the tube, when he opens his mouth to answer.

I look at Julia, alarm widening her eyes, and I see her picturing it too.

"It's good news," Dr. Brighton says to our silence. "It's what we've been waiting for."

"Right," I say. "Thanks."

As the doctor leaves, Julia steadies herself with a hand on the windowsill.

"I'm not ready," she tells me. "I want Jason to be okay, but I'm not ready to talk to him about it. I don't know how to—"

I rush to her side before she can finish her sentence. "It's okay, I get it."

"He lied to me. About Maeve. About the *money*."

In her agonized emphasis, I feel it again: Jason's lie about the money hurts her almost as much as his infidelity. It's certainly baffling—distressing, even—that he used the savings from their vacation account, but if it devastated her this much, why didn't she ever tell me about it? Her answer last night was a little insulting—*I didn't want you to think he and I were having problems*—as if I'm some child who can't handle hearing their parents fight. I could tell it wasn't the full story, too; there was something she was holding back. And now it hurts *me*, knowing she didn't trust me with the truth. Not when I asked her in the car. Not when she first noticed the money was gone.

"I'm not ready," she says again, and the pain on her face makes me shove my own aside.

"It's okay. You don't have to be."

But my assurance doesn't soothe her. Julia's gaze flits around the room like the walls are creeping closer, like we're both about to be crushed. I weave my fingers through hers, anchoring her to me.

From the corner of my eye, I see my silenced phone light up with a call, the screen glowing from where I left it on one of the chairs, but I don't move to answer it. Right now, Julia needs me more than anyone who might be calling.

"And remember, it's good," I try, "that these pieces are falling into place. The alibi, Jason's recovery. It means that when you *are* ready, he'll be here to listen."

"And what if I'm never ready?"

We both pull back a little, the question seeming to surprise Julia as much as it does me.

"You will be," I promise, squeezing her hand.

She shakes her head, uncertain, then parts her lips before clamping them shut.

"What is it?" I ask, trying to suppress my impatience. "Say it."

"It's just— How do you know? You've never been ready with Wyatt. You cut him out completely."

"That—that's different."

Heat charges into my cheeks, and I rub my jaw to mask my blush. I look toward my phone, wondering if I should answer it after all, but the screen is back to black.

"No, it's not different—see?" Julia says. "You're getting all pink. It's been a year since you broke up and you still look like that whenever he comes up."

"No, Jules, trust me, it's different. You and Jason are *married*. You have a kid together. That's so much more than me and Wyatt ever shared. So, yeah, I get it, he's hurt you so bad, you can't imagine ever being ready to speak to him about it, but you *will* be. You'll work through this."

She shakes her head again, and I nod emphatically, trying to cancel out her doubt. She and Jason can't end up like me and Wyatt— because what would that mean for me and Jules? My throat tightens just to wonder. Tears burn in the back of my eyes. Even though Jason's the one who connected us, I always thought my bond with Julia transcended his involvement. We have jokes that don't include him, shorthand he doesn't share. But what would it look like if they weren't together? How would I sit in my brother's house, unable to hold my best friend's hand? How would I stay close to Julia and to Jason without betraying them both?

"Excuse me," someone says from the door.

I swivel to find Beck there, standing beside an officer in uniform.

"Jesus Christ," I hiss. "What do you want? He was with Maeve Dorsey last Friday. If you don't believe her or their emails, have her take a polygraph or something."

Before he can respond, another person bustles into the room. Bald head, bristly mustache. It's been years since I've seen him, but I recognize him instantly.

"Lou? What's going on?"

He opens his mouth, but it's Beck's voice that booms toward me and Julia.

"We have a warrant to arrest Mr. Larkin," he says, "for the murder of Gavin Reed."

Julia's hand goes slack in mine. Beck reaches into his suit jacket, pulls out a crisp piece of paper folded into thirds.

"*Arrest* him?" I volley my gaze between Beck and Lou. "He has an alibi!"

"Sienna," Lou says. He puts up his hands like a crossing guard, like I might be stepping into danger. "The alibi's no good."

I let go of Julia's hand to rake my fingers through my hair. I point my response at Beck: "I get that you can only take Maeve's word for it, but why would she lie? She outed herself as a—as a fucking home-wrecker by admitting she was with Jason!"

"It's not that," Lou says, moving a few inches so he's blocking my view of Beck. "It turns out Ms. Dorsey's statement still left a gap in Jason's timeline."

"What? How?"

"She said he left her house around ten thirty. And since Julia has previously stated that he arrived home around eleven thirty, that still leaves an hour unaccounted for." He leans closer, lowers his voice. "Gavin Reed lives twelve minutes from Maeve's house. Twenty from Jason's."

"So?" I fire back, leaning to the side to glare at Beck. "You really think Jason cheated on his wife, then immediately went and murdered his boss? That doesn't make *any* sense."

Julia drops into a chair. I spare enough of a glance to ensure she hasn't fainted or collapsed before I whirl back to Beck.

"Doesn't it seem a lot more likely that Jason realized he'd fucked up in the biggest way, so he drove around trying to figure out what the hell he was going to do before going home?"

"I understand this is upsetting," Beck says, "but we have evidence that corroborates his involvement in the murder."

"Yeah, yeah, Gavin's phone, the bloody knife, but it isn't Gavin's blood, it's—"

"It is, actually."

"—probably Jason's, he probably cut himself and—"

Somehow my mouth knows to freeze, even as my mind is sluggish to process Beck's interjection.

"Wait." I fall back a step. "What?"

I look at Julia, who's staring up at me. Her eyes are wide and wet enough that I can practically see myself reflected in them.

Lou cups my elbow. "The results came back. The blood on Jason's knife is a match to Gavin."

"No," I say, and it feels like I'm breathing in slow motion, like my body will accept only the thinnest sip of air.

"It is," Lou says. "I'm sorry. I got in my car as soon as I heard they were coming with a warrant, and it was only in the parking garage that I finally got word about why. I'm sorry. I would have liked to give you more warning."

His voice is quiet, gentle, but his words plug up my ears, water I can't shake out.

"No, there has to be some mistake," I say.

Beck taps the warrant against his palm, its fold as sharp as a blade. For a second, I picture blood spilling from his hand, staining the white page.

"You're going to *arrest* him?" I say. "He's in a coma! What do you plan to do, wheel his bed to a jail cell?"

"We're going to hold the warrant," Beck says, "until he regains consciousness. But in the meantime, this is Officer Grady." He gestures to the cop beside him. "He'll be posted outside Mr. Larkin's room."

"Like a guard?" I run my eyes over Grady. He's the opposite of intimidating—thin as a sapling, too young to question orders—but there's a pompous tilt to his lips that makes my nerves sizzle. "You're acting like my brother's a flight risk. I don't know how many times I have to say it, but he's asleep!"

"Sienna, believe me, this is the better option," Lou says.

"Better than what?"

"Than restraining him to the bed."

"What?"

My gaze drops to Officer Grady's belt. Handcuffs dangle there, shining in the room's abrasive lights. They hang open like hungry mouths, eager to chomp onto Jason's wrists.

"This is insane," I say, walking a tight circle in the middle of the room.

Lou stops me with a hand on my arm, speaking so low that I

doubt even Julia hears him. "It's far from an open-and-shut case. We'll fight it."

His eyes are somber but kind, filled with compassion as they hold on to mine. I'm reminded of a picture, pressed into one of my mother's photo albums, of Lou with his arm slung around my father's shoulder. The picture, snapped at some party my parents hosted, is only memorable to me because of the shenanigans captured in the background: a clump of kids shrieking through trust falls. In the photo, I'm just a shape, a blurry slant above the grass, and behind me, Jason is solid and still, his body braced for strength, his arms open to catch me.

"Okay," I say, and Lou steps back, turning toward the cops.

"Detective, Officer, may I speak with you outside a moment please?"

Beck nods and waves Officer Grady forward. On the way out, Lou shuts the door. I don't know if he's allowed to do that—Jason's door has always been open until now, except for when the nurses usher us out to run their tests—but I appreciate the gesture of privacy.

"Jules." I crouch in front of her chair. She's staring straight ahead, eyes stunned and unseeing. Tears speckle her lashes. "Did you hear what he said? This is far from over. Lou's going to fight it."

When she doesn't respond, I grab her hand, shake it like she's sleeping and I need to wake her up. "Jules."

Finally, she blinks, tears spilling onto her cheeks. I wipe one away, but they keep cascading, silent and steady.

"Lou will figure this out," I say. "He'll make this go away."

Julia releases a jagged breath. "No he won't."

"Of course he will. Why would you say that?"

As her lips curl inward, sealing her answer inside her mouth, I shake her hand again, harder this time. "Hey, don't do that," I say. "*Talk* to me."

She drags her gaze to Jason, and as she watches him over my shoulder, her eyes swim with fear, as if it's not her husband she's seeing, but a ghost.

"Lou can't make this go away," she says. "Maybe at a trial, maybe he can make a case for reasonable doubt—"

"Reasonable doubt? He can do a hell of a lot better than that. But this won't even go to trial, he'll figure it out, he'll—"

"How?" Julia asks. "Gavin's blood was on Jason's knife. Jason had his phone. He was in the area at the time of the murder. The evidence is there."

"Yeah, but—there's got to be some other explanation."

"Even if there is," Julia says—and I flinch at that *if*, "the doctor said she thinks Jason will wake up soon. Tomorrow, maybe! This won't be fixed before then. He's going to be arrested for Gavin's murder."

"No."

Flames lick my stomach as I think of those handcuffs, see them snapping around my brother's wrists before Beck hauls him to a jail cell.

"We'll figure it out," I tell Julia. I drop from a crouch to a kneel, tightening my grip on her hand. "Before Jason wakes up. We'll spend all day on it. We won't sleep, we won't stop, not until we find out what happened to Gavin. We still have those names from the warehouse. I know we got sidetracked by Maeve yesterday, but that cash is still a lead, and we know Jason's innocent; we know he is!"

"I don't think we know anything anymore."

The sentence, quiet as it is, knocks me back on my heels.

"What?" My voice is barely more than a whisper. "What are you saying?"

Julia tucks her chin toward her chest, eyes scurrying across the blank tiles on the floor.

"What are you saying?" I repeat, firmer this time. "You think he did it?"

She shakes her head quickly, as if to say, *No, of course not*. But the gesture doesn't look like denial. It looks like defeat.

"I don't know," Julia says.

"You . . . don't know?"

"I just— I can't—" Julia heaves in a breath. "How else do you explain everything?"

I almost laugh. "Um, you explain it literally any other way than by believing Jason killed a man."

Julia shakes her head again, confusion stamped onto her face. "I guess. But . . . it's not just the blood or the phone, is it? There's also that paper from Jason's pocket, the one with Gavin's address on it. It's all— When you put it all together, the picture is pretty damning."

"But there's *zero* motive. Jason had no reason to want Gavin dead."

"We don't know that. There's so much we don't know. He lied to me. Over and over. He lied about the money he took from our account. He cheated on me with Maeve. And no, I *never* would have thought that Jason could commit murder, but I never thought he'd do those other things either. I don't think I really know him, Sienna. I don't think either of us do."

I gape at her, blown back. One moment she was reluctant to speak, and now her words feel like matches struck against my bones.

"I know him," I manage.

Because even though she's right about parts of it—he lied, he cheated—there's a world of difference between adultery and murder, a distance too huge for Jason to cross.

"He's my brother, my *blood*," I add. "I fucking know him. And yes, he's made some terrible mistakes, but he isn't violent. He doesn't *hurt* people. He helps them."

For the millionth time in my life, the memory whirs into motion, a film strip flickering on: Jason, at that high school party, freeing me from Clive Clayton's grasp, saving me from the threat of violence— *Shh, just relax*—that Clive had hissed into my ear.

"That's what we thought about Aiden," Julia says. "But he pushed that kid."

"One: that's nowhere close to the same thing. And two: that kid provoked him!"

"Maybe Jason was provoked. We have no idea what happened. And I'm not saying—" She massages her forehead with one hand, wipes her tears with the other. "It's not that I'm sure he killed him. I still don't know *why* he would." She lowers her hands to her lap, looks me right in the eyes. "But I'm not sure he's innocent, either."

Pain blasts across her face, as if she only feels the impact of her doubt now that she's spoken it aloud. She pitches forward, her back heaving with sobs, her face becoming so twisted and strange it's like I'm looking at her through glass spiderwebbed with cracks. And suddenly I get it, even if I don't agree. The second she learned Jason was capable of cheating on her, capable of hurting so thoroughly someone he loved, it became much easier to think him capable of the impossible, too.

Which means, right now, I have to believe in Jason for the both of us.

I look toward the door, on the other side of which stands a detective, a guard. They've been gone for minutes now, but their presence lingers like a cloying cologne. It clogs my throat, reminding me of the thick, dread-heavy air of my parents' wake. That day, Jason let me sit behind him in a chair, numb and immobile, while he shook an endless line of hands, dealing with the business of sympathy so I didn't have to. And now that Jason's the immobile one, I will swallow hot, jagged coals before I let him wake up to find he's under arrest.

But Dr. Brighton has made it clear: I'm running out of time to point the police to someone else.

"Jason is innocent," I say to Julia. Her hands lie in her lap, palms facing the ceiling. "And I promise you I will prove it."

Chapter Thirteen

JULIA

I'm not sure he's innocent.

It's been two hours since I said those words. Their echo should be long gone.

I'm not sure he's innocent.

Slumped on our family room couch, I'm studying my empty hands—which look wrong somehow. Asymmetrical. Like they belong to someone else. Even my wedding ring seems discolored: bronze instead of gold, a metal less precious than the one I intended to wear.

I try to twist the ring, but it's resistant. All these years, my finger grew inside it, and now it's part of me, like a circle of bone. Maybe that alone should have kept me clutching my trust in Jason. But something changed in that hospital today. An arrest warrant. A guard outside Jason's door. A dead man's blood on a knife my husband is never without. By the time Sienna read the fear on my face, my doubt had sprouted too big to keep swallowing down.

Now, I'm haunted by a phantom weight beside me on the couch, as if Sienna's on another cushion. But every time I turn my head, I find myself alone. This is the first time since last weekend that I've spent an afternoon without her, and I know it was my words, my declaration, that keeps her from being here now. She didn't scream at me like I might have expected. Her body didn't tighten, fists didn't clench. But the moment I said it—*I'm not sure he's innocent*—I felt something break between us.

My gaze flits to the family room wall, and there's a twinge in my side: all those roosters, red and grotesque, an undeniable pattern of blood that Sienna and Jason never saw.

Shivering, I force my focus to the giant photographs, scrutinizing the one from our wedding where I stand between Jason and Sienna on the courthouse steps. I used to play a game with that picture— close an eye and imagine one of us removed from it: with Sienna gone, it was a portrait of a husband and wife; with me erased, it was siblings on a sunny day; with Jason smudged out, it was best friends who, even then, were linking hands. I loved that the photo held three relationships at once, but now, with one eye shut, I see something different when I remove my husband: Sienna and I off-balance with each other, a picture that's incomplete. My eye jolts open as I'm struck by a terrifying thought—that if I lose Jason, to prison or infidelity or simply my own doubt, I might lose Sienna, too.

The idea is so gut-wrenching that I put my hand to my chest, struggling to breathe. Losing Sienna would feel like losing a vital organ. My heart. A lung. Maybe both of them at once. There'd be parts of me left gaping. Pitch-black places that light could never reach. I push the thought away—too excruciating to bear.

It's only been a couple of hours, but I miss Sienna already. I miss slipping beneath the undertow of her conviction, her unwavering belief in Jason—though I'm bothered by it, too. It's one thing to love someone, to trust them, but I'm beginning to think love shouldn't be blind, shouldn't limit us to seeing only the pretty parts. All this week, Sienna and I have learned some ugly things about Jason, and it rankles me that her response is now to close her eyes, to turn away, to leave me to witness it all on my own.

Not for the first time today, I picture Jason at Maeve's last Friday—nervous, maybe, as he shuffled his feet on the doormat, already sensing a buzz of something between them. I see his fingers brushing Maeve's as he huddles with her over the designs for her store. I see Maeve and Jason on the couch, their mouths, their hands, their breathy separation at the end of it all. The rushed retrieval of clothes, the vow to never speak of it, then Jason hurrying out the door.

That's where the images stop, where my mind goes staticky like an old TV.

What happened after Jason left Maeve's? Did he drive to that address in his pocket, confront Gavin about—something? At the hospital, I theorized that Jason might have turned violent at Gavin's provocation, which only made Sienna scoff. But the truth is: I don't know what Jason's capable of when pushed. I've never pushed him myself, never so much as spoken up about my own discomfort: our son's party he skipped to stay beside a stranger; our anniversary dinner we missed so he could play the highway hero. I have no idea what happens when Jason is met with resistance, when something hot gets under his skin. I've seen it in Sienna, that fire in her eyes that could burn down the world, but maybe Jason has that too. Maybe he's stifled it for all the years I've known him and last Friday night it finally erupted, turning him into something dangerous. Something wild.

But there's the question I keep coming back to: *Why?* Even if I manage to imagine the murder, I can't muster up a motive. There are loose ends, sure: the shoeboxes of cash in the warehouse; Jason's customers among those involved in Gavin's potential fraud; the promotion Jason never told me he lost. But it's still nearly as laughable as the last time it occurred to me; Jason wouldn't kill someone over money.

Then again—that's the crux of the problem, the reason I'm here, acutely alone, on this couch at all: I don't know what Jason would or wouldn't do. Not anymore.

The doorbell rings, scattering my thoughts. I consider leaving it unanswered, but then I think of the last time that bell rang—Beck, a search warrant—and I don't want to risk Aiden clomping down from his room to find a cop at the door. I haven't told him, yet, of Jason's impending arrest. I've barely spoken to him since pizza last night, haven't even seen him since I got home; I only beelined from the garage to the couch, texting him I was back.

When I haul myself up and lumber down the hall, I glimpse a familiar flash of red in the front window. Panic squeezes my neck, my footsteps stutter, but after a moment, I push forward. Because I must be mistaken; it wouldn't be—

"Maeve," I say when I open the door. She's got a nervous stance—arms crossed, shifting on her feet—but she's dressed impeccably: jeans that look tailored specifically to her legs, a cashmere sweater, a turquoise scarf embellished with red petals. Just the sight of her, so put together when I'm falling apart, makes me lean against the doorframe for support. "What are you doing here?"

"I'm sorry, I went to the hospital, but no one was there. I figured I'd try you here."

Icy fingers clamp around my heart. "You visited Jason?"

"No," she's quick to amend. "I was looking for you. Can I come in? I wanted to talk to you. About that night."

That night. Bodies on a couch. A tangle of lips and tongues and hands.

If I were more like Sienna, I'd laugh or spit in Maeve's face. I'd thunder curses at her, unleash a storm of *fuck you, how dare you, go the fuck away.*

But *that night* was something else, too. Gavin on the grass in his own backyard: stabbed, smothered, stitched.

I touch the doorframe, disoriented by the contrast of those images— sex and death, adultery and murder. How is it possible that both nights existed at once, that my husband is the common thread between them? Jason's mouth on Maeve's skin. Gavin's blood on Jason's knife.

As I stand frozen, a sick, slushy feeling mucking about inside me, Maeve interprets my stillness as an invitation. She slips over the threshold into the house.

"I know I'm the last person you want to see," she says, heading straight for the kitchen. She stops at the table where we hosted her for Thanksgiving, where she complimented the cranberry sauce Jason had made from scratch, where she asked for seconds of it, then thirds, her hungry lips closing around the berries, her smile, aimed at my husband, stained with red.

"I just— I have to apologize, again," she says, fingers skimming the surface of the table as she stares at the wood. "It's my fault you're hurting, and I'm so sorry about that."

I don't respond. Instead, I think how untrue her statement is. As much as I'd love to assign her all the blame, it's not a fair assessment of what happened. Even though she initiated things by kissing Jason, he still could have recoiled, walked out the door, done anything but kiss her back.

"And I want you to know that I'm going to pay back that ten grand." She pulls a piece of paper, folded into thirds, from her canvas tote, and I'm dislodged for a moment, picturing the arrest warrant Beck extracted from his jacket.

Maeve opens the paper and sets it on the table. It's a spreadsheet of dates and numbers.

"I've made a repayment schedule. This is your copy, for your records. I have the first payment due to you at the end of September. If that's too late, I can adjust it. Jason kept insisting the money was a gift, but I've *always* thought of it as a loan. So as soon as my store is open, I'll be setting aside—"

"Wait." My stomach grows heavy, as if it's lined with iron. "Jason said it was a gift?"

Maeve bites her lip. "Maybe he didn't use that word. He was just adamant that he didn't expect me to pay him back. All he cared about was me getting to open my store."

Unsteady, I sink onto a chair. "Your dream store," I mutter—and it's a fresh smack of pain: he contributed to Maeve's dream while stealing from mine.

"He must've had feelings for you for a while then," I add, "to give you such an extravagant gift."

"Oh—no!" Maeve says. "That wasn't it at all. He was just . . . really freaked out by what Gavin said to me in the warehouse. He kept telling me I couldn't work for someone who'd treat me like that, and then I'd say, 'Well, I need this job until I can save enough money for my store,' and then he—"

She stops as I wave off the explanation. He was rescuing her, sure; that's what he does. But would one creepy incident from Gavin—one in which he didn't even touch her—really push Jason to give Maeve so much money, no strings attached, if he only saw her as a friend?

"Maeve." I clasp my hands in my lap. "Tell me the truth. Did you sleep with my husband before that night?"

She plunks into the chair diagonal from me, eyes swelling wide. "No! I swear."

Before I can decide if I believe her, my phone trills with an incoming email. I glance at it on the table and feel a punch of dread at the sender's name: Dale Stapleton, our notoriously difficult client.

Opening the message, I'm assaulted by a string of all-caps sentences. Phrases pop out—UNACCEPTABLE, NOT HOW PROPER BUSINESSES OPERATE, I EXPECT IT BY MONDAY—before I press my forehead into the heel of my hand.

"Is everything okay?" Maeve asks. "It's—it's not bad news about Jason, is it?"

"No." I heave out a sigh, then rattle off Dr. Brighton's update before I remember that Maeve is the last person who deserves to hear it.

"Are you serious? He's really waking up soon?" Maeve pitches forward, practically salivating for details. "When?"

I swipe my gaze at her, and she's self-aware enough to wince. It's not a great look, so soon after her apology—her eagerness for the moment my husband's awake.

"Sorry. You don't have to tell me." Maeve nudges her chin toward my phone, quick to change the subject. "You can deal with . . . whatever that was, if you need to."

"It's fine. It's just a client being nasty."

She grunts in understanding. "That's the last thing you need this week."

I shrug. "He's mad we're missing a deadline. Sienna's told him— twice now—that we have a family emergency, but . . ." I trail off, uncomfortable to be confiding in her.

"What a dick," Maeve says. "Reminds me of the time my dad had a stroke—a minor one, but still—and even though I told my customer there'd be a delay in her order because I was flying home, she sent me a message, all capital letters, about how I'd better mail her the order by the end of the week or she'd 'go nuclear' in my online reviews."

"This message was all caps too," I admit.

"Of course it was." Maeve rolls her eyes. "This is how I'd respond: 'So sorry you're frustrated'—apologize for *his* feelings, not anything *you've* done—'but my family comes before your business, which I encourage you to take elsewhere if you're unable to grant us an extension while my husband's in a fucking coma.'" She pauses. "Maybe without the 'fucking,' though."

In spite of myself, I almost chuckle; I can only imagine how "nuclear" Dale would go on *our* reviews if I swore at him in an email. Still, Maeve's suggestion might be a useful template. Dale is detail-oriented—often obnoxiously so, sending us more information than the average web visitor would possibly read—and I wonder now if the "family emergency" Sienna mentioned to him was too vague, if he interpreted it as a cop-out instead of a crisis.

I open the email to type out a response.

Hi Dale,

I am so sorry for your frustration. To clarify our previous messages, my husband—Sienna's brother—has been in the hospital since Tuesday. He had an accident and is now in a coma, and as such, we won't be able to complete your updates on time. You're certainly a valued A&A client, but family comes first for us, and we're hopeful you'll be kind enough to grant us an extension as we navigate this difficult time.

Thank you,

Julia

My finger hovers over Send before pressing it. Then, with a definitive *whoosh*, the message zips off to Dale's inbox.

"Sorry you have to deal with people like that," Maeve says, "on top of everything else." Her face scrunches with another wince. "Including me. I'm sorry to, like, bombard you with this visit. I just needed you to know that I'm serious about paying you back—and, of course, that I'm sorry. It might not mean much, but I fucking hate hurting you like this."

Regret pools in her eyes, as tangibly as tears. Maeve's either Meryl Streep in the making, or she's being sincere. Either way, she's right; it doesn't mean much.

"I'll go," Maeve says, rising from her seat, but she pauses when my phone chimes with another email. "Is that him already?" She leans forward to read the screen.

I pull my phone from her gaze, then brace myself when I see Dale's name. "It is."

His message is shorter this time, its only capital letters the ones at the start of each sentence:

Oh, wow. Really sorry to hear that. I'm eager to get these updates done, but I understand you've got a lot going on. Let's touch base next week and decide on a reasonable deadline for the extension.

My brows shoot upward. It actually worked. I read his response again, savoring the shift in Dale's tone, the way I nudged him from aggressive to acquiescent with a single message. Pulsing with pride, my fingers itch to text Sienna, tell her I handled Dale myself for once, saw his caps-lock screaming and did not flag it as a problem only she could solve.

But even in the midst of my tiny personal win, there's something that feels like losing, another tether between Sienna and me that's gone a little slack. My heart chafes at the thought: I managed this without her.

"Is he still pissed?" Maeve asks.

"No. He backed right down. That was good advice, I wouldn't have—" I close my mouth, stopping short of thanking her.

"Happy to help." Maeve picks up her tote. "I'll get going."

"Wait."

Her presence makes the air feel heavy, but I can't deny she's just been useful to me—and there might be other ways she's able to help.

"They're arresting Jason as soon as he wakes up," I tell her.

Her eyes flash with surprise. "What? How— I told them he was with me that night."

"You told them he left at ten thirty. According to the police, that still gave him time to murder Gavin. He didn't get home until an hour later."

Slowly, Maeve descends back into her seat. "Shit. I didn't know, I—"

"He had a receipt in his pants from that night. On the back, he'd written Gavin's address. Do you have any idea why?"

Maeve's forehead wrinkles. "No."

"Do you know any reason he'd want to hurt Gavin?"

I expect even more confusion. I wait for her brows to squeeze together, her lips to pitch down. Instead, her expression smooths out, like a crumpled piece of paper carefully flattened. My heart kicks at how clearly I can read her expression.

She knows something.

"Maeve, what is it?"

Face frozen, she stares in my direction. "Hurt him?" Her voice is distant, as if she's only mouthing the words while someone else speaks them. "No, not really, but—" Her gaze sharpens, her eyes clicking into focus, penetrating mine. "You know Jason hates him, right?"

I straighten in my chair. "What?"

Maeve nods, the movement tight and quick, like she's never been more certain of anything. "He despises Gavin."

Ice feathers over me, a layer of frost on my skin. "What?" I say again.

But Maeve's answer only worsens my chill: "I'm sure he's relieved our boss is dead."

Chapter Fourteen

SIENNA

Two hours after leaving the hospital, I'm at my desk, making a spreadsheet of suspects.

I've typed in all the customer names from the gutter machine, and I've googled them one by one, scouring for any red flags. I'm not even sure what a red flag would look like, or why someone getting a discount from Gavin would want to kill him, but I promised Julia I would prove Jason's innocence, and the only place I can think to start is the last place we left off, when we were still trying to prove it together.

Despite the hour—middle of the afternoon, sun flooding my bedroom—I slurp my second coffee. I may have slept at Wyatt's last night, but my body, knowing I wasn't supposed to be there, kept me on the cusp of waking, a sleep too shallow for the mental sharpness I need now. I click my nails on my mug—a custom one Julia gave me: *Liquid Motatoes*, pure nonsense to anyone but us—and try to focus on my spreadsheet. Instead, I glance at my phone.

I'm surprised she hasn't texted yet. I thought, at the very least, she'd ask what my plan is. I even decided to do my research from home, drinking my own bad coffee instead of hunkering down at a café, just in case Julia changed her mind and dropped by to help. And where the hell is Lou right now? Each time I look at my phone, I check for his name, too. When I left Jason's hospital room, I thought I'd find Lou in the hall, arguing with Beck about the warrant, but the only person I saw was that stupid guard, smirking at me like there was something I didn't know.

I force my gaze back to my spreadsheet. Like the names Julia recognized, Linear and Zigoris, most of the customers from Gavin's notebook are businesses, not homeowners. At first that struck me as strange—homeowners are Integrity Plus's bread and butter—but maybe businesses are a better target for this kind of scheme; the jobs themselves might be bigger, the owners more likely to be able to pay in cash.

It's only once I google deeper, skimming pages of search results, that I find another link between some of Gavin's customers: a website on which three of them appear. I didn't think anything of the company's name at the top of the site—Higher Home Improvement—until the third time it popped up in my search, but now I pore over the page, Higher Home's testimonies section, and each time I read the name, it chimes in my mind as one I've heard before.

Higher Home Improvement bent over backwards to get us great service at the best price, says the owner of one business from Gavin's notebook. *Higher Home Improvement was an unprecedented pleasure to work with*, says another.

Higher Home Improvement. I squint at the screen, and when I navigate to the homepage, I understand why the name is so familiar. The page is dominated by an orange banner: *While Higher Home Improvement is no longer in business, we extend our eternal gratitude to our loyal customers. We've been honored to serve Connecticut homes and businesses for over thirty years.*

This is the company Integrity Plus almost merged with before Gavin turned the owner in for tax evasion—the same crime Gavin himself appears to be guilty of. Irritation scratches at me over Gavin's hypocrisy. I knew Integrity Plus absorbed a lot of Higher Home's customers after the merger fell through, but it appears they also absorbed the backdoor deals that some of those customers were enjoying.

I can only imagine the rage Higher Home's owner would feel if he learned what Gavin was up to. It's clear he hasn't moved on—after all, the Higher Home website still exists; someone has paid the hosting service each month. It's as if he's keeping it as a reminder of everything Gavin destroyed.

I pull up my spreadsheet again, add Higher Home Improvement to the list of names.

My phone dings with an email, and my hand leaps for it.

It's not Julia. Not Lou, either. It's Dale Stapleton—speaking of angry business owners—and his message is an onslaught of capital letters.

THIS IS UNACCEPTABLE, he screams in the middle of the email. IT'S NOT HOW PROPER BUSINESSES OPERATE.

Heat builds in my stomach, boiling out toward my extremities. I already told Dale, twice now, that we're dealing with a family emergency.

I write a response with my own capital letters, along with a particularly creative string of expletives. When I'm done, I read it over, finger hovering over Send. Then I turn my head to the side, because it's pure habit, turning toward Julia, and I know this is the moment I should see my best friend, should hear her muttering my mantra, feel her taking my hand. Or, no—it's past the moment. If Julia were here, she would grasp my palm before I could even begin a draft to Dale. *Let's not have another Lashley Incident.*

But right now, my hand holds nothing. It's cupping only air. And for a second, I forget everything: why my email is open, why my caps lock is set. All I feel is emptiness.

Blinking out of the moment, I delete the draft, push my phone away. Now is not the time to deal with Dale. Now is for proving to Julia that, despite his reckless infidelity, despite the money she never told me he took, Jason is still a man worth believing in.

I return to my spreadsheet, look at Higher Home on the list, and toggle back to their website to search for the owner's name. I find it on the Meet Our Team page, right at the top, beneath a photo of a man with a round face and gray hair.

As soon as my eyes focus on his name, my spine straightens.

Henry Hendrix.

I've heard that recently. My mind gropes for the memory, repeating the name until I hear it spoken in Lou's gravelly voice, the sound thinned by a phone connection. I jolt as I remember.

Henry Hendrix was the man arrested on drunk and disorderly. The man who accosted Gavin a week before his murder.

Pulse thrumming, I call Lou.

"Do you have more details on the Henry Hendrix arrest?" I ask when he answers, no time for greetings. "You said you were going to check the police report. Is that something you can forward me?"

As I speak, I highlight Henry's name in my spreadsheet—a bright, obnoxious yellow. But even that looks too cheery, too sunny and tranquil. I change it to red.

"No, sorry," Lou says. "I don't have it yet. I can work on that later, but—"

"Okay, but you said Henry complained to the police about Gavin committing fraud. So does that mean he knew about the tax evasion—the same shit Gavin busted Henry for? If so, that would be huge, right?"

Lou's pause whistles over the line. "I'm sorry, Sienna. I don't know the specifics of Hendrix's complaints, and I'm in my car right now, going to meet another client. There's been a development in their case, so I'll be unavailable for a—"

"There's been a development in *Jason's* case. Shouldn't you be with the Hillstead PD? You said you were going to fight this."

"I will. But perhaps I wasn't clear. I'll be fighting it in court."

"In *court*? Lou—the whole point is to keep this from *going* to court."

"Well, yes, that would be the best-case scenario, but I have to be honest with you, Sienna: given the evidence at play right now, I don't see another outcome."

"What are you saying?" I ask. "You think he did it?"

I clench my jaw at the echo—exactly what I said to Julia at the hospital. It's a question I never expected to ask once, let alone twice, especially of people who are supposed to be on Jason's side.

Lou's hesitation is searing. "What I'm saying is: I think you should prepare yourself for what happens next. When Jason wakes up, the arrest warrant will be served, and a prosecutor will likely bring charges against him. And that's when I'll get to work."

"Oh, *that's* when?"

"Once I can speak with Jason," Lou continues, ignoring my slap of sarcasm, "we can hammer out the particulars of his timeline, and from there, I'll start building his case. Now, I'm sorry, but I really do have to go. I'll talk to you—"

I end the call.

I know Lou can't devote all his time to Jason's case, but it sounds as if he's devoting none of it now. Doesn't he care that my brother has suffered a brain injury, that the stress of an arrest will only impede his recovery? I grab my mug, hands hot against the ceramic, even though the coffee has long since cooled. Lou's plan is bullshit, and I'm not waiting until Jason's in jail to get to work.

I google Henry Hendrix.

Wading through old news stories, I read about the man's downfall, dump the info into my spreadsheet: after Gavin turned him in to the IRS, Henry was sentenced to pay an enormous fine, on top of repaying the amount he'd evaded; he declared bankruptcy soon after; finally, his business went under. The cells in my spreadsheet bulge with text, but it's too dry, dispassionate; none of these details, two years old at this point, are the ones I really need. And Henry's previous brushes with the law are much less important to me than his one from a couple weeks ago.

I need that arrest report, need to read the witness statements, see exactly what Henry yelled at Gavin. "Fraud" is a vague complaint—could be a shot in the dark about a man who'd stabbed him in the back—but if Henry said anything to suggest he knew about Gavin's tax evasion, then that means he had even more motive to hurt him.

I could call Wyatt, pump him for the specifics he refused to give when he first alluded to Henry's drunk and disorderly. Or maybe I should try to see him. Sipping my cold coffee, I indulge the image: skimming my lips along his, withholding the kiss until the answers I want slip right off his tongue.

But then I think of his face this morning. Each time I resisted him, each time I insisted that sleeping in his arms was a mistake, his expression closed a little tighter, pinched with an almost visible ache. Remembering it now, I feel an ache of my own, my chest raw as a rug burn. I rub against the pain, applying pressure to the space above my heart, until the rubbing hurts worse than the memory, until I believe what I told him, just hours ago: *it's nothing, we're nothing.*

I'd have no self-respect, saying something like that, only to return to him now, begging for something.

Beside me, my phone chirps with another email, and when I see that it's from Julia, my breath catches. Then I squint at the screen.

She's responded to Dale.

But Julia never responds to Dale. He was rude to her in our first meeting, skeptical of her quiet presence. *You always let her speak for you?* he challenged her. Challenged us. I tried to let her answer, I counted out the seconds, hoping she'd prove to Dale—to herself— that she does have a voice, but her lips slid inward, and I had to save her with a lie about laryngitis.

As I read her email, I'm surprised to find it strikes exactly the right tone, professional but firm, as if she's been fielding the Dales of our inbox for all these years. My heart swells with love for her, with pride, and even though we're not in the same room, it feels like this email was her way of taking my hand, of muttering my mantra, of cutting in so I wouldn't cuss Dale out.

But when I look back at my laptop, my spreadsheet, my browser in the background with tabs of research, I consider how different Julia's afternoon must look from mine. Because I *didn't* cuss Dale out. I swept him to the side, a response to him less urgent than looking for leads. So what is Julia doing? Working, like it's any other day? Like her husband isn't facing an arrest?

When I left her in the hospital, I promised Julia I'd prove Jason's innocence. Still, I didn't consider how heavy it would feel, carrying that burden alone.

I swipe out of her email. Then I close my browser, my spreadsheet, and scramble away from my desk. Because if I'm going to save my brother, it won't be with Safari and Excel. I need action, need movement, and if I don't have Julia, or Wyatt, or even Lou to rely on, at least I still have myself.

Chapter Fifteen

JULIA

Maeve's statement hovers in the air, dark and ominous as a storm cloud. She's looking at me like nothing's changed, like the room doesn't crackle with charged particles, like the hair on my arms isn't standing on end.

"You—" My voice fights me on its way out, wanting to cower in my throat. "You think Jason's *glad* Gavin was murdered?"

"Not glad. Relieved," Maeve says. But I don't see the difference.

Head cocked, she watches me as if trying to determine something. "Why did you ask me whether I thought Jason had reason to hurt him? Do you—" Her eyes narrow. "Do you think he did it?"

"I don't know what I think, I'm—"

A creak on the stairs snatches the rest of my sentence. I jerk my head toward the front hall, straining for the source of the sound. But what follows is a nothingness so thorough it's like someone's holding their breath.

"Aiden!" I call.

A pair of feet thunk down the steps before reaching the floor. "Yeah?"

I spring from my chair and hurry down the hall, where Aiden's gripping the banister with one hand, knucklebones white through his skin.

"Maeve's here," I say, "in the kitchen. Did you . . . did you hear us just now?"

Aiden chews the inside of his cheek, hollowing out one side of his face. It gives him a wounded look that compresses my chest, but when he speaks, his words are gruff with indignation. "No. I wasn't listening to you. I was about to leave."

"Leave for where?" It's only now that I register Jason's garment bag slung over his arm.

"Parker's. A bunch of us are chilling there before the semiformal. His mom's driving us to the school after dinner."

"Oh. Well—" I waver between asking for details and insisting he stay. If he did overhear us, there's so much I need to explain. But I don't have the words yet, don't have Sienna to help me craft a script. Despite my recent victory with Dale, talking to my son about his dad's impending arrest is not the same as talking to a belligerent client.

"Does this mean you're feeling better about the dance?" I ask. "Last night you were worried about kids saying things about Dad."

Aiden scrunches his nose. "I wasn't *worried*. I'll be fine."

"But if someone does say something to you—"

"I know, I know: 'violence is never the answer.'"

He's quoting me, what I told him at the hospital after he explained the incident. I hadn't known what to say to him then, couldn't grapple with the fact that my son, who still seems so soft-bodied and vulnerable to me, like a turtle without a shell, shoved someone into a locker. So I'd fallen back on a cliché, a phrase that tasted strange, and he wouldn't even look at me. Instead, he glared at Jason and mut-tered, *Then why the hell are we here?*

"I'm gonna be late," he says now.

"Do you have the cuff links?" I ask.

"Cuff links?"

"The ones you were looking for the other night. In our room."

"Oh. Yeah. They're in here." He lifts the garment bag in a kind of shrug, then shifts his eyes to the banister. "Why did you ask if I heard anything? Did something happen with Dad?"

"No," I say, too quickly maybe. I hate to lie to him, but I hate to hurt him more. "No, everything's the same with your dad."

Annoyance scribbles across his face, as if he senses all my secrets. Not just the arrest warrant, but Jason's infidelity, too. I've been wres-tling with how, or even if, I should tell him about Maeve. Just the thought of saying it—*your father cheated on me*—makes my tongue feel thorned, the roof of my mouth riddled with cuts, and I wonder if it's better to never speak of it at all.

But as I look again at his garment bag, I remember I'm not the only one who's leaving things unsaid.

"Honey, let's step outside a minute." I open the door and he hesitates, eyes wary, before following me out. I wait until the door is closed behind us, Maeve no longer in earshot. "When you were look-ing for Dad's cuff links the other night . . ." I let the sentence trail off, giving him space to anticipate my question.

"What about it?"

"Well, is that . . ." I step toward him, trying not to notice how he steps back in return, a dance that keeps us apart. "Is that really what you were looking for? It seems like you were searching in places where the cuff links wouldn't be. I'm not mad or anything. Just curi-ous."

For a second, I think I glimpse panic. It rings an alarm inside me, the same one that used to sound whenever he cried in his crib. But it passes so quickly, replaced instead by frustration, which carves Aiden's features with creases he's too young to bear.

"I forgot where he keeps them," he says, voice firm, impenetrable.

"Well, what about Sunday night?" I ask. "You said you didn't leave the house, but I checked the security app, and it looks like you did go outside. Twice. So why—"

"No I didn't," he interrupts.

"It said the front door was opened, right around two."

"Why are you so sure it was me? Why aren't you suspecting Dad?"

I pause, lips parted, then glance at Aiden's Converse, my first hint that something had been off that night. He's right, though: I haven't considered it was Jason who triggered the app, nor can I imagine why my husband would go outside, twice, at two in the morning. But as I look at Aiden, he seems so certain—even as his face remains a hard mask, still concealing something.

"Aiden. Is there something you want to tell me?"

He doesn't answer. He only scrapes the porch with his shoe.

"You can talk to me, you know. About anything."

He tilts his head, and I think I see his lower lip quiver.

"Even if it's hard," I add. "Even if it's about . . . Dad."

Silence pulls taut between us, and in the steel of his eyes, I'm alarmed to see myself reflected back. All his life, I've tried to protect him from the sharp edges of everything, blunting the corners of tables, passing him scissors with the blade in my palm—but now, I see it already inside him, that cut-up feeling I know so well, like his tongue is too sliced to speak.

It guts me—even worse, maybe, than the fact of Gavin's blood on Jason's knife.

"Aid—"

"My friends are waiting for me," he says. "Can I just go? I want to hang out with them. Please?" he adds, so soft and young.

It almost makes me cry, him asking for something as simple and necessary as companionship. I nod, grazing his cheek with my knuckles.

"What time should I pick you up?"

"Ryan's dad is driving us home."

"Okay. We'll talk tonight, then? After the semiformal?"

Aiden shrugs as he steps off the porch. "If you actually still want to," he mumbles.

Walking away, his pace is leaden, and I'm more convinced than ever: my son has secrets weighing him down. If Sienna were here, she'd tell me to force them out, grab him before he goes too far, yank out the truth like a tapeworm. But I understand something Sienna never has: silence can feel like power, like control, and I want that for Aiden, at least tonight.

Which means I need to get the truth, *a* truth, from someone else. Aiden knows something about Jason—but so does Maeve.

When I return to the kitchen, her brow is furrowed with concern. "I think he heard us," she says. "Or is he always like that? Sorry, I didn't mean to eavesdrop."

"Is he always like what?"

"Short. Dismissive."

The last dance Aiden went to was his eighth-grade formal, before he was this prickly version of himself. He let us take pictures for that one, let me fuss with his tie, and after I posed with him for a photo, I hugged him tightly—something I forgot to even try to do before Aiden left this time.

"He's going through a lot right now," I say. "But go back to what you said before. Jason *hates* Gavin? Why? I've barely heard Jason talk about him."

It's embarrassing to admit that to her—that she knows things about my husband that are complete surprises to me—but as she drops her gaze, it's clear she isn't relishing that fact.

I sit back down, and Maeve takes a deep breath, holding it a moment before letting it out.

"So Jason didn't tell you about the office holiday party? The most recent one?"

I squint at her, trying to remember, but all I can conjure is a cozy image of me and Sienna. I'd been sick with a cold that night and decided at the last minute not to go to the Integrity Plus party. Instead, Sienna came over to take care of me, bringing me sugar cookies to dunk in my chicken soup, queuing up Christmas movies we could fall asleep to.

"What about it?" I ask.

Maeve's discomfort is obvious. Her hands fidget in her lap, like she's knitting without any needles. "I got really drunk. Drunker than I'd normally get at an office party. But I'd heard some bad news a few hours before, about my aunt who's sick. I wasn't in the best place."

She flattens her palms against her legs. "I'd been hanging out with Jason for most of the night—as friends. We were just friends. And we were joking about how sloppy I was getting. Spilling my drink. Knocking over napkins. It was so unlike me that it was funny, at first. But . . . laughing with Jason is the last thing I remember. Because the next thing I know, it's morning, and I'm lying in my bed."

"Jason took you home?" Against my will, I picture it: Jason's palm on Maeve's back as he guides her inside; Jason easing her into bed, tucking her in so tenderly—the way he does with me, nights when I doze on the couch and he carries me to our room.

"No." Maeve's eyes harden—lead between her lashes. "Gavin did."

I frown. "Gavin?"

"That's what I found out the next day, from Jason. I was blacked out, which has *never* happened to me before. But I guess Jason went to the bathroom, and when he came back, I was gone. He said he asked people where I went, and they told him Gavin had noticed I was a mess and decided to drive me home."

Her hands squirm on her lap again, playing with their invisible yarn. Her expression turns stormy, like she's stuck in the darkness of a memory—or the lack of one.

"My boss," she says, gaze drifting toward the wall, "who sexually harassed me in an empty warehouse. He drove me home."

"Wait." Horror skitters up my spine. "Are you saying— Did Gavin *do* something to you? While you were blacked out?"

"I don't remember." Her voice is eerily flat. She stares at something I can't see. "All I know is, when I woke up, I was still in the dress and tights I wore to the party." She blinks hard, as if forcing the movement. Her eyes return to mine, glinting with determination. "Which would mean he didn't, right?"

I open my mouth, shake my head slowly, relieved when she continues without an answer.

"When Jason called and filled me in about Gavin driving me home, he asked if Gavin had hurt me at all—and I told him the truth: I didn't even remember getting home. And Jason started freaking out. He said he'd noticed Gavin watching me throughout the party, and he thought I got drunk much quicker than I should have, given the number of drinks I'd had. He was suddenly so worried Gavin had slipped something into my drink, he wanted me to get *a tox screen*."

"Did you?"

"No. I had a massive hangover; I wasn't getting out of bed for anything. And honestly, I thought Jason was being paranoid. Because, in a weird way, that incident with Gavin in the warehouse seemed to affect Jason more than me. He couldn't get past it. He obsessed over it—like I said before, he gave me the loan because of it. And now he had it in his head that Gavin might've been biding his time at the party, waiting for Jason to leave my side so he could swoop in and . . ."

She swallows down the end of her sentence.

"But I told Jason that, to the best of my knowledge, that did not happen. As far as I knew, I got in bed safely, and alone. But he was *convinced* something happened that I couldn't remember. For weeks afterward, he kept asking me, over and over, exactly what I remembered, if any details of that night had come back."

I bite my lip. What was Jason thinking? It's an invasive question to ask even once, let alone multiple times.

"It was like he was desperate to do something about it if his suspicions were true," Maeve adds.

My tongue goes dry, sticking on one phrase in particular. "Do something about it?"

"I eventually had to tell him to drop it, because now he was freaking me out. I started having trouble sleeping. I'd lie in bed, *shivering*, because Jason's theory forced me to entertain a . . . fucking traumatizing idea."

Her hands keep moving, knitting at nothing on her knees. Her shoulders are hiked toward her ears, but as she takes a deep breath, they begin to settle, relax. Her fingers go still.

"Sorry," she says. "I don't like thinking about that. Obviously."

I wave off the apology, my mind leaping to Sienna. The story is similar to one of hers—how, after Clive Clayton touched her at that party, his fingers raking over her even as she tried to push him away, she struggled to sleep, struggled to simply close her eyes, because always, on the back of her lids, was the image of what might have happened if Jason hadn't intervened.

"But now that more time has gone by," Maeve says, "it's become harder for me to believe Gavin did do something. Not because he's some upstanding guy or whatever—we know he's a creep—but it seems like I'd feel it, you know? Like, even though my mind can't remember, it seems like my body would."

She pauses, her gaze rising toward mine, tentative. "Don't you think?"

Sienna once told me that the memory of Clive's hands was like worms on her skin. She could feel them crawling there, maggoty, insatiable, months and years later. But what do our bodies record when our minds are tucked away? I think of Jason, miles from me in his hospital bed. When he finally wakes up, will his hand remember how many times I held it this week? Will it remember that I let it go?

"I don't know," I tell Maeve.

She nods and shrugs at the same time. "Yeah. Well. That's why Jason hates Gavin."

My skin buds with goose bumps—that word again: *hate*.

"He doesn't trust him. He hates how he talks about women during sales meetings. He hates what he said to me in the warehouse. And I don't know what he thinks about it now, but for a while after the holiday party, he was genuinely worried Gavin did something to me."

With each reason Maeve gives, my heart thumps—a persistent knock that feels like a warning. Once again, I don't recognize this man she's talking about, the one who's obsessed with his boss, who despises him. Jason's feelings toward Gavin are just another thing he never told me.

"But still," she adds, "why would Jason leave my house last Friday and go straight to Gavin's, over something that happened—that probably *didn't* happen—months ago?"

"I don't know," I say again, and beneath the table, my fingers tremble. "I don't know."

Chapter Sixteen

SIENNA

As I park my car at the police station, I search the lot for Wyatt's Nissan. I'm relieved not to see it anywhere, not to recognize his bumper with a heart-shaped dent—damage I caused one day when I hit it in his driveway. It's been years since that minor collision, and he's never had the dent fixed. I reminded him, so many times, that my insurance would cover it, but he liked to joke that it was a "love tap."

Lately, whenever I've glimpsed that crumpled, plastic heart, I've felt a twinge behind my ribs, like my own heart is dented too.

I walk toward the double doors of the station, ignoring the thought that I don't belong here, that I'm trespassing on my past: times I brought Wyatt takeout for dinner during a twelve-hour shift, times I dropped him off at work—because he wouldn't get the dent in his bumper fixed, but he *would* repair his windshield after a rock nicked the glass. And anyway, I do belong here, because as Google informed me, arrest reports are public records; all anyone has to do is make a request and it's theirs to review.

Still, my hand lingers on the door handle. Even if I didn't connect this building with Wyatt, I'd feel itchy to be here, the place where Detective Beck is waiting to book my brother.

When I enter the station, it's quiet as a mausoleum. I remember this now, from my pop-in visits; it's not the bright, bustling room of police procedural sets. Instead, it's a brick hallway that bisects the building, the walls flanked by benches, pocked with doorways that lead to other halls, down which there are offices and workspaces, interview rooms and holding cells. If not for the woman tucked behind the glass-encased reception desk, the place would feel abandoned.

"Yes?" she says as I approach.

I speak toward the holes in the glass, patterned like a shower drain. "Hi, can I take a look at an arrest report? I'm not sure of the exact date—it would have been the week before last—but the person arrested was Henry Hendrix."

Her gaze flicks over me, up and down. "Are you press?"

"No. Does that matter?"

She shakes her head. "You just look familiar. One moment, please."

As she turns around to slip through a door behind her, I see her tight black bun and realize she's familiar, too. I've seen that bun at the same department parties where I originally met Beck, parties where Wyatt would introduce me to his colleagues, slipping a random fact about me into each conversation: *Sienna puts cinnamon on her french fries; Sienna thinks cats are reincarnated serial killers; Sienna said "Snuffleupagus" in her sleep the other night.* When I asked if he was trying to make me sound unhinged, he smiled sheepishly. *I'm making sure they remember you,* he said, *because I hope you'll be around for a long time.*

I rub my sternum, suddenly sore, and wait for the woman to return.

But it's like he knew I was thinking about him, sensed my thoughts circling our better days, because a door pops open, and it's Wyatt who exits, dressed in his uniform, car keys dangling from his hand.

He stops short at the sight of me. "Sienna. What are you doing here?"

"I— You're not here," I say.

He frowns at me, then looks down at himself, as if making sure I'm wrong. "Yes I am."

"No, your car. Your car's not here."

"Oh. Yeah, I park in the back now."

"Oh."

He waits for me to continue, but even from a few feet away, his piney aftershave makes me woozy with memories. My eyelids flutter shut against them—mornings when he leaned toward the mirror, sliding his razor up his neck with the precision of a surgeon; nights when he shaved just minutes before our dates, his cheek soft and scented beneath the kiss I planted there.

"Si?" he says. "Is everything okay?"

I open my eyes. "No."

I look past Wyatt, to the door that leads toward offices and cells. I picture my brother, still bruised and bandaged, led there by a guard. "No, everything's not okay. Beck showed up to Jason's room today. With a warrant to arrest him."

Wyatt rubs the back of his neck as he nods. "I know. I'm sorry. I was going to check in with you as soon as I got a minute, but things have been—"

"Labs make mistakes, don't they? The lab said the blood on Jason's knife belonged to Gavin—that's the reason they got the warrant. But couldn't that be an error?"

As Wyatt stares at me, his brow slumps with concern, and it's that—his watchful silence, his hesitation—that floods me with frustration.

"Come on, Wyatt. You know Jason. You can't possibly think he'd ever . . ."

I leave the deeds—stab, smother, stitch—unsaid.

"It doesn't matter what I think," he replies. "I'm not the one leading the case, and those who *are* have to follow the evidence. Which, unfortunately, points straight to Jason." I open my mouth to argue, but he continues. "Do I think your brother murdered someone?" He shakes his head with a humorless chuckle. "Honestly, it's hard for me to imagine. It's *Jason*, you know?"

Of course I know. But the way he said it—emphasizing my brother's name like it's synonymous with sainthood—makes me want to cup his face and kiss him.

"Exactly." I cross my arms, tucking my hands away. "See? You get it. Unlike Julia. She isn't sure he's innocent anymore."

There's a beat of silence as Wyatt absorbs this news. "Really? Wow. Shit. That must be so hard for you."

I shrug, even though his reaction is perfect. *Wow. Shit.* It honors my surprise, while announcing his own. It validates that Julia's doubting of Jason is worthy of cursing.

"Seriously," he says, "I've never known the two of you to disagree about anything—except which *Weekend at Bernie's* is better."

"The second one."

"Obviously. Dancing dead man wins every time." His mouth twitches upward, almost a smile, before sobering again. "So, what changed her mind?"

I study him, trying to gauge how much he already knows. When I showed up at his door last night, reeling from the revelation that Jason cheated on Julia, I didn't explain my presence with anything other than an urgent, distracting kiss, backing him against the wall until he pulled me even closer, his mouth closing hungrily on mine. Because it wouldn't make sense, it still doesn't: I comforted myself over my brother's infidelity with the man who was unfaithful to me. Still, Wyatt knows about the arrest warrant; he probably knows about Maeve's statement, too, and that fills me with so much shame I have to break our gaze.

"Here you go," a voice says, and we turn to find the woman back behind the reception desk, slipping papers through the gap beneath the glass. She narrows her eyes at Wyatt, then flicks them over to me. Before she can piece together our former connection, I snatch the papers.

"That can't leave the premises," she warns. She nods toward a door directly across from her desk. "But you can use that room to review it."

"Thanks," I say. Then, to Wyatt: "I'll talk to you later." But as I cross the hall to the door, he's on my heels, stepping over the threshold only half a step behind me.

"What is that?" he asks. The door closes, sealing us in this space that's little more than a closet. A desk is bolted to one wall, and I lay the arrest report onto it. Wyatt leans over it, skimming the first page, then lances me with a look of concern.

"Why did you ask for this?" he says. "I told you they checked this guy out."

"Yeah. But you didn't mention he was Gavin's almost-partner."

"So? What does that matter?"

"Everything! I want to know what he said to Gavin when he was yelling at him that night. Those names in that notebook I told you about, with the boxes of cash—"

Wyatt whips his head toward the door, as if he could see through it to someone listening on the other side.

"—some of them used to be Henry Hendrix's customers. So if he knew Gavin was cutting deals with them, after busting him for the same damn thing, that would make him furious, don't you think? Sounds like motive to me."

"Sienna, no. It's a dead end." Wyatt touches the report, as if he's about to pull it away, but I slap my hand on top of it.

"Maybe it is! But I have to do *something*. No one's doing anything. Lou's with other clients, Julia's sending work emails like this is no big deal, I can't rely on her right now—" My voice wavers, almost a break. "But Jason's relying on me. Even if he doesn't know it. And anyway, you're the one who said I can't tell the cops about the money in the warehouse, so this arrest report is all I have."

"It's not all you have. You have me. You know I'm on your side, Si, always."

I flinch at the phrase.

Wyatt rubs his jaw. "Look, I understand how hard this must be. I know what your brother means to you. But why don't you leave this type of thing to your lawyer?"

"He said he's not going to do anything until Jason wakes up!"

"Okay, but you don't have to solve this right now. I'm worried about what this is doing to you. The stress of your brother's accident, the Gavin case, now this split with Julia—"

"It's not a *split*."

"My point is: you can take a break from it all. You're allowed to regroup, you know. Jason wouldn't want you running yourself ragged. And this report is only going to work you up even more."

He looks at the car keys he's still holding. He closes his fist around them, the Hillstead PD key chain poking between his fingers, labeled with a number that identifies its cruiser.

"I have to go." Reluctance strains Wyatt's voice. "But why don't you come over tonight? I'll make you dinner, or we can order in, whatever you want. We can even watch *Weekend at Bernie's II* and you can replay your favorite parts a hundred times, no arguments from me."

For a moment, I allow myself to picture it—enjoying the movie, my feet in Wyatt's lap; reprising our old game, One-star Bartender, mixing drinks so disgusting we spit them into the sink, cracking up at each other's concoctions. But then I see my smile souring, feel the alcohol burning the back of my throat, reminded of the way he betrayed me. The shots at that bachelor party, the tequila and vodka and rum, the dizzy mix that spun him right into someone's bed.

I shake my head, clearing the images like cobwebs. "I've been over your house two nights in a row."

"Oh, shit, you're right," he says. Then he lowers his voice to a whisper, as if letting a secret slip. "I won't tell anyone if you won't."

His lips lift toward the hint of a smile, but his attempt at levity can't sway me. It only reminds me how serious the situation is: we're standing in a police station, where Wyatt works, where people in his same uniform are waiting to arrest my brother. Jason doesn't have time for me to relax, to regroup, to go to my ex's and goof around; he needs me to stay in this room and review the arrest report, then follow wherever it leads.

"No," I say, more forcefully this time. "I can't."

"Okay." Wyatt backs away, hands up in a gesture of surrender, one still closed around his keys. "I'll just say one more thing: I know it's important to you to take care of Jason. But it's important to me that you take care of yourself. Go home. Get some rest."

He opens the door, casts me one last look—a blend of empathy and affection—before disappearing into the hall.

As the door clicks closed, I pull in a steadying breath. His leaving loosens some things in me, while tightening others. My chest pulses with a dull ache.

I turn to the report.

The words swim before me, as if I'm viewing them underwater. My eyes prickle with a sting like chlorine. I blink until my vision clears.

Still, it takes me a minute to focus. First, I have to filter out the facts that don't matter to me: Henry Hendrix's date of birth, height, weight. I flip to the section where the arresting officer described the scene upon arriving—Henry had been steered away from Gavin by then, drunkenly hunched against the hostess's podium at the restaurant, but he was still shouting accusations, snatches of which the police recorded: *you should have kept your mouth shut, I trusted you and you ruined everything, we could have done it together if you'd just kept quiet, now my wife up and left, you did this, you did it too.*

My heart drums.

There's a lot to unpack in such a small snippet. *You did it too* could mean that Henry's not only holding Gavin responsible for destroying his business, but his marriage, as well.

Or it could mean Henry knows Gavin committed the same offense for which he reported him to the IRS. *We could have done it together if you'd just kept quiet.*

I take a picture of those lines, then continue reading. I slow at a statement from the restaurant server who called the police. According to the server, Henry had been at the bar for an hour before the commotion began. While the server was taking an order on the other side of the room, he heard Henry shouting, saw him hovering over Gavin's table. When Henry grabbed a drink from Gavin's table and smashed the glass at Gavin's feet, the server rushed over. He asked Henry to leave, but Henry didn't budge. Instead, he hurled more words at Gavin: *You expected loyalty from customers you stole? Smith told me everything.*

I snap a picture of that, too, my pulse percussing at a frantic pace. I don't know who Smith is—with a name so common, they could be anyone—but I'm willing to bet they're connected to one of the businesses from Gavin's notebook.

On the next page of the report, another diner described Henry to the police as "shouting at the man, calling him a fraud and hypocrite, practically foaming at the mouth," despite Gavin's attempts to ignore him. *I could fucking kill you for this*, Henry screamed, just before smashing Gavin's glass to the floor.

I shouldn't be smiling. A death threat shouldn't make me feel this fizzy and buoyant. But it's right there, in black and white, recorded by an officer of the law.

You did it too.

Smith told me everything.

I could fucking kill you for this.

I'm sure of it now: Henry knew about Gavin's secret deals. And just as I suspected, he was enraged, he was violent, and he could fucking kill him for this.

I flip through the photos I've taken of the report, drawing circles around the most pertinent lines so I can send them to Julia. But when I return to the first photo, my finger freezes beside one sentence in particular.

I didn't think much of it the first time I read it. It's a common enough expression.

You should have kept your mouth shut.

But now I picture Gavin on his back lawn, the way his neighbor found him after two days of rain—his stomach sliced, his breath jammed in his lungs, his lips woven with thread. Those details have always made one thing clear: Gavin's murder was not only purposeful, but personal, too. Because the killer didn't simply smother Gavin and flee.

He went to great lengths to keep his mouth shut.

Fingers tingling, I hold the report closer to my face. I begin combing the rest of it, unwilling to miss another quote that could be important, that could help *build a case*, as Lou said. But on the second to last page, my eyes skid to a stop. Air tumbles out of me.

It's an additional witness statement, from someone sitting at the bar that night. Only, this time, it's not the person's account of the evening that's stolen my attention. It's their name.

Jason Larkin.

Chapter Seventeen

JULIA

After Maeve leaves, the day oozes by, sludgy and slow. At some point, I return to the couch and eat—dazed, unhurried bites from a bowl of cereal I accidentally filled with water instead of milk, my mind too crowded with the echoes of Maeve's story.

When she first told me about it—how Jason obsessed over Gavin driving her home from the holiday party, how he made her second-guess her safety, how he pestered her with questions that kept her up at night—I struggled to process the details, wondering only how my husband could harbor hatred for a man I never knew anything about.

But now that I've had time to absorb the story, I recognize the role Jason played.

He kept asking me, over and over, exactly what I remembered, Maeve said, *like he was desperate to do something about it if his suspicions were true.*

Desperate to rescue her, she meant.

It fits into the pattern that has only recently taken shape for me. I can imagine Jason, sleepless and tortured by his thoughts, grinding his teeth against that nightmare: Gavin slipping Maeve a drug, then touching her in places she could no longer feel.

I can imagine, too, how that nightmare might have superimposed itself over another: the memory of his freshman sister, drunk and fumbling in a stranger's bedroom, as a senior boy held her against a wall.

I see how Jason would obsess over it—the possibility that he didn't do for Maeve what he did for Sienna, that he failed to protect her, when protecting people is what he does.

But how far would that obsession take him?

Beside me on the couch, my phone dings with a text.

JULES, Sienna's written, beneath a group of photos. I have SO MUCH to tell you! First, some context: Henry Hendrix—the Higher Home Improvement guy, the one Gavin turned in to the IRS—accosted Gavin at a restaurant ONE WEEK before his murder. These are from the arrest report, a drunk and disorderly offense. Henry knew about Gavin cooking the books!! See the highlighted sections of Exhibits A and C (aka the first and third pics) for the SMOKING FUCKING GUNS.

I zoom in on each photo to scrutinize the small print. As I read, I try to catch up with Sienna, to piece together the narrative she already seems committed to. Admittedly, my breath hitches on one line in particular—*I could fucking kill you for this*—but when I look at the other section she's highlighted, I don't understand the significance.

Why is "you should have kept your mouth shut" a smoking gun? I text her.

Her response zips onto my screen: GAVIN'S STITCHED LIPS!!

I cock my head, unconvinced.

That's just an expression, I reply—but I don't add what else I'm thinking: *So is "I could kill you."*

On its own, maybe, Sienna writes. But with everything else? The report makes Henry sound insane with rage. He THREW A GLASS! He's a violent dude who clearly had motive!! And that's not all. LOOK AT THIS.

She sends another photo, and when I focus on the part she's circled, I stop breathing. My fingers shake as I type out a response: Jason was there?

Not only there. A witness. He saw his boss get attacked—which he never mentioned to me—and made a statement to the police: *Mr. Larkin said he didn't know Mr. Hendrix personally but he'd been talking to him at the bar when Mr. Hendrix suddenly got up, crossed the restaurant, and started yelling at Mr. Reed.*

My grip on the phone loosens. Couldn't the cops use this—Jason's presence at another instance when Gavin was attacked—as more evidence against him?

And why was Jason at this bar? He's not one for solo drinking. For a second, I see him there with Maeve, the two of them smiling above icy martinis, and my stomach goes sour. I look at the date on the report, but it doesn't ring a bell. He's worked late the past few weeks, gunning for that promotion, adding customers to his schedule well into the evenings. Or maybe that was another lie.

JASON WAS THERE! Sienna reiterates, and I'm not sure why she seems excited until her next text rolls in: What if Henry's framing him?

I frown at the phone, the connection not computing, then respond with a question mark.

There's def more to figure out, Sienna writes. But it's too big a coincidence to be nothing. Jason met Henry the night Henry first attacked Gavin, they TALKED at the bar, and days later, Jason became the prime suspect in Gavin's murder. Maybe Jason told Henry he worked for Integrity Plus. Maybe Henry thought he was in on Gavin's gutter machine scheme. Either way, he could have planted the evidence in Jason's car after he killed Gavin.

I shake my head as I type my response. There's a giant hole in Sienna's hypothesis, and it's almost disturbing, how thoroughly she's able to ignore it.

How would Henry have planted traces of blood onto Jason's knife?

For almost a minute, there's no reply, not even an ellipsis that would signal Sienna's typing. When the ellipsis does appear, it flickers like a dying lightbulb. I picture her writing a word, then deleting it, writing and deleting again, face pinched with a scowl.

Like I said, there's more to figure out, she finally answers. For all we know, it wasn't even Jason's knife they found in his car. Henry could have planted his own. We haven't actually SEEN the knife. We just assumed it was Jason's because he usually carries one!

I rub my forehead. I get why she's latching onto this idea; Gavin imploded Henry's life when he turned him in, the incident at the restaurant did happen weirdly close to the night of Gavin's murder, and it's unnerving that Jason was there to witness the scene. As unnerving, in fact, as him never talking about it. Still, there's so much Sienna doesn't know.

In a rush, I type out what I've learned today. I explain the holiday party, Jason's ensuing obsession, his fears about what Gavin might have done to a drunk, unconscious Maeve. After I send the message, there's another long measure of silence. No typing. No response. I read the text again, trying to see it through Sienna's eyes. Maybe something in the story is resonating with her, too. Maybe her skin is prickling, just like mine, as she recognizes, and then rethinks, that need in Jason to always—

You talked to MAEVE?

I stare at Sienna's question—such a strange thing to focus on in light of what I've shared.

She stopped by to apologize, I write. And to give me a schedule for repaying the money. And I asked her if she knew any reason why Jason would want to hurt Gavin.

I study the message, anticipating how Sienna will respond. To be safe, I delete the last sentence. Even though it's the truth, it will only hurt her to learn I asked such a pointed question about her brother. And more than hurt her—it'll anger her, trigger her instinct to defend him against any implication of guilt.

I don't think I could handle that today, on top of everything else. Sienna's rage runs as hot as a furnace, and I've been lucky, for all these years, to never have been directly scorched. She's been annoyed with me, frustrated with me, but never furious. I've always been the hand that cools her fire—and does not fuel it.

I revise the end of the message before sending: I asked her about Jason and Gavin's relationship.

You asked Maeve? Sienna fires back. The woman who slept with your husband?

Yes. Thanks for the reminder.

Sorry, she amends. I just mean—of all the people to talk to about this!

But what do you think? I ask. About what she said.

I think Gavin's an asshole! Sienna writes. And I really fucking hope he didn't do anything to her, even if she IS Enemy Number One right now. But I don't see how it's relevant to Gavin's murder. Unless you're saying Maeve killed him? As revenge or something?

My mouth pops open. It's almost acrobatic, the way Sienna contorts all blame away from her brother. Before I can type out a response, my phone rings in my hand—Sienna, impatient as always, pressing for an answer I'm suddenly too exhausted to give.

"Is that what you think?" she asks when I pick up. "Because I see where you're coming from. The cops think Jason had time to murder Gavin because his house is only twelve minutes from Maeve's, but that just means *Maeve* could have gotten there too. And—ooh! Maybe she planted the evidence in Jason's car because she got pissed at him for saying that sleeping with her was a big mistake. And"— she gasps—"Oh my god. Maybe she even *caused Jason's accident* so the cops would find the evidence!"

"Whoa, whoa, whoa." I pump the brakes on her runaway theory. "No, Sienna, stop. First of all, they said no one else was involved in Jason's crash."

"Yeah, but he doesn't drive distracted. It's never made sense to me that he'd just—shoot off the road all of a sudden. Who does that?"

Plenty of people. But even this—the idea that Jason could be so human as to take his eyes off his windshield, to flick them toward his phone, same as any of us have done a hundred times—is something Sienna isn't willing to entertain.

"Second of all," I add, the words coming out on a sigh, "that wasn't what I was saying. Maeve isn't even the one who thinks Gavin hurt her. It's *Jason* who thinks that. Jason who wanted to do something about it."

Sienna's silence is thick, like a cloth pressed against my ear. I hear nothing on her end, not the click of computer keys, not the chirp of birds outside. It strikes me suddenly: I have no idea where she is. Normally, it's like there's a compass inside me, pointed toward Sienna's location. But now, as I strain for any scrap of sound, she's so quiet it's as if she's disappeared.

"Sienna?"

"So you're saying this is motive," she says, "for Jason killing Gavin."

My stomach clenches at her shift in tone. To anyone else, Sienna would sound icy. But I know her voice better than my own, and right now, it's the opposite of cold. Within her words is a barely contained heat.

"No—I don't know. I'm just . . . really confused," I hedge. "I don't understand why he'd go directly to Gavin's house, two seconds after . . . sleeping with Maeve, especially since the holiday party was months ago and Maeve's convinced that Gavin didn't—"

"Exactly," Sienna cuts me off. "So it doesn't make sense. But Henry Hendrix—*his* motive makes sense."

I wish it were that easy. That one afternoon had given us all the answers. That despite everything that points toward Jason, Gavin's murder has nothing to do with anyone we know.

Sienna's right about one thing, though. In terms of motive, Henry's is so much cleaner than Jason's, so much easier to under-stand: money, rage, revenge—all the things that have driven men for centuries.

"Have you talked to Beck about this?" I ask her. "Your theory about Henry?"

"I can't. I don't know how to bring up the tax evasion angle with-out revealing how we know that Gavin was cooking the books in the first place. And Lou told me yesterday that what we did in the ware-house would only hurt Jason's case."

I press my lips together. This is the first I'm hearing of Lou's warning.

"Okay," I say after a moment. "So can Lou do some digging on our behalf? Maybe he can find evidence of Gavin's tax evasion and then *he* could discuss it with Beck."

"Lou's no help right now. I talked to him a couple hours ago.

He says he's only going to start building a case *after* charges are brought, and *after* he can talk to Jason. But I'm not willing to wait that long."

"Okay, then what about Wyatt? He might get pissed that we searched the warehouse, but given your history, I'm sure he wouldn't, like, turn you in about it. And at the very least, he could tell you if he thinks it's worth having Lou pursue this lead. And who knows, maybe he'll give you some other info about the case, something else that could help us, or insight into—"

"Jules, no. I told you before: I'm not going to Wyatt—for this or anything else. I don't *talk* to Wyatt. I don't *see* Wyatt. I'm on a very strict No Wyatt Diet." As she speaks, her voice climbs in pitch, as if her throat is closing around the words, forcing her to squeeze them out. "And do you really think I'd just run right over to him, throwing away everything I believe in? You know me better than anyone. You should know I'd *never* do that."

Everything I believe in. She means one strike and you're out. One wrong and you're gone.

Except when it comes to Jason.

Irritation twists inside me at this double standard. Our partners both cheated on us. But while Sienna's response is to cut Wyatt out of her life completely, she wants me to keep standing by Jason's side—even when my faith in him has been shaken, even when I'm no longer sure that his side is the right one to be on.

And that's another way Wyatt could be helpful. If he thinks Henry Hendrix is a credible suspect, then great; I'd love to look in a direction that isn't Jason's. But if he doesn't, if he knows some reason to count Henry out, then it's validation, as gut-wrenching as it is, that I'm not wrong to be feeling so much doubt.

I'll never get that from Sienna. Not when she sees words as

"smoking guns." Not when she warps and contorts each fact until it supports Jason's innocence.

"I'm *not* turning to Wyatt," she reiterates.

And that's fine. She doesn't have to.

But that doesn't mean I can't.

．　．　．

I park in Wyatt's driveway, behind his silver Nissan. Even in the fading light, I recognize the dent in his bumper, shaped like a lopsided heart. *A love tap,* he called it when Sienna whacked it by accident, and I'm surprised to see it now, surprised he didn't finally fix it after the two of them broke up. Instead, a year later, he's still carrying the mark she left.

I ring the bell, then listen to Wyatt's footsteps inside, bounding closer. When he opens the door, his eyes are bright with anticipation, until his expression collapses, first with disappointment, then with concern.

"Julia," he says. "Sorry, I thought you were—someone else. Is everything okay?"

"Yeah, sorry to drop by unannounced."

His eyes flit over my shoulder, as if searching his driveway for another visitor.

"Are you expecting someone?" I ask. "I can come back."

"No," he says, the word a little strained. "No, I'm not expecting anyone. Come in."

I follow him into his living room, then stop in front of the couch, awkward and unmoored. I've never been here on my own before. In the old days, Sienna would plop onto Wyatt's couch, then tug me down into the space beside her. She'd joke that Wyatt was our "cabana boy" and ask him to bring us some drinks. But now I don't know whether to sit or stand. I'm not sure what the etiquette is for visiting your best friend's ex behind her back. When I got off the phone a little while ago, I didn't tell her I was coming here. Instead, I invented an excuse—driving Aiden to his semiformal—and tried to ignore the cramp of guilt.

"Have a seat," Wyatt says. As I settle onto the couch, he pitches a thumb over his shoulder, back toward the kitchen. "Do you want anything to drink? I have water and . . . well, water. Sorry. I don't have beer or wine or anything like that."

"No, I'm good," I decline, "thanks."

Wyatt sits in a chair opposite me. "How's Jason doing?" As he drums his fingers on his knees, he seems to be sharing my awkwardness.

I look at my hands, clasped tightly in my lap. "Actually, the doctor thinks he could wake up as soon as tomorrow."

"Oh, wow. That's so great." Wyatt pauses, tilting his head. "When did you hear that?"

"This morning. I guess he responded to a test in a way that seemed promising."

It's a moment before he replies, his face blank, as if processing my answer. "That's— Wow, that's great," he repeats. "Really great."

But his enthusiasm doesn't reach his eyes. Instead, there's something like confusion there—or maybe a haze of hurt. It's an odd reaction, and when he sees me examining it, he clears his throat, clears that cloudy look from his eyes.

"How are *you* doing?" he asks. "With, you know, everything."

"Not too well," I admit, releasing a small laugh. "I'm just . . . really confused. Which is why I'm here, actually. I was wondering if— Well, first: Do you know who Henry Hendrix is?"

His brow twitches—not quite a furrow, but a flicker of apprehension. "Yeah."

"Okay, well . . ." I pull out my phone, then bring up the photos Sienna took of the arrest report. "Sienna has this theory," I say, and I explain it to Wyatt, his face almost blank as he listens, like he's working to remain neutral. When I'm done, I pass him my phone over the coffee table. "It's the last four pictures. Sienna highlighted what she thought was especially important."

He scrutinizes the screen, zooming in with his thumb and finger. When he finishes studying the final picture, he hands the phone back to me, still giving nothing away.

"I don't know why Jason was at the restaurant," I say, "but Sienna thinks Henry might have framed Jason. That maybe Jason said something to him that night that made Henry think he was involved in Gavin's financial schemes. So, I'm wondering what you think, in your professional opinion. Is Henry a viable suspect?"

Wyatt sighs, dragging a hand over his face. I hold myself stiff to keep from squirming.

"No," Wyatt says. "I'm sorry, but he's not."

It isn't disappointment, exactly, that sinks through me, but it's coarse and heavy, like swallowing the pit of some fruit. It would have been so nice for Sienna to be right. I would have known, then, how to talk to Aiden tonight; I could have told him there's another suspect in the case, someone we'll make sure the cops consider. I could have given him the same hope his aunt already floats on. I could have kept him whole, for a little while longer, distracted from all the evidence I don't know how to explain.

But it's exactly that evidence that had me expecting this answer from Wyatt. And now I got what I came here for—confirmation that I'm not wrong to dismiss Sienna's theory, to suspect my own husband. I just wish it felt satisfying, or soothing, or like anything other than a crater in my gut.

"It's because there's nothing tying Henry to the crime, right?" I ask. "Not like there is with Jason."

"They checked him out," Wyatt says, "soon after the body was discovered. Because, in one sense, Sienna's right—the altercation at the restaurant definitely made him a person of interest. But as I already told her, Henry has an alibi for the night of the murder. I guess I'm not surprised she's still pushing it, though. We know Sienna's stubborn like that."

He forces a weak smile, attempting to connect over our shared understanding, but I can only frown, puzzled by his response.

"She talked to you about this?" I ask. "When?"

The change in his face is immediate. His cheeks flatten, erasing his smile, and his eyes go wide, his features somehow both slack and taut, like he's trying—and failing—not to show a reaction.

"Oh. Yeah, it was nothing, she just asked me the other day about who Beck had looked into before Jason, and then I saw her today at the station, when she requested the arrest report."

My lips part in surprise.

"It was nothing," he says again, scratching his jaw.

But I shake my head, my vision murky, as if a fog has rolled into the room. Because that isn't nothing. That's two encounters. In just a few days. When less than an hour ago, Sienna sniped at me for even suggesting she speak to Wyatt.

"We're not back together or anything." Wyatt picks at his pantleg, eyes roving across his thigh.

"Back together?" The thought hadn't even occurred to me.

I don't talk to Wyatt. I don't see Wyatt. I'm on a very strict No Wyatt Diet.

When I pictured her saying those words on the phone, I imagined her cheeks flushing—the same splotches of pink she always gets when we speak of her ex. For months now, I've thought of that blush as the burn of her anger, beneath which her pain still smolders. But now I wonder if I've been seeing it all wrong—if it was never about her sadness or rage, but instead the flush of a secret. The flush of shame.

"Wyatt. How often do you see Sienna?"

"No, it's not like that," he protests—even though I haven't accused him of anything.

You know me better than anyone. You should know I'd never do that.

"It's just . . . sometimes, you know, she— We just . . ." He trails off, shifting in his chair.

I watch him cross his legs, then uncross them. I watch his fingers pluck at the fabric of his pants. I watch him press his gaze to the table between us, then hold it there, to keep from watching me in return.

Finally, he pulls in a breath, eases it out, and his posture relaxes a little. As if determining something, he raises his eyes to mine.

"I'm sorry, Julia. I'm not supposed to talk about it."

My heart clunks against my chest. There's an *it*.

"Has it only been recently that you've been seeing her?" I ask. "Since everything with Jason?"

Wyatt skirts my gaze, looking toward the blank, black screen of his TV. "I'm sorry," he repeats—closed, it seems, to any more of my questions.

But it doesn't matter. He's said enough. And my stomach roils with the revelation: it's not just Jason who's been keeping secrets from me.

Sienna—my true other half, the person I know better than anyone—has been lying to me too.

Chapter Eighteen

SIENNA

I told myself I wouldn't come here. Told Wyatt I wouldn't. Told Julia, too. But she was right, earlier on the phone; Wyatt is the person I need to turn to. He told me Henry Hendrix has an alibi for the night of the murder, but if there's one thing I've learned this week, it's that alibis can fall apart. Jason's did—according to the police. So excuse me for not trusting their assertion that Henry gets a pass.

I'm only one house away when I yank my foot off the gas. There's a car parked next to Wyatt's. And it looks like . . .

I drive a little closer, peering through the dark at the license plate. When I'm able to read it—these numbers and letters I've seen a thousand times—my heart bucks against my ribs.

Julia.

I pound the pedal, screeching down the street.

Why the hell did she come here? As far as she knows, she's crossing enemy lines, having no idea how many times I've crossed them myself.

I drive aimlessly, turning deeper and deeper into the neighborhood. I squint out the windshield and squeeze the steering wheel, trying to get my bearings.

Julia was abrupt when she got off the phone, but she told me she was taking Aiden to his dance—which is nowhere near here. So either she dropped him off, then broke every speed limit on the way to Wyatt's, or she lied to me, driving to the one person I told her I wouldn't see.

Which means I lied to her, too.

In such a brief call, we deceived each other as easily as breathing. More than that, we've been deceiving each other for months. Me about Wyatt. Her about the money Jason took that sent her reeling. I know why I've been hiding the truth, but her reasoning remains a mystery to me, and thinking of it now, I feel the sting of her secrecy all over again.

Taking a sharp turn, I worm back through the neighborhood before parking a couple houses from Wyatt's. I stare at his front door, as if I can see Julia through it, read every word on her lips, and as the minutes pass, my shock shrinks to curiosity. Maybe it's not a bad thing, her being here. She must be doing what I said I wouldn't— asking Wyatt about my Henry theory—so doesn't that mean she's giving it a chance? That she's closer to believing, completely again, that her husband is innocent? I relax a little, calmed by the thought.

Still, it hurts that she didn't at least warn me before heading here. If the roles were reversed and it was Julia with a cop for an ex, I wouldn't consult him without her consent.

All day, Julia's acted in ways I've struggled to understand. She's sent work emails while I'm out here fighting for the both of us. She's let Maeve into her house—Maeve! The woman who seduced her husband. She's even insinuated that Maeve's story about Gavin might explain Jason's motive—as if Jason would truly kill someone over a *theory*, a fear.

Now, as time ticks by and Wyatt's door doesn't open, my stomach throbs. I feel the sandwich I scarfed down at home trying to sputter back up.

I almost miss her when she finally leaves. Julia is dressed in the deep purple sweater I bought her for Christmas. It camouflages her, making her little more than a smudge in the night, even with the yawn of light from Wyatt's front door. When she slips behind the wheel of her car, I'm tempted to sprint out of mine. I could dart in front of her, be the deer in her headlights, wild and stunned. *What the hell?* I imagine saying. But the tone in my head unnerves me. It's one I've never used with Julia before, one I save for the people who have wronged me most.

I watch her go. My eyes dry out, staring at her taillights until they're speck-small in the distance, and finally disappear. Misery ripples through me, a slow, unending wave. Something else tries to drown me: longing, maybe. Loneliness. But when I look at Wyatt's house again, I push it all down until only my determination seeps through.

He answers the door quickly, probably assuming it's Julia again. When he sees it's me, a wince ripples across his face, and I don't wait for an invitation before stepping inside.

"So," I say. "Julia was here."

In the entryway, I lean against the wall. I cross my arms, trying to appear cool and unbothered, but Wyatt looks at me the way he always does, the way that makes me feel see-through, like the tenderest, tucked-in parts of myself are all lit up by his eyes. I turn away from his gaze, walk to the living room instead.

"Was she asking about Henry Hendrix?" I say, perching on the edge of the love seat.

Wyatt nods, a strange ache in his expression. He sits on the couch, choosing the side closest to me. I shift my knees away from him, even as their impulse is to angle toward his

"Sienna," he says—and his voice is so bruised with emotion I have to cut him off.

"Did she ask if he had an alibi?"

A crease appears between his brows. "I told her he has one, yes."

"And what is it?"

He leans back, resting his head against the top of the couch. He answers with his eyes closed. "I told you, I can't share that. Just like I told you he wasn't worth investigating."

"I can't accept that. I need to know."

Wyatt picks up his head to look at me. "I wish you trusted me. I understand I made it so you felt like you couldn't, but—it's been a year, Sienna. What are we doing here?"

It catches me off guard, the speed with which he spun this into something about us.

"Give me a reason to trust you," I say. "You didn't even tell me Jason was a witness at the restaurant. But you've known since the beginning, haven't you? That's why you were all confused that Jason hadn't told me about the altercation. And then you didn't even mention it at the station, when you knew I'd see it in the arrest report. Why?"

"Because," Wyatt says, harder now, "I don't know what to make of it. Jason being there that night. Jason speaking to someone right before they attacked Gavin, and then, a week later, having all that evidence in his car."

I curl my hand into a fist, but I don't allow myself to be derailed by what I hear in Wyatt's voice, the same thing I heard in Julia's—doubt.

"It's got to be connected," I say. "I don't know how or why exactly, but I think Henry could be framing Jason. And look, I know you're not allowed to tell me his alibi. I know, as a person, you have a strict moral code, but—" A bitter sound escapes me. "You've broken that code before, right? That's how we got here, isn't it?"

I gesture to the distance between us, the closeness we lost the night he cheated, but my hand goes still at the change in his eyes, the hurt and shame that well there.

"Please," I say, softer. "Tell me where Henry was that night. Because my gut is telling me he's involved. And I can't just let that feeling go, not without knowing the whole story."

Wyatt looks at the ceiling again, quiet for so long that I wonder if he's ignoring me.

"If I tell you," he finally says, "will you let this go? Will you accept that it wasn't him?"

"If the alibi seems sound, then yes."

He presses his lips together, exhales through his nose. "Fine. He was at work that night."

"Work? What work? Gavin blew up Henry's company."

"Sure, three years ago. I imagine he's had to make a living since then."

"Okay," I concede. "So where does he work?"

"That . . . doesn't matter."

"The hell it doesn't. Wyatt, I'm two seconds away from doing some kind of"—I grope for the right phrase—"stake-out on this guy, so if I have to follow him to work, I will."

"Do not do that," he cautions. "He works at Home Depot, okay?"

"Um, you mean the place that closes by, like, ten p.m.? The cops are saying Jason could have done it because he left Maeve's at ten thirty. How does Henry working at Home Depot eliminate him as a suspect?"

Wyatt sighs. "He didn't have a car that night. It was in the shop. A friend drove him home, and they have the friend testifying to that."

"A friend?" I say. "So his actual alibi is a friend?"

Wyatt pauses. "A co-worker."

"That is the flimsiest thing I've ever heard. How do they know his *friend* didn't drive him to Gavin's first? How do they know Henry didn't get, like, an Uber to Gavin's, after his friend drove him home? And isn't that kind of a convenient excuse—his car being in the shop?"

"Sienna," Wyatt says, voice weary, "you said you'd drop this."

"If it's sound, I said. And this is anything but."

I spring up, energized by this revelation. I pace the length of the couch, cycling through options, planning my next move. Do I want to track down Henry and talk to him directly, or is it better to find the co-worker who drove him home that night?

"Beck doesn't think so," Wyatt says.

My footsteps stutter to a stop. "If it hasn't been clear yet, I don't give a fuck what Beck thinks. Not when he also thinks Jason's a killer."

"He has to fol—"

"Follow the evidence. I know. You've told me."

"But you understand, right," Wyatt says, "why Jason's a better suspect?"

I blast him a scorching look.

Still, he continues. "There's nothing physical tying Henry to Gavin that night. No means or opportunity we know of. But Jason had Gavin's phone and—"

"Gavin's blood, and a missing hour in his timeline," I finish for him. "Yes, I get it. I understand it looks bad for Jason. What I'm *saying* is: there has to be more to this story." I resume my laps along the couch. "Did you tell Julia about Henry's supposed alibi?"

"Not specifically. Just that he had one."

"And she was satisfied by that?"

The possibility claws at me—that she might have let this go so easily, exactly like Beck.

"I don't know," Wyatt says. "We didn't really get into it."

"So she didn't even press on it. Didn't ask any follow-ups." I cross my arms, stopping again. "She gives a complete stranger the benefit of some vague alibi, but when it comes to her husband, she— She—"

The energy drains from my body. I drop onto the couch, pressing my forehead into the heels of my hands. "This is so fucked," I whisper.

"It wasn't like that," Wyatt says. "She didn't accept it, or not accept it, it's just—the conversation . . . moved on to something else."

I look toward him, just in time to catch him dodging my attention. "Moved on to what?"

The shake of his head is shallow, a back and forth so slight it's almost stillness. I know that gesture, a blend of embarrassment and dread. I saw it the night he confessed to cheating on me, and seeing it now makes my stomach tumble with nausea.

"Wyatt, what?"

He rubs his hands on his thighs, as if wiping something off them. "I accidentally let it slip," he says, "that you and I have been seeing each other."

My heart plunges. Shame blasts into my cheeks, sudden as an explosion.

"No," I say. "She knows?"

Wyatt nods, but still won't look at me. "Yeah, Si. I'm sorry."

The shame spreads—not just in my face, but my neck and shoulders and chest. I feel it like a sweater of sandpaper, scratching at my torso. Then it rockets through the rest of me until I feel it everywhere else, too: this hot, scraping thing.

She won't understand why I lied. She won't understand that to speak it out loud—*Wyatt did something awful, but I still let him back into my arms*—would be to make the betrayal real. Not Wyatt's betrayal. That's always felt vivid to me, like a scab I keep picking at, a wound that won't heal. No, the worse betrayal, the one I try so hard not to look at, is the betrayal of myself.

Each time I kiss Wyatt, or clutch him close, I might as well be saying, *It's okay that you hurt me, I don't matter that much*. Each time I sleep with him, each time I lose myself beneath him, I'm letting him off easy, letting him go unpunished for the bad thing he did.

"How could you tell her?" I ask. "You know that this—us—it's supposed to be a secret."

"I know," Wyatt says. He massages the back of his neck, face tensing with pain. "But I don't want to be a secret. I honestly didn't mean to tell Julia, but I wish I wasn't being disloyal to you, slipping up like that. I want us to be something you talk about with your best friend."

His eyes are so tender, raw with hurt and yearning, that I struggle to meet his gaze. He kneads his neck, harder now, and I see that the ache he's working against is not a physical one.

"Wyatt—"

"Why didn't you tell me the doctors think Jason will wake up soon?"

I blink at the non-sequitur. "What?"

"I saw you only hours ago. You'd gotten this great news about your brother, and you just . . . didn't think to share it with me. I heard it from Julia. But not you."

"Because it's not great news! I want him to get better, but the second he wakes up, they're arresting him, and that terrifies me. Especially since I don't have proof yet that someone else did it."

"Then you should have told me *that*. Jesus, Si, I want to be more to you than just the guy you sleep with. I want you to tell me things, the same way you used to. Good things, bad things, everything you're going through. I want us to be there for each other."

"We're not . . ." I start, unsure where the sentence will take me—only certain of where it can't. "Wyatt, you know I can't do that anymore."

"Yeah, I know." There's an edge in his voice, jagged and hard. "But we've been doing this for months now, and I've held on to every scrap of you that you'll give me, because I love you so much. Because I hurt you the worst way I could. But this"—he points back and forth between us—"hurts *me* now. Having you but not having you. Having you only on your terms, and only ever skin-deep. You were always so giving in our relationship, so thoughtful. You made me a proton pack, for Christ's sake. But now? You've been selfish. And I get it, I'm not saying I don't deserve it. But I can't keep doing this, letting you punish me forever. Let's just be together, Si. Let's give it another shot, and I'll be here for you, during everything with Jason. But if you can't do that, then let's end it completely. Because I can't take the in-between anymore."

I sit back, astonished. I've seen pain skate across his face, the way it did this morning when I told him it meant nothing, sleeping in his bed—but I've never heard him vocalize it, or give my actions a name: *selfish*.

The word rattles inside me, a vibration deep in my bones, because Wyatt's right; I have been selfish. I've cashed in on his love for me again and again, without giving him anything in return. I know why I do it, too: for comfort, for distraction, for the sake of my disobedient heart—which, right now, feels sawed in half.

Part of me wants to take his hands in mine, lay down every heavy thing I'm feeling and let him hold it for a while. But the other part knows better. It would be wrong to get that close, to accept his love and love him back. It's been wrong for months now, an entire year, because Wyatt wronged *me*.

Jason wronged Julia, a hissing, slithering part of me says. *He did something terrible, just like Wyatt, and you want Julia to stand by him anyway.*

I try to dismiss the thought, but it lingers inside me, stoking some anger toward my brother. How could Jason have been so stupid, so *weak*, as to sleep with Maeve, to risk the amazing life he has with Jules? The amazing life the three of us have together? And on top of everything else, how could he put me in this position, where I have to make concessions for him, make myself a hypocrite?

I was blindsided today, when Julia lost faith in her cheating husband, even though, for so long, I've believed Wyatt should be punished for cheating on me. But that's just who I am—I hold on to things; I expect retribution; I burn—and if I'm forced to allow an exception, there can only be one. Between these two men who did something terrible, I can forgive Wyatt, or I can forgive Jason, but it can't be both, because then—where's the line? Do I have to forgive Clive Clayton, too?

I stand up from the couch, towering above Wyatt in his chair. He lifts his eyes to look at me, but the rest of him stays still, his body steely with apprehension.

He knows I have to break his heart. And I hate to do it. I really do.

But he broke mine first.

"You did this," I tell him, calling on every ember inside me, hoping to spark some flames, kindle some fire, because when I run that hot, I can't be hurt.

"You brought us here," I say. "I would have loved you forever, but now—" I stop for a moment, my voice threatening to tremble. "But you're right. We can't do this in-between. Because you don't get to sleep with someone else and still be with me."

"I don't even remember it, Si. That night is a black hole in my brain."

"You think that makes it better? That you basically ruined us in your sleep? And I know, you were wasted. But I've been drunk while you and I were dating, I've been to bachelorette parties, and I never so much as kissed someone on the cheek. Never would have dreamed of it. Being drunk doesn't change who you are; if anything, it brings out what's already there. And it shattered me, Wyatt, to find out that you were someone who could do something like that, when I thought you were—" I pull in a shaky breath. "I thought you were *good*. So it doesn't matter to me that you don't remember. Because I can't forget."

Somewhere in my monologue, he stopped looking at me. His gaze is pinned to the middle of the room, his mouth a tight knot.

"So that's it?" he asks.

"That's it."

Seconds pass, and he doesn't respond. His silence mushrooms between us.

It's fine, though. There's nothing he can say to change the past. Nothing I can do but go.

I walk toward the door, and he doesn't follow. As I step outside, the April night tries to chill me, but I focus on the heat I carry, the torch I've willed myself to be.

I head down the driveway, through the space where Julia was parked—and I focus on that, too: how she came without telling me; how she left with knowledge that should have been mine to keep or share; how her suspicion of Jason, however small, is still a betrayal, because no matter what weak, stupid, disappointing things my brother has done, murder would *never* be one of them.

But when I reach the rear of Wyatt's Nissan, the sparks inside me sputter out.

There it is: the heart-shaped dent in his bumper, and it shoves me back to the first time he told me he loved me. He whispered it in the midst of a goodbye kiss at his door, and I was so dazed, so dazzled by his declaration that when I tried to leave, I forgot to put my car in reverse. Instead, I launched forward, and even as my bumper crushed his, I couldn't stop smiling. *I was like a deranged crash test dummy, I* said to Julia later that day—telling her the truth, like I always, *we* always, used to do.

But I explained the collision to Wyatt with a lie. I said that my hand had simply slipped while switching gears—because even back then, I didn't want him to know the effect he had on me, the way he softened so many things inside me I was used to keeping hard.

It's okay, he said as we surveyed the damage. *I still love you.*

Now, tears crawl down my cheeks, icy where they should be scalding.

Chapter Nineteen

JULIA

The house is dark when I return. I left in such a hurry earlier that I didn't think to keep a light on to guide me back. While the rest of our neighborhood gleams—porchlights on, windows glowing—our house is a gap of blackness, like a missing tooth in a grinning mouth.

Still, when I step inside, I don't flip any switches, don't reach for any lamps, don't want to glimpse the blotchy roosters staining the walls. I feel my way to the family room with my hands, then collapse onto the couch, where I remain for a long time.

It took something from me, learning about Sienna's lie. Some essential energy. Some intangible thing that's powered me for a long time. It's not even the lie itself; if she wants to see Wyatt, she should. It's the ferocity of it all, the intensity with which she insisted she never speaks to him—and the way I never thought to doubt it. Doubt her.

Sienna's lie was so much smaller than all of Jason's. So why does it feel like it's clobbered me? Why do I feel like I can't even move?

I guess, with Jason, I had some warning, even as I tried for years to ignore it: *How well do you know this man?* That old seed my mother planted. Not to mention the cliché of it all: one partner betraying another, their secrets as sacred to them as any vow. But Sienna and I—better than partners; better, even, than friends—were above all that.

I can't see it in this night-dark room, but in one of the photos masking the wallpaper, there's Sienna and me, palms clasped on the beach, mouths roaring with bent-over laughter as the ocean glitters behind us. In the past, whenever I looked at that photo, at our hands linked together, I saw only the places we overlapped, the spaces we filled for each other—not the cracks between us through which some things might slip.

In a way, these family room photographs feel like ghosts. Sienna and me, standing on sand. Jason with Aiden on his shoulders. Jason and Sienna and me on courthouse steps.

How many secrets are in each picture, pressed and preserved beneath glass? How much have we kept from each other? *How well do you know this man*—or any of them?

I can't help but think of my mother, the distrust that festered in her like an infection. My whole life, she was cured of it only once, briefly, that month she dated Bob Sullivan, the man I later found stealing from her. She screamed when I told her, yelled that I'd ruined a good thing, that I never knew how to just keep quiet, and I wonder now if she understood what that would do to me, how it would make me swallow my own voice, shutter my truths and suspicions.

For the first time since it happened, I feel sad for her. That day I saw Bob pulling money from her purse, my mother learned there were two versions of the man she loved: the one who bought her flowers, made her blush, and the one I told her he was, a man who'd take from her, a man who'd waste the rare jewel of her trust. Maybe, then, when she screamed at me, she didn't do so in anger, but in horror—that the two versions could conflict so much.

In the entryway, a key clicks inside a lock. The dead bolt flips back. The front door opens.

"Mom?" Aiden calls.

At first I don't respond. I stare into the darkness, my mouth open like a fish on a line, the discussion we need to have a hook inside my lip. The pain, the danger of it, renders me silent.

"Mom?" he tries again.

"In here," I say, my voice creaky, like a door that hasn't been opened in a while.

Aiden's feet clap down the hallway, sounding dimly metallic in his dress shoes. When he flicks on the overhead light, I raise my hand to shield my eyes, then drop it to take him in. He's so handsome, so achingly grown, even if his pants are a bit short at the ankles, allowing a glimpse of his flamingo socks, a sight that nearly drowns me in affection. His hair is a little damp, sweat-slick, and I hope it's because he spent the night dancing, because he laughed and joked with friends, and, for three hours, didn't give a single thought to his father.

"Why are you in the dark?" he asks.

"I don't know. I guess I liked it."

He frowns at my answer, then swings his gaze between the family room and kitchen. "Where's Auntsy?"

"I don't know," I say again, and he frowns at that, too.

"Okay . . ." He arches his neck to loosen his tie. "Well, I'm gonna go change—"

"Come here a minute."

I pat the cushion beside me. He hesitates, eyeing the couch like it wants to eat him, but then he shuffles over, flopping onto the corner of it, as far from me as he can get.

"How was the semiformal? I ask. "You look perfect."

"It was fine."

"Yeah? Did—did anyone give you a hard time? Was Nate Hyde there?"

"No," he says, and I'm not sure which question he's answering. I give him a moment to elaborate, but his mouth is a firm line.

"Did you dance with anyone?" I ask.

He shrugs. "Everyone danced with everyone."

"You really do look great. I should get a picture of you so we can show Dad."

"Why, is he awake?"

He doesn't look at me when he asks it, but his voice is strange, caught between timid and indifferent. It's like he's trying not to care about the answer, but he's scared of it, too.

"Not yet." I reach over to pat his knee, which tenses beneath my hand. "But we got some good news today. The doctors think he'll be out of the coma soon."

He snaps his head toward me. "And then what happens?" he asks.

Like he already knows. Like he understands the story doesn't end when Jason wakes up.

I inhale deeply, wanting to delay this a little longer. But my lungs fill to capacity, tight and burning, and I'm forced to empty them. Forced to answer.

"Unfortunately, sweetie, he'll—he'll be arrested."

His gaze doesn't soften or sharpen. He doesn't spring back in surprise, or even flinch.

"Yeah, I figured," he says.

"You did?"

His eyes slink away from me, burrowing into his lap. For several seconds, each so taut and heavy, he doesn't respond.

"So they have enough evidence?" he finally says. "Wasn't there supposed to be a test or something? On, like, the blood?"

I sip more air, steadying myself. "There was. They got the results back, on Dad's pocketknife, and . . . it's a match. The blood is Gavin's."

Aiden's face darkens, brow slumping deep enough to shadow his eyes. "So he did it."

A declaration. Not a question.

It practically strangles my heart.

"Auntsy doesn't think so," I say. "She thinks there's an explanation for all of this."

I'm grateful, in this moment, to still have Sienna to fall back on, to be able to use her voice instead of my own. Maybe Aiden won't notice. Sienna and I have always been so linked that speaking for one of us usually means speaking for both. Even when her words clash with the ones I won't say, I'm content to let it go, to let her thoughts sit in for mine.

"What kind of explanation?" Aiden asks.

"Well, she's . . . looking into another suspect. She feels like she's got a really strong lead."

It's not a lie, but I know it's misleading. Still, I'm reluctant to tell him Sienna's suspect has an alibi, that everything still comes back to Jason in the end. My stomach seizes up with all I'm not saying, but surely there's no harm in it, giving my son a little bit of hope.

Aiden scowls, yanking his tie from his collar before dropping it onto the couch. He sloughs off his suit jacket, places it over his legs. I look at his wrists, where the sleeves, like his pants, are just a little too short, and nausea spins in me anew. He isn't wearing Jason's cuff links.

"Honey," I start, "are you okay?"

"Are *you*?" He slams his gaze onto me, direct and imploring, and it feels like the first eye contact he's initiated in weeks.

"Yeah," I manage. "I'm fine."

It's definitely a lie this time, and he spots it right away. He answers with a scoff.

I know I should tell him the truth, that I'm further from fine than ever, if only to show him that he can say anything, tell me any truth in return, and I will not scream at him, no matter how scared it makes me. But my throat feels like a rusty faucet, dried out for too long.

"You think he's guilty," Aiden says. "Don't you?"

His expression startles me even more than his question. He doesn't look angry, or accusatory, or even sad. His face is an odd blend of curiosity and—hope, it seems. Like he's been alone with something for a while, and he's seeing now that he might be able to share it.

More than anything, it's that hope, that need inside him, that helps me to speak.

"Aiden." My voice is just a drip at first, then a gush: "You've been suffering for days. And I know it's more than Dad's coma. More than him being a suspect." I touch his cheek, and he doesn't recoil. "Tell me what it is."

He's still for a while, eyes pointed away. I withdraw my hand from his face, and he reaches into his jacket pocket to pull out his phone. For a moment, I think he's ignoring me, about to text someone or open some game, but as he speaks, he only holds the phone in his palm.

"I lied to you," he says, "about last Sunday night. I did leave the house."

Goose bumps swell on my arms.

"I couldn't sleep. And at some point, I heard one of you guys head downstairs and open the front door—which was weird, you know? It was almost two in the morning. So I looked out my window, and I saw Dad out there, walking down the driveway."

I tilt my head, unable to imagine how this story will end. Dread fills me all the same.

"Where did he go?" I ask.

"Down to the curb. To the trash can."

Aiden rests his other palm against his phone, sandwiching it between his hands. He stares at it solemnly, like he's swearing an oath on a Bible, and my heart knocks. Part of me wants to tell him to stop, I was wrong, we don't have to talk, we can lie to each other a little longer.

I wrestle that impulse down.

"He threw something away, and then he came inside. Went back to bed. I tried to fall asleep, too, but I couldn't stop thinking about it. I mean, why get up in the middle of the night to get rid of something? And why go all the way to the curb? I know garbage collection is Monday mornings, but it's not like we don't have trash cans in the house."

Aiden clicks the button to awaken his phone. "So I went out there to see what it was."

He opens his photos, swipes until he lands on one in particular. "And I found this."

He passes the phone to me, and my hand trembles.

I shouldn't look at the picture. The conclusion arrives with so much certainty that I almost hand the phone back to him, tell him to delete it, that if his father took such care to get rid of something, it must be something he never meant us to see. But when I look at Aiden, there's so much pain in his eyes, it's like he's watching something die in front of him.

Whatever's in this picture, I can't leave him alone with it.

I hold my breath as I lower my gaze to the phone. Then I exhale in a rush, as if someone's punched me, knocking the air from my lungs.

I'm not exactly sure what I'm looking at. Pale blue fabric. Buttons. But one thing is clear in the camera's flash.

Blood.

Dried, dark splotches of it. The color of the roosters on our walls.

I recognize the fabric now. It's one of Jason's blazers. And I recall—with such blinding focus, like an interrogation light shined in my face—what he wore to the conference last Friday. A salmon button-down, which is still crumpled in our hamper upstairs. Gray slacks, from which I pulled the receipt with Gavin's address. And a pale blue blazer, now spotted with blood.

My heart isn't knocking anymore. It bangs.

"When I first saw this, I didn't know what to make of it," Aiden says. "I'm not even sure why I took the picture, other than . . . it was creepy—the timing of it all: Dad's boss getting murdered, Dad throwing this away in the middle of the night. But then, a few days later, you and Auntsy came home and said he was a suspect, that the cops had all this evidence, and all I could think about was that jacket. I couldn't sleep, couldn't pay attention in class. It was killing me."

"Oh, honey—"

"You know the other night, in your room? When I said I was looking for cuff links?"

I manage a wary nod, watching as color creeps into his cheeks.

"I lied then, too. I was just trying to see what else Dad might be hiding, if there was more evidence somewhere. Because that's what that stupid jacket is, right? Evidence. And I don't understand it. I don't understand *him*. I don't know why he'd . . . how he could . . ."

He trails off, and I don't push him to continue. Over the past several days, I've searched for answers in our laundry, in our credit card statements, in Jason's emails. Aiden, bearing his own agony, was searching through closets and drawers.

"I'm so sorry you've been carrying this alone," I say. "Why didn't you tell me sooner?"

His answer is quick and sharp: "Because we don't talk about shit like this."

The swear hardly fazes me. I'm more confused by the vitriol behind it, the way it stings me like a slap. "Shit like what?"

"Like *anything*. You never say what you're really feeling. Even now, when I asked how you were, you said *fine*. While Dad's in a coma, about to be arrested for murder, you're fine. And not just that. It's little things, too. If Dad decides to, like, bring home takeout when you already made lasagna or whatever, you don't say, like, 'Oh, I wish you talked to me first, I went to a lot of trouble making dinner.' You just put the lasagna in the fridge and don't even mention it. But I've seen your face, Mom—even if you only show it for a split second, it bothers you."

I'm stunned by this example. It's one I never would have thought of when considering the ways I've silenced myself. But it *does* bother me when Jason makes the unilateral decision to bring home takeout, especially since he should know that I usually have a plan for dinner. I've never mentioned it to him because I know he means it as a kindness. And I didn't want to risk upsetting him, seeing his face spring back in hurt.

"So why would I show you this?" Aiden continues. "I thought you'd brush it off. Or pretend it isn't obvious that this is *blood*." He zooms in closer on the splotches, until they fill the screen with a rusty hue. "Because that's what you do. You brush things off. You act like everything's fine. I even asked you straight-up the other night what you and Dad fought about in December, and you acted like it was no big deal. You told me"—his fingers hook into air quotes—"'It was nothing. I overreacted about something.'"

Again, I'm thrown off-kilter. I didn't know how carefully he was listening to me, enough to parrot my lie. I didn't know that, all this time, he's been recording my facial expressions, the lengths of my silences. Didn't realize the kind of example I'd set. That, in not speaking the truth, I'd left no space for words at all, not even from my son.

"I knew that was a lie," he says, "the second you said it. Because you don't overreact to things. Most times, you don't react at all."

My mouth snaps open, my eyes widen—and I can only imagine what he sees in me now: surprise, distress, embarrassment. I don't bother to hide it or distract him with a denial. Because Aiden's right. How many times have I rearranged my face to not give anything away? How many times have I forced a smile, a nod, even as something gnawed me inside?

"I know you and Auntsy have been trying to clear Dad's name all week." Aiden pulls the phone from my hands. I stop myself from latching onto his fingers—not to keep him from taking it, but to hold on to him a moment.

"The problem is," he adds, "I don't think Dad *can* be cleared."

The phone has gone dark, but he wakes it again, and there it is: blue fabric and blood.

Blood on this blazer. Blood on Jason's knife. Blood welling from Gavin's stomach.

"He killed him," Aiden says, and my heart splits open.

"Oh, honey," I whisper. I envelop him in an embrace—and he allows it. Even though his shoulders are stiff, he rests in my arms, so much bigger than he's ever been, so much older than I ever imagined him when he was a child. My entire body hurts, the way it did fourteen years ago, right after I'd given birth. It amazed me then, how even my tongue ached from my labor, the soles of my feet, my neck and elbows. I had given all of myself in order to bring our son into the world, and now I squeeze Aiden to me, devastated by the ways Jason and I have failed him.

Something like a whimper escapes me. I try to hold Aiden tighter, rock him like he's still a child, but he draws back until my arms loosen around his shoulders.

"You think so too," Aiden says. "Don't you?"

I look at the photo one last time—a piece of evidence the police never had. And though my chest throbs, my lungs cramp, my eyes burn, I answer my son. I tell him the truth.

"I do," I say. "I think your father killed him."

Chapter Twenty

SIENNA

I head to Home Depot as soon as it opens, no Julia in my passenger seat, no texts from her on my phone. There was a moment this morning when I almost called her. My thumb, moving by instinct, reached for her under Favorites. Then I stared at her name, stunned by the emotions it conjured—sadness, resentment, shame—and I couldn't bring myself to press it.

Instead, I looked up Home Depot locations—two in a twelve-mile radius—and after comparing them to Henry Hendrix's address, I picked the one closest to him.

The one in Hillstead. The one only a couple miles from Wyatt. And I winced at that thought, the nearness of him like a reopened wound.

As I pull into a parking space, I have to remind myself that nothing's changed. Wyatt and I didn't break up last night, because we never got back together. We were over when I arrived at his house, and over when I left it. It doesn't matter that, afterward, in my rest-

223

less, shredded sleep, I pictured myself returning to him, telling him I want him again, want him always on my side.

I'm on your side, Si, always.

That was what snapped me back to my senses, that sentence he said. He meant it as a balm, but it felt like a bruise. Because no matter how much he believes it, he's proven it isn't true. If he were on my side, he wouldn't have insisted Henry's alibi was solid when it seems anything but, wouldn't have implied I give up like Julia and wait for Jason to be arrested.

As the doors to Home Depot part, I'm smacked by the smell of lumber and must. It reminds me of Integrity Plus's warehouse, the gutter machine, the cash and notebook, the customer names that led me to Henry in the first place. This whole time, it's been a trail of breadcrumbs right to him, and no one can keep me from following it—not Julia (*How would Henry have planted traces of blood onto Jason's knife?*), and certainly not Wyatt (*You understand, right, why Jason is a better suspect?*).

I check down each aisle, alert to anyone who resembles Henry Hendrix's picture: round face, gray hair. The only men who fit the bill are clearly customers, not employees, studying the options for caulk in one aisle, doorknobs in another.

And that's good—preferable, actually. My plan will work better if he isn't here.

At Customer Service, there's a skinny, pimply teen manning the counter. He's staring at nothing, chewing on a pen cap, and there's a smudge of blue ink in the corner of his lips. My first thought is to ask for his manager, but I reconsider; someone this young (and maybe a little dumb) might be willing to cross more boundaries.

"Hi," I say, as bright and cheery as I can muster. "Is Henry working today?"

I omit his last name on purpose—Henry and I are *such* good friends.

"Henry Hendrix?" I add, like it's just occurred to me to be more specific.

The kid's pen cap clicks across his teeth as he yanks it out. "Um. Let me look at the schedule, I can pull it up on my phone."

I smile at him. So easy.

"Nah, he's not on till tomorrow," the boy says. "Sorry."

"Don't be." He's just confirmed for me that this is the location where Henry works. Now I can ask what I really need to know. "There might be something else you can help me with. Henry said a co-worker drove him home last Friday. He left something of mine in the person's car and I'd love to get it back if they're here today, since I came all this way and everything."

"Uh, who drove him home? I can check to see if they're—"

"That's the thing, I'm not sure. He's been so hard to get ahold of lately." I make a show of rolling my eyes. "You know how Henry is."

"Not really. We work different sections."

"Oh. Well, is there anyone who might remember—"

"Hey, Tony?" the boy calls to someone behind me. I turn to find a man with an orange apron over a plaid button-down. "Do you know who drove Henry home last Friday?"

"Hendrix?" the man clarifies. "He doesn't work Fridays."

"Oh, but he did that night," I step forward to say. "His car was in the shop, and his co-worker gave him a ride. I'm trying to figure out who it was because he left my—"

"Sorry, ma'am," the man cuts in. I cock an eyebrow. "Hendrix doesn't work Fridays."

"But schedules change all the time, right?" I try. Because I can't exactly say, *I heard this straight from the police.* "Sorry, I don't mean to pester you. It's just—Henry was very clear that his co-worker drove him home that night."

"Hendrix doesn't work Fridays," he says—for the third time. "If one of his co-workers drove him home from somewhere, it wasn't from here."

"Are you sure?" I bite back my frustration. "Could you check with the manager maybe?"

The man smirks. "Honey, I *am* the manager."

Then he strides away, too fast to feel the heat of my gaze.

I swivel back to the teen smiling obliviously, the ink like a bad piercing at the corner of his mouth.

"Yeah," he says, glancing at his phone. "Henry wasn't on the schedule last Friday."

They checked this guy out, Wyatt assured me. But I've been here two seconds, and Henry's alibi, already flimsy, has now completely dissolved, quicker than salt in water.

"Thanks," I mumble to the boy. Then I storm away.

How did this happen? Clearly Henry lied about his alibi—but wouldn't the police have verified his timeline? They've certainly been obsessed with Jason's.

And it's not just Henry who would've had to lie. Wyatt said they spoke to the friend who backed up Henry's claim.

So what the hell happened?

As I pound across the store's concrete floor, my phone's already in my hand. When the doors slide open to let me out, my fingers pull up Wyatt's name.

I have to tell him the cops are wrong.

But my thumb won't make the call.

I'm not supposed to do this anymore, run to Wyatt like a reflex.

I swipe instead to Julia. But the thought of speaking to her now pumps my chest with pressure, a discomfort that compresses my heart. What could she possibly do to help? What would she even be *willing* to do? She doubted my Henry theory the minute I told her about it. *How would Henry have planted traces of blood onto Jason's knife?*

As her question slices back into my thoughts, it's as if I can feel that knife on my own skin, making a hundred little cuts.

Who does that leave me with—Detective Beck? The man who fucked this up in the first place? The man with a warrant, who considers this case already closed?

I exit out of Contacts to search for Henry's address. I assumed, the first time I looked this up, that Home Depot would be a better place to start, that I'd have more luck with the co-worker side of the alibi than with Henry himself. Now that I know he lied to the police, I need another plan, another angle, another—

I crash into someone, hard and sudden. We grunt in sync, our phones clattering to the ground.

"Sorry!" we say as we stoop to pick them up.

The person cradles my elbow as if trying to keep me steady. With their other hand, they fumble for their phone. We check our screens for damage.

"It's my fault," they say, still crouched. "I was looking at my phone."

"Me too," I admit. We straighten—and then I freeze.

The man freezes too.

We stare at each other, as stopped as statues.

It's the person I've seen in pictures, in windows, in memories of parties and courtrooms. The person I haven't stood this close to in decades.

He knows who I am. The recognition flared so fast I have to wonder if he's kept tabs on me. If every moment I've spent rage-stalking his profile, he was simultaneously hunting through mine.

Sweat pools in my armpits.

How many hours have I spent in his neighborhood? How many times have I slowed past his house? Yet it's only now, when I least expect him, that he smashes into me, a head-on collision.

Something grazes my skin—a spider I want to swipe at. But no: it's Clive Clayton's hand, still on my arm, his fingers now twitching.

"Don't touch me!" I say, wrenching from his touch.

"I'm sorry," he says. "I'm sorry. Did I hurt you?"

"Did you *hurt* me?"

The question shoots across the parking lot, bounces off the hoods of cars. Clive whips his head around to check for onlookers, customers suspicious of the man who'd earn my scream. But it's early still; the lot is sparse. We're alone out here. Together.

"Sienna, I'm—"

"Oh, you remember my name! How nice of you." I speak through nausea, through fever, through chills that rock me even though I've never felt so volcanic. "Do you remember my parents' names, too?"

He swallows before he answers, his expression stiff. Practiced. "Jim and Gina."

My throat closes like a fist. "Don't," I squeeze out.

"I think of them every day." His voice has the audacity to tremble. "I think of you, too, and your brother."

"I'm warning you, stop talking."

A cloud floats in front of the sun, shadowing us, but my skin practically steams.

"I will, I just—" Something relaxes in Clive, like his spine is a rope gone slack. "God, I kind of always hoped I'd run into you someday. Although, I didn't think it would be so literal . . ."

He exhales a chuckle, light as the air around us, but I feel it like a brick to my face.

"I've thought a million times about what I'd say to you, how to apologize for what I did. I do the school circuit now, the whole cautionary-tale assembly thing."

He fiddles with the strings of his hoodie—Willow Creek Varsity Soccer, a decades-old costume he's still wearing of the popular jock.

The fabric is blindingly white, like it's never once held a stain he had to scrub out or bleach.

"I've said thousands of words to thousands of people," he says, "about that night, the aftermath. But I've never figured out the ones I'd say to the two of you."

The aftermath. That's what he dares to call it: me sobbing until I'm sure my body is splintering; Jason holding me as if his arms were steel beams; grief, that ancient wrecking ball, crushing us anyway.

It wasn't aftermath. It was ruins.

"I guess there aren't any," Clive adds. "Words, I mean." He waits for a woman to walk by before he continues. "But I'll always be sorry. I was . . . such an asshole that night, drinking and driving, and your family didn't deserve to pay the price for my mistake."

My nails dagger my palms. *Mistake. An asshole that night*—as if it was all a fluke, a one-time thing, him acting so reckless, hurting people. But it's just like I said to Wyatt last night: being drunk doesn't change who you are; it only brings out what's already there.

"You've *always* been an asshole," I say. "Not that that word even scratches the surface. You think my parents are all you have to be sorry for? You think I really don't remember what you did to me in high school? And yeah, murder's worse than assault, but don't you dare stand here and act like, other than that one night, you were a fucking saint."

"Assault?" he says—and I could kill him for looking so surprised.

"Oh, fuck you. *I* was the one who was drunk at that party, and I still remember, so don't even give me that."

"Wait. You're saying I assaulted *you*? At a . . . party in high school?"

"Your hands were all over me. You said, *shh, just relax*, because you knew I didn't want you touching me anymore. And if my brother hadn't come in and thrown you off me, who knows what you would have done!"

"Your brother . . ." He says it slowly, each syllable distinct, like he's testing out the memory to see if it fits. Finally, clarity dawns on his face. "Okay, yeah. Bill Stanton's party. You and I started to hook up."

My fingers clench harder. My nails stab deeper.

"Look, I'm really sorry," he says, "if I took things too far that night. I have a daughter now, and I'd hate to think that someone might—"

"Do *not* go there."

"Go where?"

"Telling me you have a daughter now, so you finally understand that women are people."

"That's not— I'm just saying, if I was out of line, I'm glad your brother intervened. Although . . ." Clive crosses his arms, purses his lips in thought. "I have to say, I remember now thinking that was a little weird."

"My brother protecting me?"

"No. The moment he chose to."

In my palm, there's a sharp pinch, like a needle puncturing skin. "You mean the moment he figured out you brought me upstairs? Yeah, he rushed right in."

Clive squints at me, even though the sun's still behind a cloud. "That's . . . not what happened." He opens his mouth to continue, then closes it again. He looks toward a row of shopping carts. "But if that's what your brother told you, it's not my place to say otherwise."

"What the hell is that supposed to mean?"

"Nothing. It's not my place," he repeats, eyes still pointed away— and there's something I don't like in them, an emotion that takes me a moment to identify because it's so out-of-place with what we're talking about.

Pity. Clive's eyes are filled with pity.

Not remorse for his actions. Not even denial. Instead, he looks like he's withholding a piece of that night that would devastate me to know.

But that's impossible. I was there. I remember every second. Clive's mouth on mine. His hand on my breast. My shoulder blades jammed against the wall. His fingers tugging the button of my jeans. Then Jason—out of nowhere, as if I'd conjured him through my panic alone—yanking Clive off me. Saving me. *Saving* me.

"You're lying." My palms grow slick. My nails slip against skin that's wet and warm.

"Look, I'm sorry I mentioned it," Clive says. "I'm sorry for a lot of things. I hope you're—I hope you're doing well, Sienna. Jason, too."

He turns to go, but I grab him by the arm. "Seriously? You're just going to walk away?"

Like he did from the party. Like he did from the crash. Like he did from prison. Each time unscathed. Unscarred. Unaccountable.

Clive looks at my hand, my fingers bolted around his bicep, then looks at me. "What else can I do?"

I grip tighter, but I don't answer. I hiss in breaths, huff them back out. My palm feels like an iron burning through fabric, straight to his arm.

"Hey!" he says. "Shit, you're bleeding!"

I follow his gaze, and when I see it—bright red smeared across the white of his sweatshirt—I leap back, checking my hand.

There are semicircles gouged there, each one deep and dark. But only one of my nails actually broke the skin. I wipe at it, more curious than alarmed, but the blood doesn't stop. It wells in my palm like tears in an eye.

As the sun skirts from behind the clouds, it shines on my wound. The red gleams in the light. I stare at it in awe.

"Shit," Clive repeats. And when a man exits his car and sees my cut, sees the scuff of blood on Clive's shirt, he approaches with caution, like I'm a rabid animal—unleashed and untamed.

"What's going on here? Ma'am, are you okay?"

Even as the man expresses concern, he looks so spooked. Like he's never seen somebody admire their own wound. I glance at Clive and see the same fear on his face. He's shocked by my strength, my power—how exquisite it all is. And I could do anything right now.

Leaving them there, I march to my car. I ignore the calls of "Ma'am?" and "Sienna?" that would only slow me down.

In the driver's seat, I punch Henry's address into GPS. My fingers smudge the screen with red, giving it a glossy, angry sheen, and I love it, I love it. I might never clean it off.

What else can I do? Clive asked. He can burn in hell. But beyond that: nothing. Because he can't go back to those nights, can't un-touch me, un-whisper in my ear, un-press me to some stranger's wall. He can't un-drink, un-drive, un-sentence himself to an insulting number of years. The damage he's done is permanent, fathomless; it's branded onto all of my bones, and I'll be damned if I let another injustice mark me like that again.

I'm glad Jules isn't here. She'd only try to cool my fire. She's never understood that my fire is not a flaw, not a thing to be extinguished. It's beautiful and dangerous and fucked-up and perfect—and it's fueling me now, fifty miles an hour on sleepy back roads. I won't let up, won't lift my foot from the gas, because the cops are useless, Henry's a liar, and I'm ready to do anything—I *can* do anything—to smoke out the truth.

"Your destination is on the left," my GPS tells me, and I pull up to the curb on the right side of the street. It's a rundown house—a duplex with sagging porches and drainage issues, from the looks of the swampy front yard. It's exactly the kind of place a bankrupt business owner would be able to afford.

I rummage through my purse, looking for a napkin or tissue, something to wipe the blood off my hand before I head up Henry's walkway and knock on his door.

Or maybe I should make sure he sees it. Make sure he knows exactly what I'm made of.

I waffle too long on the decision, because now the door to the duplex's garage is opening. Brake lights flash, and a car reverses down the driveway, quick and careless. When it swings onto the street, I'm close enough to identify the man behind the wheel.

Shit. He's already getting away from me.

Henry's timing is immaculate, almost like he knew I was coming, like he could feel my rage, my need, barreling closer, and decided to flee.

As he takes off down the road, I don't think, don't plan. I only follow.

We snake through quiet neighborhoods, pass through streets that are dotted with storefronts, until we're back in the bustling section of Hillstead. The Home Depot is up the road, half a mile away. Maybe that Customer Service kid was wrong. Maybe Henry is on the schedule today. But soon, he streaks past the entrance, glides through a green light, and keeps on going.

When he finally makes a turn, it's toward a building I've never looked twice at: Hillstead Community Center. He parks, and I park, tucking my car into the row behind Henry's, and if he's noticed me following him, he doesn't show it. He only sits in his driver's seat, and when I crane forward to peer through his back windshield, I can tell he's scrolling on his phone.

I drum my fingers on the wheel—smeared now with my blood. I lean back, stretch out my arms, feel my veins pulse and pulse, expectant and electric.

I craft my questions, my line of interrogation: *Where were you really last Friday night? Why did you lie to the police? Who's this friend who lied for you too? What did you mean when you told Gavin Reed "You should have kept your mouth shut"?*

Thud, thud, thud—my heart, my drumming hands. *Thud, thud—Thud.*

The rhythm stutters. Then it stops.

Because another car has just pulled into the lot. It passes Henry's, passes mine, parks diagonal from me with its bumper facing out. And on that bumper: a dent I'd know anywhere.

A lopsided, crumpled heart.

I crouch down in my seat. What the hell is Wyatt doing here?

Peering above the dashboard, I watch as he gets out of his car. He stretches. He's not in a hurry. Not in his uniform.

He strolls toward Henry's car, where Henry's still staring at his phone. Did Wyatt follow him here, too?

Maybe I got to him. Maybe Wyatt's given a second thought to my theory. Maybe—my lungs expand, light as helium—he really is on my side.

Thud, thud, thud: this time it's Wyatt, knocking on Henry's window.

Henry's head turns. Wyatt raises one hand in a motionless wave, then steps back as Henry opens his door.

I sit up a little higher, watching their body language for tension, apprehension.

Wyatt says something to Henry.

Henry's mouth moves with a response.

And then, at the same moment, they laugh.

Not quietly, or politely. Not merely a chuckle. The two of them pitch forward, as if their laughter has thrown them off-balance.

With my bloody hand, I grip the wheel. Shock blasts through me like a fire hose.

As they head up the sidewalk, toward the community center's door, Henry claps Wyatt on the back. Wyatt returns the gesture, and for a few seconds, they huddle close together, their faces turned toward each other—officer and suspect—smiling like two old friends.

Chapter Twenty-One

JULIA

I sip my coffee at the counter, staring at the blood on Jason's blazer.

I've memorized each drop, could draw each streak in my sleep. Not that I'd be able to sleep right now; I'm on my third cup of coffee since dawn. All night, after Aiden AirDropped me the photo, I studied it in the dark, eyes wet and throbbing.

Before Jason slid into bed with me last Friday, did he wash his hands? Did he watch Gavin's blood spiral down the drain? Or, even now, are there traces of it on our sheets? Specks of red I kept myself from seeing? I tilt my ear toward the laundry room, where our washer thunks with a bulky load, then return my attention to my phone.

I don't know what to do with the photo. It's evidence. I know that much. But if I show it to the police, they'll question Aiden, and the thought of that—my son forced to testify against his father—makes me feel like I'm zipped into a dress too tight.

The blood has a strange pattern. I zoom in for the hundredth time. Drops like buttons near one of the cuffs. Streaks like claw marks across the fabric. When Aiden first showed me the photo, I thought those streaks meant Jason had tried to wipe the blood from the blazer, clean his clothes of the crime. But now I see it differently: he was wiping the blood off his hand.

Maybe I should tell the police that I was the one who took the photo. I can pretend Aiden never saw the blazer, never carried this burden for almost a week on his own. But what would it matter in the end? The police already have a warrant; they're not looking for additional proof.

Proof. That word curdles the coffee in my stomach.

The knife, the blood, the blazer. Jason's hands on all of it.

I set down my mug. Pick up my phone. But suddenly, it's not Jason's hands I see; it's his face, some future version of it, scuffed with hurt when he learns I turned in the picture. It shouldn't matter to me. He lied, he cheated, he *killed*. But somehow, it's still enough to give me pause.

And then there's Sienna.

She would never forgive me. We simply wouldn't survive it. There'd be no more Movie Nights, no jokes that feel like home, no hands that always find each other, even in the dark. She'd demand I move out, deem me unworthy of the house she grew up in. Our business would go under, our partnership severed, our days and lives instantly untethered.

The thought of it almost doubles me over with pain.

Strange that I don't feel this way when I think of losing Jason. It hurts to imagine life without him; it's dizzying, disorienting—but it isn't debilitating. It's not the crippling panic of losing Sienna. Jason and I were pressured by my pregnancy to commit to each other so young, and of course I grew to love him, but maybe the truth of that love is more complicated than I've ever allowed myself to believe.

Maybe my marriage was made more fulfilling because Sienna, who I instantly adored, was a part of it. Because she and Jason were a package deal.

It's breathtaking, really—how much of my life is tied to her. Not just my husband, but my home and career, as well. For years, I've believed these threads were bound in an unpickable knot. But now, as I return to the photo of Jason's blazer, it feels so loose, so close to unraveling.

"Jules?"

I hear her say my name.

"Jules, are you here?"

At first I think I'm imagining it, but the front door closes, footsteps scurry, and Sienna appears, panting. Strands of hair stick to her temples. Her blue eyes blaze.

"He knows him. Wyatt knows him. Henry Hendrix. He seems to be *friends* with him. But he never told me that, never acted like Henry was anything more than a stranger to him. Is Wyatt protecting him, helping him cover up Gavin's murder? He told me a hundred times not to look into Henry Hendrix, even though Henry's alibi didn't make any sense—and wasn't even *real*, it turns out. Julia, what the fuck?"

A sound escapes my lips—something between confused and startled.

"Sorry," she says. "I'll slow down. Henry's alibi is that he was working at Home Depot that night, his co-worker drove him home, and he didn't have a car, so he didn't have a way to get to Gavin's. Obviously, I don't need to tell you the issues with *that*—but get this: I went to Home Depot. Henry wasn't even working that night. So I went to his house and followed him."

"You what?"

"I didn't plan to. I was just going to talk to him, but then he was leaving, and his car was getting away, and—it doesn't matter. The point is: he ended up meeting with Wyatt. Not at the station. At some random community center in Hillstead. And they were *laughing* together. Basically hugging. So I think Wyatt's, like, in on it, Jules. I think Henry killed Gavin, and Wyatt's been helping him cover his tracks."

Sienna grips the back of a chair, breathing hard, like she's fought to cross a finish line.

"That . . . doesn't sound like Wyatt," I say.

"Yeah, well, neither did cheating," she snaps, "but he did that, too."

I'll admit, it's surprising, Wyatt being friends with Henry. He made no mention of that to me last night. For a second, I allow the idea—Henry as the killer, someone who isn't Jason with blood on his hands—to lap at my mind.

But then I look at my phone on the counter, and all comfort evaporates.

"Sienna," I say.

Whether or not I show the photo to the police, she needs to know it exists. She needs to be pulled from wayward theories, from the whirlpool of her indignation that scalds her every time. That's always been my role in our relationship—to save her from herself. And now she needs to see, with her own eyes, what her brother has done.

And maybe, if I'm being honest, I need something, too. I need Sienna to share the weight of this discovery, to hold my hand as we hold on to it together.

"I know you weren't sold on my theory about Henry," she says. "But you have to see that there's so much here that doesn't add up."

"I get it," I allow, "but . . . Sienna."

"What? Why are you saying my name like that?" She squints at me, takes a step closer. "Your eyes are all red. Have you been crying?"

I pick up my phone. "Yes. I cried a lot last night. I didn't really sleep."

I open the Photos app.

"Why?" Sienna asks, before swallowing in a way that looks involuntary. A spasm of her throat. A tick of nerves. She can see on my face that I'm about to wreck her. "Because of Jason's cheating?"

"No."

I hold the phone out to her. She looks at it warily, like I've offered her a weapon.

"Aiden showed me this. Yesterday."

At her nephew's name, she frowns and takes the phone. She stares at the photo, zooms in, then out. "What am I looking at?"

"Jason's blazer. With blood on it," I say.

Then, in a flood of words, I tell her about Aiden, about Jason carrying the blazer to the garbage can in the middle of the night, how it's the same blazer he wore to the conference.

As Sienna listens, her lips separate in surprise. She looks at the photo again, brows shoved together—and I think she might actually get it this time, might finally allow the dots to connect. Already I feel lighter, less strangled, less alone.

But then Sienna shakes her head, and in that small gesture, I see her disbelief. Her *refusal* to believe. She returns her gaze to me, sharp as an ice pick, and passes back my phone.

"So—what," she says, "you think this proves he—" She pauses, expression shifting into something darker. Her voice becomes low and throaty, a distant rumble of thunder. "You really think Jason killed him?"

Think. That's the word I used with Aiden last night. *I think your father killed him,* still softening the blow—for my son's sake, of course, but more so for my own. I know, though, that Sienna won't accept *I think.* There's too much wiggle room in the phrase, too much for her to chip away at. *I think* is almost *maybe,* almost *I'm not sure.*

"I don't know exactly what happened," I start, staring at my mug. "I don't know why Jason went to Gavin's after he left Maeve's—"

"Exactly," Sienna cuts in. "Why would he?"

I lift one shoulder, a half shrug that takes so much energy, and I offer the only theory I've been able to piece together. "Maeve said Jason thought Gavin assaulted her after the holiday party. So maybe he tried confronting him about his suspicions at that restaurant first, the night Henry Hendrix attacked Gavin, but then there was all that chaos and he lost his chance. And then maybe after . . . sleeping with Maeve, Jason realized how much he cared for her, and he decided he couldn't wait for another opportunity. He had to confront him immediately."

"One, Jason doesn't *care for her*," Sienna counters. "Not like that. It was a moment of weakness. Of stupidity. He loves *you*. Two, why would he try confronting Gavin at a restaurant, *or* at his house, when he sees him every day at work? And three, confronting Gavin is one thing. Killing him is another. You can't really believe—"

"The evidence is there. The knife, the blood, the blazer. Gavin's phone in Jason's car. You can't keep ignoring it all."

"Why would he take Gavin's phone?" Sienna fires. "If he really killed him, why would he pick it up at all? Why not leave it with the body?"

"I don't know," I admit.

"And if he was getting rid of evidence, why would he trash the blazer but not the phone?"

"I don't know."

"And why would he wait till Sunday to throw it away? Gavin was killed on Friday."

"I don't know, Sienna. I don't know."

"That's because it doesn't make sense. He couldn't have—wouldn't have—done it."

She wants me to nod. Expects me to, I'm sure. Expects me to let her speak for both of us, because it's what I've always done.

Instead, I take a shuddering breath. "I still have a million questions, but . . ." I meet Sienna's gaze. "Jason did it. I truly believe he did."

Sienna squeezes her eyes shut, as if absorbing the shock of my conviction. I see the pain on her face, and I wish I could peel it off her, scrub it like dead cells from her skin. But that wouldn't be enough. Because beneath that pain, I see the flickering pulse of her fury.

"Wow," she says.

When she opens her eyes, she keeps them narrowed. "So, what'd you do, Jules? Since you *truly believe* he did it. Did you take that photo to the police?"

My hand tightens around my mug. "No."

"Oh, really? You didn't, say, show it to Wyatt last night?"

"No. I didn't see it until Aiden got back from—" I stop, the question fully registering. "Wait. How do you know I went to Wyatt's?"

I guess I shouldn't be surprised. She and Wyatt talk all the time, apparently.

"I saw you there. And I can't *believe* you would go to him without telling me first. Without warning me. I would have warned you, I would have done you that courtesy, if I had any reason to even be in the same neighborhood as one of your exes."

I huff out a breath. I was going to let it go—her lie about Wyatt; we have bigger issues at the moment. But her choice of words is insulting.

"The *courtesy*? Like you did *me* the courtesy of telling me you're back with Wyatt?"

"I'm not *back with him*. We just have sex. I've been very clear with him that it doesn't mean anything."

"Right," I say, not bothering to hide my sarcasm. "You still lied to me a hundred times about it. And for no good reason! It's not like I would have judged you for seeing him."

"*I* judge me for seeing him!" she bellows.

I glance at the ceiling, listening for the groan of Aiden's mattress. All morning I've been trying to be quiet, tiptoeing down the stairs, avoiding the creakiest steps. I haven't wanted him to lose a second of sleep—the one place where he doesn't have to endure our new, shared truth.

"That's not who I am," Sienna says. "I'm not the woman who lets people hurt her and keeps them in her life."

"Sienna, you're exactly that woman! Why else do you cyberstalk Clive, or drag me to his house to look in his windows? You can't bear to move on from him because then you wouldn't have that rage to hold on to anymore, and you *love* that rage because it's easier than pain."

Tears, big and abrupt, well between Sienna's lashes. She closes her eyes for a second, like clamping lids onto simmering pots. When she opens them again, the tears haven't dried or disappeared. They boil over onto her cheeks.

"That is so unfair," she says.

But I'm not done. "It's the same thing with Wyatt. You've been seeing him because you obviously still love him. But you keep your anger wedged between you, insisting it's 'just sex,' it 'doesn't mean anything,' because if you ever forgave him and got back together, you'd have to live with the fear of him hurting you again."

"That's—not true. And you're wrong, I don't love Wyatt. I'm just . . . used to him."

"Oh, come on! You're not just lying to me anymore. You're lying to yourself, too."

Sienna scoffs as she shakes her head. "Well, Jules, it's not like you've been honest with me either. You've known since *December* that Jason took money from your Europe account, but I only heard about it from Maeve." Fists balled, she crosses her arms. "You might *never* have told me, all because—how did you put it?—you didn't want me to think you and Jason were having problems? That's such a bullshit reason. I'm aware, you know, that no relationship is perfect."

"But you're not aware that Jason isn't." I take a deep breath, steeling myself as I admit the truth. "And that's the real reason I didn't tell you. Not because I didn't want you to know we had problems, but because of how you'd *react* to the problem. Jason's story was that someone had screwed him over on an investment, and I knew if I told you that, you'd become so obsessed with the injustice against him that you wouldn't even recognize how hurt I was. You'd seethe about this nameless bad guy, and you wouldn't once consider how *Jason* had actually been the bad guy, because it was *Jason* who betrayed me by taking that money."

"That's—that's not— I wouldn't just blindly take his side."

Air whooshes out of me, practically a laugh. "That's exactly what you'd do! You're doing it right now with him and Gavin! If the evidence the cops have against Jason pointed to anyone else, if it was any other man about to be arrested because the victim's blood was on his knife, you'd be positive he was guilty. But because it points to *Jason*, you just—disregard it?"

"Jason isn't just 'any man.' He's my brother. He's your goddamn husband."

"But he isn't perfect. And you have to see that. You have to stop *doing* this."

"Doing what?"

"Picking one view of a person and acting like it's set in stone. Wyatt drunkenly cheated on you, so he's the worst and you can't be with him, even though you still love him and you *want* to be with him."

"I told you, I *don't*—" Sienna starts, but I barrel through her protest.

"Jason's helped you through some really hard times, so you put him on a pedestal where he can't do anything wrong. But Wyatt, Jason—they're both just *people*. Which means they're more than one thing at once. Wyatt can make a colossal mistake *and* he can be the best thing for you. Jason can save you from Clive Clayton, save every single person he thinks needs his help, *and* he can end up hurting someone because he's taken that savior complex way too far."

"Savior complex?" Sienna narrows her eyes, her voice cold and slow. "You're really trying to spin Jason helping people into a *bad* thing?"

"It is if it means he gives Maeve money—money we've been saving for years—without even consulting me. And it's definitely a bad thing if it means he'd *kill* Gavin, over a *suspicion* that he hurt Maeve."

"Well, if you're so convinced it's a fucking complex, then maybe Jason was actually trying to *help* Gavin that night! Maybe he stopped by his house for some reason, found him already hurt in his back-yard, and maybe—maybe he tried to save him. Maybe *that's* how Gavin's blood got on all his stuff!"

"Sienna, come on!" This time it's me who bellows. "You need to stop with your ridiculous theories! Stuff like this, and Henry Hendrix—it's only keeping you from accepting the truth."

"Henry lied to the police about his alibi! He's *friends* with a Hill-stead cop—a cop who made it clear he didn't want me investigating him. Gavin Reed ruined Henry's life, only to turn around and do the same thing he ruined it over—which gives Henry plenty of mo-tive. And Jason talked to him the night Henry attacked Gavin at the restaurant, which has to be connected somehow. So the only thing ridiculous here is that, even after knowing all that, you're positive it was Jason who killed Gavin. God, Jules, I can't believe you'd betray my brother like this!"

"Yeah, well, he betrayed me first, multiple times. He took that money and then slept with the person he gave it to."

"But he wouldn't *kill*. And let me guess: When you were so upset about the ten grand, you didn't even tell Jason, did you? You just stuffed down your feelings."

I open my mouth to argue, but my response idles. She isn't wrong. After that night in December, I stiffened when Jason touched me, put space between us on the couch, in our bed, but I was careful not to mention the money. He didn't know how much he'd rattled my trust, or that, for weeks afterward, I studied the details of our other accounts until I knew them by heart.

"I . . . was distant with him," I finally reply.

"Distant. That's exactly my point. Your silence *is* distance, and I'm sure he felt it and hated it. So maybe if you'd actually talked to Jason about the problems you were having, you could've worked things out with him before he turned around and slept with Maeve."

Her last sentence stuns me. I blink at her as if she's just thrown water in my face. "Are you saying it's *my* fault Jason cheated?"

"No. I just know it can be hard to deal with, the way you keep everything all locked up. You didn't even give me a chance with the money thing! You kept it a secret, because it was easier to assume I'd hurt you with my response than to consider I might agree with you, that what Jason did was messed up. Because then you'd have to deal with talking to him about it. So instead, you refused to speak, just like always. You refuse to say anything a little bit hard, and then I have to—"

She cuts herself off, weighing whether to continue her thought. I lean into the counter, bracing myself.

"Do you know that I time your silences?" she says. "Three seconds. That's how long I wait until I speak for you. Not because I'm dying to be heard, but because I'm hoping you'll finally find your own damn voice before your silence becomes unbearable to every-one around you. But hey, I guess you did find it, huh?"

She sweeps her arm across the room, as if my *own damn voice* is everywhere, dripping from the walls, blood spatter from a terrible crime—but all I hear is the echo of hers.

Timing my silences? Unbearable to everyone around me? Her words hollow me out, my chest aching and empty at once.

"And that's great, Jules. I'm happy for you." As Sienna's voice breaks, the tears that fill her eyes look like shards of glass. "I just never thought you'd use your voice like this."

Tears sting me, too. All over my body, I feel sliced open, slashed apart. When Sienna lowers her arm, I see a flash of red in her hand, as if she's holding my wounds in her palm.

"What is that?" I ask, pointing to the dried blood.

She closes her fist. "Nothing." She wipes her tears with her knuckles.

"That's not nothing. Did you cut yourself?"

She shrugs—noncommittal, nonchalant.

"What happened?" I demand.

She sucks in her cheek, suppressing something. I'm about to call out her hypocrisy as she, too, refuses to speak, but then: she smiles. A slow spread of her lips. An oozing grin. An expression both villain-ous and victorious that makes me cold enough to shiver.

"I ran into Clive Clayton."

My eyes widen, a flare of confusion before I'm rerouted back to horror. "Oh my god, did you— Is that *his* blood?"

Sienna's smile instantly dissolves. "Seriously? No. It's mine. He was at Home Depot. He gave me some half-assed apology, said some bullshit things about Jason, and then I—I got so angry that my fingernail just— It—"

"You did that to *yourself*? Sienna!"

She opens her fist and raises her hand, showing me the cut more clearly. "You know what? I'm glad I did. It made me realize that I don't need your mantra. It's only ever held me back. And after I did this"—she turns her wrist to gaze into her palm—"I felt amazing. So I guess you were right about one thing, Jules. I *do* love my rage. Because look what it does for me: it makes me strong."

I shake my head, alarmed by the way she's talking, the speed with which she's spinning away from me—into dangerous territory. Today alone, she's stalked a suspect, sliced open her hand, and I'm worried, now, what else she might do, how far she'll go to confirm her belief in her brother.

For a moment, I can't look away from the blood. I don't see it the way Sienna does. I see only torn skin, broken vessels. I see suffering, not strength. And it scares me that our perspectives have skewed so far. Scares me, too, that she believes I've held her back.

But maybe, in a way, she's right. I always thought I was helping her—taking her hand, whispering words to dull her rage—but maybe I only kept her from becoming what she wanted to be: a bright and burning thing.

And every time she spoke for me, three seconds in or not, maybe she only made it harder for me to speak for myself.

"Maybe," I say, the word choked, "we've both been holding each other back."

Sienna drops her hand. "What?"

I can't bring myself to repeat it. And I can't take it back.

Sienna and I stare at each other, our faces rebounding shock, our eyes equally blurred by tears, and it's then that my phone rings, shattering our silence.

I have to blink several times before I can read the number. "It's the hospital."

Sienna lunges forward. "Answer it."

I bring the phone to my ear, force out a greeting. I try to listen to the woman's response, but my head feels fuzzy, my lungs tight, as if someone's holding me underwater.

"I'm sorry," I manage, "could you repeat that?"

As she speaks, I flash back to the call last week, the one about Jason's accident, the one that set this all in motion. I thought I knew, then, how thoroughly my heart could break.

"Okay," I say to the woman, finally understanding. "Yes. Yes, of course."

When I end the call, I meet Sienna's eyes, a glacial blue that should be cool, but has always burned like the center of a flame.

"They're bringing him out of the coma," I say.

Chapter Twenty-Two

SIENNA

It's a long time before we're allowed to see him, well into the afternoon. They have to run tests, let him rest, and it's almost unbearable—this long, final wait.

Upon arrival, we were intercepted by a nurse, who led us to the family lounge. "It'll be a little while. I'll come get you as soon as he's ready," she said, and I jumped on the phone with Lou. He agreed to make some calls, keep Beck and any guards from pouncing on Jason right away. That was hours ago, hardly the *little while* the nurse promised, and the entire time, Julia and I have occupied opposite sides of the couch, legs crossed away from each other, our silence like another person sitting between us.

Visitors have come and gone, plucking tissues from boxes, clearing their throats during calls. They made our quiet less loud. But we're alone now, and it seems like every time I breathe, the room shrinks or expands. Sometimes, it's too big for us. Other times, too small.

Julia looks hollow, merely a husk. But I am filled to the brim, emotions raging inside me. Fury, bewilderment, despair—all of it swirls around the same fact: Julia's made up her mind; she believes my brother's a killer.

But there's something else, too, a dark epicenter right above my heart.

Maybe we've both been holding each other back.

No other words have left me so devastated. They're worse than Wyatt's, when he confessed to cheating. Worse than the judge's, when he condemned Clive to only three years. Worse, even, than Julia's own: *Jason did it, I truly believe he did.*

It crushed me this morning, how different she was, just from yesterday. Her voice was firmer than usual. Faster. Like something had unclogged inside her. For years, I've waited for Julia to speak her truth. I just never imagined the words she'd say would hurt so much, or that the change would happen without me—as if I've been the one to plug her up.

I look at my hand, my cut cleaned and bandaged. Earlier, Julia gaped at it like it was gruesome, while I still saw it as beautiful, proof of my own power. Now, though, as I press my thumb against the gauze, I'm surprised to feel the wound beneath it throb.

A sound reaches us from the hall, the blunt padding of a nurse's shoes, and we snap our attention toward the doorway, tense with anticipation. When the nurse pops her head into the room, chirping, "You can see him now," we spring up in unison.

This is it. Jason will tell us everything. Julia will know how wildly wrong she was.

"He's alert enough to talk," the nurse says over her shoulder as we tail her down the hall. "Lucid, too; he's been asking about you both. But he's going to be weak, so we ask that you don't stay longer than fifteen minutes to start. And we'll need you to do your best not to agitate him."

Outside Jason's closed door, there's a tangle of suits and uniforms. Lou is here, speaking to Detective Beck, and behind them are two officers, hands on their holsters like they expect to burst into Jason's room and find him armed.

The sight of them flushes my face with heat. "Lou, you told me you'd hold them off."

He swivels toward me, offering a thin smile to Julia and the nurse before responding. "Detective Beck has agreed to let you visit with Jason before he goes in."

"Oh, you've *agreed*, have you?" I say to Beck. "How generous."

A muscle twitches in Beck's jaw. "We're not obligated by the law to wait."

"Well, were you obligated by the law to verify Henry Hendrix's alibi? Because you did a shit job of that. It took me two seconds to learn he lied to you. And you should know that Wyatt Miller is covering for him."

Lou jolts up a hand like a crossing guard. "Whoa, whoa, who's Wyatt Miller?"

"A Hillstead cop. My ex. He's helping Henry."

"Sienna, stop," Julia says behind me, touching my arm. "You don't know that."

I yank out of her grasp, whip around to face her. "Do *not* tell me what I know." I turn back to Beck. "Don't believe me? Ask Wyatt yourself. Go over Henry's alibi again. I don't know who the hell you checked with the first time, but it's all a lie."

Beck's face surprises me. He doesn't scoff at my claim, or roll his eyes, or even seem to dismiss it, the way I expect. Instead, he looks confused, almost troubled, as if he's actually considering what I've said. Over his shoulder, his officers exchange a glance.

"Uh," Beck says, and it's the first time I've seen him anything less than confident. "What did Miller say to you, exactly?"

My heart drops, even as it should feel bolstered.

Beck's question gives weight to my assumption—it *is* possible; Wyatt *could* be covering for Henry somehow. Even Julia seems to sense it. She squints at Beck, frowning.

At Jason's door, the nurse clears her throat. "Should we hold off on this visit?"

"No," Beck says, as if she'd been asking him. "No, you should both go in while I—" He turns and mumbles something to his officers, who nod and straighten. "I'll be back in a minute," he adds. Then he heads down the hall, pulling his phone from his pocket.

I look at the officers, shifting on their feet, aiming their eyes at the floor, before grabbing Lou's arm. "He's—he's taking me seriously! He's going to make a call."

Brows squeezed together, Lou watches Beck round a corner.

"You have to press him on this," I urge, "as soon as he gets back. This could be exactly what we need."

Lou pivots toward me, nodding. "I'll talk to him."

I let out a breath, my shoulders relaxing.

"Sienna, let's go," Julia says. She's beside the nurse, who's waiting for me, and her voice is flat, unmoved by my enthusiasm.

Still, when I look at her hand, dangling at her side, I see that it's shaking.

"Remember," the nurse says, "fifteen minutes to start, and try not to agitate him. If you need us for anything, we're just down the hall. Use his call button."

She opens the door, then gestures for us to enter before closing it behind us, keeping the officers out. I check over my shoulder, making sure she hasn't followed us in, and when I turn back, I'm stopped by the sight of Jason.

His eyes are tired but open. His bed is tilted up. His mouth holds a weary smile.

"Hi," he says.

I rush to him, and I'm surprised when Julia gets to his bed just as quickly. Relief dances on her face as she takes him in—alive, awake—and a smile of her own buds at the corner of her lips. Then, as Jason focuses on her, his gaze gentle with love, Julia's expression morphs into something harder, darker. A steel mask of dread.

I ignore it, sitting on the edge of Jason's mattress, taking his hand. For the first time in all our visits, his fingers respond to my grip—not squeezing so much as pulsing, but still: warm. Moving on their own.

Opposite me, Julia remains standing, keeping a distance that confuses Jason, his forehead rumpling like slept-in clothes, but I can't even care right now. Laughter froths up in me.

"You look like shit," I tell him. "But you're, like, the prettiest shit I've ever seen. I'm so happy I could smack you."

Jason attempts another smile. "Please don't." His voice is rough, grainy, like rocks scraping together. "I don't—" He winces as he shifts. "I don't know what happened. The doctors didn't tell me much."

"You had an accident," I explain. "And listen, the cops are here. They found a bunch of evidence in your car."

"Sienna," Julia hisses.

Jason tries to sit up straighter. "Evidence?" He blinks fast like he's coming out of a dream.

"They found—" I try to elaborate, but Julia cuts me off with a warning.

"The nurse said not to agitate him."

"She also said we only have fifteen minutes," I snap. "And I get that this isn't urgent for you, because you're sure the case is closed, but Beck is right outside with his fucking warrant, so we need Jason's side of the story, and then we need to fight for him. Or—I do, at least. You can do whatever the hell you want."

Julia stumbles back, as if I've pushed her.

"What—" Jason glances back and forth between us. "What's going on?"

I glower at Julia, daring her to stop me again, and it strikes me suddenly: Jason is literally between us, his bed a dividing line. All week, Julia and I have sat together on Jason's left, but now, she's poised on his right. Deliberately separate from me.

I clamp tighter onto Jason's hand. "The police found things they think link you to Gavin Reed's murder. His blood on your pocket-knife. His phone in your car. And they think you had opportunity because you were near—"

I don't want to say it, don't want to have this conversation with my brother, and despite my happiness at finally hearing him speak again, I feel a flicker of frustration.

"We know you were at Maeve's after the conference. We know you slept with her."

Julia tips her head back, glaring at the ceiling.

"What? No," Jason protests. "Why-why would you—"

"We found the email you wrote: *sorry about last night, it was a big mistake,*" I paraphrase, biting back my disappointment. At least when Wyatt cheated, he admitted it.

"No," Jason says, "that's not—"

"Jason. Don't. We talked to Maeve and she confirmed it, and I'm fucking furious about it, but we'll deal with that later. First—"

"She told us about the money, too," Julia interrupts—no longer concerned, it seems, about agitating him. Her voice is icier than I've ever heard it. It raises the hair on the back of my neck.

She crosses her arms, hiking her shoulders toward her chin. "Ten grand. The money you took from our Europe account."

Jason stares at her, face blank as he absorbs these things we discovered while he slept. Then—slowly, as if on a delay—his features warp with emotion, shifting between denial and devastation, his brow still wrinkled like he's trying to work something out.

Finally, he relaxes, his expression flattening with acceptance, and he drops his head against the pillow.

"Julia," he says. "You must be—" He stops to grimace, pulling his hand from mine to rub his temple, screwing shut his eyes.

"Should I get a nurse?" I ask, half standing from the bed.

"No," Jason groans. He opens his eyes, staring into Julia's with so much pain I almost call for someone anyway. "I did give that money to Maeve. But I—" He stretches out his hand, limply reaching for Julia, who holds herself back. "I didn't sleep with her. I *swear.*"

His last sentence is strangled and strained, more like a plea.

I glance at Julia. Her face is still stony, but her head is tilted in confusion.

"I don't get it—" I start, before Julia jumps in.

"Then why would she say you did?"

Jason leans back again, looking at the ceiling when he speaks. "She must be cover-covering for me." He swallows for what seems like a long time. I watch his throat bob in slow motion. "For what I did. At Gavin's that night."

Time stretches, liquid and languid. The temperature drops. Julia turns to look at me, but I'm still staring at Jason, waiting for him to clarify, waiting for him to walk his statement back.

"You were—you were at Gavin's?" I ask. "You were . . ." My sentence rolls away. "I don't understand."

Jason's gaze sinks to his lap. He studies his hands—empty, unheld.

"Gavin's an animal," he says.

Cold curls through me. My tongue feels frozen, stuck to the roof of my mouth.

"He makes . . . comments," Jason continues. "About women

he's dating. Women in the office. Treats our sales reps like, like frat brothers. And he was after Maeve. He cornered her in the warehouse. And when I heard about that, I thought of—" Jason looks at me, gaze murky, haunted. "Clive Clayton. In high school. The things he said about you."

Air catches in my throat. Clive talked about me? If Clive was boasting about me in locker rooms after that party, nudging his friends as I skirted past him in the hall, I suppose it makes sense that Jason wouldn't tell me. He'd want to protect me from that.

"Gavin in the warehouse—that was just words," Jason says. "But I know what words lead to. With men like him. I didn't want him to—to have, have the chance. That's why I gave Maeve the money." His eyes slide to Julia. "I thought if she could start her store— I knew I could— I was up for a pro-promotion. It would all be okay."

His sentences are brittle, each one breaking up like a bad phone connection. I'm not sure if it's exhaustion from the coma or effects from the meds they have him on, but I don't urge him to stop, don't warn him to take his time, and Julia doesn't either.

"But then you saw the withdraw-drawal," he says, still staring at his wife. "You wanted me to get the money back. I had to make you believe I couldn't. Maeve needed it more than we did."

In my peripheral vision, I see Julia stiffen. She knots her hands in front of her.

"I had to get her away from Gavin. Before he did worse. And I was still sure—with the promotion—" Jason shakes his head, the movement slight. "But Gavin gave that to someone else. And I didn't know how to tell you. You felt so . . . f-far away. But I know I was right to give Maeve that money. It was just weeks after the warehouse that Gavin did something to her."

Jason closes his eyes, resting for a moment. I feel Julia sneak a look my way, but I don't return it. I'm locked on my brother.

"She got drunk so fast. At our holi-holiday party. When I came out of the bathroom, I saw her through the window. Gavin putting her in his car—she was stumbling. Out of it. I thought, 'I can't l-let her be alone with him.' But then I—I thought of you, Julia. Counting on me, for that promotion. And I knew Gavin would—he'd be petty. Cross my name off if I intervened. And I hesita-tated too long. He drove away."

Jason lowers his gaze, burying it in the blankets. "I'd let it happen, I— Sienna." I startle as he says my name. "It was you and Clive all over again."

"Me and Clive?" I frown, inching closer. "You mean in high school? But that was nothing like Gavin and Maeve. You stopped Clive, remember? You saved me."

"No." Jason shuts his eyes again, harder this time, as if trying to wring an image from his mind. "That's not what happened."

I straighten, nerves sparking along my spine. It's the same thing Clive said to me this morning, eyes full of pity, right before blood pooled in my palm. I assumed he was lying, deflecting. But Jason's face is tight with certainty. And more than that: shame.

Nausea whirls inside me. My jaw clenches, as if guarding against the inevitable question, but I manage to push it through. "Then . . . what did happen?"

He's still shaking his head, fighting the memory, and for a moment, I don't think he's going to respond. Then he licks his dry, cracked lips, reels in a trembling breath, and exhales an answer: "I let him take you upstairs."

"You *what?*"

The question shoots from Julia's mouth, sharp as shrapnel. She's speaking for me, asking what I can't, because suddenly my throat is shrinking, my voice scuttling away.

"We got teamed up," Jason says. "Beer pong. He'd bare-barely spoken to me before. But he was being friendly. Inclu-cluding me in jokes. Then he started saying things. 'If I make this last shot'"—Jason pauses to swallow—"'I get to take your sister upstairs.'"

My heart riots—a fist against my rib cage, trying to break free.

"I thought it was a joke," Jason says. "I laughed it off. Clive was . . . popular. I was . . . me. But he made the shot. Said he was going to 'collect his winnings.' And I froze. Froze, again, when I saw him talk to you. Lead you upstairs. And it took me . . . too long, to go up to that room."

"*Why?*" The word has to claw its way out of me. "I couldn't even— Didn't you know I was drunk?"

Head tipping back, Jason chews his lip—the only answer he gives.

I hear his silence like a scream.

"Why did you let him do that?" I cry. "Why didn't you stop him?"

"I was stupid," he finally says. "I was a junior. He was a senior. I was worried I'd seem . . . uncool."

"Oh, Jason," Julia says, his name weighed down by disappointment and horror.

"Uncool?" I spit out. "He assaulted me!"

"I know. Trust me—I've thought about it. Ever since. Sienna, I'm so—I'm so sorry."

He says this to the ceiling. He can't even look at me.

Only—that's not true. He could look at me. He's tired and he's weak, but he's physically capable of pointing his eyes my way. His avoidance is a choice, and it leaves me untethered. No gaze for me to meet or hold. Nothing to keep me from spinning through a memory that's mutating with every turn.

For all these years, I imagined it like a TV show, the scene deceptively electric: bubbling voices, pulsing music, colorful lights. A good time. But then a hand reached through the crowd to tap

Jason's shoulder. *Hey, man,* someone said to him, *Clive took your sister upstairs, she looked pretty drunk.* As if burned, Jason leaped away, upending people's cups, their mouths slack with shock as he barreled through them, charged up the stairs two or three at a time. Then the scene switched, and I saw myself, pressed to the wall in a dark and disorienting room. I saw Clive, his hands hunting for something I didn't want to give. And I saw Jason again, blowing the door off its hinges, the light from the hallway like a halo around him.

But now I know: that was only fiction. And these are the facts: Clive singled me out as a prize he could win, and my brother said nothing. Clive snaked his arm around my waist as I stumbled up the stairs, and my brother watched, and said nothing. My brother waited then, long enough for Clive to kiss me, long enough for the kiss to turn sour, long enough for panic to bulge in my eyes. And when my brother burst through the door, he wasn't right on time.

He was almost too late.

I curl in on myself like somebody's punched me. I grip the blanket beside Jason's leg, a knot of cotton in my fist. I'm winded and whiplashed and trying to breathe, but the air feels like water—something to drown in. Everything's knocked off-kilter. The room is tilting, the bed is floating, my hands are empty, I'm anchored to nothing. Even Julia is so far away.

"I let him hurt you," Jason says, and my chest burns with held-in breath. "And that was all I could think, after I froze again, at the holiday party. I hesi-hesitated. Watched Gavin leave with Maeve. And I think he'd been waiting. Drugged her drink. Because she said she blacked out. Couldn't remember. No matter how many times I asked about it. For any scrap of mem-memory."

"Jason, that's so intrusive," Julia says, "to keep asking Maeve about something so personal. Something so potentially traumatic."

"And it killed me," Jason continues, as though he hasn't even heard his wife, "because if he did something to her, I could have stopped it."

Finally, I exhale, the sound as ragged as a sob.

"I started watching him," he continues. "Any time he got near her. But not just her. There was some bus-business dinner last week. A woman. He'd been bragging she was hot, was sure 'business would turn into pleasure.' So I sat at the bar at the res-restaurant. Watching. Making sure she was okay, that if he put something in her drink, I'd see it. Because then I'd know I was right. About Maeve. But—there was a fight. The night ended qui-quick."

I swallow. He's talking about the dinner Henry interrupted. That's why Jason was there. Not to confront Gavin, like Julia guessed, but to keep tabs on him. And more than that, it seems: to prove his theory.

"So after the conference," he says, "when I saw Gavin drive home with Maeve—"

"The conference?" Julia cuts in. "You mean the party, right? Gavin drove Maeve home after the holiday party."

"At the party, Gavin drove her home. At the con-conference, *she* drove Gavin home."

"Wait," Julia says. "That doesn't make sense. I talked to Maeve. She doesn't think he assaulted her, but she does think he's a creep. Why would she give him a ride?"

"He'd been drinking. At the dinner. A lot. He was planning to drive home. Drunk."

Now his gaze crawls toward me, heavy with the memory of our parents.

I drop my eyes to the bed.

"He wouldn't call an Uber," he continues. "Said he was fine."

"So *Maeve* took him home?" Julia says, still stuck on that detail. "Wouldn't people have seen Gavin leave with her? The cops haven't mentioned that."

"She was parked down the street," Jason says, still focused on me. "Left a little before him. I heard her say she'd wait for him, in her car. No one but me was listening. Watching. And this time, I followed. Had to make sure Maeve was safe. Had to *act*. Like I didn't at the p-party. Like I didn't, at first, with *you*."

I feel his stare like a sunburn. My fingers itch to peel it off.

"That's how— That's why it all happened," he says. "That's why . . ."

As he pauses, his gaze lasers deeper, until I think that even my bones are on fire. And I won't look back at him, I refuse to, because I know what he's about to say.

The room grows hazy with heat. It rushes over me, slickening my skin. The walls warp, wobbling like they're made of rubber. I clutch the bed tighter to keep from tumbling to the floor.

Jason's breath wheezes in the back of his throat, but his words are crisper than they've been since we arrived. They torch right through me, leaving no part of me uncharred.

"That's why Gavin died."

Chapter Twenty-Three

JULIA

It isn't Jason's words that gut me. It's Sienna's face.

I can read it in the pinch of her mouth, her blistering eyes: Sienna's clean, uncomplicated love for her brother is now irrevocably stained.

My instinct is to take her hand, but she's gripping the blankets so hard there's no room for my palm in hers. And I can't risk her seeing my touch as something it's not: *See? I told you so.*

Despite our fight this morning, the stance I took so starkly, I'm devastated to be right.

I look toward the door, wondering if the officers outside heard what Jason said, if these are the last seconds we have with him before they burst inside to arrest him for murder.

If so, I need to know more. Because even with Jason's confirmation, I can't understand how it all played out. Back in December, after I confronted Jason about our missing money, I didn't question the omissions in his story. I was too scared of his response, too scared of what the truth might reveal about him, about us—but my silence didn't serve me either. It still led me right here.

"How did it happen?" I ask.

"I lost Maeve's car," Jason says. "I'd parked on a differ-different street. Had to look up where he lived. Fig-figure out the route, before my phone died. So by the time I got to his house, they were alrea-ready around back. I heard voices. Heard Maeve say, 'Stop.' And I ran back there. Told Gavin . . . to get away from her. His hand. On her thigh."

The story stalls as Jason pulls in a labored breath. Then his mouth presses into a grim line, like he's bracing against pain. My eyes leap to his monitor. It displays two rows of numbers that, even after a week, still mean nothing to me.

"Jason, are you—" I start, but he forges ahead.

"Gavin said I was tres-tres-trespassing. Going to call the cops. But his phone was on the p-patio table. And I took it, before he could. Turned it off. Put it in my pocket. Forgot about it, com-completely. If the cops have it, it must've f-fallen out, later, when I took off my jacket. Blood on it. Had to thr-throw it away. Evi-evidence."

His eyelids droop as he stutters. Air rasps between his lips.

"Jason . . ." I check the monitor again. One number plummets. The other climbs.

"Gavin came af-after me. For his phone. Got aggre-aggresssive. I took out my knife—to hold him back. Let him know I was . . . se-serious. But he laughed. At me, he laughed."

"Jason." It's Sienna who says it now, concern about his choppy language, his near incoherence tugging her from despair.

"Then he ran at me. He—"

He's interrupted by a shrill beep from his monitor. Sienna and I bolt up from the bed, sharing a wild look.

"I didn't m-mean to, to st-stab him. Just wanted . . . take me seriously. Then I told M-Maeve to go. Drive away." His chest works hard to expand. His words wind down. Too slow. Too slurred. "Told her I'd t-take care of it. Him."

The door bursts open, two nurses whisking through it.

"Ladies, we need you to step outside," one says. She heads for me first. She guides me toward the exit, then swings back around for Sienna. When she has us corralled near the door, she presses on our backs to push us through it.

"But—" we protest, looking back at Jason, who's blocked by the other nurse.

"Outside," the woman repeats.

Then she shuts the door in our faces—the barrier not enough to keep us from hearing the shriek of Jason's alarm.

Panic pounds in my chest. We stare at the door, our noses only inches from the wood. And though things are messy between Sienna and me, raw and uncertain, the air feels so hazy that I fling out my hand to her—the same instant she gropes for mine—and it's like we're grasping for oxygen in a roomful of smoke.

When our fingers knot together, it feels more natural than breathing.

"Sienna," someone says, and when she doesn't respond, I turn to find Lou Ackerman behind us with Detective Beck, back from whatever call he hurried off to make.

"Not now," Sienna says, voice weary.

"Is everything all right?" Lou asks.

Sienna shakes her head, holding tighter to my hand.

I answer for her. "We don't know. Jason's monitor started beeping and—"

The door opens, the nurses emerging. I crane my neck to peer beyond them, and what I glimpse hollows me out: Jason's eyes are closed again; his head lolls toward his shoulder; his nostrils are plugged with tubes.

One of the nurses, the woman who led us here before, steps forward. "He's okay."

Sienna and I slump into each other, our shoulders pressing together, shoring us up.

"His oxygen level was down," the nurse adds, nodding a dismissal to her colleague. "And his heart rate was elevated—which isn't unusual in his situation."

"But he's okay?" I ask. I need to hear it again, my thoughts sprinting toward Aiden. I woke him before we left this morning, told him they were bringing Jason out of the coma, asked if he wanted to come. He said, *I'm not ready to see him*, and I'd allowed him his space—but what if that's all he'll have left of Jason now? Empty, endless space.

"He's okay," the nurse confirms. "We've got him on oxygen, and he's resting."

"Excuse me," Detective Beck says. He's trying to edge into the room, but the nurse—Diane, I read on her lanyard—puts her body in front of his.

"You can't go in there," Diane says, but Beck still tries to nudge forward.

"I've been held off long enough. And Sienna—" He turns to her. "I talked to Wyatt, who cleared everything up. I don't appreciate you badgering my officers for information, no matter what personal relationship you have with them. It seems you could have saved yourself, and me, quite a bit of time if you simply left the investigation to the police."

"What does that mean?" Sienna asks—but the fire's gone out of her. Whatever theories she came here with, they've blown away like ashes.

"Now, Mr. Ackerman," Beck says to Lou, "I'm sure you won't mind explaining to everyone"—he gestures to me, Sienna, Diane, encompassing the three of us with one lazy sweep of his hand—"that I have a right to serve the warrant."

He attempts another step into Jason's room, but Diane stands firm. "Do you typically serve warrants to people who are unconscious? We've given Mr. Larkin a sedative." She closes Jason's door, then pivots toward me and Sienna. "It's just to let him rest."

Beck throws up his hands. Frustration fumes off him as he backs up to pace the hall. I look at Sienna, expecting to find a flicker of triumph—Beck's been thwarted for now—but instead, she appears tortured, like she's waiting for a knife to slice into her, inch by unhurried inch. I squeeze her hand, reading the nuance of her expression. She finally understands that Jason's arrest is inevitable. And worse, so much worse: she believes now that it's justified.

"You're welcome to go back in," Diane says to me and Sienna. "He's sleeping, but if you just want to be with him, you can." She rests her palm on the door handle, the offer lingering.

Sienna's fingers unlink from mine. I study her face, watching the color drain from it.

"Are you all right?" I whisper.

There's a sheen of sweat on her forehead, and now she's clutching her collar like it's trying to strangle her.

"I can't," she says, and she spins around to run.

I follow without hesitation. Doors whiz by, the floor squeaks beneath our feet, and Sienna charges into the empty family lounge, where she puts her hands on her knees, gulping for air.

I place my hand on her back, which heaves beneath my palm as if she's retching. But the only sound from Sienna is the whoosh of her breath.

"I can't," she says again, hunching lower.

I hunch too, keeping my hand firm along her spine.

"I can't go in there again. I don't know how to sit with him. Or look at him. I don't know how to see the brother I loved."

Sienna pants, out and in so violently that my hand is almost pushed from her back.

The words slip from my mouth: "Cool your fire." I regret them instantly. Whatever thrashes inside her now, whatever keeps her gasping for air—it's all real, and warranted, and it shouldn't be stifled or extinguished.

"Sorry," I say, "you don't need to—"

"We've lost him." Sienna stands upright, forcing me to straighten with her. She spins around to meet my eyes. "We've lost Jason."

"No. The nurse said he's fine. That it's normal what—"

"I don't mean he's dead. Just—the brother I knew, the brother I thought I had, is dead. He watched Clive take me upstairs, even though he *knew* I was drunk! Just like he watched Gavin take Maeve home when she was blacked out. And he *killed* him, Jules!"

The last sentence fires from Sienna, a stray bullet ricocheting around the room. She recoils, as if feeling the kickback of it, a bruising punch to her body.

I feel it too—the impact of the accusation. I know what it's cost Sienna to say it, what she's lost of herself in the process.

"Let's just recap," she continues anyway, her voice hard. "From all his rambling at the end, this is what I got: Jason took Gavin's phone, Gavin got mad, went after him, Jason took out his knife to protect himself and ended up *stabbing* him. Then he told Maeve to leave so he could *take care of it*. Take care of it! Like the man bleeding in front of him was a spilled drink he had to clean up. And then we know exactly how he *took care of it*. He suffocated him. He—" She drops onto the couch, digging her forehead into the heels of her hands. "Oh my god, he sewed up his lips! *Why?* Why did he do that?"

She picks up her head, eyes expanding with horror, picturing it for the first time: Jason with the needle, Jason with the thread he wove in and out of Gavin's mouth, stitching it shut, an act of revenge against—what, exactly? The words Gavin once said to Maeve in the warehouse? Why did he bother with that final, gruesome step?

And where, during the panic of "taking care of it," did he even get the needle and thread?

In the cresting, overwhelming wave of all the evidence against him, the *why* of Gavin's stitched lips is a question I sidelined. Now it sticks in my mind, gumming up my thoughts.

"How could he do this?" Sienna cries. "Whoever that man is in there, back in that room, I don't know him. I can't—"

She's cut off by her own sob. She tilts her head back, as if trying to reverse her tears, even as they drip down her cheeks.

"All this just to soothe his own guilt! Over me and Clive. Over Maeve and Gavin at the holiday party. Oh, and let's not forget his reasons. He didn't intervene with me because he didn't want to seem *uncool*. And with Maeve, he didn't want Gavin to deny him a *promotion*. Such stellar motives! No wonder he stood back both times!"

It's jarring to hear her speak like this, critical and caustic, when it comes to Jason. But his confession shattered something inside her, hammered against the glass that's protected the picture of him she's held all these years, ever since he rescued her from Clive.

It's horrible to witness, the breaking of everything she believed in.

As tears slice down her face, I sit beside her. Her cheeks are drawn, her eyes narrowed, head shaking back and forth. I wrap my arms around her, and she's so rigid, her shoulders as hard as marble.

"You were right," she says, staring at the wall across from us. "You tried to tell me he did it, and I wouldn't listen. I excused every piece of evidence, even though *everything* pointed to him. I don't know why Henry Hendrix lied about his alibi, or why the hell Wyatt's protecting him, but *clearly* I was wrong; Henry, Gavin's deals, his goddamn cash in the gutter machine, had nothing to do with it. It was always Jason."

She pivots toward me, gaze wet and sorrowful. "You were right," she says again, her body softening a little. Then she rests her head against mine, curving her arm around my back until we're locked together. In an instant, tears pool in my eyes, spilling onto my cheeks.

There was a moment, this morning, as we sniped and snarled, threw flaws in each other's faces like grenades, that I worried we might never sit this close again.

"And I lashed out at you," she adds, taking my hand with her bandaged one, her fingers almost tentative as they slide between mine. "I said . . . awful things."

"You said true things, too."

Your silence is distance. You keep everything all locked up, refuse to say anything a little bit hard.

I should have known: even at my quietest, Sienna always heard me. Even when she couldn't make out the words, she could see them there, bulging in my throat.

"So did you," Sienna says. She pulls back a little to wipe her nose with her free hand, and I recognize the fear that wrenches her face.

Maybe we've both been holding each other back.

Is that one of the true things I said?

I look down at our hands. Our grip on each other is looser than usual. Our palms, untouching, cup a pocket of air.

"But hey—" Sienna says, forcing mock cheer into her voice. "At least we know Jason didn't actually cheat on you. At least he's *just* a murderer, right?"

She laughs, bitterly, before crumpling forward, collapsing into sobs. I rub her knuckles and don't bother to shush her, don't mutter soothing sounds. I let her cry, feeling each of her tearful gasps like a fist in my chest, pressed against my own pain.

It should be a comfort—the idea that Jason didn't cheat. It should probably unclench something inside me. But mostly, I'm confused. Why would Maeve tell us that, instead of what really happened? Why cover for Jason, if it meant spinning a scenario where she shared the blame?

"God, those *emails*," Sienna says. "*Sorry about last night, it was a big mistake.* Of course you assumed it was an affair; why would you ever think he'd write so casually about *killing* someone? And no wonder Maeve didn't want to talk to him—she'd seen him *stab a man* the night before, and then he was just like, 'Go home, Maeve, I'll take care of it!'"

Sienna lifts her head, tears shining on her cheeks. "And Gavin died from suffocation, not blood loss. Which means he was still alive when Maeve left. Which means when Jason emailed her the next day, talking about his *big mistake last night*, she probably didn't even know he'd killed Gavin. She probably thought he cleaned up his wound and left." Sienna bats at her tears. "It's so fucked-up."

I nod, slowly. But I'm only partially following Sienna's words, distracted instead by my memory of those emails. If I'm recalling correctly, it's another puzzle piece that isn't fitting the way it should. Just like Jason's insistence that Maeve drove Gavin home that night, or Jason's motive for stitching a dead man's lips.

I lean away from Sienna, pulling my phone from my pocket. To get to the screenshots we took of the emails, I have to bypass the photo of Jason's blazer, and I pause on it a second as Sienna peers at the screen.

"I know," she groans. "Even *this* wasn't enough for me. Because you were right, I've been so blind when it comes to—"

"No, look," I interrupt, swiping to the screenshots, then zooming in. "*I want to apologize again about what happened last night. And I need to know that you're okay. You're not answering my calls, so if I don't hear back from you soon, I'm coming over.*"

Sienna scoffs—such a small sound, but I still hear her tears in it; they thicken her throat, her voice, even the air between her lips.

"Yeah, great move, Jason," she says. "She's not answering your calls because she's fucking traumatized, so maybe leave her alone."

I nod again. But as I read Maeve's response, a chill crawls over my skin: *Don't come over. I told you when you left the house last night that you need to stay away from me from now on, and I meant it.*

I review it another time, silently, and I become so still that my body forgets to breathe.

Sienna flicks her gaze from the screen to my face, then back again. "What?" she asks.

I point to the line that's frozen me. *"I told you when you left the house last night that you need to stay away from me."* I look at Sienna, who still seems stumped.

"We assumed 'left the house' meant Maeve's house," I explain. "But she must be talking about Gavin's. Only—Jason said he told *her* to leave."

"It's probably a typo. She probably meant 'when I left.'"

"Maybe," I agree. "Or maybe she didn't leave when Jason told her to. Maybe she saw everything that happened."

Sienna frowns, wiping her nose again. "Does it matter?" she asks. "Jason confessed."

I give myself a moment before I answer, playing back everything he told us. Sienna's right; he did confess, more or less. Any prosecutor would probably be satisfied. Jason accounted for opportunity (he was there, in his boss's backyard) and means (his knife in Gavin's stomach). And even motive: he was desperate to rescue Maeve, whether she needed to be or not. Moreso, like Sienna said, he was desperate to rescue himself—from the guilt of his past, from the men he didn't speak out against, the women those men might have hurt.

Even still, there was one thing missing from his account of that night.

"He didn't say he killed him."

Sienna's brow wrinkles. "Yes he did."

"No," I press. "He didn't."

"He was talking about not helping Maeve at the holiday party," Sienna says, "not helping *me*, initially. And it"—she spins her hand through the air—"whipped him up into a frenzy when he saw Maeve drive Gavin home from the conference. He said that's why he killed Gavin."

"No. He never said, 'That's why I killed Gavin.' He said, 'That's why Gavin died.'"

Sienna frowns at me, considering my correction. "Okay, but—given everything else he *did* say . . . is there really a difference?"

My heart chugs in my chest, steady but insistent, because there might be. There might be.

"I don't know," I admit. "But I really think we need to talk to Maeve."

Sienna's lips purse in thought. "Okay." She reaches for my phone. "Let's call her."

Turning on Speaker, she holds it between us as it rings. Once. Twice. But the third ring is truncated, cut off mid-trill.

"She declined the call," Sienna says.

She tries again, jabbing Maeve's name on the screen. This time, it goes straight to voice mail, and I feel something harden like cement inside me.

I glance at the hallway, down which Beck is back where he started, waiting for Jason to wake. Except now he has the warrant he's been itching to serve.

I picture Aiden back home, his pain turned physical, cramping him into a fetal position as he replays our talk from last night, when both of us were convinced his father's a killer.

But there was so much, then, we didn't know. So much we still don't.

I spring up from the couch, tugging Sienna until she's standing too. "We need to go there," I say. "To Maeve's house. Now."

Chapter Twenty-Four

SIENNA

As Julia rings Maeve's doorbell, the cut beneath my bandage pulses with pain.

Maybe I didn't clean it right. Maybe I'm headed for infection. Either way, the pain has a crooked rhythm, a beat as erratic as a broken heart.

Half a minute passes, no answer at the door, no footsteps inside. I lean over the porch railing, trying to peer into Maeve's window, but gauzy curtains obscure my view.

"What do you want to do?" I ask Julia—because this was her plan. I don't blame her for teasing out the details, analyzing each word her husband said, but I've been looking for loopholes all week, testing out theories that absolve my brother of guilt, and today, Jason proved me wrong—in such unbearable ways.

"You lookin' for Maeve?" a voice calls to us. On the tiny lawn of the adjacent town house, a woman pats down soil in a flowerbed. "She left about an hour ago."

"Do you know where she went?" Julia steps forward to ask.

"Nope. She had a bunch of moving boxes and painting supplies, though. If that helps."

"Oh—thanks," Julia says. Then she frowns at me: "Moving boxes?"

I shrug. "Maybe she's bringing stuff to her store?"

Julia's eyes brighten. She snatches my bandaged hand. "Let's go."

As she hustles down the porch steps, I don't share her urgency, but I feel something glow inside me, warming the places that Jason's left cold: right now, it's the two of us again—heading somewhere together.

"Where did Maeve say it was?" Julia asks. "Near the Barnes & Noble?"

"Yeah, in a strip mall. Next to a yoga studio, I think."

We get there quickly, breezing through green lights, slanting sharply through turns, and when Julia pulls into the parking lot, it's easy to identify which store is Maeve's. The others have signs, decals, neon OPEN lights, but Maeve's door, still months from welcoming the public, is blank.

Before I've even snapped off my seat belt, Julia's out of the car.

"Maeve!" she calls, knocking on the glass door.

Inside, Maeve turns, a paintbrush in her hand. She doesn't seem surprised to see us. Instead, her expression is odd: a mix of relief and impatience, as if we're late to a party she's throwing. Still holding her brush, she heads to unbolt the door.

After she opens it, she flicks her gaze between us. "He woke up?" she asks.

Julia's nod is curt. "He woke up."

Maeve steps aside, and we file into the store—a small, nondescript space with stained industrial carpet. It's mostly empty, except for Maeve's painting supplies and some boxes, one of which is open, revealing stacks of her totes. One bag in particular, embroidered with intricate ivy, rests on the floor, as if Maeve held it up to the wall, imagining how it would look on display. The walls themselves are a dingy white, but the one Maeve walks to now is splotched with different colors: lavender, light blue, forest green.

"You're painting?" I ask, uselessly, my mind still fuzzy, half of it back at the hospital.

"Color swatching." Maeve dunks her brush into a cup of water on the floor. "It's early for it, but I was struck this morning with all these ideas, and I thought, 'Why not? Why not today?'"

"Why did you ignore our calls?" Julia asks.

Maeve tilts her head. "You called? I'm sorry—the service is spotty here. But tell me about Jason." She crouches to fill a tray with another color, a red so thick and vivid I can't help but think of Jason's knife in Gavin's stomach, his blazer spotted with blood. "Is he okay? Is he"— she sets down the paint can, reaches for a fresh brush—"lucid?"

"More or less," Julia says.

"Oh, thank god. I didn't want to say this before, but I was worried about memory issues. You see these horror stories on TV, and brain injuries are so scary. But that's great. Although—did the police arrest him? I know you said they have a warrant."

"Not yet. The nurses had to sedate him." Julia pauses, watching Maeve closely. "But before that, he told us some things."

I can't help but scoff. Maeve looks up at me, her face quizzical.

"No, just—" I start to explain. "Jason being a killer is hardly 'some things.'"

Julia is close enough to swat my thigh, a gesture Maeve notices, despite how quick and slight it was. Still crouched, she lingers on me and Julia, on the space between our hands.

"Wait, so . . . he confessed?" Maeve asks. "To killing Gavin?"

"More or less," I say, borrowing Julia's phrase, bitter between my lips.

Maeve stares at us, mouth open, eyes still and glassy as a doll's.

As if this is news to her. As if she saw Jason stab a man but never concluded he proceeded to kill him.

"Oh, come on," I say. "We know you saw at least some of what happened."

Maeve's mouth snaps shut. With some effort, she swallows, lowering her head. Then she turns her attention to her brush, which she dips into the red paint. As she stands, she sneaks a glance our way. "I take it Jason told you we didn't really sleep together."

"Was that the truth?" Julia asks.

Maeve drags the brush down the wall, making a mark the size of a cell phone. Julia's jaw is steely as she waits for Maeve's answer.

"Yes," Maeve admits, scrutinizing the paint. "I never would have slept with Jason. And even if I wanted to—which I didn't—he never would have cheated on you. Not in a million years. Honestly, I was surprised you believed it so readily."

Irritation flares beneath my skin. "Of course she believed it, Maeve—you had a whole fucking story. Showing Jason the plans for your store. Kissing him. Fucking on the couch. Who makes up something like that?"

But as I say it out loud, I hear how insubstantial the story really is, how it relies too much on clichés—the sudden, unexpected kiss; the sex so urgent they can't even make it to a bed. Even Maeve's reason for Jason being at her house is stupid. Wouldn't the designer have sent the plans via email? Couldn't Maeve have accessed them on her phone? The whole explanation was sloppy from the start, but we believed it, of course we did, because who would fabricate a story where they're one of the villains?

"Why did you even—" I start, but Julia touches my hand, stopping me.

"Jason also told us," she says, "that you drove Gavin home from the conference."

It's almost imperceptible, the way Maeve's brush stutters. But when she draws back from her second red stroke, the swatch has an errant edge, a notch that exposes an unsteady hand.

"Why would you do that?" Julia asks. "I get that you didn't think Gavin assaulted you, but still—he did that disgusting thing in the warehouse."

Maeve doesn't answer. She only dips down to swish her brush in water before setting it back on the tray.

"And you weren't *positive*," Julia pushes, "that nothing happened after the holiday party."

Maeve snaps upright. "That's exactly the reason. Because I wasn't positive. Because Jason had shoved the idea down my throat, even when I told him to stop."

"Wait," I say. "Shoved it down your throat?"

Maeve crouches again to pick up her brush, and as she whips it toward the wall, she spatters the carpet with bright red drops. "For weeks after the party, he harassed me. 'What happened, Maeve? Have you remembered anything? What about cuts and bruises—did you have any of those?' I told him to stop. I told him nothing happened. But every few days, he'd bring it up again at work, this sad, droopy look on his face: 'Hey, Maeve, uh, did you, uh, remember anything yet?' He just wouldn't take no for an answer."

Something dark and sticky stirs inside me—a hot, swirling tar. *Harassed me, wouldn't take no for an answer,* as if Jason's questions were their own kind of assault.

"I told you, Julia." Maeve slashes the wall again, a third swatch of red. "It freaked me out. It kept me up at night. I'd have nightmares where Gavin was . . ." As she trails off, she shakes her head, adding another streak, a thick tally mark. "So at the conference dinner, when I saw Gavin getting wasted, brushing his hand against the waitress's ass, telling her and me and basically every other woman he saw that they should come to his lake house after—which no one had any desire to do—I saw an opportunity. Because I couldn't exactly confront my boss at the Marriott. But I *could* act like I wanted to go home with him. And when I got there, I could get him even drunker, get his defenses down, ask him about the night he took *me* home. Silence Jason's question for good."

"Okay," Julia says. "That sounds like . . . kind of a risky plan, though."

Maeve whirls back to her, and when the paintbrush catches my eye, my mind lurches toward Jason again. The knife dripping with Gavin's blood.

"I had it under control," Maeve says. "*I* was in the driver's seat—literally. And when we got to his house, I made sure we never went inside. I wasn't going to let him corner me, have a repeat of the warehouse. I told him I wanted to sit outside and enjoy the view of the lake. So we went to the patio, and I set my phone to record the whole thing, in case he admitted it. In case he gave me something I needed to take to the police as proof. And I crept toward the question: 'The night of the holiday party, it's a little fuzzy to me, but we had fun, didn't we?' He just kind of laughed in response, but I knew I was close."

"But something went wrong," I say, my voice thick. "Jason said he heard you tell Gavin to stop, and that's why he came to help you."

"*Help* me?" Maeve's eyes flash. "I didn't need his help. Gavin kept putting his hand on my thigh, but he was wasted, his eyes were practically crossing—he wouldn't have had the coordination to over-power me. But then Jason grabbed Gavin's phone and took out his fucking knife. Which Gavin thought was hilarious. And when Gavin launched at him to try to get his phone back, he— I don't know. It was so fast. They struggled a little, and then there was just"—she looks at her paintbrush, face appalled, as if finally recognizing the color—"all this blood."

She drops the brush onto the tray, where it lands with a clack, leaving a red spritz on the plastic. I close my eyes, seeing Jason's blazer.

"And then he told you to leave," I force out. Even after hearing the story from Jason himself, it doesn't feel real. Maeve's version confirms that the cut on Gavin's stomach was an accident, but: "He told you he'd take care of it." Which led to suffocation, stitching—acts that could only be on purpose.

Disgust warps Maeve's face, her mouth pulling back into a sneer. For a few moments, she holds it there, as if stuck in the memory. Then, unfreezing, she nods. Slowly. Carefully.

Then she closes her lips, creating a tight seam.

I almost jolt at the gesture. It's one I know so well, one I've seen Julia do thousands of times. But right now, Julia's lips are parted, her eyes slitted with suspicion as she watches Maeve keep something back.

"Why didn't you tell us this on Friday?" Julia asks. "Why make me think my husband cheated?"

"Right," I say, backing her up. "Why didn't you just tell us what really happened?"

As I ask it, though, I know I wouldn't have believed her, even if she had. Words, a story, would have never been enough for me, not when I was already ignoring evidence and facts.

Maeve crosses her arms, drumming her fingers against her bicep. "You assumed there was an affair because of the emails. So I went with it. Because what would have been worse? Breaking your heart with infidelity, or by telling you your husband was guilty? It's a decision I made in the moment, and I did feel awful for hurting you. But the alternative would have hurt more."

"Those emails, though," Julia says. "You told Jason he needed to stay away from you."

"Well, yeah. Why would I want him anywhere near me after he killed someone?"

Julia and I look at each other, and I see it in her eyes: we're making the same calculations. As I turn back to Maeve, the acid in my stomach heats up.

"But Jason told you to leave, right?" I try to keep my voice even. Cool. "After he cut Gavin. He said he'd take care of it, and you left. So how did you know when you wrote the email on Saturday that Jason had killed Gavin . . . if his murder wasn't reported until Sunday?"

One of Maeve's arms drops, the other still crossed in front of her like a safety bar. "I mean, I guess I just assumed that's what he'd . . ." She lifts one shoulder, a casual shrug.

"You assumed 'take care of it' meant killing him?" I ask. "Instead of, like, tending to the wound?"

Maeve's mouth closes. She pushes her gaze toward the wall. "I don't know, I—"

"And another thing," Julia says. "Jason said he told *you* to leave. But in your email, you said, *I told you when you left the house.* So . . . who left first? Him or you?"

Maeve digs her teeth into her bottom lip, staring at the swatches of color, the single stroke each of lavender, light blue, green. The overabundance of red.

"I left first. I must've made a mistake in the email."

The heat inside me spreads. She's lying. I sense it in the slant of her eyes, angled firmly away.

"Are you sure about that?" I ask.

I step toward her, close enough to see a speck of paint on her cheek, a drop of blue, like a drawn-on tear. Even still, Maeve skirts my gaze, her own skittering around her store before landing on the single tote bag on the floor. I lock onto it, too—its elegant design, its vibrant colors.

Its intricate stitching.

My breath hitches. My words fall out in a whisper: "You sewed Gavin's lips."

Julia grabs my hand, and I grip hers back.

We watch Maeve's mouth seal shut. That skillful, perfect seam.

It's a long time before she looks at us. The accusation hangs in the air like smoke. But when she finally turns her head our way, the answer blazes on her face. She doesn't look guarded or cornered. Doesn't even look caught. She's glaring at me with an anger so vivid, so familiar, it's like staring into a mirror.

"I wouldn't have done it," she says, "if it weren't for your brother. Everything that happened that night—it's all because of Jason. I had a plan. I had it under control. And I'd told Jason to stay out of it. But as soon as he heard me offer to drive Gavin home, he yanked me aside, insisted that Gavin would hurt me, and I told him to back off, I could take care of myself, because what about how *Jason* had hurt me? Not just hounding me about the holiday party, but the way he'd scurry over to tell me every sick little thing Gavin said in those sales meetings, as if I could fix it for him. But I wasn't in those meetings! The time to fix it was *there*, in the moment, in that room. But when I asked him why he never told Gavin to stop, he said, 'It's awkward, he's my boss, I'm worried I'll seem too difficult.'"

The sentence almost flattens me. I recognize its rhythm, a close replica of another Jason said: *I was a junior, he was a senior, I was worried I'd seem . . . uncool.*

My heart hammers. The cut on my hand throbs.

"Just think about that a second," Maeve says. "Jason would rather be complicit in Gavin's behavior—which created a hostile environment for any woman who worked for him—than risk seeming *difficult*. He'd rather give me ten thousand dollars to help me get away from Gavin than actually talk to his boss about his actions."

Maeve scoffs before she continues. "And yeah, I took the money; this store is my dream, and I had every intention of paying it back. And even though it bothered me, the way Jason acted—or didn't act—with Gavin, I still considered him a friend. But then the party happened. And the hounding. And the nightmares. Then, as soon as I'm ready to take matters into my own hands, Jason can't have that. He follows me to Gavin's. He leaps out like some white fucking knight, wielding a *knife*, and ends up stabbing him. And then he has the audacity to tell *me* to leave, that *he'll* take care of it. But I hadn't gotten my fucking answer from Gavin yet. So I demanded that Jason leave. I told him to stay away from me for good, that for months all he'd done was make things worse, and I didn't need him—not now, not like this; the time when he could've helped had come and gone and he'd done *nothing*."

Maeve laughs, icy and humorless. "You should've seen his face after I said all that. He slinked back to his car, all wounded. Meanwhile, Gavin was still *bleeding on the ground*, so I bent over him to check he was okay, and then he—" She pauses, raising her hand to skim her knuckles across her lips. "Then he reached up, blood on his palm, and tried to kiss me."

"*Kiss* you?" I spit out—an involuntary response.

Maeve nods, her gaze growing distant. "I pushed him back down. And then he said—" She stops again, grimacing like she's going to be sick. "*Aw, come on. You liked it last time.*"

I suck in a breath, instantly queasy. Julia clasps my hand tighter.

"It was as good as a confession," Maeve says, before mimicking him again: "*You liked it last time.*" She stares at the wall as she speaks. "It was enough for me to know he'd done something to me the night of the party. And I was . . . shocked. Couldn't even move. But then he said"—her lips pull back in disgust—"'We both know you wore this dress for me tonight.' And that was it, I couldn't let him speak again, couldn't let him say another thing I'd probably never get out of my head. So I put my hands over his mouth, and I don't know how long I held them there—it must have been a while, a long while, I must have been pressing so hard, but I— I don't even remember him struggling. In my memory, it's just that sentence, over and over: *You liked it last time, you liked it last time.*" She trails off, shaking her head. "When I took my hands away, his mouth was still open. Gaping at me. As if, at any moment, he might say something else. And I thought of all the other things he'd said—to me in the warehouse; to men in meetings; to countless women, I'm sure—and then . . . I thought of the sewing kit in my bag. The needle and thread I bring everywhere."

My stomach sloshes.

I hold my fist to my mouth.

I'm overcome by horror. Not only of these images—Maeve's hands, Gavin's mouth, first smothered, then sewn—but of Gavin's words, too: *the last time*, vague as a drunken memory, specific enough to incite such fear, such rage in Maeve.

Next, I feel a surge of bitterness. For more than a week, Maeve has kept this from the police. She lied to them, lied to us, let Jason remain a suspect.

And yet, beneath that bitterness there's relief, a rush so powerful it nearly collapses me. Jason didn't kill Gavin. He made terrible choices, he hounded Maeve, he stayed silent when he should have spoken—but he's innocent, at least, of murder.

I take out my phone, turning to Julia. "We have to call the police. Let them know Jason didn't kill him."

"You can't do that," Maeve objects. "Haven't you been listening? Jason started this. And he escalated things with the knife. Things I had *under control*. If you tell the cops, you won't be saving Jason. He still stabbed Gavin, whether he meant to or not. He'll still be arrested. Assault with a deadly weapon."

My thumb lifts off the phone screen, my pulse ticking in my throat.

"And Sienna," Maeve pushes, "look where we are." She sweeps her arms around her store, its walls blank but for the swatches of paint, like an idea still forming. "I'm so close to having what I've always dreamed of. You're going to let *Gavin Reed* take this from me? After everything he already took? Jason says you get so angry about every injustice. Well, doesn't that count, Gavin assaulting me? Isn't that an injustice, too?"

It is. I know it is. Heat prickles the back of my neck, thinking of Gavin. Because fuck him. He brought this on himself. If he didn't want a woman to take his life in her hands, he shouldn't have toyed so viciously with hers.

In another situation, that might be reason enough for me to keep quiet.

But if I do, then it's Jason who takes the fall. And despite how disturbed I am that he did nothing, did nothing, and then did too much—terrifying Maeve with questions, probing her for information she had no obligation to give—I'm still at the place I started last week, unable to let my brother go down for a murder he didn't commit.

Maeve's right, though. If Jason had acted earlier, none of this would have happened at all.

Indecision wrestles inside me. There's no perfect answer. Blame and guilt are so tangled here that it's hard to see which strand of it belongs to whom. And suddenly, I feel so weary. For too many years, I've housed a well of rage in my body, and I've never let it run dry, not when it boiled over, boiled me up, not when it left me sizzling and scarred. I believed my anger was the same as action, as if I could redirect the course of justice with the strength of my rage alone.

I obsessed over Clive, furious he took my parents from me and now is one himself. But what do I want? For his daughter—who squeals as he tickles her in videos, who laughs as he tosses her in the air, who's innocent in everything Clive did—to lose her parent, too? See him locked away in prison, the way I've always wished?

I punished Wyatt—with distance, with mixed messages, because I couldn't bear to believe that someone good could do something bad, that he could fuck up a love that had felt infallible and still be a kindhearted man.

But people do that, I guess. They fuck up. They do bad things they can't take back. Maybe what really matters is whether or not they wish they could.

I look at Julia, the person who sees me clearest, who's always recognized my clenched fists as the lit matches they are. That's why she made me a mantra; she knew that, otherwise, I'd let my fire consume me, let myself burn away to ash.

What was it she said this morning? *You have to stop doing this, picking one view of a person and acting like it's set in stone.* I balked at it then, but she was right. And now nothing feels set; everything is shifting. Everything is so many things at once.

My eyelids droop, my hand still stinging with the wound I inflicted on myself. I've been so righteous, so angry, for so long now, and I didn't realize until just this moment how much energy that's taken from me.

It's wrung me out, wanting black-and-white justice in a world so full of gray.

Maeve clocks my hesitation. "The truth hurts Jason, too!" she says, desperately repeating a previous point, the one she thinks will spear me most. "But if you tell the cops about me, it would be *you*, his own sister, giving them reason to convict him."

Once again, I look to Julia, who nods at me gently. The tiniest nudge. It's been minutes since she's spoken, but she isn't silencing herself. She's been giving me space to make this choice—a clear choice, the only choice—because she knows I needed this moment to waver, knows it's about more than the guilt or innocence of Jason and Maeve.

"It's not up to me," I say, unlocking my phone, "to decide what happens to you, Maeve. Or what doesn't." I bring up the number for the Hillstead PD. "But the truth still matters."

As I connect the call, Julia nods again, gaze shining with tears I feel in my own eyes.

"Even if it implicates my brother."

Chapter Twenty-Five

JULIA

When I finally make it home again, stars stipple the darkness, reminding me too much of pinpricks, needle pricks, as if the night is a gaping hole someone's tried to sew shut.

I smell like the police station—coffee and stale rooms. Sienna and I were interviewed separately, Lou Ackerman ferrying back and forth between us, Detective Beck shuffling papers, slurping from Styrofoam cups, clearing his throat into his fist. The whole time, Beck seemed unhurried, uncomfortable, like he was hoping we might reroute the narrative to the one he preferred.

Now, entering our family room, I find Aiden on the couch, loosely strumming his guitar. He sets it aside, then scooches over, wordlessly inviting me onto the space beside him.

"What happened?" he asks. I texted him from the station, warning him it would be a while before I'd be back, but I'd kept the message light on details.

I settle onto the couch, which is so much softer, more forgiving, than the hard-backed chairs in the interview room.

"Dad's doing okay," I start. "We were able to talk with him a bit, and . . . Auntsy and I learned so much today, Aid. But the most important thing is—" I take a second to savor the news I get to share: "Dad didn't kill Gavin Reed."

Aiden twists toward me, his knee jabbing my leg. "Wait, are you serious? Even with the— He's actually innocent?"

The hope on his face deflates me. Because no, Jason isn't innocent, even if he isn't guilty in the way we thought. I wish I didn't have to explain it, all the nuance and new details. I wish we could curl up on this couch together, blanket ourselves until morning, and not say anything at all. There's something so safe in that—in simply not speaking—and it's why, despite everything, I understand my husband, the man who stood silent at parties, silent with men in meetings.

But silence can be harmful, too, and I know, without any lingering doubt, that telling Aiden everything is the right thing to do.

I don't leave anything out. I mention the money Jason stole from our account, the truth of the argument Aiden overheard in December. I even tell him about the party, years ago, where Jason watched a senior boy lead Sienna upstairs—because, in so many ways, that moment was the trigger to everything else Jason did.

As he listens to it all—Jason's obsession with Gavin, his hounding of Maeve, the ways Jason failed the woman he called his friend— Aiden's jaw shifts up and down, like he's chewing his own tongue.

"And I talked to our lawyer," I say at the end. "It's very likely that, even if Maeve confesses, Dad will still face charges."

When Lou named them at the station, I should have felt relieved—anything's better than a murder charge. But mostly, I felt removed, like I was watching a show on TV.

"At the very least, there'd be an assault charge," Lou said. "Maybe second-degree, maybe third. If it's third, it's a misdemeanor. Then there's obstruction of justice. False statement and withholding information—he was previously questioned, along with everyone else at Integrity Plus—and that could be anything from gross misdemeanor to mid-level felony."

"Meaning?" I asked.

"I'll work to get the charges reduced as much as I can, but with all of that together"—Lou's pause sapped the air from the room—"it's possible he'll see some prison time."

My tears were hot and sharp, stinging like splinters in my eyes. They snapped me into my reality: my husband could be going to jail. That possibility has taunted me all week, a shadowy, peripheral fear, but I never looked at it too closely; I'd spent the days more concerned with who my husband is, what he's capable of, than what I might do if he's gone.

As I relay Lou's words to Aiden, I wait for his reaction. But his face has gone blank, a concrete expression that does not crack.

I continue. "Maybe this is the wrong time to say this, but honey, if you ever see something, like your dad did at that party—both parties, actually—or if anything ever looks off to you—"

"I know, Mom. I wouldn't just stand there. I'm better than that." His words whip out in anger, but his voice is thick, as if he's holding back tears. He looks up at the ceiling, eyes glassy, and he swallows. He shakes his head and scowls.

When he was a child, he used to cry so easily—at movies, at bad dreams, at a rip in his favorite shirt. I never stopped to note the last time it happened, the last day he shed tears over something fictional or fixable. It seemed he would always be that way—my sweet, sensitive boy—but now I watch him twist his face, squeeze in a breath, shred himself to pieces inside to try to seem whole. I feel how much it hurts him, as if his muscles, his nerves, live inside my body, the way they did when I carried him, basically a child myself, with so much left to learn.

"You can cry," I say softly.

He closes his eyes. His throat bobs again and again.

"You can." I slide closer to him, put my hand on his shoulder. "Aiden."

I take his chin between my thumb and forefinger. I tilt his head down, hoping he'll open his eyes and meet my gaze. But he keeps them shut.

"What's going to happen to our family?" he whispers.

I pause, unprepared for that question. I know he means all four of us—me, him, his father, Sienna. I don't know what's going to happen to Jason and me, how we'll repair our trust, how we'll say all the things that need to be said—but even more, I don't know what will happen to me and Sienna. There hasn't been time, yet, to discuss what I said to her this morning: *Maybe we've both been holding each other back.* It hurt so much to speak those words, but it hurts even worse now, knowing that neither of us have denied them.

I stroke Aiden's cheek, answering him as truthfully as I can: "I'm not sure, hon. But Dad and I love you. So much."

A tear slips from Aiden's lashes and onto his cheek. His lip quivers.

"It's okay to cry," I remind him. "Crying's important."

Finally, his mouth splits open with a sound that startles me, like he's choking and gasping at once, losing air and gaining it at the very same time.

It's a primitive sound, one that resonates inside me. Its vibrations knock my own tears loose. And when Aiden topples forward, then crashes into me, I catch him. I cradle him in my arms, smoothing his hair with my palm, and we cry together—for Jason, for our family, for everything we each have lost.

. . .

It's the next afternoon, as Sienna drives us to the hospital, that we learn Maeve confessed.

"Cell phone data puts her at the scene," Lou tells us, voice tinny over Speaker. In the back seat, Aiden leans forward. "They recovered the recording, too."

"What's going to happen to her?" Sienna asks, face taut as she stares at the road.

"I imagine she'll make bail," Lou says. "Maybe get her charge reduced to manslaughter."

"Do you think she has a case for self-defense? Gavin tried to kiss her. He implied he'd assaulted her before. I know she didn't need to . . . smother him, but . . ."

As she trails off, I'm proud of her for even asking these questions. A week ago, if she'd learned that Maeve had been willing to let Jason take the fall for a crime she committed, Sienna's rage could have powered entire cities. But now I see in her squinted gaze the facts she's trying to balance: the ways Maeve was harmed by men, and the ways she harmed them back.

"Uh, I don't know," Lou says. "If she'd called the police the night it happened, maybe. But she waited a week. That's obstruction of justice, a whole other charge."

Sienna and I exchange a weighted glance. That's one of the charges Lou told us Jason would likely face.

"What about Jason?" I ask, looking at Aiden, who's perched so far forward in the back seat that his head is in line with mine. "What's going to happen to him?"

"Well," Lou says. "That's the other reason I'm calling."

. . .

By the time we arrive at Jason's room, his arrest has already been made. Assault. Obstruction of justice. False statement. Exactly as Lou said.

On the surface, it doesn't change anything. Jason's still in his bed. An officer is still outside his door. But there's a new soberness to the room, different from the anxiety that's hovered here all week. It's a funereal air, even as Jason's improving, his cheeks more pink than yellow, his voice smoother, like it's been polished overnight. For a while, we stumble through small talk—the temperature in the room, the night nurse's clammy hands—and when a different nurse comes to check Jason's vitals, we fall into a silence so heavy that the woman, clearly embarrassed for us, smiles at the awkwardness, humming as she leaves.

Finally, I ask something that's been bothering me. "Where did you go after Gavin's that night?"

The police made so much of Jason's timeline, but in the end, the story of Gavin's murder didn't explain why it took Jason three hours to get home from the conference.

Jason hesitates, eyes filled with apprehension. "Does he know what happened?" he asks, nodding toward Aiden while staring at me, like he can't bring himself to look at our son.

"Yeah, I know everything," Aiden says, and I reach out to rub his back, loving him so much for answering on his own.

Jason nods, solemn, but less ashamed than I'd expect. "I went to Integrity Plus," he answers me, "to use the phone. Mine was dead, but I needed to know that Maeve was okay. I left her a message, telling her I'd stay at the office for a while so she could call me back there. Because when I left Gavin's, she spoke to me like *I* was the monster, but— I needed her to understand. I'd only wanted to protect her. That's why I was there that night in the first place, it's even why—" He coughs, weakly. "The accident. I remember it now. For days, she still wouldn't talk to me. By Sunday night, I knew she'd killed him. And I had no intention of turning her in. But she wouldn't even look at me at work. Wouldn't answer my calls. So I stopped by the senior center in Hillstead—she volunteers there Tuesday nights—and I waited for her to come out. She wouldn't talk to me then, either. She drove away so fast. I tried to call her on the road, wanted to see if I could meet her at her house instead. But then I—I dropped the phone, and when I tried to pick it up . . ." He lifts his hands, a helpless gesture.

Sienna and I share a disturbed glance. The room buzzes with silence, audible as an alarm.

Aiden is the first to break it. "You were, like, stalking her, Dad."

"What? No, bud. I just wanted to help. She had no one else to talk to about it."

"It wasn't your place," Sienna says, "to decide what she needed to talk about. Just like it wasn't your place to harass her—"

"Harass her?"

"—about what Gavin might have done to her. Not after she told you to drop it."

"But," Jason says, "you didn't see the way he touched her as he put her in his car. His hand lingered, and it seemed like— I could just tell he— How could I not try to find out what happened? Or try to stop him from doing it again?"

"God, you still don't get it!" Sienna cries. "You should have stopped him *then*. At the party."

"Exactly," I say, and Jason's gaze ping-pongs between us. "It's one thing not to speak up when Gavin made comments in meetings—"

"Even though you definitely should have," Sienna cuts in.

"But when you saw what looked like Gavin taking advantage of Maeve—*that* was the time to act. Not when Maeve decided to drive

Gavin home. Even if you didn't understand her choice, you should have respected it. Respected her. Because all you did was make things"—I shake my head, nauseated—"so much worse."

Surprise blooms like a bruise on Jason's face.

"I *do* respect Maeve," he says. "I know I should've stopped Gavin the night of the party, but that's why I was trying so hard to—to make things right. After." Tears glaze his eyes, making them glisten in the light. "I made a mistake, and I wanted to fix it so badly. And I never meant to *hurt* him, but . . . I know. You're right, I know. I made things worse."

At that, he grips his forehead with one hand, and a sob overtakes him—a single sound so intense my eyes zip to his monitor.

Sienna crosses her arms, clenches her jaw, but when she speaks, her tone has softened. "Jason, I understand *why* you did this. And the feelings, the history it sprang from."

Her pause stretches out, heavy with meaning.

"But there are some things you can't fix or make right," she adds. "You just have to live with what you've done. And decide whether you'll let it define you."

Jason bites his bottom lip, stilling its tremble. He straightens his shoulders against the pillows. "Are you talking about . . . the other party? With Clive?" He slides a guilty glance toward Aiden before returning to Sienna. "Are you saying there's no way I can make that right with you? That you won't be able to forgive me?"

Pain darkens Sienna's face, like a cloud blotting out the sun. She's quiet for a while, swallowing twice before she answers.

"I'm going to work on it. Forgiveness. Not defining people by their mistakes. Not just with you, but—" She looks away, clearing her throat. "You know what? This is a lot; I need some water. You guys probably want some time alone anyway."

"Wait, I'll come with you," Aiden says. "I need water too."

He coughs into his fist, but the sound is forced. I feel his discomfort, even though he asked to come here today. I suspected, even before we left the house, that he didn't really want to, but I took it as a good sign that he did it anyway. There's so much hurt and confusion scrambled inside him, and I know I'll have to work to make him feel safe enough to share that with me, to let him know that, whenever he's ready, I'm here and he'll be heard.

As Sienna slings her arm over Aiden's shoulder and guides him into the hall, it's the first time since last Tuesday morning that I've been alone with Jason. I wonder, given his arrest, how much alone time we have left. I wonder what it might feel like, seeing him in a prison jumpsuit, if it would be worse or better than seeing his hospital gown.

"What about you?" he says, a hitch in his voice. "Will you be able to forgive me? I'm so sorry for lying to you about the money. And for taking it without asking." He dips his gaze, studying the blanket. "I know that trip meant a lot to you. I still really want to take you."

Images gather, a montage of memories we might have shared: exploring the grounds of the Sacré Cœur, strolling through outdoor markets in Sorrento, standing on the Cliffs of Moher. Europe has never felt so far away, and I haven't forgotten that Jason gave to Maeve by taking from me.

"Why *didn't* you ask me?" I say.

Jason bites his lip. "I didn't know how to explain it, why I knew that Maeve needed to get away from Gavin. I couldn't tell you it reminded me of Clive in high school without telling you what really happened with Sienna at that party."

I frown at him, unsatisfied by that answer.

"Either way," he adds, "it was wrong of me. I just—" He meets my eyes again. "Julia, I need to know we'll be okay."

I sit on the side of his bed, giving myself time to think through my response. Because even now, my instinct is to agree, to hold my-self back from making waves. *We'll be okay*, I almost say. As if Jason's need is more important than mine. But I want to be done with that, shrinking myself for other people's comfort.

"Jason, it's not just the money or the trip. Yes, that's a big deal, but it's so much more than that. You slept beside me for three nights knowing you'd *stabbed* a man. Then you knew Maeve killed him. And you never said a word."

"I was protecting her."

"I know you think that. But you did so at the cost of our relation-ship. Our trust."

He stares at me, unblinking, eyes wet and fearful. Finally, he nods, accepting that truth.

"You've done that a lot, actually," I continue. "Hurt me, hurt our family, while you claim to be helping others. I won't go through all the examples now—this is a longer talk we'll need to have—but you have a pattern, Jason."

Again, I watch him process my words, his expression torn be-tween confusion and consideration.

"And I know I haven't been perfect," I add. "I've lied to you too, in my own way. It's not the same, at all, but I never told you how much it hurt me, how betrayed I felt, after you used that money."

Guilt tightens Jason's face. "You might not have said it," he says, "but I felt it. You hardly looked me in the eye for months. And it killed me, knowing I'd hurt you so much. That's why I couldn't bear to let you down about that promotion."

"But I didn't care about the promotion! I cared about the betrayal. Which is exactly what I'm talking about—it's my fault you didn't know that. There were so many times I locked my feelings away. But it only hurt me, hurt us, even more to do that. So I can't keep quiet anymore. I won't."

Jason puts his hand on mine. "And I don't want you to. I want to know how you're feeling, even if—especially if—you're upset with me. But . . . we'll be okay, right?" he asks again, still looking for this to be easy, to be over.

"I don't know," I tell him. "We've been married for fifteen years, but I don't know how well we really know each other." I let that linger a moment—the truth I've only just begun accepting. "Like Sienna, I'm willing to work on it, but we don't stand a chance if we can't be honest with each other. Even if that honesty hurts us."

He raises my hand to his mouth, kisses it with lips so dry they scratch my skin. A tear slips from his lashes, and I catch it by cupping his cheek. He leans into my palm, eyes closed, like my touch is something precious, something he never wants to lose.

"Julia, I promise," he says, "from now on, I'll be honest."

Somewhere inside me, my mother tries to intervene: *Never trust a man.* She always said it like it was a decision I could make—and only ever a wrong one. But trust isn't chosen; it's earned. And as I look at Jason now, vulnerable and earnest, it's possible to imagine that somehow, with time, he will earn mine.

Then again, maybe he won't. Maybe, in the end, we'll let each other go.

I still worry what that means for me and Sienna. The fear of losing her still grabs me by the throat. But I push that panic aside, table it for later. Because Sienna isn't here right now; she *shouldn't* be here, in any decision I make about my husband. In this moment, it's only me and Jason, a man who, for better or worse, is promising honesty.

"I'll be honest too," I say back. And even though it's just words right now—not enough, on its own, to save us—that promise, exchanged in a hospital room, witnessed only, perhaps, by the guard outside, feels more significant than any other vow we've made.

Chapter Twenty-Six

SIENNA

Wyatt's doorbell is warm beneath my touch. I drove here first thing, after dropping Julia and Aiden at their house, and as Wyatt opens the door to me, my heart gavels against my ribs.

"Can I come in?" I ask.

"Of course," he says, clipped and cautious, and I don't blame him. Last time I was here, I told him we were over.

I don't move to the living room, or his bedroom, like I normally would. Instead, I stay in the entryway—this in-between space—crossing my arms, leaning against the wall.

"I saw you with Henry Hendrix at the community center yesterday. Looking like old pals."

Wyatt blows out a breath, then leans back, too, against the opposite wall. "So that's what Beck was talking about. How did you see us?"

"I followed him."

No sense denying it. I don't want to be like Jason, so caught up in his own reasons, his own needs, that he couldn't hear his son, who was brave enough, back at the hospital, to call his actions what they were: stalking.

"Jesus, Si. We talked about this. We made a deal—an alibi in exchange for leaving him alone."

I note his word choice. "*An* alibi. But it wasn't *the* alibi, was it? Because I checked with Home Depot; they said he wasn't working that night. So, what—did you lie to me?"

He bites the inside of his cheek, focusing on my collarbone instead of my eyes. His silence gives him away.

"Wyatt," I continue, "you lied to me on the same night you were asking me to be open and vulnerable with you again, to tell you everything I was feeling, and I don't get why you'd—"

"Because *I* was his alibi," he cuts in. "Part of it, at least."

My arms unknot, one of them falling to my side. "What?"

"I was with him the night of Gavin's murder. First at a . . . meeting. Then at a diner for a few hours. He's been having a rough time lately. You know about his run-in with Gavin, his arrest. His wife recently left him, and he'd heard from a former customer that Gavin was making the same deals he'd reported Henry for—which now we're looking into at the department. So he and I had waffles while he talked things out, and then I drove him home."

"Wait, go back." I skip over the confirmation that, at least in some small way, I was right, Henry did know about Gavin's deals; that doesn't matter anymore. "What meeting?"

He gives me an expectant look, as if waiting for me to figure it out.

"The same one you saw us at yesterday," he says.

"Okay, but—what meeting is held at the community center?"

Wyatt blows out a frustrated breath. "It's AA, Si. Alcoholics Anonymous. I was protecting Henry's privacy. I figured if I told you he was at work that night, you'd drop it. But clearly you didn't."

My head rears back. "Wait, what? You're in AA?"

My mind whirls through images: the beers we used to drink after sex; the IPAs that were always stocked in his fridge; even One-star Bartender, our favorite game. Still, enjoying alcohol isn't the same as having a problem.

"You're not an alcoholic," I add.

"I didn't think I was," Wyatt says. "But as soon as I tried to actually quit drinking, I . . . had trouble. I'd come home from work and feel like I *needed* a beer. Not wanted. Needed. I've been going to meetings for a few months now. They've really helped."

His explanation only confuses me more. "You quit drinking? When?"

He slides his hands into his pockets, eyes strained with pain and shame. "A year ago. Pretty much the moment I woke up in a stranger's bed."

My breath sputters out, a quick puff of surprise. If it weren't for the wall behind me, keeping me in place, I might stumble back.

"I— I never asked you to do that," I say.

"I know. But if something can affect me so much that I'd betray the one person I—that I'd betray *you*, then that thing is toxic for me and it has to go. So I cut it out, immediately."

I stare at him, dizzy with this revelation. Wyatt quietly quit drinking—not as a ploy to keep me, but because drinking had made him lose me.

"When I met you," he says, "you'd already been torn apart because someone got beyond wasted and did something inexcusable. And then I got beyond wasted. I did something inexcusable. I hurt you too."

My lips part, air draining between them. Somehow, I never made this exact connection between Wyatt and Clive—two drunk men on their drunkest nights, completely upending my life.

"So, yeah." Wyatt shakes his head. "Never again."

He steps away from the wall, closer to me, and my skin prickles with the nearness of him. He extends a hand like he might touch my arm, and even though my body responds, tilting toward his palm, he stops himself. My heart stutters, drumming a clumsy beat, and my eyes, fastened to Wyatt, are unable to blink. My arm aches where he didn't touch me. My mouth throbs from not being kissed.

"Anyway, I'm sorry I lied to you," he says. "I just . . . believe in the program, and I take people's privacy seriously." He clears his throat. "I'm sorry about Jason, too. I heard about his arrest. I can only imagine how you're feeling."

It takes me a moment to speak, to switch gears from how I'm feeling about Wyatt to how I feel about Jason. "Well," I finally say. "He did everything they arrested him for. So."

The truth of that is lacerating. When Jason asked me at the hospital if I'd be able to forgive him, there was part of me that wanted to grant him a clean slate, tell him there's nothing he could do to change how I see him. But I knew that wasn't true. Moment by moment, he was vanishing before me—or not him, exactly, but the man I thought he was. Soon, he'll be so faint that I'll see right through him, until the only version left is the one he really is.

"But I know how much you love him," Wyatt says. "He was something to you that no one else could ever be. And I'm sure this feels like you've lost him. But no matter what he did, he's the same man who made you blueberry pancakes while the two of you were drowning in grief."

Tears seep to the front of my eyes. They spill onto my cheeks. Because Wyatt's right: I do feel like I lost Jason, but I love him, too. It would be impossible to stop. As much as I've tried to fight it in the past, love, for me, has always been a simple, unfixable thing. If I love someone—in that bone-deep, drop-everything way—it's forever.

I'm surprised Wyatt knows this about me, surprised he even re-members the story about the pancakes, or understands my pain so specifically.

I shouldn't be, though. Like Julia, Wyatt has always seen me so clearly, and over the years, he's memorized me with the greatest of care.

"I'm just—" Wyatt looks down, rubbing the back of his neck, as if worried he's overstepped. "I'm sorry for what you're going through. I hate to see you in pain."

I flush with warmth that has nothing to do with anger. I keep my gaze secured to Wyatt, until he lifts his own to meet it.

"Because you love me," I say, stepping closer to him.

His brows inch together as he studies my face. "Because I love you."

I knuckle a tear from my cheek. "And you fucked up at that bach-elor party, but you would never do that again."

Because he is the same man who cherished our anniversary chopsticks, even after I told him, time and time again, that we were over. He is the same man who gave up drinking, even without my asking or knowing.

"No," Wyatt says, voice low with sincerity, heavy with regret. "I never would."

I kiss him. My lips are wet from crying, but he responds so in-stantly, cupping my face in his palms, it's clear he doesn't mind. We soften into the moment, our bodies melting together.

"Wait," Wyatt says, pulling back. "That doesn't mean I wouldn't fuck up in other ways. I never want to hurt you, it's the last thing I want to do. But I can't promise I won't."

I lean toward him, closing the space he's made. The space I've made, too. The barrier I've tried to wedge between my heart and his.

"It's okay," I say. "I can't promise I won't fuck up either. And I'm sorry for hurting you all these months. For being selfish and careless."

I skim my lips along his, then whisper against his mouth, words I've fought against for so long, words I thought would make me weak: "I love you, Wyatt."

He answers me with a kiss.

. . .

As ever when something momentous happens, Julia is the first person I tell.

Entering her house that night, I hold up a bag of chocolate-covered pretzels. "I brought *motatoes,*" I say—but the old reference falls flat, neither of us smiling. Already, it belongs to another time. Another set of people.

"And I'm back together with Wyatt," I add.

Julia's grin beams across her face, brightening her eyes, the room, the moment.

"You are?" she asks, voice verging on giddy.

"Yeah, someone kind of smart told me that Wyatt can make a colossal mistake and still be the best thing for me." I shrug. "I think she was right."

"Oh, wow. Well." She looks at her fingernails, playing it cool. "Whoever she is, she sounds amazing."

I carry the pretzels into the living room, where I slump onto the couch. Julia follows, already reaching into the bag.

"Yeah, she's a real angel," I say.

She smiles again, softer this time, and there's something a little sad about it. Out of habit, I start counting: *One . . . Two . . .* But I don't get to finish.

"There's something I have to tell you," she says. "I don't know what's going to happen with me and Jason. I told him I'm willing to work on things. But I truly have no idea how it's going to end. He kept so much from me, I don't trust him right now, and honestly, I wouldn't blame him if he didn't trust me either. Because you were right yesterday. Too many times I hid what I was feeling. I created distance without even knowing. And—I don't know. I really don't know what will happen."

I grab her hand. "No one expects you to have all the answers right now. Not to mention he's been *arrested*, so we don't even know what's going to happen in general yet."

"Yeah, but I'm not even sure what I *want* to happen. I married Jason all those years ago because I was pregnant, and he was . . . well, he was Jason. But also: I knew if I married him, then I got to be *your* sister-in-law. Your family. But I can't make any decisions this time based on how much I want *you* in my life. That wouldn't be fair to Jason. Or Aiden. Or even to me."

I sit with that a moment. "Yeah, of course. That makes sense."

"So—" Julia slides a careful look at me. "You're not mad?"

Two days ago, I might have been. No—two days ago, I *would* have been. My fists would have clenched at her doubt in Jason, which I'd interpret as disloyalty. My nails would have stabbed into my palms. Now, though, I look at my hand, at the cut I gave myself just yesterday, and I know there's nothing my anger would have done for me but leave me with self-inflicted marks.

And that familiar heat, that sting, those sparks—I don't feel them right now. I feel only the sadness I see in Julia's eyes. In many ways, I'm bonded to my brother no matter what he does. But that's not the case for her. Or, at least, it doesn't have to be.

"No, I'm not mad," I say.

"But—say we don't work things out. What will that mean for you and me?"

I look at her hand, which is curled in my palm. She hasn't loosened her fingers. Hasn't gripped me back.

"It won't mean anything," I insist.

"Come on. Things would change."

"Yeah. Where you live, I guess. How often we see each other."
I swallow around the instant lump in my throat. "But I love you in
ways that have nothing to do with Jason. That won't change."

"But." Tears thicken Julia's voice. I keep my eyes on our hands.
"What about yesterday? What we said to each other. I'm scared it's
true. We thought we were holding each other together, but all this
time, we might have been holding each other back."

My answer flies out of me, sudden and certain: "So what?"

When I look at her face, I find it creased with confusion. "So
what?" she repeats. "You think we should just . . . keep holding each
other back?"

"No, I'm saying, I think it *was* true. In the past, I spoke for you so
you could stay quiet and safe; you regulated my emotions for me so
I didn't have to manage them myself. But now that we know those
patterns, we can break them, right? I mean, look at me! I'm working on things with Wyatt! And look at you! You were the one who
pushed Maeve to tell us the truth. Not to mention how you were
with Jason, yesterday and today. We can do things differently. With
other people. With each other. Don't you think we can do that?"

Julia meets my eyes, her own cautious, if not a little skeptical. "I
want to think so."

"Good. Then think so. Because you're my soul mate, Jules."

"You're *my* soul mate," she says back—no hesitation. Finally, she
links her fingers with mine, holding tight to that simple truth. Our
heads tip toward each other, her left temple grazing my right. We sit
in silence, staring at the wall across from us.

"There's something else I have to tell you," Julia says. "And I don't
know if you'll be as chill about this one."

Even with my speech still warm on my lips, I brace myself.
"What?"

Julia squeezes my hand, as if locking me into whatever she's about to say.

"I *hate* the rooster wallpaper. It looks like blood. I'm going to take it down."

As if to punctuate this proclamation, she plucks a pretzel from the bag and tosses it at the wall. It hits its target in spectacular fashion, smacking the fat red body of one of the roosters.

"Wow," I say. "Okay. Didn't realize you were such a cockblocker."

In the span of one glance, we lurch toward each other, collapsing into laughter that's embarrassingly big for such a dumb joke. It feels so good, though—laughing—after everything we've gone through this week. Our stomachs spasm; our eyes sparkle with tears.

I took it for granted, this luxury, these simple, stupid joys we experience together, but I feel now how truly miraculous it all is. And as we lean even closer, as we tighten our grip on each other, I am certain of one thing: whatever happens next—between Julia and Jason, Jason and me, me and Julia—I will hold her hand, but I will not hold her back.

Acknowledgments

I usually save this one for last, but this time, I'm putting him first: thank you to my husband, Marc, who—for more than two years—listened to me complain, cry, and stress about this book. I can't count the number of walks we took where I yammered on about a plot problem and he gave me smart suggestions that I (frustratingly, I'm sure) vetoed over and over until something finally clicked. His patience is astounding, and his creativity and problem-solving are gifts I've benefited from for four books now. My stories simply would not be the same without him.

Endless thanks to my editor, Kaitlin Olson, who handed me the biggest creative challenge of my life when she asked me to strip this story down to the studs and re-create it from the ground up. It was, of course, exactly what it needed, and I'm immensely grateful for her guidance, encouragement, and insight along the way. She saw the heart of Julia and Sienna's story before even I did, and it's because of her that I eventually saw it too.

As always, I am so thankful to have the most wonderful agent, Sharon Pelletier, who helps me sharpen my ideas, strengthen my sto ries, and whom I feel blessed to have in my corner. Also, she deserves at least a million dollars for the number of anxiety-laden emails she fields from me, so if anyone has a spare million, please send it her way.

Huge, heartfelt thanks to everyone at Atria, especially Megan Rudloff, Maudee Genao, Elizabeth Hitti, Ifeoma Anyoku, David Brown, Stacey Sakal, and Sara Kitchen, and thanks once again to Kelli McAdams for creating such a beautiful, eye-catching cover.

Thank you to Dr. Matt Rade, who explained the ins and outs of a medically induced coma to me. He was extremely generous with his time (Phone calls! Emails! Texts!), and it is only because of him that I (hopefully) looked like I knew what I was talking about when I wrote about Jason's condition. Any errors or inaccuracies are completely my own and should have no bearing on whether you trust Dr. Rade with your life.

Thank you to Kevin Cook for answering my police procedural questions and for letting me know from the start that the plot I had in mind was actually possible.

I can't express how grateful I am for the support of other writers. There are so many names I could list, but my publisher might get mad at me if I lengthen this book by about twenty pages to do so. Instead, I'll say this: if you and I have so much as exchanged DMs on social media, if we've chatted about writing and publishing, or if you've helped spread the word about my books in any way, I appreciate you. Special thanks to Samantha M. Bailey, Kathleen Barber, Kimberly Belle, Michele Campbell, Heather Gudenkauf, Janice Hallett, Robyn Harding, Darby Kane, Sarah Langan, Vanessa Lillie, Catherine McKenzie, PJ Vernon, Jeneva Rose, Alex Segura, and Ashley Winstead.

Special-special-with-a-side-of-cupcakes thanks to Andrea Bartz, Layne Fargo, and Halley Sutton for helping me rethink, replot, and rework this book. Their suggestions and support were game changers in so many ways.

Authors would be nothing without readers, so thank you—yes, you, the person who is holding or listening to this book right now. I can't tell you how much it means to me that you've invested your time in this story. Thank you, as well, to all the booksellers (especially those at River Bend Bookshop, Book Club on the Go, Bank Square Books/Savoy Bookshop, and Ink Fish Books), librarians, book bloggers, BookTokkers, and bookstagrammers who do miraculous work connecting readers with writers. Thank you to Barnes & Noble for their tremendous support of *The Family Plot*. And special thanks to bookstagrammers Kayla (@kayreadwhat), Gare (@gareindeedreads), Christina (@a_politicallyreadgirl), Briana (@brianas_best_reads), Jody (@redreadreviews), and Kendall (@sunflower_book_lover) for all their generous promotion efforts.

Thanks once again to my parents, and thanks especially to my dad, Paul Collins, who consulted about all things home improvement business. I modeled Integrity Plus (minus the shady shenanigans) off the company my grandfather started in the 1940s and my father later took over, and my dad was especially influential in helping me craft the warehouse scene.

And finally, thanks to my past self, who didn't give up on writing this book, even when she really wanted to.

About The Author

Megan Collins is the author of *Thicker Than Water, The Family Plot, Behind the Red Door,* and *The Winter Sister.* She taught creative writing for many years at both the high school and college level and is the managing editor of *3Elements Literary Review.* She lives in Connecticut, where she obsesses over dogs, miniatures, and cake.